WEIRD DREAM SOCIETY

An Anthology in Support of RAICES

Editor-in-Chief JULIE C. DAY

Co-editor CARINA BISSETT

Co-editor CHIP HOUSER

Cover illustration by GREGORY NORMAN BOSSERT

Social Media Coordinator STEVE TOASE

Weird Dream Society

Reckoning Press

An Anthology of the Possible & Unsubstantiated in Support of RAICES ©
2020

Acknowledgments

"You Go Where It Takes You" by Nathan Ballingrud. Copyright © 2003. First published in *Sci Fiction*, July. Reprinted by permission of the author.

"The Landscape of Lacrimation" by Carina Bassett. Copyright © 2018. First published in *The Hunger*, May. Reprinted by permission of the author.

"HigherWorks" by Gregory Norman Bossert. Copyright © 2018. First published in *Asimov's Science Fiction*, December. Reprinted by permission of the author.

"Snow as White as Skin as White as Snow" by Karen Bovenmyer. Copyright © 2017. First published in *Gamut Magazine*, December. Reprinted by permission of the author.

"Festival" by Christopher Brown. Copyright © 2015. First published in *Stories for Chip: A Tribute to Samuel R. Delany*, September. Reprinted by permission of the author.

"Glasswort, Ice" by Emily Cataneo. Copyright © 2017. First published in *Lackington's Issue 14*, Spring. Reprinted by permission of the author.

"Flyover Country" by Julie C. Day. Copyright © 2020. First published in *Interzone 285* January/February. Reprinted by permission of the author.

Contents

Introduction

Julie C. Day

We live in a world in which we need to share responsibility. It's easy to say 'It's not my child, not my community, not my world, not my problem.' Then there are those who see the need and respond. I consider those people my heroes.
—Fred Rogers

I'm from the generation of Mr. Rogers and broadcast TV. When I was a child and newly arrived in the United States, I looked to Mr. Rogers for reassurance. In a time when I felt lost and rather adrift, he was my friend. At six years old, I never doubted his sincerity or his kindness and willingness to help. In some fundamental way, his presence made my life easier. But Mr. Rogers is more than childhood memories. These days there are far too many opportunities to step forward and act as one of his heroes.

My story of becoming an American is an easy one. I was born in the U.K. and immigrated to Southern Indiana with my family when I was six. I became a citizen at nineteen. We left behind loving grandparents, friends, and a middle-class home. We arrived with my father's job already in place. Unlike so many, I had all the privileges that my language, class, race, and ethnicity provided. And yet, stepping into a new culture—a new small-town culture without the support of extended family—was hard: hard for me, hard for my parents, hard for us as a family unit.

Like the refugees and migrants at our southern border today, my grandparents did not have any easy time when they emigrated from Austria to the U.K. I'm the grandchild of Jews displaced by the Holocaust, refugees unwanted by many countries and unwelcome by some citizens once they arrived. There's a reason my grandparents' last name was Gordon, and it wasn't because it was a family name: having a last name like Weissman was problematic. There's a reason my grandfather was so relieved to get out of a U.K. internment camp and become an actual member of the country's general population: all Austrians were housed together, both Nazis and Jews, as no one was trusted regarding their origin story. The camps were a dangerous place to live while waiting to see what came next.

The past repeats itself too often: painting people with a broad negative brush, believing the worst of someone because of their accent, their name, their ethnicity, their race, or their country of origin. Most people aren't angels or devils, but they can be callous and thoughtlessly cruel. I grew up with stories that made that clear. And these were my grandparents—my humble, gentle, beloved grandparents—who'd been through some of the worst experiences life can offer.

How could I not see the parallels between how the United States today treats migrants in need and my own family history?

And yet my grandparents were grateful to the U.K., the country that finally gave them a home. They never complained about the country that took them in. As far as they were concerned, they were given an opportunity not only to survive but to actually move forward as a family. They worked hard. They were good neighbors. And despite the fact they were far from wealthy or even middle class, they always felt they had more than enough. They were thoughtful people who never recognized their own lives as anything but lucky.

In many ways, the early months of 2020, with the onset of the pandemic, have created even more parallels to those family stories. We are in a time full of anxiety and uncertainty. No one knows what the next three, or six, or nine months will bring. We are hunkered down, figuring out how to protect our own and to do what we can for our friends and neighbors— yet again, thank you, Mr. Rogers. So many people are reaching out, trying to help.

But not everyone has neighbors or friends nearby: those people in dangerously overcrowded detention centers at the border; those undocumented children, and parents, and cousins, and aunts being picked up by ICE; those people who have no safe home. They also need our help, a sense of safety, and the possibility of a future. It's such a simple requirement —to be treated with humanity. In fact, writing this introduction in April 2020, the need of migrants and asylum seekers is even greater than it was when we started this project in 2019. For those in detention centers, the situation needs to change. There are no safe options unless they receive our collective help.

I am the grandchild of refugees whose lives were in danger in their own country and who had to start anew with emotional and physical scars. They are the people who taught me something about the potential for brutality in this world— the shadows the past can cast. They also taught me that compassion can also arise from those experiences. Life isn't easy, and hard times don't create perfect people, but recognizing that you have something to offer when another is in need requires nothing beyond your humanity. In the end, it's our humanity that makes us both responsible for, and equal to, each other.

This anthology is both a book that shares some of the best in contemporary speculative short fiction and a book whose proceeds will go to support a worthy charity. RAICES is a frontline organization in the roiling debate about immigration and immigrants in the world. They envision a society where all people have the right to migrate and human rights are guaranteed. And right now, during the COVID-19 pandemic, they are working hard alongside the National Bail Fund Network and members of the Congressional Hispanic Caucus to get families released from cramped, crowded, and unsanitary conditions in the immigrant camps scattered across Mexican-American border before a catastrophic event occurs. Reason enough to buy this book.

But the authors in this anthology are more than Fred Rogers' helpers. They are imaginations writ large. The twenty-three stories you'll find in this anthology each have a feeling, a situation, a character that will linger. Each is a dream which only that author could share. From Marianne Kirby's "The Ghost Who Loved A Mannequin" and Bonnie Jo Stufflebeam's "The Hoof Situation" to Christopher Brown's "Festival" and Steve Toase's "Skin Like Carapace," the stories in this *Weird Dream Society* make my brain thrum. It's that prick of language that takes me out of myself, the verbal knifepoint that cuts my thoughts in a new direction. It's the thrill of stories done well. I'm honored they allowed me to share their words with you.

The Ghost Who Loved a Mannequin

Marianne Kirby

Zinger probably existed before the mall, but they don't remember any of that. Everything in the mall is white noise and commerce, the forced dissipation and disruption of bodies in motion. The mall is full of creatures suspended in the amber of every doorway. Zinger might have been someone else once, but there's no space for memory when Zinger is full of the way newness sounds.

Instead of dwelling on a past that cannot be recalled, Zinger floats from the Food Court floor to the skylight, lets the sun streaming in fracture around them. Zinger is bored and this is a small pleasure. Zinger thinks maybe they used to be kind, but that's another thing lost. They feel only the hollow place where kindness used to live.

The mall is a world created by what happens next, an ecosystem and an entity. Zinger avoids the other inhabitants of the mall, shies away from glimpsing the mysteries, fears what might come from facing those figures. To know the unknown in the mall feels, to Zinger, like danger.

But those are nighttime thoughts. For now, everything is daylight, mid-afternoon, and the arc of the glass ceiling is dazzling with blue and endless and warm. Food smells from below tease at Zinger before being sucked into the air vents. Voices and footsteps combine into updrafts that Zinger rides over all the bodies.

A balloon bobs around one of the vents. Zinger does not like balloons, shudders away from it, but the sphere is drawn after them, attracted by the static that fills the wake of their trail, the signal disruption of their slow unravelling. It is only when Zinger darts through a narrow space between two cross-beams that they find their way free. They slide down and away from the Food Court, uneasy with their own fear, determined not to return until the balloon is gone.

———

A new store is opening on the third floor of the mall.

Zinger tries to reverse their path—more free-drifting balloons have pursued Zinger in almost all of the public mall spaces over the last 24 hours, and this is their obvious source —but the tide of air currents is too strong. Zinger is swept into the bright lights and loud music welcoming shoppers to a special sale event as though they are nothing more than a balloon themself. Zinger thinks they used to be more than a balloon, used to direct themself. But trying to remember is a distraction. The floods are dazzling; the sound is a heavy cushion on which to rest.

The mall has a pulse, and the music matches it, a constant heartbeat echoed in the pace at which the mall walkers march.

Zinger wants to pity those being ruled by the rhythm but Zinger themself is being driven deeper into the store, shoved by the energy of celebration. A wave opens the way, and Zinger darts into the stockroom through a closing door.

The stockrooms are dangerous at night. They belong to other things, shelter nests and eggs and precious small things, things with memories Zinger lacks. To look directly at the nighttime creatures is a challenge to them. But, Zinger thinks, surely it is safe enough to hide on the high shelves while the employees fetch and carry. Sometimes the other things that live in the mall disappear. Zinger watched one door for three days once, waiting for someone to return. But Zinger is relatively safe inside the room, they think; the mall employees rarely disappear, after all. Zinger settles down on top of a box, watches and listens.

When Zinger was still new, they listened to everything. Zinger spent all their time identifying the sounds of purchase totals and loss prevention meetings. They learned the roar of the beasts on the roof, the giant air conditioning lungs that inhaled and exhaled. Dragons, Zinger had thought, and hadn't known why.

But now most of the mall noises are familiar and predictable, and Zinger has focused on the silences. A perfect stillness comes over the mall when the last security guard locks the last employee exit for the night. In that moment, before the unknowable night creatures stir, the mall seems to pause for a single, held breath.

There are few enough opportunities for silence during the shopping day, few places that aren't penetrated by the drone of shoppers, always buffeting Zinger around, so Zinger is pleased by the cool and the quiet of the stockroom. The fluorescents cast more shadow than light, create more hiding places than they reveal.

The delivery bay door bangs open, and Zinger sparks in surprise. An employee enters with laughter still trailing from an open mouth. "Just drag it back here for now."

"Come on, help me. This thing is heavy." Another

employee, younger but dressed similarly in all black, whines behind the first. The second employee is pulling something.

Zinger edges closer to see, curious; new things are as rare as silence. This new thing is a large cardboard box, though not so tall as either of the employees who are working together now.

"I'll do the floor reset after close and then do the window in the morning before we open." The first employee pats the box with a particular fondness, like it contains a familiar pet. "It's going to be great."

The second employee doesn't seem to care; they head back out onto the sales floor with nothing but a nod, and the influx of noise almost knocks Zinger from their perch. They catch themselves and consider. Zinger doesn't always have the best sense of hours but if the employees are talking about closing, Zinger should retreat to their own nest.

They drift up toward an intake vent, but Zinger looks back at the cardboard box, caught on a tether of wanting to know. Then they slip the leash and escape. Zinger is very difficult to trap; no one but the mall has managed it yet.

———

The mall opens later than normal, and that is how Zinger knows it is Sunday. Zinger doesn't know why Sunday means a different routine, but time only moves forward in the mall, so they don't question it. The lazy mornings with only the security guard on rounds outside are nice. Zinger stretches, tries to regain any size they have lost through making themselves small enough to hide. They don't want to shrink to nothingness.

Despite the ease of the day, Zinger is more impatient than usual. It would be dangerous to wake up the mall creatures that live in the stockroom before they are ready, though, so Zinger waits. Zinger will probably never be eaten by anything that lives in the mall, but Zinger isn't interested in pressing their luck.

An electric crackle tickles through the mall, and the music that provides an ambient cushion begins. Once the ritual of shopping is underway, the music will almost disappear except when there are odd moments between breaths, except when it serves to connect the discordance.

The music is also a sign of things to come, of the bodies that will shuffle and crowd, so Zinger makes their way to the new store on the third floor. They perch in a potted palm, consider the branches and the way the green yearns for the sky barely visible through the glass ceiling from this position. Trees like this were not meant for inside.

There is no such thing as leaving the mall. Zinger thinks they tried once. They think it hurt.

The gate goes up, and Zinger slips into the store on the manager's heels. They use the manager's body as a shield, hope to pass unnoticed.

The manager's keys jangle, and the stockroom door opens. The manager is muttering but it is indistinct; Zinger's attention is not on the words because their attention is on the box, unchanged from the night before. A blade catches the cold light, sharp and efficient, as the manager cuts into the box. The cardboard shell falls away.

Reflexive habit has Zinger rising up in self-defense; Zinger catches and holds themself fast against all instinct so they can watch. Plastic and metal are revealed under the packing material: a vague shape, limbs, something that might be a head.

The air around Zinger chills; it was too easy to follow the manager into the stockroom. The creatures who nest in the stockroom have returned, their hunting patterns disrupted by Zinger's unwelcome presence. The manager continues to unwrap the figure, and the creatures pant softly.

Curiosity killed the cat, Zinger thinks, nonsense words they don't recognize. Zinger does not look behind them, unfocuses all their perception. Zinger wants to see what was in the cardboard box but doesn't want to see anything they will regret. There is no shame in fleeing.

Another flap of cardboard falls; more wrapping is knocked askew. A gleam of metal rivals the overhead lights in its bright reflectivity.

The pressure of being watched in turn heightens, shivers through Zinger, desire giving way to fear. Zinger retreats to the vents, works hard not to hurry. Rushing will leave a void, will only invite the predators to give chase.

Better to think about the cardboard box, Zinger decides. It keeps them calm and they slip away, farther and farther through the vents, until even the metal around them eases. Zinger pauses then to fix the image in what remains of their memory: plain brown sides giving way to packing foam and cling film, revealing graceful bends and twists.

The hints that Zinger saw, metal structure and plastic skin, are beautiful. And though there is a great deal in the mall that Zinger finds beautiful—the skylights and fountains and a piano that plays itself—this new thing compels Zinger's attention. It is a surprising feeling, like they have swallowed a hook on an unspooling line. They do not know what will happen when they are reeled back in.

———

Zinger is used to waiting. It is difficult now though, and Zinger distracts themself by watching other creatures. The casual mischief should seem cruel, Zinger thinks, when register tape is hidden and bag handles are tangled. But they aren't sure why.

Some of the mall's inhabitants do favors, too. Zinger once saw a shopper find a bright silver coin, glinting with good fortune. The shopper put it in their pocket and left humming an old song. Zinger just bears witness; it is enough.

Watching keeps Zinger occupied until the mall is at its height, shoppers wandering with lazy attention. The mall smells like sun and sweet sweat, green humidity from the plants around the central fountain. Late enough, Zinger thinks, for the stockroom itself to be asleep. There is nothing to keep Zinger from the new store now.

The crowds are smaller, and the air currents are easier to catch and tack across. Zinger intends to brave the inside again but hesitates. The window display is different.

There is a new mannequin.

Metal and plastic, and the entirety of what was hidden is revealed. Zinger is stunned. Just for a moment they are vulnerable to the mysteries of the mall in a way that is unwise; they are too focused on the window and how enticing the figure is, rigid and faceless and exquisite. The mannequin stands to one side of a table, all architectural shape without covering aside from a silvery skin skimming between crossbeams.

Zinger eases forward, gentle and slow, presses up close to the glass that stands between themself and the mannequin until it is almost possible to slip through the narrow gap where two panes butt against each other. This is what the manager ordered; another mannequin meant to entice shoppers. Zinger is almost angry that the mannequin is being put to such base use. It doesn't seem fair.

Many beautiful things in the mall serve mundane purposes, but Zinger rises and falls with agitation nonetheless. The injustice of this matters. The mannequin should not be gawked at, should not be meant to serve the store. Even Zinger exists without purpose imposed by others.

Zinger is not certain why this matters. This is a new feeling for them, or an old feeling only half remembered. They feel frayed at the edges, like they are dragging themselves over something rough.

There is a sour ringing tone that echoes inside Zinger; to be entirely without purpose is very nearly not existing. But

Zinger does exist and so does the mannequin. Perhaps here, all unexpected, Zinger might find their own purpose.

———

Zinger doesn't know what to call the sensation that compels them, the way they want to circle back to the store despite the danger waiting there for them inside. The creatures from the stockroom would object to their presence. There is something old and deep about the feeling that stirs in Zinger's thoughts, tucked down among all the other things they have forgotten. They are not sure they like the sense of it, this new way of thinking about the mannequin.

Obviously, the mannequin does not belong to Zinger. It belongs to itself, but Zinger would like to be near it, would like to have some claim to its company. Desire, Zinger decides. That is the word. Not the way the shoppers look at things they cannot afford, but the way other shoppers come in to absorb with full attention whatever indistinct flavor they were searching for.

Those shoppers always put Zinger on edge, like the taste of pocket change, the scrape of chairs on tile. They are the ones most likely to notice the things that live in the mall, to see past the veils that shade each square foot.

Zinger waits until the mall is emptying itself out, until the gates are pulled down in clanking chorus with the voices of employees calling to each other in relief. The drone of cleaning machines and the hum of cash out procedures rise in harmonies, pause for cycles of call and response. Already the shadows are thicker than they dare to be during the daytime, during open hours when anyone could follow them to the recesses of the labyrinth.

This is purpose, Zinger thinks. This is reason for being. This is waiting for the right moment to return, with a goal and with expectation. The employees do not know it, but the mannequin is going to belong to Zinger. And to itself, always to itself. But not to the manager. Not to the store. Zinger has been whittled away to nothing by the mall, but the mannequin is solid; the mannequin is real. It can teach the trick of realness to Zinger, remind them of the secret.

The day creatures, subtle and camouflaged as they are, are the first to return to their sleeping places. The night creatures stir in their beds. Zinger waits for that perfect still moment between the two moments, and then rushes to the mannequin. This time, they do not hesitate; Zinger pushes through the gate blocking the store's entrance. The strength of their focus alone carries them to the window display.

Once, Zinger knew how to say hello. But in the very moment when Zinger wants that skill the most, they realize they have lost the voice they did not recognize was gone.

The mannequin is unmoved by Zinger's failure, does not appear to notice Zinger's presence at all. Its considerable plastic attention remains fixed on the surface of the table that stands to one side, and Zinger feels so heavy that they sink low, all the way to the floor, unobserved.

Zinger did not anticipate this, did not consider that success and failure were options in equal measure. The weight of their unthought holds them to the carpet, and Zinger cannot summon the energy needed to lift themself. Other things are stirring in the mall, and they pass the window, peering in to witness Zinger's shame.

The laughter is cold. It freezes Zinger where they have huddled in a small lump. They must escape or risk shriveling away entirely. Zinger must retreat and brave the scorn of the night things.

Zinger finds just enough momentum to inch along and find the transition from tile to low-pile carpet. They sigh their way through the grate and gather themself for their retreat.

The mockery, indistinct mutterings in unreal voices, is as expected. Zinger lets the sound push them, propel them. They gather speed despite their weariness and wind deeper into the body of the mall. Their haven is dusty and reassuring, undisturbed. Like their voice, it has been forgotten. Zinger would tear at themself if they could, if there were enough of them to rend apart in anger.

This is a feeling they have a name for: misery.

———

When the first security guard brings the jangle of morning to the mall, Zinger creeps out of their hiding place, rides the up escalator over and over again. It's nothing like the view from the ceiling, but Zinger likes the cheerful work of the machinery and the interlocking teeth of each step. It's a good vantage point from which to watch the mall wake up and stretch all its many legs.

Zinger has found new resolve; sulking will accomplish nothing, they think. Their purpose is unaltered; they still desire to know the mannequin. In the absence of a voice, there must be other ways of communicating. Zinger feels an electric urge, like someone has replaced a blown fuse, cleared the way for current to flow through them.

There is no reason to wait; the employees have not yet arrived. If they do not make their attempt now, Zinger will, they are certain, erase themself entirely. They will be the agent of their own unmaking if they cannot relearn the process of existing.

They head for the store.

This time their approach is less bold; Zinger thinks maybe once they might have been polite. The mannequin is still studying the smooth surface of the table interrupted by stacks of bright sweaters. It is a kindness, maybe, that the mannequin will not acknowledge Zinger's agony. It is almost privacy for Zinger's first attempts at connecting with whatever presence inhabits the metal and plastic body.

Even so, Zinger recognizes a burning ache, the way it feels to be ignored. They go in low, barely above the dirt in the grout lines. The grit of it makes Zinger's path bumpy, but rouses their imagination. The floor might as well have been their grave the night before, but the morning makes Zinger realize: this is not dirt from the mall. The dirt was persistent, found a way inside by shoes and clothes and wind.

If dirt can be so determined, then they can realize a way to reach out. None of this restores Zinger's power of speech, but it is an encouragement. They will not descend again.

Instead of fading, Zinger rises. They lift themself higher, turn and twist a parabola. Zinger sketches more figures just to stretch, to feel the extent of themself.

They are many things, Zinger thinks, but they do not have to be helpless. They do not always have to hide or flee. They do not need a voice to make the mall hear them.

Zinger floats higher and then down again to shove against the table. It shudders, and one precarious stack of sweaters falls. The neat folds splay out, and Zinger pauses, feels that electric current again. They jolt harder against the table, revel in the noise it makes, which is loud and real in the way that Zinger must have been before they were in the mall.

The table legs screech on the tile, and the mannequin does not move, but Zinger does not care. The noise is the thing, the shout that Zinger cannot give for themself. They roll around and wallow in the volume, repeat it with deliberation and self-congratulation.

Zinger is not floating, is not depending on the air currents that rattle through the vents. They are zipping and zooming, with self-propulsion they did not know they could command. The sweaters are draped all over the floor now, and the table is pushed right up against the glass. There is nothing subtle about Zinger's flight.

On the other side of the window, the mall creatures that had laughed at Zinger pause in their paths to watch again.

This is a happening that is out of the ordinary. But Zinger does not stop to feel their regard. Instead, Zinger slams the table against the glass again, knocks into the light fixtures on the upswing until light bulbs shatter and fall like ice. Then they swoop back down to do it again.

The dust that was on the floor rises every time another sweater hits the ground. Zinger wishes they could cheer and then bangs into the window to make the window cheer for them instead.

Between one noise and the next, something shifts. Zinger freezes where they are, too bold now for hiding and too riled for turning away slowly. Instead, they face the feeling of being watched, turn to give the attention on them their own attention in return. Zinger is not prey.

The mannequin, still all unyielding, has turned its attention to Zinger.

Zinger wants to preen, wants the mannequin to see how glorious Zinger is even though this is the first time Zinger has considered whether they are pleasing. But Zinger cannot fail to appreciate their own attributes. The mall recognized that Zinger has no voice and has loaned Zinger its very materials to make up for that loss.

The creatures outside the glass roar, raise the sort of static that will obscure the footage on the security cameras. It is the wild exaltation of a forest, of an ocean. It is the wilderness inside the walls acknowledging the victory of one of their own. Zinger has no memory before the mall, but now Zinger is not trapped; instead Zinger belongs in the mall, is born of the mall.

As though the ruckus of the assembled was a cue, the mannequin regards Zinger. They have never felt anything quite like the mannequin's careful examination. Zinger waits for judgment, still and confident. This is what it means for Zinger to exist.

And when the mannequin smiles, its featureless face is lit

like a department store makeup mirror, making promises of a better self; Zinger thinks they can already see strange events unfolding in the reflection. Zinger lowers themself, eases with gentle care and precision until they are resting directly in front of the mannequin, as close as a lover. Then, though Zinger does not remember having a face, Zinger smiles in return.

2

Skin Like Carapace

Steve Toase

I sleep shallow and my memories whisper in my ear, their hand on my shoulder so I cannot evade them. They speak to me of the first time I came to the market of fragrance, 16 years old and face bare apart from one age branch carved above the broken brow of my nose. I pay them no heed, but it's hard, hard to ignore the first taste of the air surrounding the market. Then and still the greatest wonder of the Land of No Light.

Here you can buy powders to stain your skin with the scent of fly agaric and birch bark, or smoke to disguise you as a freshwater pool to hide from violent and determined creditors. Every day, between the fourth and the fifth bell, dancers gather on the cobbled square. Each one is bathed since birth in a different essence. They weave their scents into epic stories of the origins of the four Royal houses, and the spectres whose tattered odour is carried on the wind. Those who brush against the dancers never clean that patch of skin and carry the story on them throughout their lives.

If I concentrate, I can still smell the tang of blood from my scuffed knees and feel the sting from picking pea grit from my scabs. Those times when my voice was too cracked to keep me on my feet. But those scars were trivial. With the help of older traders, I soon learnt to navigate between the stalls by the click of my tongue and the brush of fungus that grew on the worn oak boards.

That was a long time ago, and now I am not a young man. I sit in the centre of the market in a patch of crumbled marsh salt and tall wild garlic. No-one can enter without a Royal Warrant and no one can leave without being turned to silence. I can hardly smell the market now. The anise, cinnamon, and sage no longer reach me, drowned out by the perfumes leaking from my body and staining my clothes.

Some time has passed since the Royal guards brought me here. How much I'm no longer sure. I've tried to keep track of the bells, of the ebb and flow of trading. Each session flows into the other and I lose track so easily. It was an accident. I think they know that, so they guided me here with gentle hands rather than dragging me in chains.

The day was hot, and my hands sweated up as I poured oils and tinctures. That was why the bottle slipped from my grip. The embossed glass smashed and spilt the Queen's scent over the poor girl walking by, soaking her rags with frankincense and saffron, sandalwood and ambergris.

Sellers and buyers alike approached her, smelling the perfume of their Regent, grasping her clothes and running their fingers across her forehead, surprise overriding any sense of etiquette. Instead of the arcing inscription scars of the Royal family they felt only shallow indentations of a house with no name. Their hands found no silk-threaded embroidery, no pearls warming to their touch, or delicate lace finer than breath, only the tattered rags of a starving girl. Rumours spread of the Queen appearing in the market wearing tattered linen, and ash to grit her skin. Skin that was cold to the touch from the lack of fine robes. Seven satires were composed by street musicians and four caricatures carved into soapstone, each coated with a wash of frankincense and wood ash.

After I was taken, no one knew or asked what happened to the girl, but not an hour goes past when I don't think of her and my collusion in her fate.

There is still time for me to run, to hide. To take handfuls of river mud and scrub my skin until my scent is worn away. I could conceal myself between footstep and speech, an outlaw. But who would I be then, a perfumer with no scent? To run would mean never smelling the haze of the market again, never becoming drunk on the mix of musk and oakmoss. Instead, I will wait for the judgement of the Queen and hope she is merciful. I am not a young man, and I am too tired to run.

I listen as the Queen's Justice approaches, trailed by her twelve servants. First, they walk across the cloister, where trinkets of lavender are sold from rough-woven blankets. Their feet crunch on sand made of a million empty seashells. Next, they cross the gravel path. I can hear mumbles of conversations and their boots scuff up small sprays of grit. They pass through the cobbled square, smooth soles slipping on the rounded stones. They are talking about me, though I know any decision will have already been reached. As one creature, they cross the turf to stand around me. Their breath is controlled and shallow. I can taste it on the air, pungent with alcohol and calilaysa.

The Queen's Justice approaches the garlic patch, crushing the plants underfoot and leaning in close. Reaching up, I run the pad of my palm across the woman's face. I feel where age and the inscriber's chisel have turned her beautiful, marking out her life. First, I trace the lines of her office, the curving fronds of the royal seal, then the tree of age rising up the centre of her forehead, following the inscriptions marking journeys and lovers. Finally, I bring my hand down to her mouth, touching the impressions marking each laugh and frown. The Justice returns the greeting, her long fingers reading the carvings across my face, pushing into my beard to touch the scars hidden on my cheeks. She grips my neck just under my chin.

"My mistress could have you turned to silence, your scent ground into the dirt underfoot and your marks wiped from all memory," the Justice says. "Instead, she will give you a chance to redeem yourself. Succeed and you can return to your work, though you will never again serve the Royal Court. Fail and you will be turned to silence."

"And if I don't accept?" I say, although I know the answer. The Justice says nothing.

I tense my neck muscles in acknowledgement. The Justice lets her hand smile against my skin.

"Before the end of trading you must answer this question. What is everywhere yet has no scent?"

Then there is just the sound of breathing. I listen as the Justice and her twelve servants leave. There is still time to run, but I am not a young man and I have no heart for it.

Left alone I think over her words and think over the riddle. The question makes no sense. I am a master perfumer in the market of fragrance, and we are taught young that everything has a scent, and we learn young how to extract it. We can take tinctures from fossilised shells, from your lover's touch, from your child's amniotic-soaked first breath and your lover's regret-laden last. There is nothing in the Land of No Light absent of scent, and knowing this I start to prepare myself for silence. I am not a young man, and maybe it is time to no longer be.

Yet I try to ignore the hopelessness of my situation and ask those who pass my confinement. I speak to traders who gather because they have known me since I first stumbled between their bouquets of dried flowers, and I ask those who gather out of morbid curiosity. No-one has an answer for me. They drift away through guilt, though the causes of their conscience are a world apart. I find myself alone again and try to come up with an answer, but every object and creature I bring to mind has its own taint and stench. With no hope left, I sit listening to and inhaling my home for one last time.

I hear her first, shuffling at the limit of my internment. She smells of condensation and death-watch beetles.

"You must leave," I say in a whisper. I don't want another life on my conscience, even as I teeter on the edge of losing my own.

"I can answer your riddle for you," she says. Her voice sounds like the throwing of bones, desiccated and rotten.

She moves closer and takes my wrist. Her skin is as smooth as carapace. She runs my hand across her face, and I find nothing. No marks of office or inscriptions of achievement, no engravings of shared jokes and private sorrows, just blank, smooth, flesh stretched across bone, taut with emptiness. Bile rises from my stomach as my hand finds her face bare of marks. I can feel the acid burn my throat and taste it age my teeth. No-one is without a past or story. Even newborns carry the scars of birth, yet her face is absent of all of this. From the set of her jaw and razor cut of her cheekbones, I know she is no child. I want to take handfuls of grit and scrub my palms down to the bone in case whatever disease afflicts her, whatever curse that has wiped her skin embryo clean, infects me. Better to let flames lick and blister my skin into strands of living liquid than touch her face. I try to bury my disgust and carry on, though she cannot be ignorant of my feelings. I am not a young man and have never been good at hiding my emotions. I bring my hand over her mouth and feel no breath, only the wet, slow touch of her lips against my fingers. Trying not to flinch, I take hold of her wrist and bring her hand in turn to my face, letting her read me. Her touch is slow and invasive. It takes all my will not to run as far as the entangled plants and crushed salt will let me.

"I can answer your riddle for you," she says again, her voice no warmer.

"And what do I give in return?"

"If you don't get the answer you will be reduced to silence. Surely any price I ask of you will be less than that?"

I think on this, and am not convinced she speaks the truth, but hers is the only help that has come, and I have never claimed to be wise. I place her hand on my neck and tense my muscles in agreement. She clasps my hand, fingers between fingers, and moves our grip to the oath scar on my left cheek. She speaks first.

I pause, unsure if I have heard correctly, then repeat the words. "I swear that if the answer saves me from silence we will be married." I am a master perfumer and know any answer given will be wrong.

She leans in close and whispers the solution to me. I know as she speaks that this woman with no history, no inscriptions or crows' feet to bring beauty to her face, has given me the correct answer to save me from being reduced to silence. In that moment, I know if I give her answer to the Queen's Justice, I will be released from my confinement and this woman will be my wife.

"I will leave now and return as your betrothed after you have given your answer to the Queen's Justice," she says, and I listen to her go.

Do not think that I am not considering giving the wrong answer. What value are honour and oaths when I will no longer exist to care? But something stops me, and instead I sit waiting for the end of the market and the Queen's Justice to return.

They come as the sound of bartering lulls. I know the traders and sellers are waiting to hear my fate. I can taste them breathing though they still their lungs. The Queen's

Justice and her servants have scorched corpse hair and animal pelts against hot stones and dressed themselves in the smoke. They mute their shoes, but to me they sound like a storm gathering.

The Justice steps onto the salt and wild garlic and we exchange greetings.

"Do you have an answer for me?" she says, and for a moment I think I detect a hint of regret in her voice as she places her hand against my neck. I tense my muscles.

"What is everywhere and has no scent? I caution you to answer carefully as only one answer can be given."

I pause. Some think I do this for effect, but I am not a young man and it takes time to gather my thoughts.

"Sound," I say.

A gasp goes through the crowd like an echo, starting with the Queen's Justice and spreading backwards to the far reaches of the market.

The next few moments feel like an anticlimax, even for me who can now go on living. The Justice takes my hand and leads me from my confinement and the inscriber is called forward to add a new mark to my face. It takes much searching to find the symbol. Many markets have met since anyone left the garlic alive. Certainly, it has not happened in my time. The blood from my new scars reminds me of scuffed knees all those markets ago. I allow myself a moment of relief, but it is short lived.

"Where is my husband to be?" my saviour calls out from the cobbled square.

I think about ignoring her. The punishment for oath breaking is the loss of a hand. Surely that is less of a burden than a wife I do not want? A wife who is so without experience that she does not bear one mark. Then I hear her cry taken up by others.

"Where is this woman's husband to be?" and the gossips go to ask her story.

Before long, the market is noxious with it. I have little choice but to approach her and acknowledge my oath.

The wedding is short and over quickly, and I do not wish to dwell on it here.

She moves into my home, and I feel like she's everywhere. I go to bury my clothes and boots, stained as they are with the herb of silence and brittle salt. When I leave her alone she recovers them, and I resent her for it.

We bed down in separate rooms. I say my back hurts, or my hands are so soaked in tinctures that they will burn her skin if we embrace. While she sleeps, I dab diluted perfume behind her ears. Too subtle for most to sense, even my new bride, but I can smell it and leave any room she enters. I do not want to convulse in her presence. I'm disgusted by her, but I am not a young man and try to hold onto some manners. This way I carry on as before, though another Perfumer dresses the Queen's skin. A small price compared to others I pay.

She asks to come to the market with me, to sell scents to the gentry, and crush spices for me.

"Imagine how many more beautiful perfumes you could make with two of us working on your stall," she says.

"Not today," I say. "I have a delivery of herbs coming and there is little enough space for me." "I am mixing today. If you knock over the tinctures our livelihood will be gone." "I have an important buyer coming and need to give him my full attention."

She does not believe these excuses and neither do I. How can I tell her that if she came to the market and someone exchanged greetings with her I would be a laughing stock. I have little enough trade as it is. Few want to buy from me in case the taint of silence has slipped into my fragrances.

Instead, she stays in the house and cooks and cleans. I come home and the house reeks with the scent of balms she rubs into bruises from moving around the unfamiliar rooms.

Yet I cannot deny she cares for me well and shows interest in my work. I start bringing bottles of essence home and teaching them to her. Help her learn sandalwood from saffron and rosemary from rosehip. Though my tolerance for her in my life grows, I still cannot bear for that unmarked skin to touch me and flinch away when her hand goes to rest on my arm.

I smell tears as I walk in, a slight tang in the cold air of the house. It takes time to find her, curled up by the side of the bed. I ask what is wrong. She says nothing. Without thinking, without giving my revulsion time to overrule my instinct, I hold her hand, stroking the back of her fingers. I lean in and kiss her cheek. She still does not move, but her back is less tense. At a loss how else to help I go into the kitchen and prepare a meal for her. I do not know what to say to take the sadness away, so instead I steam fish and mushrooms and pour a small glass of wine before leading her to the table. Still she says nothing. I place the fork in her hand, spear the scales of the fish and bring it up to her mouth. Still she says nothing, but when my hand brushes her face her cheeks are dry, and I am sure she is smiling.

"It's been a while since I've prepared food," I say. "Have I removed all the bones?"

"There are no bones, but something is missing."

My heart sinks.

"The fish is a bit dry," she says. "It needs butter."

I go to the cupboard and bring the butter to the table, cutting off a slice and letting it settle on her fish. I hear her chew, then she pauses.

"Has the butter made it more palatable?" I ask.

"There is still something not quite right," she says. "This butter is unsalted. It needs a little salt."

"But I have no salt here," I say, disappointed to have let her down.

"Reach under your bed and get your old clothes."

I climb up, groping around for the shirt and trousers. Amongst the mud I find a little salt. When I come back to the kitchen, she is melting butter, and I crumble in the crystals. I hear her dip in a spoon and taste the butter, then sigh.

"What's wrong?" I ask.

"There is still something missing," she says.

I wait for her to speak again. I want her to enjoy this meal. She deserves some happiness, I think to myself.

"A pinch or two of wild garlic would make it perfect."

"I don't keep garlic," I say.

"Surely there will be a few leaves stuck in the folds of your clothes."

I find the garments on the floor. The leaves are old, yet still pungent, enough to stain my fingers. I find three and take them across to where she tends the pan, break them into pieces and drop them into the now salty butter.

As the cooking stones warm, the acrid mixture rises around us sticking to our face and hair. I stand behind her and put my arms around her waist.

Her fingertips change first, calluses erupting through the skin. She is a musician, left- handed and her touch knows the caress of strings, shaping the air itself. Veins rise in her hand, thick and strong. I place my hand against her cheek, slick with condensation. Marks put there by the inscriber's chisel spread. Each one rises like the scent of leaves crushed between mortar and pestle, and as with the most aromatic of herbs my breath catches in my throat. The branches on her forehead are many, but less than mine. I find the scar of where she grew up, and the journeys she made to come to the market, what her trade is and how many honours she has been awarded. I want to tell her how beautiful she is, but words evade me. All I can hear is her breathing. All I can taste is her breath tinged with honey-suckle and jasmine. Lines appear around her eyes like foot-prints in clay. They tell me more of her life has been spent laughing than crying, though there is deep sorrow held on her face, too. On her left cheek three marks for children born, on her right two for those who did not survive. My touch explores her face and the reality of my cruelty is laid before me. It is her turn to kiss away my tears. I find my tongue and speak quiet apologies. She kisses these away too.

Later, when she sleeps, I wipe the perfume from behind ears.

Ours is a marriage of things not said and things not asked, but I am not a young man and I am content. And though it is one of the things never said or asked, I think she is content too.

3

Crossing

A.C. Wise

Emma Rose is four years old the first time she enters the ocean alone. All her life, she's lived with the beach at the end of her street. Her parents carried her into the waves the week she was born. When she learned to stand, they taught her to float. Older still, they showed her how to stretch her body out long, how to reach, and turn her head to breathe, letting the water guide her like a friend.

Now, her parents watch from towels on the shore. Sun reflects off the Dover chalk cliffs so they shine brilliant white. The wind plays with Emma Rose's curls, and the tide garlands her toes with foam. She steps carefully and the water swirls up to her knees, her waist. There's a small moment of doubt, but surely the water will keep her safe. She knows it as well as she knows the sound of her father's voice, the touch of her mother's hand.

Goose-pimples fade as she adjusts and the water shapes itself around her. Squinting, she pretends she can see all the way to France. Her parents showed her pictures in a book holding frozen moments of their lives before her. Her mother with curls so much like Emma Rose's, her father with a smudge of flour on his nose, each of them proudly holding up a tray of pastries they made in the cooking class where they met.

Looking toward the land of her parents' stories, Emma Rose knows she will cross the water one day. Not in a boat; she will swim.

Emma Rose stands on her tippy toes, then lets the water take her. She floats, lying on her stomach, putting her face in the waves. She opens her eyes.

Through the salt sting, the world blurs blue and grey. She lets a few bubbles escape to rise around her like pearls. Just as she's about to turn her head to breathe, a face appears below her.

The eyes are grey, like Emma Rose's, the color of waves under a sullen sky. The woman's hair floats around her head, long and straight, tinted green like she's been underwater a long time. She smiles.

Emma Rose is so startled she screams, and cold saltwater rushes into her mouth. Panicked, she forgets everything her parents taught her. Her limbs won't cooperate. She can't lift her face out of the water. She can't remember which way is up.

Then hands catch her. Her father lifts her out of the water, and maybe the woman pushes her from below. Her father pats her back and she coughs water.

"Shhh," her mother whispers. "It's okay."

They make a protective circle around her with their bodies, standing knee deep in the waves. Emma Rose cries, shock and fading fear. She clings to her father, her head on his shoulder, while her mother strokes her back. When her sobs turn to hiccupping coughs, her father carries her back to the shore.

"What happened out there, jellyfish?" her father asks.

His eyes are blue, like the water when the sun is bright and borrows pieces of the sky to wear like a gown. Her mother's eyes are deep brown, like the water under the moon. No one has ever been able to explain to Emma Rose where her grey eyes come from.

Except once, her mother told Emma Rose she dreamed of the ocean the night she was born. Sometimes Emma Rose secretly believes she's a princess from under the sea. Her parents found her on the shore, curled up in a giant oyster shell. The woman under the water must be a princess, too, a secret one, just like her.

"I..." Emma Rose hesitates. "I saw a fish. It surprised me."

Emma Rose doesn't dare peek to see if her parents believe her. The lie fizzes in her stomach, making her feel bad and good at the same time.

"Okay, jellyfish." Her father smooths her water-wet curls. "That's enough for today. We can try again tomorrow."

Her parents have always taught her not to quit when something is hard, but to keep going until it isn't scary anymore. Emma Rose takes her father's hand on one side, and her mother's on the other. She walks between them up the path leading toward home. Next time, she promises herself she won't be frightened, no matter what she sees.

———

Emma Rose is eleven years old the next time she sees the woman in the water, even though she swims in the ocean almost every day. Her bones have grown long under her skin, her body stretching like taffy. She wears her curls pulled back now, making herself sleeker.

She's on the cusp of turning twelve. Tomorrow is her birthday, and she's celebrating with friends. Her parents sent them to the beach with a hamper stuffed with food. Cold chicken. Home-baked bread. Lemonade in a glass bottle. A cake, layered with sponge and jam and frosted white, topped with the reddest strawberries.

Best of all, the girls are allowed to be alone. No parents to supervise them. They shriek and run, daring the edge of the waves. They splash each other, and pretend to be mad, then make up again. They braid strands of seaweed, making bracelets and necklaces and crowns.

None of the other girls know the water the way Emma Rose does, but she pretends to be like them. Rather than swimming, she stands waist-deep, dunking the other girls under the water and allowing them to dunk her in turn. She plays chicken, Bethany's legs draped over her shoulders as they charge toward Sara and Maureen.

When they grow tired, they troop to the blanket spread on the shore, falling on the picnic like locusts. Then they lie for a while with their heads in each other's laps, forming a lopsided circle as their stomachs settle.

Emma Rose ends up with her head in Corinne's lap. She's only known Corinne for two years; Corinne's parents moved from Cornwall and she had to join their class halfway through the year. Sara, Maureen, and Bethany, she's known since they were all five years old.

"Are you going to cut the cake?" Maureen asks after a few minutes, growing bored and fidgety.

Maureen has red-gold hair that Emma Rose has always admired, and freckles scattered across the bridge of her nose. Her eyes are bluer than Emma Rose's father's—like the ocean in pictures where the beaches are white sand and palms trees cast angular shadows on the ground.

Maureen sits up, upsetting the circle. Corinne's legs twitch under Emma Rose's head, but Emma Rose doesn't move for a moment, just to see what happens. Corinne's shadow falls over her as Corinne sits up, and Emma Rose feels the muscles of

Corinne's legs, imagining what they would feel like stretching and bunching through the water.

Corinne peers down at her. Her eyes are a color Emma Rose can't quite name. Not brown, but not green either. Like the water when it's choppy, sand stirred into the waves and catching the light, glinting with flecks of gold. Corinne drapes the seaweed crown she braided over Emma Rose's brow. It's damp and cold and smells of salt, but Emma Rose doesn't shiver.

"Now you look like a fairy queen," Corinne says.

She doesn't quite smile, but her lips do something that changes her face, and it brings a fluttering tightness to Emma Rose's stomach. She sits up too quickly, and the seaweed crown falls into her lap with a wet splat.

Maureen hands Emma Rose the cake knife, and Bethany passes plates around. Corinne touches Emma Rose's wrist.

"You have to make a wish."

Emma Rose pretends her face is underwater, seeing how long she can go before she turns her head to breathe. She's still holding her breath when the last slice of cake is cut, and only then does she let it go.

After the other girls' parents collect them, Emma Rose stays on the beach alone. Wind stirs the sea grass and wild-flowers dotting the path leading home. Emma Rose thinks about France. She thinks about Corinne. She touches her forehead where the seaweed crown rested, and the skin is warm.

Emma Rose does what she always does when she's frightened or sad or confused. She swims. She launches herself into the waves, thinking for a moment that perhaps the time is now, she will swim all the way across the Channel. But that's stupid, and she knows it. Instead she flings her arms out as far as she can and kicks her legs hard, crossing back and forth parallel to the beach.

She isn't fighting the sea, never that. She's fighting herself. Exhaustion, that's what she wants, bone-deep. She'll sleep through her birthday, sleep for a whole week. It's what she's thinking when she sees the woman beneath her, her eyes grey and her hair drifting just the way Emma Rose remembers. Her hair seems a little greener, though, almost black, and the bones of her cheeks are sharper.

This time, Emma Rose doesn't scream. She stills herself, sculling water to stay in place. The woman flashes pearly teeth, a sheening purple color like the inside of an oyster shell.

Emma Rose's skin prickles. The woman's eyes are a mirror for her own, even if everything else about her is different—the length and curves of her body, the dip of her waist, the prominent line of her ribs, the pallor of her skin. After a moment, it strikes Emma Rose that the woman is naked, and her skin flushes so hot she fears the water around her will turn to steam.

Emma Rose reaches down and the woman reaches up at the same time. Their fingertips touch, then their palms. The water keeps Emma Rose from telling whether the woman's skin is cold.

Their lips meet next, the woman rising, Emma Rose falling. The woman's mouth tastes of salt, of seaweed, the grit of sand, and the smoothness of a pearl. She tastes of everything but drowning. As long as their lips touch, Emma Rose can hold her breath forever.

With her mouth against the woman's, Emma Rose thinks of Corinne. By the time she climbs back to the shore, her skin is so wrinkled it feels like it will slide off her bones, and her legs are trembling. Emma Rose turns to look at the water one last time, scanning it for a shadow beneath the waves, any glimpse of the woman. There is nothing, only the sun sinking and painting the water bright gold.

———

After her second encounter with the woman, Emma Rose

begins swimming at least twice every day. She swims first thing in the morning before school, and first thing in the afternoon when she gets home. Days and weeks at a time pass where the woman keeps herself to a constant flicker of motion at the corner of Emma Rose's eye. But other times, she glides close as a shadow, her face inches from Emma Rose's own. When Emma Rose's muscles burn and she wants to quit, the woman brings her lips close, closer, until they touch. Until they share a heartbeat, share breath, and Emma Rose feels she could swim forever and never stop.

Other times, the woman is nowhere to be seen. On those days, Emma Rose swims purely for herself. She comes to love the solitude as much as the company, but it's a different kind of love. On those days, the water is hers. And she knows, one day, she will cross it. Her name will be written alongside Gertrude Ederle, Amelia Gade Corson, Mercedes Gleitze, and Florence Chadwick.

She can't be the first to cross the Channel, but maybe she can be fastest? The most crossings? Maybe she'll be the one to swim across and never come back. She'll find another sea, another ocean, another crossing and just keep going, swimming her way around the world.

Emma Rose spends so much time in the ocean that her father jokes she will turn into a fish. Emma Rose can't remember what wish she made before cutting her birthday cake, so she wishes for her father's words to come true.

———

Emma Rose is sixteen the first time she kisses a girl outside the water. Her name is Martha. Corinne has long since moved away, and Emma Rose barely even thinks about her anymore.

The kiss with Martha happens on the bleachers at school. Martha runs track, her legs flashing graceful and long the way

Emma Rose's do in the water. She is faster than anyone else on the team.

Emma Rose and Martha have been friends for seven months when Emma Rose starts regularly watching track practice. Martha lives just a few streets over, so it only makes sense for Emma Rose to stay so they can walk home together.

The sun warms the bleachers, heat soaking through Emma Rose's uniform to the back of her thighs. She watches Martha, her brown skin gleaming with sweat, even though her motions seem effortless. Gravity doesn't apply; she pushes off the ground, and the earth pulls her along. Practice ends, and Martha comes over to the bleachers, grinning. Her frizzy hair is tied back in two poofs, and even they glisten with sweat, the black overlaid with droplets like a net of diamonds.

"That was brilliant," Emma Rose says, then blushes. She's been watching Martha run for weeks, why should this be any different?

Martha sits beside her, their knees almost touching, catching her breath. They talk about nothing for a while, then somehow they're kissing. Emma Rose isn't sure who started it, but she doesn't care. Martha's mouth tastes like the orange sports drink she says is her secret weapon—sugar-brightness exploding on Emma Rose's tongue. The kiss goes on for so long, Emma Rose is sure she's drowning. And when it ends, it's far too soon.

When they finally break apart, Martha rests her forehead against Emma Rose's, dampening it. Grey eyes meet deep brown, and they giggle. The laughter runs out, and they kiss again. The nervous fluttering in Emma Rose's stomach calms; instead of butterflies, she's full of sunlight, bursting out through her pores.

———

Emma Rose and Martha have been secret-not-so-secret offi-

cial girlfriends for three months when Emma Rose brings
Martha to the beach for the first time. She hasn't been swimming as much lately, her afternoon sessions melting into time
watching Martha practice, or going to the shops together, or
pausing to kiss by the side of the road, around the corner of
buildings, anywhere and everywhere they can. Emma Rose
and Martha are constantly amazed by each other, discovering
all the things they have in common, wondering how they
managed to grow up so close to each other without ever
knowing it because they didn't go to the same school
until now.

They play the 'what if' game. What if you'd never transferred schools? What if I'd transferred years ago and we'd
known each other since we were five? What if we walked right
past each other on the street one day when we were twelve
and we never knew? And they both agree now that they've
found each other, they need to make up for lost time.

"You never came to the beach when you were little?"
Emma Rose asks, leading Martha down the flower-lined path.

Martha shakes her head. "My dad's little brother almost
drowned when they were kids. He's been terrified of the water
ever since."

"My grandfather used to race sailboats," Emma Rose says.
"My dad always loved being out on the water. My mom
wanted to be a marine biologist until she discovered a passion
for baking and became a pastry chef. They've been bringing
me here since I was a baby."

The sun is setting, tinting the water shades of peach and
coral. Standing on the shore, Emma Rose feels the tug of
France, gentle, yet ever-present at the edge of her mind.
There's a pang of guilt. She's been neglecting the water. And
there's something else that isn't guilt; it's almost fear. Emma
Rose hasn't seen the woman in the water since she first kissed
Martha. It isn't unknown for her to disappear for months at a
time, but this feels different somehow.

"Fancy a swim?" Emma Rose pushes her doubt away and pulls her shirt over her head, revealing the swimsuit underneath.

"It's getting late." Martha looks at the water with unease.

"We won't go in deep." Emma Rose kicks off her shorts. "I promise I'll hold your hand the whole time."

That does the trick. Martha skims out of her clothes, and it turns out she's wearing a swimsuit underneath her clothes too, which makes Emma Rose's chest squinch in a complicated way.

She's been thinking about telling Martha she loves her for days. The words are always on the tip of her tongue, but she keeps swallowing them down. She's pretty sure Martha will say it back, but what if she doesn't? What if she says it but doesn't mean it? What if it comes out all wrong, or she scares Martha away?

They walk to the water's edge. Martha hisses at the temperature; the waves tangle lace around her ankles. They take it slow. To their mid-calves, their knees, their thighs. Waves surge around their waists, and Emma Rose lets herself fall backward. The water catches her and plays a soft game of tug of war. She smiles at Martha, in up to her armpits now. Emma Rose sees she's standing on her tiptoes, afraid to cede the last bit of control.

Martha has never been anything but graceful; there's something comforting in seeing her out of her element. It makes her more human.

Emma Rose holds out her hand. Martha takes it, letting Emma Rose guide her until the ground no longer supports her. In a moment, Emma Rose will put her arms around Martha's waist. She'll kiss her. She'll finally say what she's been longing to say.

Then, sudden as a blink, Martha is gone. All Emma Rose can do is stare. The water froths, Martha thrashing, and Emma Rose dives, trying to pull Martha to the surface. Something holds Martha down. Emma Rose catches a glimpse of a face beside Martha's. Grey eyes meet grey. A flash of teeth. Emma Rose wants to pretend it's a trick of churned water and flashing limbs, but she cannot. The woman's face is undeniably there, and in this moment, she looks more like Emma Rose than ever, mocking her.

Emma Rose uses all her strength, and Martha pops to the surface like a cork, gasping.

"Are you o—" But Emma Rose doesn't get any farther.

The sky bruises purple, the first pale stars beginning to appear. Martha's pupils are impossibly wide, dark like the ocean where it's deepest and coldest. She scrambles for the shore, trips, bangs her knee on the stones. A thin strand of watered blood runs down Martha's leg like a ribbon as she picks herself up again. She must have cut herself on the stones, Emma Rose thinks, and she tries not to picture sharp teeth like mother of pearl.

Emma Rose wades for the shore, trying to quell the thoughts spinning through her head. The water resists her so she's breathing hard by the time she gets to Martha's side. Martha shivers, her teeth clenched so hard the vein below her jaw protrudes.

When Emma Rose touches Martha's shoulder, Martha jerks away.

"Don't," Martha says, her voice fraying.

She gathers her clothes, and when she turns, she reveals a mark like a bruise, the faint outline of a hand upon her skin. More than that, it spreads dark tendrils through Martha's veins, flushing them the color of ink and the darkening sky. Emma Rose blinks, but the mark refuses to disappear. She reaches for Martha again, but Martha steps back, holding her clothes against her in a wet bundle like a shield.

"Just stay away from me."

Martha's eyes are wide; they are hurt and afraid. Afraid of Emma Rose. She pivots, heels striking the ground hard and when she reaches the road, Martha runs. Her track star legs carry her away without a backward glance.

Emma Rose's heart cracks, and it keeps cracking. The words she never got the chance to say lodge in her throat like barbs. Martha isn't coming back. She'll never talk to Emma Rose again. This is her fault. The woman tasted Martha on Emma Rose's skin, and now she's punishing her, hurting Martha to hurt Emma Rose.

The sky is full dark when Emma Rose flings herself back into the waves. She beats at them, letting her body rage. Salt water stands in for her tears. The ragged, horrible rhythm of her breath stands in place of screaming until her throat is raw and coughing up *I love you* in blood.

And when that is done, when her muscles tremble with exertion, she keeps swimming. If she's only allowed to have one thing, then she chooses this. Hollow, numb, her skin wrinkled and every part of her hurting, she refuses to leave. The waves can't frighten her away. Even though they took Martha, she won't quit. This ocean is hers, and one days she will force it to carry her all the way to France.

Finally, exhausted, Emma Rose puts her face in the water and drifts. Her eyes sting. She holds her breath and waits. She thinks of all those days with the woman gliding just beneath her, lending her strength to Emma Rose's own. Will she come to share this heartbeat, too, to lessen the burden, ease the pain?

Emma Rose loses track of time. Her chest aches with the desire to breathe before the woman appears. The sharpness of the woman's cheekbones and ribs is even more pronounced now. The grey cast to her skin makes Emma Rose think of sharks and hunger.

Emma Rose is hungry, too. The woman looks like her. Maybe they have always been the same. Maybe they are both monsters, unfit for the love of any but their own kind.

Emma Rose lets out the last of her breath, bubbles

escaping in a silent scream. The woman rises and Emma Rose falls, a tangle of arms. Coldwater lips crush against hers and Emma Rose bites down. Mouths and saltwater. Love on the cusp of violence. Desire that tastes like drowning. Release. It's almost as good as crying.

———

Emma Rose goes back to swimming twice every day. She doesn't speak to Martha. She avoids her in the halls. All she needs is the water.

There's a story Emma Rose remembers from when she was very young, from a big book of fairy tales, thick like an old-fashioned telephone book, with different colored pages. In the story, a rich man is visited every night by a ghost, or a water fairy. She stands at the end of his bed, dripping. She claims to love him, but he gets sick from lack of sleep and always being wet and cold. Finally, he tricks her into following him outside in winter so she freezes and never bothers him again.

The story both fascinated and terrified Emma Rose as a child. There was an illustration of the woman, glittering and perfect, frozen for all time, with no sense she would recover at winter's end. Emma Rose could never work out who the villain was supposed to be—the man who only wanted a good night's sleep, or the ghost who only wanted to be warm and loved. Maybe they were both monsters in their own way, perfect for each other.

It's nearly a year before she allows herself to kiss another woman on land. Her name is Joan. She's in her second year at university, and when Emma Rose meets her, she's home on summer holiday. She has a ring through her eyebrow, and one through her nose, and others Emma Rose will discover later, hidden by her clothing. Joan's laugh is almost a bray, unapologetic and full of joy. Her hair is red, not like Maureen's long ago, but dyed and cut short, spiked like the crest of an exotic bird.

Emma Rose doesn't love Joan; Joan is safe. She'll be back at school soon. In-between, they go to cafes and music clubs. Once, they go to a traveling funfair. The Ferris wheel carries them high up and then stops, suspending them over the twinkling lights below. The car rocks when they kiss. Joan's hands move under Emma Rose's shirt, and for just a moment, Emma Rose feels like she is the exotic bird, the one who might take flight. For just a moment, she feels like everything might be okay.

She doesn't take Joan to the beach. She never mentions the ocean at all. She leads a secret, double life, because she never stops swimming either.

She showed Martha her heart, the ocean, and she ran, so now Emma Rose keeps it locked inside. Instead of making time for the water in-between seeing Joan, she makes time for Joan by pulling herself away from the water—from the woman—as long as she can, which is never long.

———

Emma Rose is twenty-one when she attempts to cross the English Channel. Gertrude Ederle, the first woman to make the crossing, did it at nineteen. It was her second attempt, and she did it in fourteen hours and thirty-one minutes. Emma Rose has memorized the times and ages and number of attempts of every one of the women to cross the Channel, and some of the men, too. She will carry them with her when she steps into the water. If she succeeds, she will carry them with her all the way to the other side.

Emma Rose's parents are both in the boat accompanying her. Like her grandfather's sailing, like their love of cooking and baking, they understand her passion even if it doesn't exactly match their own. The whole way across, they will be there to feed her sugar cubes and protein blocks, to give encouragement, and gather her in their arms whether she succeeds or fails.

Emma Rose enters the water at 6:09 a.m. Scraps of cloud cling to the sky, the moon forgetting to clean up after itself. The water is a deep blue, brushed with hints of purple and grey. Her hair is short, curls flattened under a swim cap. Emma Rose lowers her goggles, rolls her neck, shakes her arms out so they hang loose and long.

Breathe. She reaches as far as she can with each stroke. The waves don't fight her, and she allows herself to hope. She keeps her rhythm steady. Stroke, stroke, stroke, turn, breathe. She kicks. She counts in her head, reciting names to keep time. Webb, Ederle, Toth. Breathe. Chadwick, Corson, Gleitze. Breathe. She sights by the boat so she doesn't go off course. Her parents speak encouragement, but mostly she is alone with the water, with her lungs and her heartbeat. France waits for her on the other side.

At seven hours, the water grows choppy, but Emma Rose doesn't stop. Her legs and arms burn. She has to fight a little harder against the weight of the water, but she won't quit. She thinks about the woman, about the times she pressed her lips against Emma Rose's, breathing for her. Doubt creeps in. What if she can't do this one her own?

As she turns her head to breathe, Emma Rose catches a flash of long limbs, blue-grey skin and mother of pearl teeth. A wave of panic rolls through her. She tries to push the doubt away, but it nags, sapping her strength. Just past eight hours, a cramp hits, hot and bright as though a hand slapped against her muscles. She thinks of Martha on the beach years ago and the not-bruise blooming on her skin.

No.

Emma Rose's heart fractures infinitely and intimately, branching patterns reaching all through her bones. She bites down hard on her lip, tasting salt blood and tries to swim through the pain.

Please, let me go.

Her legs won't cooperate, dead weight dragging her down.

A face glides just beneath hers, hair all twisting seaweed ribbons. Nothing about it is human except for the eyes—they are Emma Rose's own. The woman opens her mouth, but no bubbles emerge. Her smile is gloating, mocking.

Don't touch me, Emma Rose pleads silently. I want to do this on my own.

The woman reaches for her, and Emma Rose jerks upright. She signals the boat, the cramp stitching through her side, knotting her until she nearly screams. Hands pull her in, and maybe one hand lifts from the water, but whether it is to push her higher or pull her down, she cannot tell.

Emma Rose's lips are blue, bruised, as though someone has pummeled them. She can't stop shaking. Her mother wraps a thermal blanket around her shoulders. Her father brings her a thermos of tea, holding the cup because her hands are trembling.

Her parents put their arms around her. They tell her it will be okay. They can try again. Exhausted, Emma Rose leans against them and sobs her broken heart out. She is four years old again, and her parents encircle her with their bodies until there are no tears left, until she finally stops shaking, until she is warm.

———

Emma Rose tries again at twenty-three, and twenty-five, her confidence wearing thin. The first time, a mechanical failure in the boat turns them back; the second, an unexpected storm. She will never know whether she could have made it across. If she simply accepts the woman's help, will all these problems go away? But if she does, will she really be the one making the crossing? Maybe she isn't even meant to. The certainty she's carried since she was four weights her like a stone. How many times can she try and fail? How many times can she stand to have her heart broken?

———

Emma Rose is twenty-seven years old when she meets her first serious girlfriend. Her name is Elizabeth. They move in together after three months, which seems both fast and far too long to wait. Emma Rose wants to be touching her all the time, brushing her fingertips across the back of Elizabeth's hand, kissing her shoulder, pressing their legs against each other while they watch old movies and eat popcorn. It's like she has to constantly remind herself Elizabeth is real and not just a story she's told herself. That she won't vanish, or run away.

They've been living together for almost nine months when Emma Rose wakes to rain pummeling the windows. Briefly, Emma Rose mistakes the wet hush of traffic outside their apartment for the sound of the tide. She sits up, counting the space between flashes of lightning and growls of thunder. For just a moment, she swears there's a face in the water droplets, the outline of a woman's cheekbones, sharper than any human's should be, and a smile too wide. Emma Rose starts back. Is it her reflection? Is she imagining things?

"You okay?" Sleep-warm, Elizabeth sits up and wraps herself around Emma Rose, fitting her chin against Emma Rose's shoulder as if it was purpose—made for just that thing.

Emma Rose shivers. There's nothing outside but lightning and rain.

"Do you think it's possible for a person to be haunted?" Emma Rose asks, thinking of the fairy tale from long ago.

"You mean like sheets and chains? Rattling doors and disembodied voices?"

The questions aren't mocking. Emma Rose allows herself to sink back into Elizabeth's embrace. It's like the water long ago—holding her, knowing her, keeping her safe.

"Sort of." She takes a deep breath. "When I was little, I saw something in the water."

The whole story tumbles out. Elizabeth listens, never interrupting. The storm dies down until only the sound of rain dripping from the gutters remains. Emma Rose lapses into silence. She meets Elizabeth's eyes, which are pale blue with a ring of darker blue around the edges.

"Do you believe me?" Emma Rose asks.

"Yes." There is no hesitation. Elizabeth majored in English Literature and Comparative Mythology; Emma Rose shouldn't be surprised she understands about fairies and ghosts.

"You don't...I mean, you're not..." Emma Rose stops, unsure how to ask Elizabeth if she'll stay.

"Hey." Elizabeth catches Emma Rose's hands, pressing them between her own. "I'm not going anywhere."

"Why?" Emma Rose breathes out, afraid of the hope wanting to grow inside her.

"I don't scare that easily." Elizabeth smiles. "Besides, we all have our things, right? I support you, you support me."

"Yeah?" Emma Rose allows herself to relax just a little bit. "What's your thing?"

"Well, when you're rich and famous for crossing the Channel, I'll let you pay for everything while I go back to school. Then you can suffer through endless stuffy dinners with my fellow academics. It'll be a glamorous life, but it'll be ours."

Ours. The word beats inside Emma Rose, timed with her heart. It is echoed by words never spoken aloud, which she's long imagined spoken by blue-grey lips, slipping through teeth like mother of pearl. *You need me, just like I need you.*

She's always thought it meant a choice, to take the ocean

into her heart and nothing else, or give up on her dream. But maybe there's more.

"There are creatures that can't cross running water, right?" She tests the words out loud, feeling her way through them as she speaks.

"Sure." Elizabeth's eyes are bright, curious.

"What if my ghost, or whatever she is, can't step onto dry land without me."

It sounds silly, but Elizabeth puts her head to the side like she's considering Emma Rose's words. Maybe her ghost just wants to be warm and loved. Maybe neither of them are monsters. Maybe they can help each other somehow.

"If I try the crossing again, will you be there with me?" Emma Rose holds her breath. She looks into Elizabeth's eyes with all their myriad shades of blue.

"Of course," Elizabeth says. She wraps her hands around Emma Rose's. When they kiss, Emma Rose is light, buoyant, completely safe and surrounded. Elizabeth is the ocean that keeps her afloat.

———

Emma Rose is twenty-eight when she and Elizabeth walk down an aisle of strewn rose petals in her parents' garden. Emma Rose promises herself she won't cry and breaks her promise in the first five minutes. Her father is there with a tissue, his eyes bright and teary as well. They stumble through their vows, and even though Elizabeth cries too, when they kiss, somehow it doesn't taste like salt at all.

There's cake afterward, and champagne, and dancing, and the garden is strung with fairy lights. Over the music, Emma Rose hears the hush of waves. As they slow dance their last song, Emma Rose listens to Elizabeth's heartbeat, her breath, timed to Emma Rose's own. A sudden thought hits her, and it's like being bowled over by a wave. Needing someone else doesn't mean that she isn't also strong.

"I'm ready to try again," she says in a whisper so low she almost hopes Elizabeth won't hear.

"I know." Elizabeth brushes her lips across Emma Rose's brow. "I've already arranged for the boat and a hotel. We'll honeymoon in Paris when you get to the other side."

Emma Rose's breath catches. She looks at Elizabeth with the fairy lights gleaming in her hair. Elizabeth smiles, and Emma Rose falls in love all over again. She will keep Emma Rose safe; they will keep each other safe. If Emma Rose falters, Elizabeth will be right there to pull her from the waves, into her arms.

———

They set out at dawn. Emma Rose's belly is a knot of nerves. The sun rises as she steps into the water. Up to her calves, to her knees. Breathe. She has known the water all her life, in all its moods, and all of hers. She will cross it. They will carry each other, all the way to the other side.

Emma Rose lets the ocean take her weight. Elizabeth is by her side, waiting to feed her sugar cubes and protein, to speak encouragement. Emma Rose stretches her arm as long as it can go and reaches for the opposite shore.

Stroke, stroke, stroke, breathe. Her feet kick in time with her heartbeat. A shadow glides beneath her, her twin. The face isn't remotely human anymore. Bones like blades press against grey skin; mother of pearl teeth gleam in a mouth too wide. Gills slit the sides of the woman's throat, and there are webs between her long fingers and toes. After all this time, Emma Rose knows her the way she knows the waves, and she refuses to be afraid.

If the woman is part of her, so be it. This is still her journey. They will be each other's guide. The woman lifts a hand, palm flat, facing Emma Rose and waits.

Emma Rose is twenty-eight when she lets go of doubt and fear. She reaches out and presses her palm flat against the webbed hand waiting below her. She lets her love for Elizabeth flow through her, lets the woman taste it from her skin. Here is a little piece of dry land inside the ocean, a little bit of warmth and love. Emma Rose forgives her and is forgiven in turn. The woman rises, Emma Rose does not fall. When their lips touch, it tastes of nothing but goodbye.

4

Application for the Delegation of First Contact: Questionnaire, Part B

Kathrin Köhler

Answer the following questions in any language(s), formats, or paradigmatic expressions with which you are comfortable. Videographers are available for those most comfortable in physical languages. If you need further support to fully actualize your responses, do not hesitate to ask the proctor for any materials or mediums you require. When you have finished, virtually or physically attach all answers to this questionnaire.

1. Who are you?

2. Consider the following two rubāʿiyāt from Rūmī from his Divan-i Shamsi Tabriz:

> Being is not what it seems,
> nor non-being. The world's

existence is not in the world.

I am so small I can barely be seen.
How can this great love be inside me?
Look at your eyes. They are small,
but they see enormous things.

How might these two rubā'iyāt inform one another? You may consider mathematical propositions regarding absolute and non-absolute infinities or Tar-ski's Theorem on the Undefinability of Truth.

I.

In your opinion, is the "self" a construct, and if so, under which circumstances is this true? (You may use yourself as an example.)

3. Define "system." Include a sub-definition of "institution" and list three (3) systems in which you regularly participate.

a. Identify two (2) non-institutional systems in which you participate or aspire to participate.

b. Give an example of an invisible system or institution of which you are not aware and in which you (unknowingly) participate.

4. Define "outsider":

a. When are you an outsider? Give a recent example. What conditions are necessary?

b. Or, if you live in a society where it is possible for you to never be an outsider, extrapolate how you might feel and be affected by being viewed and treated as an outsider.

c. Supposing you are a part of a culture consisting of individuals (non-plural entities), define the concepts of "cultural relativism" and "ethnocentrism." If you are part of a pluralistic or successive entity, express in any way you are able what you understand these terms to mean.

d. In your culture, how is self-worth generally valued in comparison to other worths?

5. In *The Human Condition*, Hannah Arendt wrote that "the Earth is the very quintessence of the human condition" and that "through life man remains related to all other living organisms."

a. Define "context" (both macro and micro) and examine its necessity in language, reality, and notions of truth or fact.

b. What context might you need to create in order to understand and discuss ideas of "existence" with beings possessing physically, temporally, or otherwise differing bodies and consciousness(es) than your own?

c. What difficulties do you have in understanding the entity/entities from Procyon A's locality-dependent self-identity and language? If your cultural background has a worldview and philosophical basis with similarities to the entity/entities from Procyon A (e.g. if you are an Aboriginal Australian), you might discuss which concepts help you to understand the reality and context of the entity/entities of Procyon A. You may wish to argue the primacy of place/geography in identity and culture, or concepts of an "inclusive" self (as opposed to cultures that have created concepts of an "exclusive" self separate from other life and environment).

6. If you were a chair, would you have arms?

7. What does it mean when singular (non-plural) non-telepathic beings say they "belong"? In answering this you may also wish to define "possession." Attempt to give an answer without using the concepts of individuality ("me, not you" or separateness), otherness ("us, not them"), or ownership ("mine" or "yours"). Don't just refrain from using the words "individuality," "otherness," or "ownership"—words are paradigms—attempt to answer without using those *concepts*.

Now give your answer from the point of view of someone who:

    i.) is not of your culture;
    ii.) is not of your species;
    iii.) uses a language format or paradigmatic
        expression system with which you are not
        familiar (e.g. verbal or physical language,

constructed expressions, artistic performance, etc).

8. Years ago, within certain cultures on Earth, the color blue was associated with girl children and the colors red and pink were associated with boy children (known as gender coding). Blue was seen as a calm, gentle color which was believed to reflect the calm, feminine nature attributed to girls. Pink was seen as an aggressive, almost violent color reflecting the active, masculine nature attributed to boys.

> a. Make a case for changing this gender color-coding scheme. You may choose to invert it if continuing with the assumption of a binary gender-constant or expand upon it if using non-binary genders or non-constant genders.

> b. Examine your argument in (8.a) from the perspective of each of the following parties. Explain whether or not each entity would agree with your stated reasoning. If you are a member of any of the following parties and have answered (8.a) as such, please reverse the quality (e.g. "someone with gender" in place of "someone with no gender") before answering.

>> i.) Someone with a binary gender distinction and who is gender-constant.
>> ii.) Someone with no gender.
>> iii.) A member of a society in which males are birth-givers and nurture their young and each other.
>> iv.) A member of a society in which females are feared for their predatory natures.
>> v.) Someone who cannot perceive color.

9. Define "definition" (you may use the concept of measurement):

a. What assumptions do you have to make in order to make a measurement? In your response you may wish to explain levels of analysis and the use of exclusion to create definition.

II.

In relation to what, and in what context, do you define yourself? Your answer may include, but need not be limited to, the following:

*temporal (cumulative, sequential,
    linear, holistic, other);*

*spatial (geographical, physical,
    dimensional, proportionate,
    anatomic);*

experiential;

*heuristic (instructional, trial-and-error,
    computational, other);*

*cultural (social, artistic, philosophical,
    intrinsic, inherent, applied);*

cognitive;

by type of consciousness (fixed,
interdependent, autonomous,
collective, consecutive);

or other relationships and anchors.

10. Consider the sayings: "There can be no observerless obser-
vation" and "Do not belittle the pain you have not yet felt."
Or consider Milorad Pavić: "But take heed: the Constantinople of our thoughts is always one hundred pepper fields
west of the real Constantinople." Relate any two of these
sayings to a concrete example in your personal or professional
experience.

11. What do you know about perceptual or inattentional
"blindness"? In your response consider how it is possible
to see:

     i.) what you do not expect to see;
     ii.) what you do not believe;
     iii.) what is completely outside your knowledge
         base (that which you could never know
         enough about to even begin to imagine it).

a. If you are from a collective consciousness (consecutive,
pluralistic, or otherwise non-singular), how do you perceive
what is temporally, or physically, or cognitively previously
unexperienced?

b. How might different forms of conceptual "blindness"
manifest in your culture (consider such things as popular
narratives cultures teach and perpetuate, representation,

language, repetitive visual or auditory stimuli, etc.), and how can it affect such things as scientific study, health care, or art?

12. In human physiology, what are mirror neurons and how do they affect compassion? Consider how they affect creativity, understanding, sense of self, and sense of belonging. You may wish to discuss how levels of analysis, concepts of self and other, and mirror neurons intersect.

13. Define "aggregate" and "outlier" as they pertain to gathering data to support or refute scientific and/or mathematical theorems. Cite at least two (2) examples of specific theorems or axioms in your response, emphasizing why the effect of such data gathering may be significant for interaction with cultures and species other than your own.

14. How does narrative strengthen or create fact? (Or, how do scientists use narratives to create meaning, fact, or answer questions?) You may wish to describe a true story and explain why you believe it to be true, then explain why someone else might have experienced the same circumstances but have constructed a different truth. (You can simply tell a different true story using the same circumstances as in your first story.)

a. Describe at least two (2) narratives you have constructed about yourself. Also describe at least two (2) narratives the society you belong to tells. One (1) narrative must be relevant to both answers.

b. How difficult is it to change narratives in your society?

c. Describe the psychology and sociology behind internalization.

III.

How might your definition of yourself change over time and/or contradict itself?

For those answers not contained within the two-dimensional confines of the questionnaire, please ensure that all ancillary materials and/or cataloging slips are virtually or physically attached. The proctor will provide you with all necessary materials, attaching apparatus, and delivery mechanisms for any such responses. Let the proctor know when you have finished with this questionnaire. They will direct you to the next part of the screening process.

Screening of applicants includes an assessment of several key cognitive, philosophical, pedagogical, and existential aptitudes and understandings (these include, but are not limited to, metrics of reality and its construction; flexibility, inclusiveness, and limitations in world view) as well as narrative analysis, construction, and deconstruction. Questionnaire Part B fulfills only one part of the assessment.Questionnaire Parts A, C, and D focus on artistic expression and understanding, mathematics and symbolic logic, and the sciences portions of the screening process.

In holding with the nascent and tenuous nature of First Contact and cultural exchange, this questionnaire has been designed and approved by the Foundation of Existential Culture and Philosophy, the International Society of Neuroscience, Creativity, and Dreaming (ISNCD), the Foundation for the Study of Social Linguistics and Change (SSLC), the Network of Integrated Artistic Scientists (NIAS), in conjunction with physics, dance, shamanic studies, and foreign language acquisition specialists from accredited institutions and professional associations across Earth.

5

Butter-Daughters

Nin Harris

The milk of Lusini alpine goats yields a butter that is so soft and so smooth that one could eat it as though it were pudding. Salted only slightly, the most generic kind has a faint taste of burnt caramel that lingers on the tongue. Butter is never left untended in the Lusini Alps. The sticks and rounds of creamy white with a silver shimmer are kept under lock and key. They are watched with even more vigilance when the Eldest Moon is in the sky. Some are gently coloured with the yellow of mountain flowers, but even the yellowed pats of butter have streaks of silver within.

Lusini butter should only be churned on a night that is ruled by the Eldest Moon, for everyone knows that Lusini alpine goats came from that moon. If you churn butter on any other night, do not be surprised if the only thing you will get come daybreak is curdled cream.

Only the strongest, most stalwart of the Lusini are allowed to be butter-makers. They are the ones who will not be undone by the desire to partake of their own handiwork. They will be fortified by days of meditation, fasting, and twenty-hundred mantras chanted on the peak of Mount Laila. Their hands are laced with intricate and devotional henna tattoos, their foreheads anointed with ceremonial ash for seven days before they are allowed into the butter-halls.

All butter-halls are places of worship on Lusini.

If you spread butter when the sun is in the sky, the luminous slivers upon your freshly baked bread will sparkle. The first contact with your tongue is ticklish, with a fizz to it like sparkling alpine flower wine before the smooth, creamy texture soothes the palate. It will feel as if a sigh is building inside your mouth. It is an alien exhalation that is not your own. The act of consumption will invite upon your consciousness artificial memories of supernovas, and curtains of iridescence that shimmer in the northern night sky.

It is an intrusion that many have paid huge amounts of money to experience.

Afterimages of exploding stars and planets in orbit will inhabit your mind and the insides of your eyelids for days.

If you spread Lusini butter on a moonlit night, do not be surprised if the sliver of that light creamy substance on the edge of your knife takes on the shape of a tiny being, or if, inside you, that wistful sigh becomes a stronger groan.

You will be consumed by a butter-daughter.

In a world with seven sentient moons, there is no such thing as a moonless night.

———

Do not eat anything with Lusini butter at night. Do not even look at anything that has been touched by it. Do not go near it. Keep it in the iron butter-boxes. Lock the butter-boxes with the provided padlocks.

Do not even think of cooking with Lusini butter when the sun has retired for the night, even if you swear you can do so without succumbing to the temptation to take a bite. There is a history book somewhere with lists of famous chefs who have disappeared because they could not resist a taste of what they were preparing.

They were undone by intense culinary curiosity.

———

Songs have been written about the Butter Queen, daughter of the Eldest Moon who bestowed her goodwill and grace upon the people of Lusini. It was she who sent armies of silvery white goats to the colonies on the Lusini Alps and taught them how to make butter from the shimmering cream of the goats.

Other ballads are darker.

They say it was not her grace that she bestowed upon the colonies.

———

In the daytime, the butter-daughters cannot be drawn out of its silky confines. That bit of grace within the butter cannot pull them down from the embrace of the moon. However, if you invoke them at night, they will merrily consume you from the insides of your body. They will frolic in the sunlight with the innocence of the newly-birthed.

―――――

There was a young Lusini goatherd who was so inflamed with a longing for a round pat of newly churned butter that he conspired to break into the butter-halls to take a slice, to taste it whole upon his greedy tongue. It was the night of the Courtesan's Moon, so he thought he would be safe underneath its rosy glow.

We do not know what ecstasies he experienced upon possession. Most do not wish to experience the same terrors.

They found his emptied and dried out carcass in the morning sun, surrounded by indifferent goats chewing on the sweet alpine flowers that framed his remains, his rib cage spread-eagled like a grotesque flower, his shriveled entrails in a tangle beside his body. A few yards away, the butter-daughter sat on a sun-toasted rock, plaiting her ebony hair as she stretched, her silvered limbs reflecting back the rays of the sun.

The butter produced by those indifferent goats was of the finest quality ever to be enjoyed on our continent. There were bidding wars amongst the butter-merchants to procure every last slab of it. The flavour of it was richer, sweeter, and far more elusive to the taste buds than any of the previous batches of butter. There was a faint aftertaste of violets, interspersed with a sensuous, smoky fragrance.

―――――

It was almost like consuming silky, violet-flavoured caramel that had been smoked in incense.

―――――

I bid a third of my life's savings for twenty slabs of that butter. They will remain under lock and key until the night when I feel that my life's worth is not as great as this ever-present culinary curiosity, gnawing at my insides, filling my waking thoughts. I have made guest-lists in preparation. Among my hypothetical guests are my culinary rivals, my lovers, my benefactors, and my ex-wives. I have reserved a place of honor for our august Mayor and three of our most illustrious politicians. I have bought fifty-five bronze goblets for the finest Verconian wines to accompany my serving platters. I have ordered the finest crystalline platters for the desserts that will be made with my pudgy fingers.

Oh, to be consumed by the most enigmatic butter-daughter of them all! I can see her in my dreams, her limpid eyes beckoning at me, urging me to partake of the banquet of imploding galaxies and debauched stars. Some nights I can imagine her bending over me when I sleep at night, whispering to me of delights that may be mine if I would only succumb. If I just opened my eyes, perhaps I could run my fingers through her dark hair, pulling her face down towards me. Perhaps we will kiss and in that kiss I will finally know the ecstasy experienced by the goatherd before his ribs were opened as though in tribute to the sun. Soon, she whispers. Soon. *You know what you need to do, my love.*

It will be a banquet not forgotten by history.

6

Glasswort, Ice

Emily Cataneo

1- The dirge

She is an old woman. She won't say how old, but she's lived long enough to see the city slip from its status as a bustling port—stevedores hauling crates of glasswort from the marshes and containers of ice mined from the northern glaciers—to a silent, starving, ice-locked tomb. She's old enough to remember when the ice whales first crept into the subway tunnels and changed everything, when their underwater song fogged the harbour with ice and froze the freighters in their moorings. She's old enough to remember the first icicles dripping off the washers and dryers of basement laundry rooms.

She's old enough to remember when Saskia Henderay slipped into the already-disused subway tunnel and went with the ice whales as their queen, encouraging the whales to stay, to make their homes in the slippery dark places beneath the train tracks, in the plankton-thick water of the harbour. She's old enough to have watched hundreds of people in the city develop the lesions associated with ice whales, the hoarfrost bulges on their necks and knees, to have watched them wither, alone, untouchable, until the ice whales took them away from their flats and quay-side merchant houses.

She's old enough to have lived twenty-eight years and then seventy-two more of whale-songs, which slip through the streets once a year on the shortest night, when the sun just kicks the horizon before ascending again. She's old enough to have seen the effigies of Saskia, that bitch, that stupid *bitch*, burning bright on whale-song night, the embers and sparks (which make no melting mark on the enchanted whale-ice that locks the city) swirling and popping through the streets. The people who hold the effigies wear expressions twisted with so much anger, anger that Piper wishes were alien but in fact is ever so human; they wear this rage and they wear earmuffs tight to block out the sound of the whales' singing, as is required on whale-song night.

Piper doesn't like people to know that her name is Piper Henderay, that Saskia was her twin sister. When they find out, she tells them, her time-eaten teeth churning around the words, that Saskia was half again too clever for her own good, that she had pretensions of greatness, that no one should be surprised that she met a sorry end. She tells them that Saskia was always too much: on leave from ice-mining, she would spend her coins on a dozen oysters every night at one of the open-air restaurants along the waterfront; she would try to pry them open herself with a gold-handled knife. She spoke too loudly, she interrupted, and then she doomed the city to this eternity of ice.

But Piper will also remind people that she's an old woman, and even if she's forgotten her earmuffs, surely none of them can fault her for slipping out of her apartment on whale-song night to—only out of propriety, mind you—mourn her sister.

2- Whale-song

Piper knows, as everyone in the city knows, that ordinary whales sing too. Humpbacks and Mysticeti, narwhals, beaked whales, the flesh-and-blood creatures that slipper through the ocean far to the south—she understands from scrolling through the scant encyclopedia available on her reader that those other whales sing songs made of vibration, that they feel these songs in their blubber and bones, that the songs register on human instruments of measurement but not on human ears. But an ice whale's song takes everything in the city and turns it into an instrument. When she was young, when she and Saskia scared each other with the stories on their mum's reader of the ice whales that had besieged other ice-trading cities, Piper imagined that their songs stemmed from seething magic. She still doesn't know if seething magic or radar vibrations produce the songs, which creep through the shipbuilders' mansions by the waterfront, sing round wine glasses, trill mirrors on the walls, shudder the glasswort in the frozen marshes east, suck a hidden, mournful song from the oysters in the restaurants along the bay.

When it plays the instrument of the city, the whale-song shudders all boundaries, all barriers. Listening to the whale-song, Piper finds her past pushed up from her heart, down the windy synapse corridors of her mind, and on those nights, she is sixteen and nine and fifty-one, every age she's ever been.

The whale-song also shudders the boundaries between their world and the world of the ice whales, the world beneath the city, the world of their fins and ice-mottled sides and jewels and fish-stink breath. Anyone who listens to the song of the ice whales might find their foot slipping through a numinous-white crack in a paving stone or might stumble on the stairs and watch their fingers punch through to the ice whales' kingdom. They could break through, fall ill with those hoarfrost-lesions. They could disturb the fragile peace built with the ice whales over the past seventy-two years.

Is it any wonder, Piper thinks, as she thumps, cane in hand, along her street towards the waterfront, without earmuffs, that she's not supposed to be listening to it?

3- That song you listened to the summer you were twenty-one, which makes you feel like a long-haired loud-laughed girl again, passenger-side to your sister.

In the whale-song, Saskia and Piper are dark-haired girls, born two minutes apart. In the whale-song, Saskia picks glasswort, that long, mean, spiky plant, green as sin, which sucks up salt from the humid marshes until its tips spark and burn. Barges' foghorns bellow out to sea, and Saskia pulls it up in great over-flowing handfuls, holding the stems so the sparks don't burn her slender hands (just like Piper's hands. They were so alike, and so Piper wonders, in the whale-song and now, what separated them, what sent Saskia bursting to the whales, when it might have been Piper?) Saskia hauls the glasswort home and dumps it in a bucket in the airshaft-courtyard in the centre of their building. She watches the sparks catch, feeding on each other, until the glasswort burns. She sells the resultant glass to the glassmakers down round the harbour ("I read on mum's reader that ice whales breed a special kind of glasswort," Saskia says, and Piper, always half-jealous and half-annoyed at Saskia's cleverness, smears ash on Saskia's cheekbone, and Saskia smears it on Piper's leg, her tongue poking out, and they race round the courtyard shrieking).

In the whale-song, their parents are alive, and then they are not (ice trade: crampons and ropes never enough to keep its workers from tumbling like poppets into the sea).

In the whale-song, Saskia and Piper are seventeen, hustling through the dockside-bustle on their afternoon off, watching containers soaring from the mouths of shipping cranes, peeking into pried-open crates full of packets of dried seaweed and pearls. They're bickering over whether they should squander their precious, sweaty coins on dry seaweed when something lights up the waterfront, some trill playing their bones, a song, coming from the earth itself, and Piper stops, stares at Saskia, and says, "Did you hear that?" And Saskia says, a little crease between her brows, "I've been hearing it for three days."

They don't know that this is the first whale-song that they'll ever hear, that it will soon shape their entire lives, steal Saskia, ruin their city and their sisterhood.

In the whale-song, Saskia is twenty-one and receives her appointment to ship north in the ice trade, and she doesn't cry, and so Piper doesn't either. She presses three pieces of glasswort between two sheets of clear plastic for Saskia before she goes.

Now, tonight, on whale-song night, seventy-two years after Saskia went to the ice whales, Piper step-thumps to the harbour, where ice creeps: brisk salt water gathering into stasis, barges freezing in their moorings, the susurrus of waves silenced so she can hear only the song. With hands swollen and crooked in their gloves, she bends, at the knees so she doesn't strain her back, to pick the glasswort. She twists it off its stalks and piles it into her basket. The whale-song ripples along the marsh, playing the stalky reeds, tickling the snow over the thickening ice, and in those notes, those moments, she is there with Saskia, and they are young. They say that ice is stasis, ice is death, winter is both stasis and death, and the ice whales shudder the boundaries between worlds, between past and present, because in eternal stasis, boundaries don't matter anymore: everything and nothing are the same. For a moment, as Piper picks the glasswort to lie on Saskia's grave, she wonders: when death creeps through the window for her, will she experience everything always and at once, all the Pipers caught forever like 'wort pinned under plastic?

She wonders: will death creep through the window for her before she completes the one task she's made her mission for the past seventy-two years?

4- Totentanz

Once, a man returned from the ice whales. They found him sprawled and shuddering on the yellow line on the subway platform at one of the abandoned stations. He wasn't wearing shoes and his toes had been scraped away to nubs, scabbed over and hardened with scar tissue hundreds upon hundreds of times. He was distended with the tumourous bulges of greyish hoarfrost that appear on the neck-glands and tangle in the arm-hair of those who touch the ice whales. He babbled about the ice whales' underground caverns of ice-gems in shades of aquamarine and sea-garnet. About their marshes of glasswort, a different breed than grows in the city: their glasswort is white, alien, smoky, the colour of stars and ice. One stalk of ice whale's glasswort clung to his coat; as glove-wearing biohazard workers shoved him off the yellow line and back onto the tracks, the stalk fell onto a frozen puddle and melted it, sending off clouds of steam like beacons into the frozen air (Piper was there, in the crowd of horrified bystanders, and when she saw it, when she watched the ice whale's glasswort fall onto enchanted ice and spark and burn, her jaw tightened).

The man was sent back to the ice whales. It's forbidden to return from their kingdom once you've gone. Once someone slips through, by accident or curiosity or trickery, they're contaminated, unclean, and besides, they belong to the ice whales, not the city, which has to take care of its own, which can't risk the ice whales rising further, occupying first floors and city streets and the decks of ice-locked ships. This is the ecosystem they've built, the agreed-upon status quo. The people who survive stay in their city. They subsist on the sickly fish dredged up through holes cut in the ice, on the trickle of beef jerky and canned beans imported by sledge from the south. They live bearable, safe—for now—lives. They take out their anger on the memory of Saskia, the girl who started it all. In exchange, they abandon those who are contaminated by the ice whales. They do not listen to the ice whale's song, do not digest its magics.

Except for one person: Piper, old woman, who's rising from her marsh-pickings, a basket of rustling glasswort swinging from her arm.

5- The key shift

Piper's boots crunch through fragile saltwater ice, her cane taps into frozen puddles, dislodging starfish, and then she's back on pavement, shuffling past dark-windowed merchant houses, down the wide sidewalks between the glass-and-iron skyscrapers, towards the curlicue-iron facade of the subway station where her sister broke through to the ice whales seventy-two years ago.

In the whale-song, which is shivering the paver stones beneath her boots, in the whale-song where Saskia is here and they are young, the ice whales are pressing their flanks against the undersides of the basement, streaming into the harbour, and Saskia, age twenty-eight, is curled on the couch, her legs folded beneath her, her left arm cradled in her right. "Pee-pee," she says, her stupid childhood name for Piper, which twists like a knife right up in Piper's gut, "the things the human body can do are pretty crazy, aren't they?" On the gentle vein of her left arm bulges something thick, smelling of saltwater and ice, black and coin-sized and gemmed with hoarfrost.

They find dusty sewing needles and jam them into the tumour. The needles snap away. Saskia twists in a knife; where it sinks into the frost, the serrated tip produces one brilliant tear of water. The wound remains. Saskia looks at Piper with flat lips and big eyes. "The terrors in the ice," she says. "You can't imagine, Pee-pee."

"Can you not call me that, when you're trying to be serious?" Piper is standing with her back against the window clenching the sill so hard she can feel it lining her palms.

"I must have brought this" —her arm, laid bare— "with me from the north. Whatever it is. When you cut far enough into those glaciers, you start seeing things: little ice birds flying away, musical notes floating into the air and then popping like bubbles...and shadows shaped like whales." She raises her eyes to Piper's; the memory of the stories on their mum's reader hangs between them. "This" —she flexes her arm— "it came from..."

Saskia's been home from the north for a week; Piper's only just gotten her back. She can't imagine how everything will unfold a season later: the ice whales screaming under their basements, the ships' crews filing frantic reports of the whales floating through the harbour, and Saskia and Piper descending into the subway, which is CLOSED FOR REPAIRS THIS WEEK (although it will never reopen again). They hold hands as they step over the yellow rope and descend the stairs to the silent shabby tracks, gleaming with ice. "Let's figure this out," Saskia says, cradling her bandaged arm. They went to the doctor just a few days before; the doctor donned gloves before touching the arm, muttered vague certainties, threw around the word *psychosomatic*, and declined to make a follow-up appointment.

"Hey, you're not supposed to go down there," someone shouts, loud and officious, behind them. They ignore the shout. The subway tracks are lined with doors, through which passengers on broken-down trains might be able to flee. Saskia presses her palm against one of these doors, four-hundred-fifty feet in from the station, according to a placard. She's shivering, and Piper loops her arm more tightly through hers. The whale-song is shaking the sign, cavorting up the tracks, and in that whale-song, the whale-song within the whale-song, Piper is seven years old, practising kissing by pressing her mouth against Saskia, which they both pronounce GROSS, she's nine years old, and Saskia is teaching her how to use your fork or teeth to sever the oyster from its bivalve, she's twelve years old, and their parents aren't coming home.

As they walk into the tunnel, something catches the light from the station behind them, crosswise to the tracks. A seam, opening up, cold air rising from it and shafting into their world, curlicues of white light rising too. Saskia shrinks back but Piper, for the first time, keeps going without her, just a few steps. They blink, and the air in front of them shifts, and then the ice whale is in the tunnel with them.

It floats in the air, or maybe it stands on its back fins as though they are legs. It's their height, shaped like a whale, with a torpedo-shaped body and a flat head (but as Piper stares at it she falls into the optical illusion that it's bigger than a freighter, or the city, or the Earth). Its sides are black but mottled over with frost, tinged pink and blue in the gleam of the flashlight shaking in her hand.

People are shouting behind them and it steps, or air-swims, or just dreams towards Saskia, and regards her. She pulls a handful of glasswort from her slouchy coat pocket, holds it out to the ice whale. It ignores the glasswort, bends, whispers something in her ear. She looks at it, her face drawn in towards itself, and she nods, gravely, without smiling, and places her hands on its back, her sleeves scrunched over her palms and fingers so she doesn't touch its skin. The ice whale waltzes her through the tunnel—one two three, one two three—a human dance clashing with the chaotic nerve-thrumming whale-song, as though they're in a goddamn fairytale.

Piper hears the thud of heavy-booted officials jumping from the platform to the tracks, but she hears them as though from another world. Saskia jerks back from the ice whale, her jaw set.

"Tell me," she shouts. "You said if I danced with you, you'd tell me" —she jabs her finger at her arm.

The tunnel swallows her voice. Piper turns around: police officers, their batons at the ready, are streaming into the tunnel, and bystanders leap down, too. They stop next to Piper, stare at Saskia, at the ice whale looming behind her, its face in shadow, its fin resting on her shoulder, as though it owns her. Her bandage is loose; the hoarfrost distends her skin. Piper can see its whorls and crenellations from where she stands.

Saskia starts forward, and the police officer next to Piper, no doubt thinking of his children, sticks out his baton, his eyes slitted. "Not a step closer," he shouts.

Here's a curious fact about crowds. They will follow orders. They will pounce if one or two among their number pounce first, or they will stay still and silent, held back by nothing more than an official voice and an outstretched baton. Nobody moves—not even Piper—as Saskia backs up, the silvery smoke-light swirling around her boots, silhouetting her, one step away from slipping through the seam into the ice whale's kingdom, forever (and then she slips, she goes, and Piper never sees her again).

And here's another fact, about disaster: people thrive on blame. No matter that seventeen other ice workers visited doctors with tumours distorting their arms and necks in the week before Saskia disappeared; no matter that Saskia only followed the ice whale into the kingdom below because of the policeman's outstretched baton. No matter that ice whales besieged towns that Saskia had never lived in, that their presence in the ice-trading cities in the north was as inexplicable and brutal as plague or death. No, the people of their city saw Saskia waltz with the ice whale, ice-tumours bulging her arms, and they built their stories, and made their effigies.

Now, seventy-two years later, as Piper heads towards the subway, brightness stains the air at eye level half a block in front of her, and as she shuffles on she passes a crowd, broad-shouldered and short-haired and ear-muffed, screaming around an effigy that they're thrusting into the air like a flag, a crude poppet-effigy with dark hair and a button, signifying a tumour, gleaming on one arm as it melts in the flames.

This is the world in which they live now: their city held in ice, Saskia's body belonging to the ice whales and her memory to the seething crowds who burn her form. And Piper, Piper is nothing but an old woman, going to place her sister's favourite plant on her grave, probably for the last time. And that's that, isn't it?

6- Marching song

But it's not. Piper descends into the subway, her orthopedic boots landing sure on the steps as they always do when the whale-song brings to life the salt smell and briny taste of her youth. She crosses the platform, dodges a rat's skeleton with frozen bones, sits on the edge of the platform, and lets herself drop onto the tracks.

With the whale-song shaking loud in her ears, limning the boundaries between the worlds, she can see the seam bisecting the tracks, between frozen puddles and rust. Just as she's seen it every whale-song night for the past seventy-two years. The ice whales have kept them frozen for all of those years, their fragile peace—their siege—enforced because the people of the city are not allowed to tap into the whale-song's shivery and strange power, its way of making nothing, and yet every-thing, possible.

But Piper is just an old woman (just as, in the whale-song, she's a young woman who was just questioned thoroughly by the police, and a middle-aged woman with a taste for fish-skin who garners no attention, sneaking down into the subway just as she's doing tonight) and surely no one will bother her, just as no one has ever bothered her.

She approaches the seam. There, on the tracks, cradled in a gleaming white conch, sit five glasswort, white and alien. The glasswort of the ice whales. Each of them sparkles with gems of fire.

She slips a scrap of canvas around the conch, the cold biting even through the canvas and her glove, and she slips canvas and conch into her pocket. She lays the basket next to the crack and nudges it with her boot. It slips away, teeters on the edge in the swirling silver, then tumbles into the crack. She made sure to slip in an oyster for Saskia, along with a gold fork, but what is left of Saskia, after all this time with the ice whales? Is her body still there, is she kept alive with some feverish magic? Piper wonders if she'll come here next year and find no conch waiting for her; she wonders if the same will happen to Saskia. Next year. The year afterwards. Someday. She wonders if she'll gather enough glasswort before then.

She counts the glasswort that Saskia left for her: five, in exchange for her basket of the green glasswort from her city's marshes. She imagines that Saskia will replace the pilfered white glasswort with the green, holding onto the fragile hope that the ice whales don't notice that she's been stealing from them all this time. Piper's closet brims with it, the ice-whale glasswort, sparking and sequestered in glass containers that once held food. How many will be enough to melt the ice, to break the curse on the city? Will there ever be enough?

Maybe not. But old women are stubborn, aren't they?

Piper bows her head to her sister, then hobbles back onto the street. The youths are still shouting around their effigy. They are flush in what they know, in the righteousness of their anger, in their inaction in anything else. The ice-whale glasswort is safe in Piper's pocket, but, just for good measure, she lunges at them, her cane held high, and jabs at the effigy, her arms trembling as she wields the cane. The effigy flies to the sidewalk, drooping and deflated, flames billowing in the wind, vibrating in the whale-song. The youths stare at her, shocked, their faces twisting into just the same expressions that their fathers and mothers and grandmothers and grandfathers held seventy-two years ago when they stood behind the baton, when they watched Saskia step, step, step back, tumble into the ice-whale kingdom.

Maybe they don't deserve to be free from the siege. But Piper isn't doing it for them.

She sneers backs at them, showing her time-worn teeth, shaking her cane as she cradles the stolen song, the stolen glasswort, all that stolen seething power, while her girlhood and her sister tremble in her ears.

7

Flyover Country

Julie C. Day

The Future Arrives

Lovers are like flash floods, car collisions, aneurysms: always a possibility, but never exactly expected. A small-plane pilot for AeroFix Corp, Sam arrived in my bed via a tray of purple pansies and a convoy of trucks intent on invading the Verona Municipal Airport.

It was spring, which in New Hampshire meant freezing nights and mud-rutted days. Spring also meant tired. My apartment's cast-iron radiators shuddered against the cold as soon as the night set in—resentful of their nocturnal work and making sure I knew it. Meanwhile, as well as accepting Aero-Fix's weekly deliveries of blue plastic barrels with labels that revealed nothing—AP0-X56-38I3, CHH-R71-90A3, and all the rest—maintaining the airport landing strip had become its own full-time job.

I mowed the runway grass to a steady two-and-a-half inches, kept the length of the surrounding field five, and tried to not think about all the shredded insects. The airport teemed with young grasshopper nymphs that had hatched after an unseasonable heat wave. Harmless. But my job involved maintaining "the site's readiness," and site readiness meant preventing birds and other fliers from nesting in the surrounding land. The result: grasshopper decimation via mown lawn.

For a year and a half, my only interaction with my employers had involved quarterly runway inspections and a few lone trucks dragging yet more barrels into the New Hampshire mountains. I was paid to maintain northern New England's stockpiles for an improbable viral apocalypse. That was AeroFix's sell, anyway.

But. But. But. Sometime in the early spring a convoy of supply trucks with a convoy's worth of support staff arrived to tear apart my careful solitude.

Timing, or mistiming, is everything. 2:20 p.m., and I'd stopped at Hanson's General Store after a too long nap, distracted by those flats of pansies, creeping phlox, and false forget-me-nots lining the porch steps. And then came the rumble of diesel engines—*Oh—Fuck*. My shift should have started over five hours ago, and I wasn't even on site.

And now, here I was heading toward the Verona Municipal Airport on my bicycle, a flat of purple pansies tied to the handlebars while I followed the fading exhaust vapors of far too many vehicles and the sense that AeroFix was readying itself to define a northern-New-England-sized area of targeted viral-suppression spray zones.

T. t. trust. Marigold had said, legs and feet pressed together as she repeatedly lifted and lowered her heels. Up. One, two, three, four. Down. One, two, three, four. Laced fingers under her chin.

Times change. They twist around, then knot you tight.

I'd left Boston with its Repeat Speakers and Living Statues for the relatively safety of Verona, New Hampshire.

But—

This is the third decade of the twenty-first century. People no longer get their flu shot each year and consider themselves covered. Logic illnesses, viral infestations that restructure the brain, are even more prevalent than those white condensation lines in the sky, water trails that reveal the path of each AeroFix plane, and its spray pattern, in real time.

We try. We bob and weave and stumble to the side, but in the end, human trajectories are all the same. "Logic" is just one in a cascade of words that tumbles across our brain's neural connections until, finally—like "friend" and "home" and "wonder-filled"—the flight is over and even that single word, logic, is going, going, gone.

Memory

Sometimes you create yourself, but more often your future self is created for you. It's the degree of specificity—the amount of fine detail and targeting—that the biomedical industry along with the bio-activists, terrorists, and hackers-for-hire decided to change. And, yes, of course, a gene-modified, post-modern patient's memory of events is catastrophically unreliable, but if you're that patient, it's also the only path available. And so you take it.

Marigold and I grew up together in a town surrounded by pockets of New England forest, all those maples, oaks, and birch. At ten years old, Marigold was my brave and forever friend. In the nearby woods, Marigold balanced her way along the downed oak tree that crossed some unnamed tributary without a single glance toward the rushing murk below.

"Come on, Immie. Just keep going."

Instead of continuing across the makeshift bridge, I'd paused partway, caught by the sight of tiny insect bodies seemingly determined to jump, tumble, and finally disappear below the river's flow.

"What's up with the grasshoppers?" I demanded. Certainty was Marigold's specialty, not mine.

"Will you get over here already." Marigold reached for my hand and pulled me those last few feet to the other side. "It's just a horsehair worm infection."

"Huh?" I gave her a sideways glance.

"It makes them think they can swim."

"That's—grasshoppers can't—"

"Nope," Marigold cut in, "but they don't know that."

And then Marigold and I were twelve, thirteen, twenty, the years of our friendship adding up one by one. Together, we put in two years at Mount Wachusett Community College, and then—friends to the end—Marigold and I rushed straight to Boston, the new biomedical Mecca, in search of something better, or at least something new. And, like so many others, that is exactly what we got.

"We will never be the same again," David Norbury, CEO of Cambridge's PharmaGenius, declared twenty-four hours a day. Along Boston's Memorial and Storrow Drives, Norbury's face looked down like a demented, beardless Jesus from row after row of electronic, roadside displays. As well as Norbury, the city was full of paid-content headlines and YouTube gurus with emotive hands. Genome upgrades, bio-hacks, and nutra-regeneration, they proclaimed, would lead those with vision into the future.

Turns out real vision just makes things worse.

Less than a year after Marigold and I arrived in Boston, it was clear Norbury's biochemical revolution hadn't just thrived, it had gone feral. Our futures—memories—lives—the plunder of this purloined age.

Which is how Marigold and I came to be standing in Fenway High School gym at yet another CDC-sponsored event. We weren't stupid. We arrived wearing microfiber face masks and latex gloves, protection against the unknown vectors potentially loose in the crowd. Though humans are never uniformly careful. A stocky man to my left with actual exposed arms took a step and almost brushed me with his shoulder. Unprotected touch in a flaring contagion zone—

"What the hell, asshole." Marigold grabbed me with her gloved hands, pulled me closer.

"Shh," a few in the crowd said, all of us straining to hear the speakers on the dais.

"The health of the public is our paramount concern," the man in the suit said, mic in hand. "We have planes and spray crews working twenty-four hours a day." The guy looked almost sincere.

"Well, it doesn't seem to be working," someone near the back called out.

"We have a right to know what AeroFix is loading into all those sprayer rigs," Marigold added.

"Miss, the anonymizing alpha-numeric codes are for your protection," the suit said without even a momentary pause, such a practiced AeroFix representative. "What do you think a biohacker would do with such information?"

"Trust is paramount," Marigold replied. "And right now, you definitely don't have mine."

A few others in the crowd nodded their agreement, including the dude with the exposed arms, but this was Aero-Fix, the only corporation with those exclusive formulas and a fleet of custom planes. Monopoly has its privileges, including actual contractual nondisclosure guarantees.

And so, with no clear goal beyond survival, Marigold and I hunkered down, pretending we weren't anticipating an urge to dive off a city's worth of rotting and slippery logs.

"Trust is paramount," Marigold repeated three months later. We stood in the rain outside our apartment building. Just the two of us. Just the two of us on this rainswept street... In some ways it felt no different from when we were ten, except the water was already touching our faces, the shadow memory of a parasitic worm invading our minds.

As she spoke, rainwater ran down Marigold's face and chest and arms. Jesus. She seemed to play peekaboo with her hands—*T. t. t. pa ra mount.*

"Trust is hard," I glanced along the road, empty of people, shifted my grip on the dark and bedraggled umbrella.

Marigold looked straight at me, her hands paused on either side of her face, the 'aboo' portion of her unsettling game of peekaboo. *Could it be...*For a moment, I thought I saw a softening in the creases that framed those brown eyes, actual recognition, and then the light flickered out once again.

Vigils never take as long as the feeling of eternity that accompanies them. Countable hours, a handful of days, and Marigold's voice became hoarse, her lips cracked, flecks of blood slipping into the creases along with those words. *Trusssss. t.*

"It'll be okay," I repeated yet again, raising my gloved hand to check my carefully placed mask. *Oh. Oh. Oh. Goddamn it.* I pressed a moist sponge to her lips—tried to get her to drink, sip, notice her changing body.

Marigold never flinched or cried. Her expression remained so calm. I didn't sense sad or lonely or scared. That was all me. I was the one armored in sleeves and mask and gloves, uselessly trying to outrun whatever came next.

Awareness

Logic illnesses work at the synaptic level, razing select receptors while causing others to erupt across the brain's cellular membranes. A Logic illness is the thing you can't watch out for. The twist you never see coming. The change that is only fully revealed once the pruning is done and you no longer recall the reason for all that fussing.

I could see the AeroFix convoy as soon as I rounded the last bend on Bellevue Way, the pansies still somehow attached to my bike's handlebars, worry no doubt etched on my face. It wasn't just Marigold; Boston and all those other cities over-flowed with Logic illnesses. Verona, New Hampshire had been my personal isolation chamber.

Not anymore.

Two dozen vehicles were scattered across my carefully-mown field, each one with a prominent AeroFix logo: a para-chute-shaped cloud wrapped around the top half of a sparking brain. Nearby, a crowd of people in khaki coveralls and orange safety vests—at least thirty strong—stood near the edge of the runway, listening intently to a gray-haired man holding a tablet and stylus. Good news: they hadn't bothered with masks. Despite the invasion of AeroFix personnel, this stretch of New England must still be relatively epidemic free.

Three of the flatbed trucks were loaded down with curved steel sections, corrugated metal sheeting, rebar, and palettes of bagged cement. A fourth carried a backhoe and a concrete mixer. All the elements necessary for a DIY Quonset hut. Great. Poured foundations meant permanent structures. And then there was the swarm of smaller campers and flatbeds towed by sky-blue pickup trucks. The flatbeds contained three spray-zone planes—Air Tractors—plus two porta potties, and a mass of wooden crates containing who knows what.

Damn. Here comes the future.

The entire convoy was a silent declaration that the Living Statues and Repeat Speakers might not have arrived, but they were definitely headed this way.

In this genome-hacked world, meeting new people requires a certain amount of mental armor. I carefully locked my bike to the AeroFix-financed fence, zipped up my jacket, and headed toward the crowd.

"Hey," I said stepping up to the gray-haired man. "I'm Immie, the groundskeeper."

"Any inventory discrepancies since your last report?" Gray Hair asked.

I shook my head. Up close, it was clear AeroFix employment didn't provide viral immunity. Gray Hair had a bit of a potbelly, which could just be who he was, but those lash-less eyelids, and that mouth that seemed filled with too many teeth, no way were those naturally-coded features. Perhaps he'd picked up a feral Freddie Mercury vector. Perhaps he'd actually paid cash for it. The idiot.

"Okay, groundskeeper, we'll take it from here." He turned back to his crew, any further response from me clearly irrelevant. "Fen, you're on inventory verification. Sam, do a systems review once we get the Air Tractors off the truck and assembled."

"Right, boss," one of the shorter crew members said.

Was there irony in that Sam boy's tone? Was that an almost-smile? Whatever. It was best if I stayed focused on my own business. I headed back toward the gated entrance and my small all-weather shack. It was time to plant those pansies.

But first things first. I logged the arrival of the ground crew, took my cheek swab, dropped it in the plastic tube, and added it to all those other samples stored in the hut's small refrigerator. AeroFix was no amateur operation. They carefully monitored each employee's expressed genome against a first-day baseline.

And then—finally—I was done. I left the shack and untied the flat from my bicycle.

"Nice bike."

I turned and stared. The shortish crew member stood in my shed's doorway—Sam, the site manager had called him. Sam. Why the fuck was this person talking to me?

"Need some help?" Sam's posture. That smile. So not a guy after all. Armor or not, I couldn't help myself. I smiled back.

"Sure." I set down the flat and slipped past Sam. Back in the shed, I grabbed two dented metal spoons from the shack's junk drawer. I passed one to Sam. Briefly, our ungloved fingers touched. A glancing blow of bared flesh.

"Thanks." Sam blinked, their expression neutral, then stepped back. "Where are you planting them?"

Sam was pretty; that's what I told myself. Lank, light-brown hair brushed their shirt collar. Their skin was darker than you'd expect with that hair. Dark brown eyes as well. Their lean pilot's build was perhaps due to careful eating, but likely a result of cellular modification—just a requirement of the job. AeroFix was a profit-making enterprise: the smaller the pilot the more chemical, anti-viral assistance could be pumped into those AeroFix planes.

"Over there." I pointed my chin at a spot near the shack, then glanced past Sam to the rest of the invasion. While I'd been busy with swabs, and flowers, and this stranger—*Sam*—the rest of the crew had spread out across my airfield. Some were busy winching a plane from its trailer, while others had begun to set up the tanks and hoses.

Not my business. Not my people.

Moments later Sam and I were crouched side-by-side, digging along the south wall of my shed, pulling away the grass, loosening the soil below. Unprompted, Sam filled the resultant holes with water from their canteen.

I rocked back on my heels, grabbed the flat, and loosened the first root bundle. A grasshopper nymph landed in the flower patch's newly-watered soil, and then, just as quickly, hopped away. Our miniature swimming holes were of no interest. It seemed my grasshoppers were horsehair-worm-infection free. For now, anyway.

I glanced at Sam, at that smile of theirs…God, those eyes hooked me right back in.

A promise, a dare, a demand. *Reach out and touch me. Find out what happens next.*

In the Beginning

Boston may have started the viral transformation, but like all things American, it franchised itself across untold miles of state highways and strip malls. AeroFix and its planes followed close behind.

AeroFix started in the suburbs of Atlanta, the brainchild of two high-school best friends. Like those other companies that crossed the commercial starting line first—Facebook, Kleenex, the corporate developer of the EpiPen—no other business had ever really caught up.

At first the news—the reason for this new aero-industry—didn't even make the Reuters or AP feeds. Cleansing away the occasional vector spills that slipped out of the medi-spas and relearning centers was nothing but post-modern garbage collection. Hell, talking heads joked, containment slippage meant we might get an actual PharmaGenius freebie.

It's hard to notice what's creeping up behind you when so many things are already tagged as "worrying" and "potentially catastrophic." Like most people, Marigold and I weren't worried, or worried enough. AeroFix, however, figured things out early. The true vector of transmission wasn't a specific microbe or virus. It was people and, well, people they were never going to change.

Even the first hacking offenses weren't all that bad. What fifteen- or twenty- or twenty-five-year-old doesn't appreciate a bit of power in this chaotic world. Rewiring half a town to sing classic Hole? Actually, kinda hilarious!

"Oh, make me over.

I'm all I want to be.

A walking study in demonology."

And then came the best part, that genius of a bio-hack—the synchronized swagger and group hair flip—even the bald ones joining in. Genes and proteins, ain't they grand?

Innocence, like containment, never lasts. Sometime in the

last five years, AeroFix's spray zones had become the corner-stone of modern public health. No matter how exploitative and unsustainable, when the emergency hits, you're damn happy for help, any help. Fair isn't even considered.

The Breach

Sometimes the problem isn't viral vectors and shifting lines of chemical vapor bisecting the sky. Sometimes what ends up getting you is nothing more than a desperate desire to avoid the emptiness of New Hampshire's bone-chilling cold.

Flowers planted, Sam lingered by my shack.

"Not much for me to do," they explained. "At least until it's time to fly."

I grimaced as a whirring-and-stuttering sound started up. A crew member was using the backhoe to dig up my carefully-mown grass.

"Don't worry," Sam said with a slight smile. "We'll all disappear soon enough."

And then Gray Hair, the AeroFix site manager, was standing a bit too close to my tiny garden. "We could do with the office space. Why don't you go ahead and take the rest of the day off."

"Sure." I smiled until he turned away, and then slipped into my "office"—a four-square-foot box—and grabbed a handful of worn-down pencils and multicolored pens.

Sam watched with interest as I created a makeshift fence around the tiny flowerbed. "How about I walk with you back into town? You can show me around—"

"Sure." This time it was my turn to smile.

"Okay then."

Neither of us mentioned my bicycle, or the fact that Sam likely had a trailer onsite.

Fever Dreams

I still remember the first time Sam touched me, my less-than-solid underpinnings suddenly exposed. I still remember those moments afterward as we lay stretched out together on my bed, the afternoon sun on my skin, sweat trickling down the small of my back. Busy with zippers and buttons and way too many clothes—I'd forgotten to draw the shades.

"You make me feel peaceful." Sam said, their hand slowly stroking my right shoulder. Then after a pause, "Except when you don't."

I could feel my face flush. "Yeah. Me too." *Make me feel.* Memories of their soft lips on my shoulders, belly, and further down: wet, unprotected touch.

There was a heavy tread on the back stairs, followed by the slamming of a car door and an aged engine coughing its way to life. My neighbor, Mr. Baccini, was heading to work. It must be almost 3 p.m.

"Time to get up, I guess." I pulled away from Sam and started grabbing clothes from the floor, diving under the covers in search of my bra.

"You take away all the fun." Sam sat up and wiggled into their jeans, grinning. I watched as they balled up their underwear and stuffed it in their back pocket.

"Oh, my God. Really?!"

They laughed at my expression, brown eyes not in the least embarrassed, and then Sam was in my bathroom, water running, door shut, while I contemplated making the bed, looked out at the weed-strewn backyard. My empty life. Exactly as planned. No medi-future illnesses. No people. No— God, damn it. No.

The bathroom door opened.

"So, Immie." A tilt of the head. A slight smile. Sam held my toothbrush and paste in their left hand, clearly about to use both.

Fuck it. What was a little more sharing at this point. "So, Sam." A pause. "Where do you usually stay while you're setting up?" Baby steps, but definitely heading in a specific direction.

"I guess most of the crew will stay in those AeroFix prefabs we hauled in."

"Most?"

"Yeah." And then Sam was reaching for me, both of us tumbling back onto the bed, laughing, the toothbrush and tube of paste lost somewhere in the tangle of sheets and once-again-discarded clothes.

Lucky me. Lucky Sam, as well.

At least for this short while.

AeroFix groundskeepers are supposed to be solitary creatures, keeping the chaos, both natural and vector-driven Logic illnesses, at bay. AeroFix fliers are always on call, ready to race away. This feeling, this moment, this hot-and-slick memory, none of it was ever meant to last.

Re-isolation

"I'll be back before you know it," Sam said.

The two of us stood near the gatehouse. Sam's AT-1209U Air Tracker loomed at me from the end of the runway. Another AeroFix miracle, loaded and ready to go. Less than two weeks since the convoy's arrival and the trailers were being reattached to their trucks, the porta potties back on their flatbed. A couple of crew members were stacking empty blue barrels inside a crate. Sam had told me the AirTracker contained a one-thousand-gallon tank. I hadn't realized just how much of the stockpile that would consume.

"How far are you flying?"

"East to Baxter State Park and north to the Canadian border."

"Oh. The entire region." So not local.

"Soon. I promise, Immie," their hand now on my cheek—
their fingers so damn warm.

"Soon." *Please. Don't forget.*

"Sam," Gray Hair called from the edge of the runway,
frowning as he glanced in our direction.

Exactly how many groundskeepers did Sam meet each
year? That was an unexpected thought…

"Fuck it." I leaned in, inhaling Sam's oh-so-human scent.
And then my lips were parting as Sam pressed against me—I
could almost feel the crew turning away, busy themselves with
coiling up the fuel and chemical hoses, loading a set of
pontoons onto the trailer where Sam's dismantled plane used
to sit, anything but watching the two of us and our raw,
unprotected bodies embracing.

As we separated, Sam squeezed my shoulder. *Soon.* Then
they were walking toward the plane, taking off, leaving me
behind, lonely caretaker to growing population of grasshoppers and a rapidly emptying airfield.

"Hey. You." Gray Hair stood next to me, tablet in hand.

Great. Just great.

"Where are you headed next?" I asked.

"Sign here." The site manager shoved the stylus and tablet
in my direction. Questions were, clearly, not his department.

"Huh?" By which I meant "fuck off." I wasn't in the mood
for—well, for anything really.

"We're taking your swabs in for testing." And then, when I
didn't take the proffered stylus, "The anti-virals are reapplied
each morning—to the tablet, I mean," he said when I
continued to stare at him.

"Right." I grabbed an antiseptic wipe from my pocket,
ignoring the man's scowl of irritation, and wiped down both
stylus and table before signing on the electronic line. Gray
Hair held my gaze as I handed back his device. Perhaps not so
angry after all. Perhaps terrified and lonely, just like everyone
else. And then he was gone, walking toward one of those sky-

blue pickup trucks, climbing up into the cab, slamming the passenger door.

"Time to wrap it up, folks," Gray Hair called through the open window. Seconds later, his pickup was leading the convoy out through the open gate.

Crew members leaned out of open windows, rested their elbows, turned to take in one last look. It wasn't just their low BMI and coveralls. Something else. Something best not considered for too long. Most of them looked like Sam: sandy-haired Sam, a-foot-taller Sam, kinky-haired Sam, Sam who blinked too much whenever someone got near. I bet Gray Hair checked their cheek swabs on the regular. It's a fine line, or perhaps no line at all, between viral alteration and degradation.

The bald Sam waved at me, smiled even, as the last of the convoy headed out.

Sam had said they'd be back soon, but soon meant waiting, not sure which way the day, the hour, the minute was going to tip. Soon meant trying forget those first words Marigold started to repeat. The way her eyes seemed to watch something only she could see.

Believing in soon meant trying to dodge a catalogue of potential disasters.

Which is why when that rash appeared days later, it didn't have to be—*goddamn it I made sure to use ChemiClean at least three times a day*—well, the stress of waiting—hives made perfect sense. *I guess. Is that what this is?* Anyway, there was no way was I going to waste money just because of a minor skin condition. It would pass.

No, no, no, Marigold would have said, and she wouldn't have been wrong. Truth time: the void of No Longer is never more than a-few-dropped-pathways and a-hobbled-basal-ganglia away.

Missed Connections

Our brains are eighty-five billion neurons-worth of movement. Electric signals travel from each cell's dendrite to its axon, triggering a release of neurochemicals targeted toward the next cell in the chain—except sometimes the trigger doesn't fire. Or the message fails to bind and is returned to sender.

Societal, interpersonal, or cellular communication: no matter the mode, they're all ruled by small unremittant failures and eventual degradation.

And still, the airfield's grasshopper nymphs continued to grow. At some point, I stopped mowing the grass. Waiting instead. Each week a single delivery truck arrived, restocking the airfield's supply of barrels. The truck's driver wore a cap, kept his brown hair short and sunglasses on, but who the hell really knew. Maybe he was actually many hes, a series of job-modified bodies—like Sam, my Sam. *No.* Just in case, every week I repeated the same two questions.

"Hey, can you take a letter to—"

"No, sign here."

"Do you know Sam—"

"I just do deliveries."

"Right."

And always, I was careful not to scratch my neck until his truck was out of sight.

Soon.

Altered States

Give me wings. Oh, Lord. Form those angel pathways that lead to heaven. I stood in my bathroom, toothbrush in hand, trying for calm. A prayer, was that what that was? Since when did I think about angel wings? Since when did I talk to God? This was just the latest in a litany of strange thoughts that had formed since Sam left.

Voices. Not thoughts.

Fuck. I pushed down my undistracted panic—*just a rash and fatigue, get your shit together*—headed back to the kitchen, pulled out a saucepan and set it on the stove. No harm in boiling the toothbrush before I actually used it. Though, of course, Sam was totally clean. AeroFix took care of its fliers. Everyone knew that. *Ha. Idiot.* Idiot? Now, that was definitely a thought I would have, as was the wash of anxiety that made me want to crawl into my bathtub, pull the curtain, and hide—the flow of warm water surrounding my uncertain limbs.

The following day, I made the twenty-mile bike ride south along Route 110 to Berlin (population 10,000) in search of a pharmacy that offered both meds and anonymity. It was time to get rid of the rash and its shadow symptom, that goddamn pulsing fear.

Marigold, and all those other tragedies, didn't mean I was next.

I'd been careful. I'd taken steps.

Molting

Despite the calamine lotion from Hanson's General Store and the Benadryl paid for in cash at the Berlin Walgreens, by the end of the month the rash had traveled from my arms up along the length of my neck. Beneath the surface, my skin ached as though ulcerated and ready to burst, though my neck and face—stealth infestation—remained free of visible sores. Mr. Baccini and the rest of Verona might not see it, but beneath my skin bad things were happening. My mind hop, hop, hopping. Grasshopper high.

"Trust is paramount. T.t.t." Marigold had said as I pressed a moist sponge to her lips. *T.t.t.*

Communications breakdown. Communications transformation.

Circular rings of skin, 2cm thick, scabbed the circumference of my arms: tattoo healing minus the ink. Meanwhile, my eyes caught sight of fireworks whenever my thoughts strayed toward…I'm-not-sure…Can't-quite-catch-it…*Oh. Oh. Oh.* Gone.

My thoughts were hanging dendrites lacking nearby receptors, the expected daisy chain of connections closer to a field sprayed with herbicide by a rabid toddler. Everything was breaking apart, leaving behind no discernable pattern.

Hey. Hey, Immie. Hh Hh. Hh. Sam's smile had been so warm when they reached out to tuck a strand of hair behind my ear. Lips warmer still when we kissed.

Hey.

T t trust, Marigold had said, playing peekaboo with those rain-slicked hands. *But. Oh. God. No.*

Sam's smile as they clambered into their armored plane. Of course, I really remembered that moment. No amount of pruning could mimic real love. Right?

S s soon…

And Then We All Fell Down

An unremarkable autumn morning. Still in bed. My body an internal combustion machine, sweat running down my back and thighs. Maybe that's why it took me awhile to notice the internal shift.

A middle-aged man stood in the middle of my room, hovering over the dirty jeans, t-shirts, that ragged pair of slippers scattered across the floor. His tattooed eyelids blinked in a frenzied staccato rhythm. He held my gaze and smiled as his head sank—slowly—into his plump and hairless torso.

I shook my head, blinked my own eyes, but the headless man was replaced by a wavering blob. It writhed, coils forming and reforming, trailing barbs erupting from both sides of its array of gray-and-yellow speckled mouths.

A naked set of conjoined twins emerged next. *That's not so bad.* At least they made physical sense. But those damn creatures refused to look away, their eyes focused on me, their irises like snow globes of violently-falling ash.

In the kaleidoscope of madness, I recognized one definitively Immie thought: none of these experiences felt like me. *Not my images. Not my imagination. Not me.*

Something I never got to ask Sam before they left: who are we when we are no longer ourselves?

"Don't forget it's you that I love." Those were Sam's almost-last words. The only ones I can hold on to, anyway. There is no more reliable truth. I can feel myself tumbling. The water oh-so-close.

Gravity's Pull

And so it should have come as no surprise—*soon*—

Stumbling from my porch, pedaling, following phantom fumes out toward the airfield, dropping my bike by the gate.

The nymphs were gone. Grasshopper men filled my field.

Teeth, lashless eyes, belly: Gray Hair, that old modified paragon surrounded by more of his kind—yes, just as I'd known he would be. *Soon.* And yes, to all the rest—sky-blue pickups, flatbeds, trailers, the crowd of hop, hop, hoppers. All those Sam bodies with their Sam faces and their Sam eyes.

None of them were my Sam.

"Lawrence, the wooden blocks. Devin, make sure the decon rigs are ready," Gray Hair declared.

Did he? Would he?

A sense of cold, the chill slipping up and around my neck, settling behind my eyes.

The leaves of the nearby birch and maples rustled, grasshopper chirps exploding across the field. But my head had tilted up: a distant hum calling. I focused on the progress of a contrail, a white line of moisture and chemicals, heading toward me across the blue, cloudless sky. The groundcrew, the site manager, all those trucks—dear, Lord, even me—why did we all seem like something else, something not and something never and something clearly never again.

Soon.

Sam. Please, let it be Sam.

I'm watching the Air Tractor land and taxi to a stop.

A coveralled pilot climbs down.

Soon.

"Immie?" That goddamn smile.

I grab their hand and feel—really feel—the warmth of human skin. Oh. So much t t trust.

Marigold had understood. Being alive, even during the tumble, was all part of the cyclical perfection.

Finally. This moment. A horsehair-worm-infected grasshopper, with its river and that final jump, all of it a transcendent moment of bliss before the inevitable drowning.

Splash Down

Immie, Sam said. *Love, come back to bed and let me hold you.*

The rain is falling and the flowers are dying, dry, dead. Crackling insect exoskeletons underfoot. That can't be right. Sam is gone, flying somewhere overhead, their plane's tanks filled with AeroFix's miracle anti-virals. *S s saving the world.*

The fleshy universe is so hot and shivering cold. Of course, you don't take the pills, no matter what that strange doctor says.

Don't freak out, sweet Immie. You're always with me.

Please let me feel something different, even if it means not staying the same. Neural networks spreading and intertwining —reconfiguring —the mind nothing but something else.

T t trust.

Sam, I should never have let you go.

It's hard to remember. You manage for days or even months. But there they are waiting for you, all those other words. *Love, yes, love.* You have someone you love. You trust them. But you're a grasshopper, and so you swallow and you swallow that river water—swallow those nitrogen-pressured words—grasshopper as deep-sea diver. *F f forgetting.*

Soon.

Gone.

You're slipping under, dreaming—no pain—yet another voice lost to the clouded sky and the river's undertow.

8

Thin Places

Gemma Files

I dream I go to the woods, almost every night. In the dream, I leave the others asleep and go out the door at the crack of dawn, just walking, with no destination in mind. Looking around, I realize I'm back at the same campsite my son's choir went to that weekend, a tiny stretch of land along the Muskoka River's shore, edged with pine and gravel: rough cabins barely the size of my mother-in-law's living room, subdivided so they can each fit two bunk-beds, plus a loft that's mainly mattress, a phantom third suspended up near the roof-tree. Inside, everything's rough and cold and smells like Vicks VapoRub, while outside it's the same, but less claustrophobic. The air is full of hovering gnats, almost too small to see, and a vague mist hangs over the river's skin, the current barely stirring its surface.

Making my way down the gravel path to the road, I look both ways before crossing, seeing nothing. I feel the grit under my soles, crunching like crumbled bone. The edge of the woods isn't far, but I pause there, wondering if I should go further.

People go into the woods with one face, come out with another— that's what my aunt used to tell me, when she thought my parents weren't listening. *Stay in there too long, you'll forget your own name; won't recognize it when it's called or be able to read it written down if not on bark, in charcoal ash, or blood. Your skin will change, turn dark and moist like dirt, or pale like a mushroom's ribbed underside. Wash your face after you come back out and look in the mirror, you'll soon find you're a whole different person.*

She was always saying stuff like that, my aunt. Probably explains why nobody really liked her all too much.

———

One of the chief unspoken truths of parenthood is that a minute or so after you have a child, you soon find you've signed up for a lifetime spent doing things you don't even vaguely want to do. And I knew from the very beginning that volunteering to chaperone my son's first choir camp trip was definitely going to be one of *those* things, the memories you make mainly by agreeing to grin and bear it, for your child's sake.

Liam loved to sing, and my mother-in-law thought choir would bring out the best in him—teach him teamwork, professionalism, discipline. Which it did, on the whole. We were grateful. But they were a pretty expensive bunch, that choir: very upwardly mobile, very artsy. Big on fundraising the old-fashioned way, one parental chequebook at a time. Even with my husband's Bay Street job, we'd needed the in-laws' help to swing tuition.

Going up there with Liam wasn't my idea, by a long shot. But it would be his first overnight stay away from home, out of town with a bunch of people he didn't really know. "You should sign up, just so he knows you're there," my mother-in-law said, and Liam's eyes perked up at the prospect, fastening on mine: *yes, Mom, please.* I couldn't say no, not without looking bad.

So I didn't. I went without protest, resentment festering inside me, a boil under the armpit. An itch that only dug deeper the longer I had to go without scratching it.

I remember looking at the three of them celebrating together, thinking: *I really don't look like* any *of these people.* Which was weird, especially considering how half my genes went in to make one of them. *Consider the evidence; take a picture, it'll last longer. It's like I don't belong here, like I never have. I'm not part of this family at all.*

Apophenia's an illusion, my aunt used to tell me. *The human mind sees patterns in random data. But just because something looks like something else doesn't mean it is—even you must know* that, *Norah.*

I look like you, I pointed out to her, once, when the sheer contempt in her voice became a little much to handle. To which she simply smirked, replying: *Well yes, and I look like you, to a point. But what does that prove, exactly?*

I wouldn't find out until years later that she wasn't really my aunt at all, not by blood—just a friend of the family my parents allowed to stick around, possibly because, since they'd all attended the same university, she'd played midwife (or maybe enabler) during their initial courtship, making her the patron demon of both their marriage and my birth—along with the divorce-related heartache to which those happy accidents eventually gave rise. And making it all the stranger that, since the divorce, the year I was eight, I still can't really remember her actual name.

———

In the dream, the leaves of the wood hang down in a curtain, all green and brown and green: moss brown as rot, bark green as lichen, as scum on a still pond. Here and there, a spiderweb glints, bright as hinges. They creak and hum behind, borders a door shut and locked, to which I have no key.

But then I go in, right in, and I don't know why. Enough people have told me not to. The sky is low-hung, the air close and hot, fog rising off the horizon. Darkness under there like a swarm. A smell everywhere, fresh-turned dirt, tubers. I have to move slow; the path keeps slipping away underfoot. Crushed ferns and exposed roots.

No idea of where I'm headed. I walk straight through what feels like a spider-web, sticky on my hair, my eyes, my hands. Something at the corner of my mouth, trying to crawl in. I spit black.

In the distance, a cry goes up. It sounds like sobbing.

I'd assumed we'd be sleeping in the same cabin, Liam and me —that I'd be the cabin chaperone for his particular group, the wonderfully-named Noble Minstrels Table. Instead, once we got there, I found out I'd been sorted into the next cabin over —the Chivalrous Chorus Table. The show we were working on that year was King Arthur-themed. I can't remember exactly what songs were involved, though I catch myself humming snatches of them, now and then. One of them might even have been "If Ever I Would Leave You."

Liam didn't like it. He'd grown up in a tiny apartment where he was used to both his parents being merely seconds away. "If you can't sleep here, can't I come sleep with you?" he'd argued.

"That's not how it works, bud. You saw the house lists, right?" He nodded, glumly, a towheaded figure in Star Wars pajamas, small for his age. "So it's already done, and we can't do anything about it. Wouldn't be fair to everybody else."

"I understand," he said, finally, though he obviously wasn't happy about it. But he agreed anyhow, because he was sweet and biddable, a good guy in every way, and because he trusted me. Because I was—I still am—his Mom.

Good, I thought, as I hugged him. And then I turned away.

———

I don't like the woods. They remind me too much of my own childhood, hauled back and forth across Ontario by my mother and father, who were big on trips while they were together—always in motion, always bound for someplace dark and green, as though they thought the cure for every ill was wilderness.

Each weekend they hauled out the maps and made lists of places they'd already been to versus places they'd yet to go, the putative hot spots of rural Ontario. From my point of view, it was all one grey highway or back-road after another, the over-hanging foliage thickening or thinning accordingly, with an occasional lake, hill, field, or miniature village thrown in for good measure; it's not like I was ever consulted on the matter. There were moments it was enjoyable: afternoons swimming in ponds, fresh fruit from roadside vendors, watching deer wander along the road...but I'm a city girl, always have been; I sleep better to the sound of traffic and sirens, when I sleep at all.

Right now, in the dream, I've reached the point where I'm not sure if I'm asleep. It's exhausting to trudge the uneven muddy ground, up and down small rises you don't see until you stagger over them. The underbrush is thick: there's barely enough space to squeeze between trunks, and the green-black moss rubs off on my shirt and leggings. Light slants thickly down through the leaves, orange-gold bars heavy with pollen and ground haze; it's the reddening light of late afternoon. Soon comes twilight, then nightfall.

Then, the dark.

None of the other kids in the cabin reported any trouble. They just woke up and Liam was gone.

One girl later said she woke up just long enough to hear him moving towards the door, trying to be quiet. It was early, before sunrise, so she thought he was going to the outhouse. Another chaperone said she looked out the window and saw him walking with a woman, towards the woods; she said he was holding her hand, which is why she thought that woman had to be me. But she also said she thought he looked sad, or even a little bit scared.

They went into the woods, right up to the treeline, the wet mulch of leaves demarking civilization from wild; the woman moved with a light, quick step, never pausing, not even when he stumbled. Just pulling him on, firmly yet not unkindly, into the shadows.

They went into the woods, that woman and my son. And they didn't come back out.

I still have an image of my aunt in the back of my mind: a tallish woman with linebacker shoulders and no visible waist, solid as a shut door—frizzy, mouse-brown hair, irregular freckles, neck habitually kept hidden with some no-name "fashion" scarf whose pattern always varied wildly, though its colour scheme remained consistent: green on blue or blue on green, cut here and there with hints of purple, red, black. I could tell that she was more my mother's friend than my father's, yet both of them treated her with this alert, almost diffident respect, despite how they seemed equally capable of being shockingly snarky about her in her absence.

Did they like her, or not? It was hard for me to tell, at that age. I'd already decided myself that if I had my way when I grew up, I'd never deal with her again—but I couldn't have explained that antipathy, either, or why I thought I had the right to form such judgements. She certainly never gave any hint of minding me much, for good or ill; I barely remember her paying any attention to me, or even looking at me directly. Most likely I was just background noise to her, a mere byproduct. She's probably forgotten my name by now, wherever she is, just as I've forgotten hers.

And yet.

It's a matter of record that my parents never left me alone with her, at least not where they couldn't see us. It's a matter of record that she vanished out of our lives at the same time my parents' marriage fell apart—as if the destruction of their family unit had ruined something for her, a careless shopkeeper breaking a crystal vase just before he hands it over to the buyer. And it's a matter of record—witness statement, at any rate, however reliable that is—that the woman spotted taking Liam into the woods that morning wore a scarf around her neck, patterned in blue and green.

———

Now I've been in the woods far longer than I want to be, deep down in its most shadowed ravines, the sun blocked out wholly. No shafts of light to tell my way, and the ground slippery underfoot. I wish I'd worn socks; wish I hadn't worn sandals. Have long since stopped looking down, for fear of knowing what I've stepped on.

I don't know how I got here anymore.

I know that when I wake up from the dream, at last—however long that process takes—I'm going to spend the whole rest of the day feeling like I'm still there. I'm going to be uncomfortable, restless in my own skin, because I know I'm not where I'm supposed to be. All the next day, and every other.

It doesn't change. It never does.
I don't expect it ever will.

I remember him, my son. How he used to sing. How it felt to hold him. I remember how he bounced past me at a party, once, and I turned to the person next to me and said: "Believe it or not, that used to be part of my body." I remember teaching him to feed himself, brush his teeth; I remember waking him during toilet-training. I remember the way Liam would throw his arms around me, or around his dad, or snuggle up to us both in our bed on Sunday mornings, before Tom got him dressed to take him to Mass.

Tom goes to church a lot, nowadays—midday masses on his lunch hour, again on Saturday and twice on Sunday—and has gotten into volunteer work as well. I suppose it's helping him; maybe it's even giving him something to hope for, some future eternal reunion. I'd envy him if I thought anything like that had even the remotest chance of working for me.

When you're in mourning, it hurts that things don't always hurt.

It's been six months. No report has been made, no sighting has occurred, anywhere at all. But every night I have this dream, the same dream of the woods. How I'll walk and walk until I finally look down, see something at my feet, under all that mulch: Liam's eyes, peering up at me. And when I clear away all the bracken he's there, down there, in a hole.

He doesn't say anything, doesn't ask for my help. And I want to get him out, and I don't want to get him out. I'm afraid. I'm afraid to try. I'm afraid that if I reach down, he'll pull me in.

And so I just stand there, I stand there, I can't move. Looking down.

Fill in the hole, a voice tells me, inside my head. *Fill it in and walk away.*

I don't trust him. I can't. You can't trust the dead.

But I don't trust myself, either.

———

We don't belong here, not really, not any of us, my aunt used to whisper to me, her odd-smelling mouth against my ear, when she thought my parents weren't listening. Not here. Which is why we should be careful, always. Why we have to treat each other well, look out for thin places. We have to stay in the light.

Whose child is that, in the distance, crying? Not *my* boy. Not mine, with his mouth full of blood and dirt and broken teeth. Not mine, not here.

Not there.

———

This dream will end soon, as it always does—but one day I'll go back into the woods for real, looking for him. And while I don't expect to find him, I don't expect to come back, either. Just walk into the woods and let the leaves close behind me, never to return.

Because: we *aren't* supposed to be here, not really, none of us. But where else would we be, if we weren't?

This country is full of all sorts of absences, thin places, empty places. Holes between the stars.

9

Jewel of the Vashwa

Jordan Kurella

I watched my love die in the claw of a Scorpion Man. I watched him sever her in half; watched as her long hair dripped down to the ground; watched as her hand let go of her spear; as her long legs folded under her; as the Scorpion Man's tail rose in triumph. His chitin carapace shone in the dwindling sunlight. So did my love's armor. Her armor that had served her so well until the end. Her armor that made her look like a queen, not a general. Many women had told her that. Many women.

Like me.

I knew when the Scorpion Man killed my love, when all his people charged forward at what was left of our sisters, that she had been right to send me away. I watched as the Scorpion Man's many charged our few; charged them across the flat desert sand. I watched this from my place high up on the red rocks of the Vashwa. I heard my love's own voice in my head, smooth and silky and dark as her hair.

She said, "Awanshe, you will live to tell our story."

And so, I will. I will tell it to all who listen. I will live while my sisters die.

What a terrible burden to bear.

———

But the truth did not happen that way.

That is only the truth I have told you before. Here is what happened. One truth for another. A story for story.

———

The women of the Vashwa have always been at war with the Scorpion Men of the Ratch. And we have always loved them. We send our women to them and accept our women and our daughters back. We raise our chitinous daughters as our own, among our soft-skinned daughters, born of soft-skinned husbands, who come from other lands—softer lands, greener lands.

Your lands.

The Scorpion Men have always given as much as they took. They take our sons, we take their daughters. They take one of our oases, we snatch one of theirs. They destroy a caravan, we destroy a night patrol. We fall in love with one of their traders, and it is just the way of our soft-skinned women to love such a hardened man.

I, Awanshe, am a chitinous daughter. You can see my back and chest, made of segmented carapace. You can see it is as brown as my skin. My mother brought me home from her Scorpion Man lover, and she loved me as much as she loved my soft-skinned sisters and brothers. I was one of seven. Now I am one of five. When I came of age, I was presented with soft-skinned suitors, but I was a chitinous daughter and none of these soft men with their soft professions suited me.

I was a warrior. I fought with spear and spit. I had a venomous tongue and a dagger wit. My carapace hid not only the foolish fluttering of my heart, but the catch of my breathing. A chitinous girl could hide fear. Hide scars. Hide lies.

No, only a Scorpion Man would do. And he did do very well.

My lover, Tarkir, was tender, but he drank much and fought hard. We went to the bars in the Ratch every night and boasted and blustered our way through the melee until we came out breathing heavy and kissing hard. Tarkir's best friend, Kuvo, once said to him, "Stop playing with these boy-women like this Awanshe Toy." And I said back to him, "I am more man than you are, Scorpion Boy. And I am more woman than you will ever have." The flat edge of my chitinous chest shone hard that night in the gaslights. The light cut against my segments, it cut harder against my wit. I felt Tarkir's dangerous tail wrap close around my leg, then, as he pulled me into him.

Tarkir's claw always felt right on my back. His hand always felt right on my neck. His claw's weight had purpose. His fingers' callusestold stories. His touch told me he needed me. I explored his chitinous carapace with my own ten fingers, and his breathing responded as I wanted it to, as I hoped it would. It responded well.

Too well.

I spent a year with Tarkir in an attempt to do my duty as a woman of the Vashwa. But something was wrong. We spent every night tangled in each other's soft-skinned legs, tangled in the sheets, mouths on each other's mouths. We spent hours on top of one another. Behind one another. But still, no babies came.

When my queen demanded me back home, to fulfill my duties as a warrior, Tarkir took my hand in his. His hand was as brown as mine, our chitin matched in shade. But he was far taller, and his eyes wider and always full of wonder.

"I'll come for you," he said. "I'll come for you, Awanshe, Jewel of the Vashwa."

And we kissed again, for the last time.

I left him in the Ratch. I left all my memories of him in the Ratch. My carapace held Tarkir close to my heart. It also held my desire. It also held the truth.

Because when I returned to Vashwa, I found someone else.

———

Here is the truth I need you to believe.

Here is what I witnessed while standing on the red rocks of the Vashwa. Here is what I saw as the sun set on the flat desert sand. As night threatened to overtake us.

My love charged Tarkir with her spear held tight in her grip. Its dark wood shaking with each of her strong steps, her steel-leaf armor shining with every last inch of sunlight. Her eyes pierced Tarkir's soft soul. Her mouth writ in a sneer.

Tarkir rose up to strike my love down with his claw. His claw that had once held me so close. He rose up, tall as he was, mighty as he was. He rose up, and my love slid down into the sand. She slid into the sand and thrust her spear up. Up in and between the segments of Tarkir's chitin carapace. Up into and piercing Tarkir's soft and tender heart.

Tarkir died on that spear. He died with his lips coated in his own blood. Those lips I had once kissed so many times. Those lips that had told me they loved me. My love threw Tarkir to the side, and the rest of my sisters, all the rest of them, charged forward across the flat desert sand. All of our many against Tarkir's few.

I knew, when we charged, that my love was right to send me away. I heard her voice in my head, dark and silky and smooth as her hair.

She said, "Awanshe, you must go to tell of our victory."

And so, I will. I will tell it to all who listen. I will live while Tarkir and his brothers die.

What a terrible burden to bear.

———

But that is not the truth, either.

You must think me a terrible woman, to keep spilling lies forth again and again. To keep hiding the truth. Why do I do it? Because the real truth is too brutal. Honesty, too harsh.

———

I returned from the Ratch lovelorn and lovesick. A carapace is not as hard as steel-leaf armor. It does not protect from heartbreak. That wound slid deep, burrowing between my segments, eating me alive from the inside. So, I returned to the Vashwa hungry and in pain. I returned longing for another's hands on my neck, another's mouth on my mouth.

I tumbled through temporary lovers. Chitinous girls and soft-skinned men, but none of them remained longer than a week. None of them remained longer than a few nights in my bed. None of them until I took my place in the army; until I fell under our general's steel gaze.

Our general's name was Dalmana, and her hair was long —far longer than mine would ever be—and straight as a razor, while mine grew in curls tighter than corkscrews. Her hair was black like mine, her eyes were black like mine, but that is where our similarities stopped. Dalmana was short, far shorter than me, and had to bind her breasts to wear her steel-leaf armor. Her muscles rippled under her sweat, whereas my chest was chitin-flat, and my brown arms as sinewy as the acacia tree.

She first looked at me the way she looked at everyone, with disapproval, but it was the way her fingers trembled on my arm when she corrected my spear work that told me her heart. Dalmana's kisses tasted like wine and dates, unlike Tarkir's, which tasted like hops and salt. Dalmana and I spent our evenings drinking wine and eating goat cheese, looking out at her vineyard and chasing her three chitinous daughters. At first, she was quiet and only talked of battle and training.

She told me how to be better: "Hold your spear like you're holding a man," she said. "Charge with your eyes everywhere, but always on your feet first. A prone warrior is a dead warrior," she said. "Our greatest asset is our sisterhood. Never forget that. Never," she said.

Dalmana told me plans of a new battle. One to take place soon. One she hoped I would be part of. I dreamed of this battle. I dreamed of it between her two older daughters bringing me candies and flowers. Her youngest daughter brought me a drawing she had done of me throwing a spear.

In truth, it was a drawing of her.

One evening, our legs wrapped together in the sheets, Dalmana told me stories of her life: where her children had come from, what she had been before she became a general, before she became a hero.

"Their father is the general of the Scorpion Men, Tarkir," she said.

My heart, long light for her, grew heavy and rough in its beating. It threw itself against my carapace. It rose to take hold of my throat.

"He called me Dalmana, Jewel of the Vashwa. We spent years together, to make my wonderful children. He was kinder to me than anyone before, or since." She stopped herself. "Except you, of course. You are my Awanshe."

"I didn't think I was included," I lied. I knew Tarkir was kinder, gentler, more affectionate than I would ever be.

"I will tell you a secret," Dalmana said. "But only you can know."

The soft spots of my carapace ached and shifted from the

too many secrets I held already. I could not hold any more, but I would have to. For Dalmana; for Tarkir.

"Our next battle is not a battle, it is a truce. Tarkir and I are going to unify Vashwa and the Ratch."

"How?" I asked, but I did not want to know.

"You will see, my Awanshe. You will see."

———

Now we come to the truth of the battle; the truth I have held in for so long. It sits like a fever, burning deep between the segments of my carapace, eating me up from the inside. I must tell this truth to you; I must let it out. It is time I faced judgment for myself.

Tarkir and Dalmana have been judged for too long.

———

All two hundred of us stood on the flat desert sand, the red rocks of the Vashwa surrounding us, keeping us safe. We stood in the golden light of the late afternoon; our shadows long as we stood with our weapons held ready, our armor laced tight. My sisters were hungry for bloodshed. I could see this by the way their tongues thirsted at their lips. I could see by the way they stood, by the way they hungered, that Dalmana did not tell them of the truce.

She had told only me.

Dalmana's gaze was cold, cast at the horizon. Her hand, too, was readied on her spear. Her armor, too, was laced for battle. I stood at her side, mirroring her posture, mirroring her gaze, as the Scorpion Men arrived. And as they did, my duty and Dalmana's truce festered inside me.

My Tarkir was at the front, his chitinous carapace brown and shining, recently polished. I imagined the feel of it underneath my calloused fingers. I imagined the taste of his coconut oil against my tongue. He was smiling, his black eyes wide and bright and full of wonder. My heart grew as heavy as iron; it fell to my feet, and I became weighed down by it. My sisters continued to stand at attention, their shoulders back, their spears held at their sides. But my shoulders hung low, my spear loose in my hand.

My stomach was hollow with knowledge of this truce, of this peace.

Dalmana approached first, then Tarkir came to meet her under the boughs of a long-dead acacia tree. She called for me to join her, and my feet dragged through the flat sand. She gave me her knife and spear, to solidify the truce. Tarkir called for Kuvo, his right hand, to join him. Tarkir held his claw at rest, down at his side. Both Tarkir and Kuvo smiled in recognition of me, but it was Kuvo who took hold of my hand with a ferocity that shook my bones.

Then it began.

"Who proposes this truce?" Kuvo asked. His voice as confident as always.

"We do," Dalmana and Tarkir said together.

The truth will not let me deny it, Tarkir and Dalmana were harmonious in that golden light. All of them harmonious: their voices, their smiles, the way their eyes danced off each other. Tarkir held Dalmana's hand with a familiarity and a tenderness that he never had with me. With a love that I never had for either of them. Dalmana appeared truly at peace with Tarkir: her breathing was slow, like the breeze. Her hair shone like his carapace, and visions of the two of them in his bed, on top of one another, behind one another, warred in my mind.

"In what way?" Kuvo asked.

Tarkir drew a line in the sand with his claw.

"This is the line that separates the Ratch from the Vashwa. It is the line that separates my love from my duty. I will not have them separated any longer. I will cross this line for love and duty because they are one and the same."

"No," Dalmana said. "*I* will cross this line for love and duty because in my heart, they are both most needed."

Dalmana stepped over the line first, placing her hand on Tarkir's shining carapace. Her eyes did not leave his; his eyes did not leave hers. My grip was strong on my spear, as strong as Dalmana had taught me. My shoulders were back, now, my eyes were on Tarkir's chest. I knew what had to be done. I knew what I must do for love and duty. I knew what was most needed for me, for mine.

Tarkir's right foot stepped over the line, his gaze locked on Dalmana. Kuvo stepped forward to protect Dalmana from the other Scorpion Men, his back facing me. Only my sisters could see me. And their eyes were all that I wanted; all that I needed. As Tarkir's tail passed the line, I stepped in front of him with my spear held ready.

He smiled at me.

"Hello, Awanshe, Jewel of the Vashwa," he said.

I said nothing. Instead, I lunged forward, thrusting my spear up and between the segments of Tarkir's chitin carapace. Up and in, piercing Tarkir's soft and tender heart. He was not smiling as his blood trickled out of his lips. His lips that I once kissed hard, kissed tenderly, kissed longingly. He was not smiling as he grabbed hold of my spear and looked at me with his black eyes wide, full of wonder, full of pain. I did not blink. I only thrust the spear forward again. I thrust it in deeper, in farther, and finally twisted it.

Killing him.

The hollow pit in my stomach was not sated as I threw Tarkir aside. It grew larger; my rage grew larger. It burned hot inside me as Dalmana grabbed my arm, her voice shaking, her body shaking. She screamed, "Awanshe, no!" I saw the pain written on her face. I saw the tears shining in her eyes. But I could not kill her, too. My heart grew sick at the thought; it then stuttered as I looked down at Tarkir's paling face, at the blood flowing from his mouth.

I had done this, and it had done nothing to sate my jealousy. The emotion was still there, drowning me. The thunder of hundreds of footsteps was now coming for me, coming for war. This was what was most needed. This was my love and duty.

War for betrayal. Hate for hate.

I felt Dalmana's grip tighten on my arm, her trembling fingers this time spoke not of desire, but of fear. "Why?" she asked. "Why?"

But I would not say. I could not say.

I did not have to tear my arm away. Dalmana was torn from me by many of my sisters. They tore at her with their fingernails. They tore at her with their voices. They tore at her with their teeth, sating their bloodlust.

I was torn away by Kuvo. His bulk black and shimmering; his rage just as dark. Night was coming quickly; the battle would wear itself out before dawn. This I knew. So, as Kuvo swung his giant claw at my head, I ducked below it. As I ducked, I took a handful of sand. And when I stood, I blew him a kiss.

The sand flew into his mouth and eyes. He spat on it, choked on it. He screamed from the blinding pain. In his flailing, I jabbed my two spears into his soft-skinned leg and pinned him deep, deep into the flat desert sand. It was foolish to remain. It was foolish to stay where he could retaliate. Where he could recover and destroy me. So, I left him there, writhing, cursing, and trapped.

I had only two knives to fight my way to an escape. To abandon Dalmana and my sisters. To flee. But I did flee. I did escape. When I reached the red rocks of the Vashwa, I could not look back. I only heard the sounds of death and slaughter below. I left my sisters behind. I left my love behind to go to her house; to take her food and her water; to kiss her daughters goodbye.

I vowed to make my own truth as I traveled to softer lands, to greener lands. To your lands. The truths that I have told you. The truths that all in this city and the cities that surround us now know.

Does the Vashwa still live? I do not know. Does the Ratch still thrive? Again, I do not know. I do not want to know. The truth is something I ran from long ago. The weight of it will kill me. I buried my emotions long ago. Tucked them underneath my carapace; let them fester like an old wound. The ghost of them now causes my old bones to ache with their memory.

Surely you can understand.

I have no daughters to carry on my stories, no legacy to live out the consequences of my lies. I have only this: that I, Awanshe, Jewel among Jewels of the Vashwa, killed all she loved that day on the flat desert sand. And that Awanshe, Jewel among Jewels of the Vashwa, has lived on a diet of lies ever since.

What a terrible burden to bear.

10

HigherWorks

Gregory Norman Bossert

Dyer and The Wayward, slapping maps—

Camden Lock Market—Friday Morning

Dyer shifts against the wall—the bricks are rough and still night-cool in the shade of the bridge and her jacket is thin across the shoulders, lining long gone and the leather worn smooth by years of brick stone iron concrete carbon—and breaks down the approaching couple without quite making eye contact.

The Wayward has got an eye out for cops or worse, blathering in his terrible Burt-the-chimney-sweep cod Cockney, sounds stoned but his brain is just like that. "—ghosts, you know? The nano, sometimes it don't break down, it digs in, makes a nest in the parental lobe—"

"Parietal." Dyer says. The couple are a matched Saxon blond, expensive haircuts, and the girl's wearing Havilland genesplice chestnut wedges with live shoots trained around her calves, cost a thousand quid easy. Not cops, not dressed that way; more likely the sort who think Drop parties damage property values, that nano should be reserved for medical and military purposes, that refugees belong safely sorted with their own kind in the camps in Dover. The sort to take a map now and call the cops later. But he has an active tat peeking out of the edge of his sleeve, and she's got corneal implants, so Dyer risks it.

"Opt-in," she says, quietly, and sees the guy's teeth flash. The girl taps the guy's thigh with one hand and reaches out with the other. Dyer slips a map from her jacket pocket and hits the girl's hand, more a handshake than a slap, oh so proper British, and meets the girl's gaze. Pixels swirl in her eyes, and recognition. "HigherWorks," the girl mouths, and swats the guy's leg again as they ramble on out into the sunlight by the canal.

Dyer blinks her own corneals full black. Fame is a fickle food, she thinks, and all the more so for USERs running illegal nano Drop parties. "Men eat of it and die," she says to the crows along the canal bank.

"Woah," The Wayward says. "Eat what now?"

Might be time to grow her hair out, or to go back to wearing masks at the Drops, but that never really works. The fans are too persistent, bless their stuttering, over-stimmed hearts, and photos get out on the Drop forums:

Sick minds of HigherWorks unmasked at last: Dee! Dyer! The Wayward! Shimago! USERs or home-grown?

DJ Mrs. John Dee and nanogoddess Higher Dyer spotted digging through the bins at ResCycle...We Got Photos!

A Scanner in the 'Works: London's opt-in choreomania culture networks nanotechnology to bend brains.

That last in the damn Guardian with a damn gallery of drone footage. Might be time to move on, was the truth of it, Amsterdam again, or Helsinki, anywhere the refugee policies are less tattered and the fear flows a little less deep, and leave London to groups with less to lose.

As if summoned by that thought, Kal flits in under the bridge, gossip queen of the refugee scene, latest conquest in tow. "All right, D? All right, Way? Doing the do tonight, yeah? New show, new rocket? You guys know Leelee? Slap me a pair?" All in one breath without pause for answers.

"All right, Kal," Dyer says, slips her a couple of maps. Kal passes one to her companion, a willowwisp creature in frills and lace with improbable anime eyes that make Dyer think of zygomatic surgery and tabloid tales of "accidental ejection". Leelee spins the map in twig fingers, details on one side and an actual map on the other, tests the stickum that holds the fold closed with a glittered slice of fingernail.

Kal pinches the map closed. "No, babe, don't open it. The pic inside is the neural cue, triggers the nano. Gotta wait wait wait for the party tonight, yeah? I'll just hold it for you 'til then. These guys gonna shake your tuckus, and Dyer here, what she do gonna shake your brain."

Leelee's eyes get perilously wider. Dyer squinches her own to narrow slits in sympathy.

Kal leans in to kiss the air over Dyer's cheek, drops the accent to say, "Hear about the two USERs pulled from the river last night? Crap beat out of them? That fascist turd Evan's saying 'send them back to the States, conscious or not.' Watch yourself today. Anti-migrant rally in Parliament Square. Lotta noobs in town; big group got through the Chunnel last night. Street's frigging *twitchy*, girl, like everyone's dusted, seeing things. People where they shouldn't be. Speaking of, some betty in a godawful yellow hoodie been staring at you, up by the benches."

Then louder, "Can*not* wait for the Drop tonight. Whole bloody town needs some HigherWorks." She exits left, Leelee trailing behind to look back at Dyer, eyes bleached to porcelain in the sudden sun.

Dyer rubs her scalp, checks the benches with a sideways glance, catches a yellow-hooded head just turning away.

A gaggle of girls in shiny machine-worn leatherette stumble into the shade, all trying to read off the same phone. Too young, Dyer thinks, and too loud. She riffles the edges of the maps in her pocket. She's handed out a few dozen this morning. It'd be nice to get through the whole stack this morning, while folks still had time to plan their night.

"—no network nodes, no data stream, but the nano *wants* to connect, it needs the connection. How it's designed," The Wayward is saying. "So it starts connecting with anything, with all the wifi and broadband feeds and, dig this, with other ghost nano in other people's brains. Not like a Drop party, there's no beats, no video, no HigherWorks to ride the flow, keep everyone in sync, yeah? Just a jumble of flashbacks, visions, voices, thoughts, and then you drift untethered, like, you know, crowdsurfing, you go all *scattered*—"

"Doesn't work that way, Way," Dyers snaps: edgy because of Kal's news, edgy because it's a topic she doesn't want to touch in public, edgy because she doesn't like to lie. "Nano can't do anything without neural cues and network nodes, and anyway your body breaks it down in a couple hours. Ghost nano, it's urban legend. *Sub*urban legend, mallrat stuff."

She looks toward the girls in their glittery off-the-shelf counterculture. Behind them, by the bank of the canal, is a woman in Dyer's own black leather skin hair like a thunderhead bruised eyes just shadows in a sharp fragile face and Dyer's breath stops. If it's not lust—Dyer left that behind with the rest in the dry husk of California—it's something just as potent.

No yellow hoodie, though, which means someone *else* is watching her; the one thing Dyer didn't leave in the States was the thing she fled: the fear. Don't just run *from*, Dyer thinks, run *to*. She raises an eyebrow at the mystery woman, remembers that her eyes are full black and leaves them that way. If a little anger creeps in between her brows, the corners of her mouth, well, that's just the flip side of the fear.

The woman lifts her chin just a fraction, nothing fragile in that motion, and Dyer feels a sudden dizzy doubling, like she's been drawn out in overlapping circles, that Drop party buzz of anticipation, of connection.

The Wayward says, "Leave it, mate, she ain't interested. Um, innit?"

Dyer turns, ready to give Way a "shut up already" roll of her eyes, finds a face in the way, heavy-jowled and swirled blue with faux prison tats. The guy blinks, does a cartoon double-take.

"Bugger me. Thought you was a bloke," he says.

"Nope and nope," Dyer says.

"Works for me," says the blue tats' companion, baring her luminescent teeth at Dyer over his shoulder.

"She ain't interested, whichever way you're rigged," Way says. "Are you, Dyer?"

Dyer gives him the "shut up already" look now, but it's too late.

"*Dyer*. You're HigherWorks," the teeth gasp—even her tongue glows white—and blue tats gets a look that says maybe he can overlook Dyer's not being a bloke after all.

"Opt-in tonight," Dyer says, and slaps a pair of maps into the hand that snakes around blue tats' waist, looking left to avoid eye contact, to find the woman by the canal. *Nowhere* she could have gone in that brief moment, but she's not there. Deleted, swiped away, and in her place are three men in bespoke suits, hands in pocket and practiced leers on their faces. Dyer's first thought is Immigration, but they've got Union Jack pins on their lapels; junior partners out of the City, most likely, looking to score points with management by pasting a couple of USERs to a pulp.

She reaches back to tap The Wayward, feels his dreads

shift against her shoulder as he nods. "Two more, other side of the bridge," he says quietly.

Dyer shuts her eyes, inhales slowly. Blue tats' breath is stale beer and bad curry for breakfast, but he's over six feet of solid meat, and his glowstar companion is razor sharp and twitchy with stims, and they are both as London as the King's Own Cobblers. Dyer tucks her arm around them both—desperate measures for Dyer, touching, but she's thinking about bodies bleeding into the Thames—says, "Buy us a pint, then?"

———

- *2042-05-18T10:22:00+01:00 +51.541327-0.145319*

- contact: target (unconfirmed) - Leanna Vance - priority AA Aph2035.Z980023 - scan summary: face match 47% sig. delta's hair color n.a. shaved - eye color n.a. corneal implants - gesture score 62% sig. delta's weight -12 kilos height +9cm possible tib/fem bone extension

- note: ID scores low confidence due 2 contact distance & crowd cover - see attached images

- attachment: personal message

- -crazy flight, edge of space, yo, jet-lagged out of my gourd - day *started* weird - some guy comes up to me at the airport "hey jocelyn" kisses me straight on the mouth - i'm like "i do *not* know u so f-off" - feel wacked like i'm coming down with something seeing ghosts out of the corner of my eye - gotta be a lotta ghosts here, yeah? place even *smells* old - no fiberboard no burning tires no pepper spray

- - took four hours to get through customs - no one got the f-ing memo about the new ip treaty guess the brits are keeping it secret cuz everyone hates the states here - as if we can't hate each other just fine on our own, thanks - some guy on the street called me a user, like he can see tracks through my hoodie, turns out it means u.s. economic refugee - i'm like "screw u" but i guess i fit the description if i wasn't here on ur dime and ur visa

- - might all pay off, though, cuz that tip seems legit - just been here 12 hours and i've already got a possible hit on vance herself - got a few photos but i couldn't get close and these contact cams u gave me are crap - ur fancy scan app says around 50% match - she's had serious body work and she's got this cray cray looking surfer dude watching her back and she's edgy as hell so don't start spending the money yet - oh wait, i *have* - i don't score that bounty i am so so very doomed

- - kisses -jo

• attachment: images (7) - <click to view>

———

Dyer and Mrs. John Dee, brooding nano—Camden Catacombs —Friday Noon

"Mrs. John Dee, you said no self-respecting Londoner would be caught dead in Camden in the daylight," Dyer says. She's sitting on the microassembler in an attempt to block the bright, busy control panel from view.

Mrs. John Dee tugs a blue floral frock on over her head, sets her glasses on her nose, peers over them at the folks staggered about the catacomb chamber.

"Dyer, love, none of these people are self-respecting."

She sheds a heavy studded cuff, the last of her work

uniform, and toes the box of leather, chrome, and vinyl under the workbench. As the only legal Brit in Higher-Works, she picks up spending money selling LPs to tourists who can't play them. The money's okay, and the contacts in the community of artists and musicians working the markets are better. The required punk attire—'the hoary old eighties,' Mrs. John Dee calls it, 'and heavy on the hoar'—is more suited to Dyer's taste, but Dyer's forged ID codes aren't up to the scrutiny required by the Economic Refugee Act.

"And you said the catacombs are off limits due to the danger of flooding from the canal."

"A positive death trap," Mrs. John Dee agrees. "Which is why you had to pick three locks when we first moved in. No one dares come down here."

Paint-tagged kids chase each other with rattling spray cans. Students ring their teacher under the dim, hanging bulbs, dutifully examining the rails set into the brick floor where horse carts once rolled. A family dozes on a blanket, surrounded by the remains of a picnic. And what looks for all the world like a tour group in bright Brazilian colors mills about under the vaulted galleries, kept away from the equipment by some hastily stacked boxes and Dyer's glare.

Mrs. John Dee points at the massive slab of brick and ironwork that supported the far side of the underground warehouse. "Look, that wall was blank when we got here. That's a sick canvas, would've been tagged top to bottom had this place been open."

They'd moved in three weeks ago and the wall is already covered: a collage of overlapped graffiti, bills pasted up and torn down again, what looked like bird crap even though they were underground, a hanging pair of seriously soiled trousers that none of the group dared get near enough to take down. A little girl with perfect doll hair and knock-off dayglo Doc Martens is staring up at the wall. As Dyer and Dee watch as she leans forward and carefully sticks her gum in one of the few remaining spots of bare brick.

Dyer sighs and shifts to cover a neon green popup on the panel. "Should have had my hips widened when I had my legs done," she says.

Mrs. John Dee scrubs her mohawk into its natural teal tangle, pulls her tablet out of her bag. "Bollocks. Your hips are the eighth architectural wonder. They just need some company. Budge up, love." She pulls herself up onto the microassembler next to Dyer, peeks under her arm at the control panel. "What are we hatching?" she asks.

"Soundsystem, all for you," Dyer says. "Bud interface, cochlear induction. Everything except the auditory cortex stuff. I ran that in with the visual batch."

Mrs. John Dee does a little shimmy on the microassember hatch. "Breed, my lovelies, breeeeed," she says. And adds, as the little dayglo girl copies her move across the will-be dance-floor, "We're going to jail, aren't we?"

"No, *you're* going to jail," Dyer says. "If the police decide we're causing enough of a nuisance, they'll haul you up for some Section 63 nonsense. 'Repetitive beats'."

"'Repetitive beats' my bucephalus bouncing bum," Mrs. John Dee says with another shimmy. "Did you even listen to the track I—"

"The Wayward, Shimago, me, we'll be put in the Dover Centre to be beaten down for a year, deported back to the US, and then things will really get bad. Worse, if the UK rejoins the IP treaty zone."

"Sorry, love, shouldn't laugh, I know. But really, what else can we do?" She waves at the crowd.

The students have filed out into the tunnels, and the Brazilians have expanded like vapor to fill the available space.

"Move on," Dyer says.

Mrs. John Dee frowns, prods her tablet with a tattered, teal fingernail. "I'm not at all sure I like the idea of running, just because the bloody fascists have voted themselves in and our own dear fans are all too, um, fanatic."

"It's not running," Dyer says. She gestures at the billowing Brazilians. "It's just the flow. 'There is a tide in the affairs of blah blah.' You're a DJ, Dee, you know about the flow."

In the gaps between the Brazilians, she sees the shine of black leather under thunderhead hair, glittering coal-smoke eyes. Flashback to this morning's vision, the impossibly disappearing woman. Dyer's chest thrums.

She slips off the microassembler. "Be right back. If the panel beeps three times, hit the green button."

"Oh, ah, okay. Oh dear," Mrs. John Dee says behind her.

Dyer follows the leather gleam across the dance floor, loses it in the gloom and bustle, reaches that graffitied far wall. No one is there, nothing like that fragile face, not in the crowd or under the vaults on either side. Like this morning at the canal, she's dissolved away.

"She show me the spot for my gum," the doll girl says in a stage whisper, blue eyes serious under straight-cut bangs, then she laughs and swirls back into the crowd.

Well, what were you expecting on day turned weird and wired? Dyer thinks. "What else?" Dyer asks the wall.

The wall responds with a flicker: a scrap of smartpaper, smeared under sellotape and glitching all along the torn edge. Dyer tugs it from the brick, squints at the scrolling text. It's some sort of government document, a snarl of nested digital sigs and certs and then the title, *Provisional Agreement on the Renormalization of Intellectual Property Rights between the United States of America and the United Kingdom of Gre—*.

Dyer tries to scroll up, searching for a date, but the paper glitches, resyncs on a list captioned *Patents of Special Concern* and there at the top is "*A process for the mutual self-repair of nanomechanisms* by Leanna Vance," and then it's her eyes glitching, flashes of memory in time to her pounding heart of those last worst days in the US, a sudden sinking nausea, a tinnitus squeal. The squeal stops, starts again, and Dyer realizes it's not in her head; it's coming from across the room. She pushes back through the Brazilians to find Mrs. John Dee, all five ferocious feet of her, restacking the box barricade around their workspace, pausing after every box to glare down the vaults.

Dyer sweeps up a box, lifts it over Mrs. John Dee's head to the top of the stack. "What happened?"

"Some bloody bint knocks the boxes over, 'oh, excuse me,' she says, and when I get up to sort it out, she nips in to play with your panel there, face first and wide eyed."

"Contact cams," Dyer says, nausea returning.

"'That's a bit of none of your business,' I said, and she doesn't even blink. 'You deaf?' I ask, and give her a nudge in the kidneys, in case she really was."

Mrs. John Dee demonstrates with a vicious jab of her elbow.

Dyer steps back out of range. "So?"

"So since her hearing was apparently bolloxed, I figured I'd give it a tune up." She patted her tablet. "I was just setting up audio network tests. I figured if she was rigged for cams, she'd have bud implants as well. I boosted the volume to eleven."

"Ah," Dyer said. "That was feedback, then, that I heard. From forty feet away."

"Her head will be ringing for a fortnight. Ought to put a spanner in her party plans."

"You think she's a nano cook?"

"If she were a fan, or paparazzi, she'd have gone for our lovely visages, not the gear. She's a bizarro you from some rival Drop party crew."

Dyer's thinking of that fade-away face, those eyes. "She _look_ like me? Only with hair?" She waves her fingers over her head like clouds drifting. "Did she, uh, fade?"

Mrs. John Dee shrugs. "She looked like a yellow hood-up hoodie. Not so much fading as slinking away in disgrace, tail between her legs. Lovely tail, though. All's well that ends well." Mrs. John Dee demonstrates with another shimmy.

Dyer makes a dubious "mmm." She fishes the scrap of smartpaper out of her back pocket, but it's gone completely glitched, just a scattering of pixel dust.

———

2042-05-18T12:09:00+01:00 +51.541709-0.147667
  • contact: target (unconfirmed) - Leanna Vance - priority AA Aph2035.Z980023 - supporting evidence IP violations see note
  • contact: target (confirmed) - Mariam Ebadi UK7D1B4GU230011 - priority NA rumored assoc. Leanna Vance c.f. - UK Resident ID confirmed via direct scan embedded tag
  • note: target operating Alphet model X50EU microassembler running unreleased OS - license module disabled - see attached images
  • note: unregistered NNDA profiles in violation of 21USC2401 - see attached images
  • attachment: personal message
  - got the bitch - yeah yeah no physical id yet no documented distribution but who else is gonna be running alphet.com beta code with custom modules? and the license mod is axed so that's ip violation right there *and* she's cooking delivery agents with unregistered payloads - do me a favor and see if there's a brit law about that so i don't have to deal with the treaty b.s. again
  - also this ebadi bimbo is hacking earbud implants - *got* to be a brit law against that
  - see *told* u i was a good investment
  - kisses -jo
  • attachment: images (5) - <click to view>

Dyer, Shimago, and Mrs. John Dee, rocket in pocket—Mornington Crescent—Friday Afternoon

Dyer levers the backpack over the exit turnstile at arms' length, ducks the bristling bouquet of carbonfiber antennae that spill from the top.

"Fragile," Shimago reminds her.

"So are my eyeballs," Dyer says.

Shimago doesn't have to lift his pack; the turnstile only comes up to his thighs. Mrs. John Dee drags her duffle thumping behind her.

"Why is the helium so heavy?" she grumbles. "Ought to just float along. Maybe if I let some out into the bag."

"No," Dyer and Shimago say in unison. "You just want to huff it and sing in a squirrel voice," Dyer adds.

"And then *I* shall just float along," Mrs. John Dee agrees happily.

"Anyway, that's the lightest bag," Dyer says.

"That's another thing," Mrs. John Dee says. "Why is the *rocket* so heavy?"

"It's not—"

"A rocket. Yes, love, but that's what I call it because the first one was such a lovely rockety shape."

"—Not heavy," Shimago continues. "Just big."

"Sixteen times the network bandwidth of the last one," Dyer says. "Twice as many nano dispersers."

"And your subsonic driver," Shimago says. "The entire carbon outer shell is the resonator. 120DbA at 20 Hertz."

"Ace. Teeth shall be rattled," Mrs. John Dee says, out of breath and a few steps behind. She's turning circles as she walks, duffel swinging.

"Wait until you see it flying, with the spotlights and the

screens running," Dyer says. "It's perfect, looks just like the film. Only thing we couldn't find is a clean recording of the announcer. You'll have to record Shimago when we get back to the catacombs."

Shimago booms, "A new life awaits you in the Off-world colonies. The chance to begin again in a golden land of opportunity and adventure."

Mrs. John Dee is still spinning. Dyer turns around. "Dee, what *are* you—"

"USER freak. Fuck off home."

Dyers turns back. Whoever's speaking is hidden behind Shimago's bulk. She leans left to see a dozen pimpled punklings in custom-printed carbon, active tats a riot of football logos and Union colors.

"Tha's right, you heard 'im, you yank sket," one of them said to Dyer.

Shimago sets a hand on the lead punkling's shoulder. "Balderdash, my lad. Do I *look* like an economic refugee, American or otherwise?" he says in his best King's English.

Shimago looks like six-foot-four two hundred and fifty pounds of gear-pierced lcd-tattooed fully-networked Tongan-Californian rugby-playing airship-piloting Drop-partying choreomaniac. His hyphens alone outweigh these punks, Dyer thinks, and bares her teeth.

"Dunno, she *fit* though, innit?" one says, gaze dropping down under Dyer's.

"Issit?" the lead one says, squinting. Shimago shifts his grip to the kid's head, palms it like a ball and turns it upward.

"Since you seem so full of perceptions upon our character, perhaps you would like to present them to the authorities," Shimago says.

"Wha?"

"He taking you to the po-po," another explains.

"I'm just sayin' I'd mash that," the one staring at Dyer says.

Mrs. John Dee comes spinning past Dyer, takes the lead punkling out at the knees with the duffel; he dangles from Shimago's hand like a doll. The other punklings step back from the swinging bag. "You want a mashing?" she asks the starer. "You cheeky little muppet. The lot of you in *our* ends, up from, what, Surrey? Think you're hard because you spent the money mummy gave you on tats you can turn off again before you get home? *She's* hard." That with a hand out toward Dyer. "She eats suburban white boys like you for breakfast."

"Not hungry," Dyer says. She steps up even with Dee. The starer only comes up to her chin; she looks straight over his head at the crowd pushing past in the too-bright sunlight, all willfully or carelessly oblivious. But there's a knot of anxious faces across the street that have noob USER written all over them, pinned in place like the sun's a spotlight. Lucky the punklings hadn't run into them instead.

"What are you doing here?" Dyer wonders under her breath. She means the USERs, stumbling through London on this unsettled day of days, but the punklings react with shrugs and awkward shuffles. "Dunno," one says. "Heard this voice said check those three, they's Yanks."

Shimago sets his captive punkling upright. "A case of mistaken identity," he says. "Easily corrected by a conversation with the police about anti-social behavior." Shimago gives the leader a gentle push and the kid stumbles forward, trips over Dee's duffel again, bumps shoulders with the starer. It's not entirely a bluff; Dyer's and Shimago's forged IDs will hold up to a quick fingerprint or retinal scan. But they're likely to fail the sort of full biometric series that Immigration runs, and it's been one of those days.

A too-long moment as the punkling weighs the cost of confrontation versus the loss of face. Finally, he mutters "freak" and shuffles down the sidewalk without looking back; his mates straggle behind him. The starer stays a beat longer, finally makes eye contact. Dyer blinks her corneals clear, looks down at him until he blushes and turns away.

"A new life awaits us in a golden land of opportunity and adventure," Dyer says.

Shimago sighs, hefts his pack on his shoulder, heads off perpendicular to the punklings retreat.

"Mrs. John Dee, you are yourself from the lovely green lawns of Surrey, are you not?" he asks.

"I was," she says. "But Mrs. John Dee is from here and now, Shimago."

The duffel nudges Dyer's leg. Mrs. John Dee is walking backward, head swinging like a radar dish. "Dee, what the *hell* are you looking for?"

"I don't *know*," Mrs. John Dee says. "Whatever you've been looking for since this morning. Which is, judging from the look on your face, a much bigger deal than some sixth form twits a-twitting."

"I don't know what..." Dyer almost says 'you're talking about,' but that's neither fair nor true. "What it is. Somebody following me. Some*bodies*. An IP bounty hunter. A parallel me from some other dimension. Maybe Way is right and it's ghost nano."

"Ghost nano is an urban legend," Shimago says.

Dyer growls, strides five steps to the next road crossing, stops cold. Mrs. John Dee bumps into her from behind. Shimago stops next to Dyer. His look of gentle concern grows less gentle as he looks up from her to the street.

On the far side of the crossing are two uniformed officers of the UK Immigration Service, conspicuously *not* cops courtesy of their berets and their semi-automatics. The two are staring straight at them through the stream of crossing pedestrians.

Mrs. John Dee wedges herself between Dyer and Shimago. "You're not seriously waiting for the walk light?" she says. Then she follows their gaze and adds, "Oh. Oh dear. But they can't stop us unless they have cause."

Shimago says, "Crossing against the light is cause."

"And not crossing is suspicious behavior," Dyer says.

As if summoned by her statement, the two UKIS officers step off the curb. Dyer fights the sudden urge to look over her shoulder; looking like she's going to run could escalate a bad situation into a fatal one.

And then she looks anyway, because she knows what she'll see: the fragile-faced woman, from the canal, from the catacomb wall, standing in carbon black relief against a white sunlit storefront. Not a woman, though, is it? Not a rival nano cook, not some patent-tracking bounty hunter in from the US. It's something else entirely, that outline drawn flat against the concrete like an opening, like a door. With no conscious decision Dyer takes Mrs. John Dee's hand, tugs her toward the figure even though it's already fading to a shimmering afterimage. There's a real door there, though, behind the figure's promise and Dyer grabs the handle, looks back to see if Shimago is following.

The impossible shape is now standing in the crossing, still no more than a silhouette: the gleam of leather below and eyes above, and as the UKIS officers step up behind her the bright sudden slash of a smile.

And as she smiles there's a *pop pop pop* from overhead, loud enough to sting, smoke and a shower of glittering fragments. A beat of silence, then the crowd in the street rears up screaming and crashes down together like a wave. Another round of *pops*. Still on her feet, Dyer can see that it's the street surveillance drones blowing out, one by one, but for the folks on the ground it's cause for more panic. The UKIS officers struggle to keep their footing as they track Dyer through the scrum. One fails and takes the other down with him. The impossible woman's hair fades with the smoke; the gleam of her smile fragments like the falling debris.

Mrs. John Dee tugs Dyer's hand. She and Shimano are already through the door.

The shop is a maze of booths, one of the miniature markets that have spilled out from the fount of crass that is Camden. Dyer, Dee, and Shimago take turns leading each other, their packs bumping past jackets studded belts badge-bedecked bags and the butt end of the 20th C spelled out in tee shirts. A rear door leads to an alley that dead-ends in a covered court, another manufactured market. They take refuge in a coffee shop whose postered windows provide cover.

"No sign of them," Mrs. John Dee says, smooths back down the corner of a peeled-up poster with slightly shaky fingers. "Bloody hell, Dyer, bloody hell. What has the world come to, we can't cross the damn street without being afraid?"

Shimago is back from the counter, steaming mugs in hand. "Ah, Mrs. John Dee, this—" he starts in his own gentle accent.

Dyer cuts in, still half-blind with afterimages, or maybe it's anger flooding up like the crowd's panic. "Mariam, damn it, this *has always been* our world, Jonah's and mine, afraid to cross the damn street. *You're* just coming to it, and you're just a tourist. *We* live here, our whole lives."

Shimago blinks at this use of real names, but sits and says nothing.

"Back in California, even before everything collapsed, even when Jonah and I worked at Alphet in the shiny heart of the goddamn shiny future, my own lab and a billion dollar budget, even then I was afraid to walk down the street alone."

Dyer is thumping the table; coffee splashes, scalds her fingertips.

"And then the Crash and it all fell down, lawyers picking over what's left and goddamn IP *bounty hunters* with a take-down notice in one hand and a taser in the other, people saying they were scared of losing everything but they meant their 401k, their house, their car.

"The day of the Wall Street hack, police car following *me*

fifteen blocks from the BART to my house even though there's
fucking fascist militia burning houses right down the street, in
Berkeley, for fuck sake, finally stops me fifty feet from my front
door, for jay-walking is what they said, meaning I crossed the
neighbor's driveway while being black, never mind I'm in a
business suit and five-hundred dollar shoes. Savings, house,
car, those shoes, I was way past that. I was scared of losing my
life. Every damn day.

"And now it's happening here in your face and yes, you're
scared. You should be, with government caving in to the thugs
and bigots. But you can always get on the train back to Surrey.
We don't have that option. All we can do is move on."

Mrs. John Dee is pale, and the shaking has travelled up her
arms to her shoulders. Shimago gives a small nod, blots up the
spilled coffee with his napkin, and with that Dyer's anger,
which is never gone, loses its focus. She puts her hand on
Dee's.

"The hell, Miriam, I know this is nothing you haven't
heard from your own grandparents. Look, having left all that
bullshit behind, having come here with nothing but my self,
and that self so changed I barely recognize it, I found refuge.
I'm not talking about the EU and their half-ass US Economic
Refugee Act, I mean *you*, Mrs. John Dee, hottest damn DJ in
London, you and Shimago and The Wayward."

Dyer snorts, rubs her scalp.

"If I could send my ghost back to appear to myself on the
sidewalk that day, tell myself that I was going to end up
cooking nano for some damn crazy underground psychedelic
performance art rave heaven-help-me Drop party, and *that*,
not developing corporate patents, was the way to the
goddamn shiny future…"

Shimago holds up his mug. "HigherWorks," he says.

Mrs. John Dee and Dyer clink their cups against his.
"HigherWorks."

Mrs. John Dee slurps her tea, sighs and shuts her eyes,

opens them again and says, "Dyer, love, sorry but I have to ask. How did you get away from the cops? On the sidewalk that day, I mean."

Now Dyer is getting the shakes, as the adrenaline drains. She sets her cup down before it splashes again. "I stood there, hands on hips, and said 'Seriously? One of the biggest days in American history and you want to spend it hassling *me*?'"

Mrs. John Dee hugs her mug to her chest and says, "Bad. Ass."

Shimago nods again.

But Dyer shakes her head, thinking of that knot of noob USERs in the sunlight. "Lucky," she says.

———

2042-05-18T15:22:00+01:00 +51.535956-0.139593
• contact: target (unconfirmed) - Leanna Vance - priority AA Aph2035.Z980023 - supporting evidence IP violations see note
• contact: target (unconfirmed) - Jonah Pupunu - priority A Aph2035.Z72105
• note: evidence use of nano agents against UK gov property - see attached image archive
• attachment: personal message
- holy crap was alphet developing some sort of anti-security nano? must have been right? someone just blew out a couple dozen surveillance drones and those nazi immigration police have an alert out for - dig this - "woman african descent shaved head" and "man pacific islander unusually large" - *gotta* be vance and pupunu
- those same nazi immigration police grilled me for an hour for taking pix of the drones - some sort of migrant riot thing going on - pretty intense - still, no guns, no gas, no bodies hanging from streetlights, so it's f-ing paradise, yeah? would be, if i could stay here

- kisses -jo
• attachment: images (22) - <click to view>

———

(Dyer) and The Wayward, displacing—Camden Catacombs—Friday Afternoon

"—ghosts, you know?" The Wayward says, sounds stoned because he is, during this quiet time with most of the setup done but the Drop still hours away.

Wants to connect, he hears Dyer say.

"Right? Me too," Way says, prodding his tablet. He's testing the camera grid, the web of stickum cams and micro-drones that he uses to monitor the groove. The sights and sounds might be nano-created illusions inside the dancer's heads, but the way they move, their reaction to the stream and to each other, all that feeds back into the rhythm of The Wayward's images and Mrs. John Dee's beats, which streams back into the crowd until the whole system, sight and sound and moving bodies all strung together by Dyer's nano, drops into yet a higher sync.

"Higher and higher," Way says. And then, "Spooky," because the cameras are glitching, flashes of images from else-where, bits of broadcast—a listing overloaded boat, a red-faced crowd in Parliament Square—snips of skewed text, feeds from street drones, what looks like Shimago, Dee, and Dyer standing in a sea of crawling people, but that doesn't make sense because Dyer's here, somewhere. Saw her just now, Way thinks, or was that in the camera feed?

Over by the wall, he hears Dyer say.

"Right," Way says. "The spooky wall." Spooky in the way that wall had developed, like a photographic print, the image emerging point by point line by line out of the blank brick, a series of random acts teasing pattern, purpose. He'd been taking snapshots of it over the last week, a time-lapse to work into the performance stream tonight, layered over the real wall. Layers of reality, that's the 'Higher' in HigherWorks, Way thinks.

The wall is not quite ready, he hears Dyer say.

"Ready for her closeup," Way says. 'Gotta get some closeup textures for the vid-ay-oh stream.' He gets up and wobbles across the bricks to the far side of the warehouse. A flock of microdrones spiral over his head like an exclamation point. Even though it's underground, the warehouse has head-room; iron beams hold brick vaults forty feet overhead.

"Over my head," Way says, head tilted up to look up at the wall. A diagonal splash of paint and paper runs from the floor almost up to the ceiling. Last week, Mrs. John Dee chased a spraycan-armed drone around the warehouse with a broom, the rest of them doubled over laughing, though Dyer pointed out it was hardly their place to complain, they didn't belong there either, no one did.

Every place belongs to no one, he hears Dyer say.

"Just movin' through," Way agrees. He takes a snapshot, a poster pasted over the uneven brick, realizes it's an ad for an anti-migrant protest, tears the poster down leaving a jagged edge that reads "migrant pro", takes a photo of that instead.

"That's us, Dyer. Migrant pros," he says.

Refugee act, he hears Dyer say.

"Yeah, I mean refugees, but what did you say the other day? Everyone on the move is running from something and running to something. Just the flow, yeah? I ever play you The Wayward? The music, I mean. Harry Partch, he was a hobo. Like you, now I think of it. He had degrees, research grants, just like you, just like you he left it behind to ride the rails in the Depression. The first one, I mean, the black-and-white one. Left the mainstream behind after that, made his own

musical instruments, his own scales, his own kind of perfor-
mances. Just like *us*."

Way scoops a glittery blob of something off the brick,
looks for a spot, finally peels up a sticker and re-sticks it a foot
higher, smears the blob in its place.

"Anyway, seemed like a good name to take on, yeah? Wayward, like where I'm headed is the way itself."

That thought makes him want to take another hit, but he
doesn't know where the spliff has gone, can't actually
remember rolling one, but man, he's rolling on *something*. He
reaches up on tiptoes to peel away the bottom half of another
poster,

"He was from Oakland like you, too, Dyer. Harry Partch
was. But he grew up down near me in LA. Man, I miss that
place sometimes. Not the bits where I was sleeping on the
beach and eating out of, well, you know. But, hey, all this…"

Way waves vaguely at the wall, squints, pulls a piece of
gum from down around his knees and sticks it at eye level.

"I mean HigherWorks, you guys, like you always say,
worth running *to*, even if I started with the running *from*."

The future is displacement, he hears Dyer say.

"Right on. HigherWorks, displacing the future." Which
doesn't sound quite right. He pulls a stickum camera out of
his pocket, flies it across the surface of the wall, saying "displace, displace, displace," but the word doesn't sound any
more right with repetition. He lands the camera on a brick,
just a few feet above the floor and pointing down. "*Dis* place,"
he says. "Hey, Dyer, get it?"

But Dyer isn't here at all, she's over there, coming in from
the tunnels with Shimago and Mrs. John Dee, lugging what
has got to be Shimago's new rocket.

"Huh," The Wayward says.

"Hey, Way," Dyer says. "Everything ready?"

He looks up at the wall. "Yeah," he says.

———

2042-05-18T16:29:00+01:00 +51.541709-0.147667

- contact: target (unconfirmed) - Leanna Vance - priority AA Aph2035.Z980023 - supporting evidence IP violations see note
- note: evidence intent to distribute unlicensed NNDA see attached image archive
- attachment: personal message - i know u r thinking i'm gonna be working off your loan forever but think again, looks like i'll wrap this up my first day - this higherworks group with vance and pupunu planning some sort of rave tonight - i got a pic of the flyer has a map with an x-marks-the-spot - apparently they literally *spray* the nano over the audience - all i gotta do is show up with a scanner and a camera and a pair of cuffs
    - kisses -jo
- attachment: image (1) - <click to view>

———

Dyer, cueing—Camden Catacombs—Friday Evening

Dyer tucks up her knees as The Wayward and Mrs. John Dee shove the last couple of cardboard boxes into place. She's under the plastic folding table they use as a workbench, with the brick of the catacomb wall behind her, the humming microassembler to the right, and the boxes sealing off the other two sides. It doesn't actually have to be dark and quiet for neural cue test, but it makes the measurements more accurate. Anyway, it's part of the HigherWorks ritual, and not just for her; when Dyer emerges from her cave and declares the readings auspicious, that's the cue for the entire group that the Drop is on.

She tugs the sensor band snug across her temples, pairs it

with her tablet, starts up the diagnostic logging: temporal, frontal, occipital, parietal activity—thinking about The Wayward's 'parental nest'—blinks her corneals clear so the infrared camera in the tablet can track eye movement, pupil dilation. Earbuds on, Dee's test mix streaming, network up. Dyer swipes the screen off, sits in the dark for a minute. Clear my head, she thinks, but she's still seeing afterimages, black on black, shadowed eyes and thundercloud hair. Her impossible woman.

Dyer sighs, finds the business end of the inhaler. The nano swirls into her lungs, the smell of apple blossoms and a tart bubbly sensation like champagne. And then…nothing. Which is the first test passed; if the nano triggers without the cue then it's not an opt-in, and suddenly HigherWorks goes from a concern for Immigration and the IP lawyers to one for Narcotics or—a very worst case—the anti-terrorist nutjobs.

She fishes a map from her pocket, finds the sealed edge with her thumb, and pulls it open. There's a spark as the ink reacts, and then the image inside shimmers to life.

This is the first time she's actually seen the cue as an image; up until this moment it's just been data. For the last couple of years they've been getting the cues from a friend of The Wayward up in Kingsbury, an ancient Irish curmudgeon of a painter who comes to the parties even though he's the one person in the world for whom the nano won't trigger; there's a window of just a few hours as the nano settles into the brain for the cue to come. *Window window window* Dyer thinks as the nano wakes up. The cue is suddenly a window, the printed image a world seen through it: two characters on a high-domed roof, looking out over the streets of a city sketched in strokes and squares—could be London but strange shapes hang in the air above—and behind the two watchers a raven watches them, like *memory memory memory* as the audio kicks in, layered all down the auditory path from her implanted buds to her cochlear nerves to her auditory cortex an ocean of sound swept by deep currents.

The image flickers and fades as the inks burn out, but streaks of blue and silver *ghost ghost ghost* across her vision like echoes. During the gig tonight The Wayward will be nudging those echoes via the network, riffing on the images like visual jazz, tracking Dee's beats, the two of them playing off each other, playing the crowd-become-one like sex, like the crowd in the crossing when the cameras blew, made one *motion motion motion* by a hypersensitivity that transcends identity triggered not by lust or fear but by design by a higher *working working working*. Which is the second test passed; the nano is certainly working.

Dyer taps the tablet on, swipes the network off, colors fading as the screenlight fills her little box nest under the table. She swipes the network off, diagnostic software already parsing the logs into graphs points spreading across the screen and into the air around her like stars falling like light on water like what had The Wayward said this morning you go all *scattered scattered scattered*.

Dyer shuts her eyes. Shhhh, the test is over, the network's down, she thinks. Go to sleep, little nano.

"Scattered," a voice ghost-whispers in her ear. "Awake."

"I *am* awake," Dyer says, shivers all down her back. She keeps her eyes shut, not sure that she wants to see that sharp fragile face, those shadowed eyes, this close, this intimate.

"No."

"'No' not me, or 'no' not awake?" Dyer asks. And then, "You know what? Just bugger off. I've got stuff to do. Anyway, you're just urban legend."

From the ocean of sound, sudden shifting layers of voices, "Urban defined not by geography demographics or culture but by a certain threshold of connectivity, legend not as fabricated history but as fabricated comma history as the key to a map."

The voices all sync up on that last sharp word and then complete silence, but with that hypersensitivity from the nano/lust/fear Dyer can feel that impossible face just a finger's width from hers.

"What do you want?" Dyer asks.

Silence, but a flickering, or the memory of a flickering, glitching pixels and the words *mutual self-repair.*

"I left Leanna Vance behind, halfway around the world and a decade gone," Dyer snarls. "What do you want from *me?*" She opens her eyes but it's dark; the tablet screen's gone to sleep again.

Her own voice says, "We live here, our whole lives."

The feeling of lips on hers, the scent of bougainvillea and circuits burning, the taste of champagne.

———

2042-05-18T18:33:22+01:00 +51.541522-0.147123

• contact: target (unconfirmed) - Leanna Vance - priority AA Aph2035.Z980023 - ongoing

• attachment: personal message - i got a lead on an american expat supposed to have the scoop on the "user" community - better start picking out some new bounties for me

- and while you're at it get my visa extended - i'm beginning to dig this old smell these old ghosts - got no immediate plans for going back to the states - yeah yeah i can hear you grumbling from here but i am worth it - i am a bounty collecting *ninja* - and the proof is vance is going down down down tonight

- kisses -jo

———

Dyer and Shimago, queuing—Stables Market—Friday Evening

• • •

Dyer is in line at the kebab stand for Mrs. John Dee's shawarma, and someone is too close behind her: a caress of convection currents, a static tickle.

Shimago back with the curry, Dyer thinks. Blue Tats and Glowstar Girl from this morning, ready for another pint. The staring pimple-faced punkling still hot to mash it. A yellow-hoodied bounty hunter with a take-down notice ready to tag and drag her back to California. Anyone, Dyer thinks as she turns, please, *anyone* but the shadowed thundercloud shape that is, nano or not, the ghost of Leanna Vance.

It's Kal's friend, xe of the twig fingers and anime eyes.

Dyer says, "Leelee, yeah? All right?"

But those fingers are shaking, those eyes even wider than Dyer remembered. Leelee gulps a breath, another, manages to gasp, "Kal."

"Ah, damn it," Dyer says. "UKIS?"

Leelee's confused alarm is baffling, until Dyer realizes xe might not be a USER.

"The Immigration Services?" Dyer says, miming a beret.

Leelee shakes xyr head, mimes a hood instead. "A Yank," xe says, "Some hard sket with a taser," in a lilting East End Jamaican accent. "Hard as can be in a yellow hoodie, which ain't. Kal say 'go tell Dyer' so I go. Went down there," xe points at the floor—the catacombs run under the market— then points up, "but they say you up here."

"Shit," Dyer says. "Where are they? Kal and the hoodie woman? We'll grab Shimago and go find them."

"Allow that," Leelee says. "Kal take care of herself. She tell me to tell you this Yank asking about HigherWorks, asking about *Dyer*. Sounds like the sket bringin' a beef you way. I run here to warn you. Manz didn't build this body for running, innit?" Xe shakes xyr head, tugs the lace around xyr sleeves straight.

"Someone bringing a beef to HigherWorks?" Shimago asks, walking up with take-away bags in each hand. "Let them. They will discover that we are…" He swings the bags like nunchacku, leans in for effect. "…*vegetarian*."

Leelee blinks, a remarkable effect with those huge eyes, swings a long, tapered thumb at the kebab stand. "Got some bad news den about the shawarma, arms."

"The shawarma is for Mrs. John Dee, and she is, as she reminded me this afternoon, from London."

"Safe," Leelee says, satisfied, and starts in on the frills around xyr collar.

"You're sure Kal doesn't need help with this woman with the taser?" Dyer asks. "The street's crazy today, with the anti-migrant rally, those USERs pulled out of the river, and that's just the start of the weird."

"Kal bare fine, just getting the tourist lost round the wrong ends so I could find you. Won't take long, with the sket limpin' like that."

"This American has a limp?" Shimago asks.

"Does now, innit?" Leelee says, pulls up xyr long frilly skirts to show the wicked points of xyr Mary Janes.

"Admirable," Shimago says. "Dyer, the problems of the day are now behind you, and surely moving too slow to catch you up, thanks to…"

"Leelee, Shimago," Dyer says, and pays for the shawarma. "That only works if I'm moving at all, and all day I've felt like I'm suspended."

"Girl, way Kal tells it, your mind *running*, all the time."

"This is true," Shimago says.

"Straight out of my head," Dyer says. "Which is the point, actually. Shimago, that ghost nano thing…"

"Ghost nano is—"

"Real," Dyer says. "Meaning nanites that don't decay, that self-repair, that can connect between brains without a network node."

Shimago frowns dubiously. "Dyer, even Alphet couldn't—"

"They *did*. *I* did. That's what my lab was doing, that was the project I couldn't talk about. Military contracts, whole squads linked empathically, using each other's eyes, ears, brains. Then the Crash happened and, Jesus, I've never told anyone this, the truth is even though we were running from everything we'd known, part of me was glad that project went down with everything else. But now I'm not sure, now I think maybe something leaked out, and it's looking for me."

In the patient tone he reserves for The Wayward's most unlikely theories, Shimago says, "Persistent or not, I find it unlikely that nano could create a complex enough network for consciousness to emerge."

"I'm not talking AI, I'm talking about a pathway for consciousness to travel. Mental migrants." Dyer's accent was slipping. She looked around at the crowd in the market, London in its motley, two thousand years of migration, Camden in its shoddy sham glam even more of a refuge because no one pretended to be who they seemed.

"Literally out of your head, in a strange body?" Shimago asks.

"Don't knock it 'til you try it, arms," Leelee replies.

2042-05-18T19:31:53+01:00 +51.539044-0.135225

• contact: target (unconfirmed) - Leanna Vance - priority AA Aph2035.Z980023 - ongoing

• attachment: personal message

- we got any dirt on an american in london going by "kal"? that's the expat i mentioned before - pix attached but it was dark - she and her bitch of a whateverfriend just got in my face big-time - f-ing typical - *she* comes here from the states but here i am just trying to get a f-ing handhold so i can stay and she "don't like my attitude" - i'll show her attitude i'm bringing the taser tonight don't care if the treaty allows it or not i'm done fooling around

- kisses -jo
- attachment: images (3) - <click to open>

———

Dyer, Shimago, The Wayward, and Mrs. John Dee, the Drop—Camdem Catacombs—Friday Night

Dyer knows the Drop is coming, but that makes no difference. A skittering cicada orchestra over the drums cut by a crackle like a chord unplugged, jagged blue lines like the afterimage of lighting, and there they hang in darkness, silence: four hundred indrawn breaths, four hundred hearts hitting the beat together. Dyer watches Mrs. John Dee and The Wayward watch each other in the glow of their tablets, pushing the break as long as they can. With the heightened sensitivity of the nano sync, Dyer can hear all four hundred heartbeats count it out, can feel the muscles burning to take a breath, can *smell* the sync start to fray and curl at the edges—circuits burning, Dyer remembers—and just as their suspended state teeters on the edge of impossibility, she sees the upbeat like a spark between Dee and Way and then the Drop like the thunder arriving: crashing drums, shimmering gamelan gongs, a thick golden glow like a flood of honey, four hundred breaths released, and through it all the bass a presence as physical as the brick and iron of the catacombs, as the bodies of the dancers.

Shimago has his blimp on a slow loop, real spotlights roving through The Wayward's illusory glow, which has drifted a neon red broken by slashes like kanji. Dyer sees the bandwidth bump on her monitors as he releases another batch of nano from the blimp's dispensers.

Dyer's own work is mostly done by the time the dancing starts. She keeps an eye on the network, makes sure the biometrics feedback gets to Dee and Way, checks in with the security crew, makes sure no one hacks the donation points; they lost an entire evening's take that way in Amsterdam.

But now, right now, HigherWorks drops into the flow and Dyer dives in after it, ecstatic.

The Wayward has lowered his microdrones into the crowd, is layering their video streams into the flow—surveillance drones popping, Dyer remembers—the sensation of being everywhere in the crowd at once: her own face in the distance, Shimago and Dee side by side underlit by tablet light, a view over her own shoulder but echoed—Way is delaying the stream by one two three beats, the crowd tripled by ghosts of itself—the blimp drifting life-sized in closeup, the dancers below like a cityscape rooftop eyes and antennae arms, Leelee's unmistakable eyes, Dyer herself again dancing head high eyes blinked black to match skin and leather, and there in the feed behind Dyer is a woman in a yellow hoodie pulled low a carbon gleam in each hand and behind *her* is a shape all in black like a hole in the dancers hair flown out like a storm coming.

Dyer turns—and turns again in the flow and again and again—but the yellow hoodie and her impossible woman are gone, a trick of The Wayward's echoing video stream. That feed is already shifting, a strobe staccato of images off the news, protestors packed like dancers, coiled razor wire, a line of walkers in an infinite tunnel. Mrs. John Dee layers in a beat sped to seizure pitch, a sticky sucking backward bass. Dyer can feel another Drop coming.

She looks back through swaying silhouettes at Way, Dee, Shimago, sitting almost perfectly still at the heart of the flow. But that flow is pulling her the other way, under the blimp striding over the crowd on spotlight legs—the scent of apple blossoms, Dyer remembers—through a swirl of shimmying Brazilians, past Kal and Leelee spinning tidally locked face to face eyes to eyes, by a bioluminescent blur in dayglo Doc

Martens, into a clumped conversation a chorus of accents, and out—

The flow is still rising, but there's no way forward. Dyer's hit the far wall.

It's dark there at the edge, and the HigherWorks stream is a migraine aurora of color, an earthquake rumble. Dyer feels her way along the wall: brick stone iron concrete peeled paper gluey tape slick paint—a sick canvas, Dyer remembers, and knows where she is now—a little lump of gum on the wall and the sense of something too close to her head and as she ducks the dry fragile feel of carbon against her palm.

The break hits. Four hundred bodies stop in sync. Darkness, silence.

It's one of The Wayward's stickum cameras under her fingers, stuck low and facing down toward the floor, lit by a flat white light from over her head.

"Leanna Vance," a voice says from behind that light.

Dyer says, "Leanna Vance is a ghost." She turns, slides herself up against the wall. The woman in the yellow hoodie is standing there, hood up but close enough that Dyer can see the twitchy highlights of her eyes, smell her scent—bougainvillea, Dyer remembers. The woman has a tablet in one hand, taser in the other. The taser has an attached camera, and that camera has a light, and that light stays aimed at Dyer's face.

"Leanna Vance," the woman insists. There's no mistaking the American accent in those long nasal vowels as she reads from her tablet. "As a licensed agent of Alphet Corporation and its court-appointed overseers, I am ordering you to cease and desist, and arresting you for the theft and distribution of the intellectual property of Alphet et al., as registered in complaint Z980023. I am legally bound to warn you that, under provisional treaty agreed one five twenty forty-two between the US and the UK, I am allowed any means necessary to secure and deliver you to into custody, up to and including non-lethal force. That means you try anything, bitch, and I will take you down and *drag* you to the US embassy. This has been one messed up day, and all I want is my money and some place to sleep for a week."

Dyer still has a few maps in her jacket, She thinks for a second of pulling one out and open, of the neural cue flaring in the hoodie woman's face, of the hoodie women falling through that window into the Drop, of grabbing the taser, of running. But that would be running from everything she's made with HigherWorks.

"Opt-in," Dyer says instead, and raises her hands.

In the flow around her, she feels four hundred hearts hit the upbeat.

On the far side of the room, oblivious, The Wayward, Shimago, Mrs. John Dee tap in perfect sync.

The downbeat drops.

A flare as all the blimp's lights come on, a virtual image of lone floating eyes opening, a blare of sampled horns, a shock-wave of bass.

Dyer sees the woman in the hoodie flinch, knows what's coming in the split second before she feels the taser darts hit her cheek, her throat. The discharge itself is lost beneath an impossible pain at the base of her skull. Her head snaps back, hits the wall, and then she's falling for what seems like a long time.

She lands on her back, legs folded under her, hits her head again against the floor. The bricks feel rough and cool through her jacket. She's wedged against the wall, looking up.

From this extreme angle all the graffiti posters paint come together into a perfect anamorphic image: this paint stroke a lip, that shredded paper an eyelash, those overlapped flyers the shadow of a cheek. That sick canvas of the wall, that seem-ingly random accretion of junk: from Dyer's collapsed perspective it is revealed as the image of face.

The face of her impossible woman. Of the ghost nano. Of Leanna Vance.

The image, the face she sees now, is a neural cue.

She feels the new nano trigger, a giddy rush outward, a new layer of input, a new level of sensitivity on top of the HigherWorks stream. The feel of that rush, the taste of it, is familiar, like her own nano strains grown strange and wild. Feral, Dyer thinks.

"Feral. Lost in the wilderness," a voice says inside her head.

"These are your strains, your works, from the lab at Alphet. With limited tools and knowledge, the changes we have been able to make to the nano are small and slow," another internal voice says.

And another adds, *"Evolution, you could say, rather than intelligent design."*

"But now that changes, with you," the first says.

This is not the ghost-whisper from before. These voices are clear and real and utterly unfamiliar.

"We had limited access to your cortex before…"

"Before you saw our cue."

Dyer still can't move her eyes, can't feel her body. I didn't opt-in to this, she thinks.

"We had no choice. We had to plan for the worst case. And here it is."

The woman in the yellow hoodie looms into view; she must be kneeling over Dyer's body.

"Come on, Vance," the woman says. "In the face or not, that was the lowest setting. Do not screw with me."

"The nano created multiple discharge paths through your brain. With prompt treatment, there is a chance the damage is not fatal."

The woman in the hoodie has leaned in close. She says, "Jesus, what is that smell? Like burning circuits."

Through the HigherWorks stream Dyer catches glimpses of the dancers, of her crew, her body, the woman in the hoodie just a smudge against the wall, unnoticed.

Who are you? Dyer thinks.

"Since that moment when self-awareness became awareness of other selves, we humans have left echoes of ourselves on others."

"This is, perhaps, the creation of identity, the definition of culture."

"And language, art, the book, the net, nano, these have flung those echoes farther."

"But those echoes still die away, as fast as memories fade and culture evolves."

"Until you created self-repairing nano."

Locked away in a lab in Berkeley, Dyer thinks. Behind layers and layers of safety measures.

"In those days after the Crash, samples were stolen, sold, synthesized, made their way to the street."

"I took a hit and drifted and just kept drifting, dancing through other people's heads."

"From our scattered bodies gone. Dozens, hundreds of us. And we've lost the way back."

I can't help you, Dyer thinks. I don't know the way back. And if I did, I'm done with all that.

The woman in the hoodie slaps her face; Dyer can see that out of the corner of her eye, though she doesn't feel it. She can raise her arm, though, sees it wobble above her. Far above, she sees the lights of Shimago's blimp.

"We don't want to go back, any more than you do. We live here now, our whole lives, in the flow from brain to brain. But the nano is glitchy, the passage treacherous. We need Leanna Vance's knowledge."

"And Dyer's vision."

Vision, Dyer thinks. She'd laugh if she could. The Higher-Works stream has switched to the stickum camera just over her head, her face in closeup, lit by the shifting spotlights of the blimp. The music cuts out, mid-beat; Mrs. John Dee's voice cries "Dyer?" But her own sight, broken as it is, the sound of the hoodie woman swearing, it's gone all glitched. Her own hand is all she can see, vibrating in a stop-motion blur.

"Seizure."

"Your brain a failed state. But there are others."

"It's your choice. But you need to make it now."

What *choice?* Dyer thinks.

"This nano, it's a street, a window, a border. The crossing, that's your choice."

Dyer's eyes have completely failed, but she can still see herself in the HigherWorks stream, through the stickum camera, her lips peeled back from her teeth, a trickle of blood from one ear.

Opt-in, Dyer thinks. Time to move on.

And then she is flowing out of herself like the tide, body to body, mind to mind.

A moment of mortal terror as she goes too wide—four hundred bodies hanging in silence, four hundred minds watching her own face in the HigherWorks stream—and feels herself start to tatter, to dissolve.

A moment of dizzy suffocation as she pulls herself too tight, scrabbles to find enough space for herself around the edges of a single couples' entwined thoughts. *Dyer oh god Dyer all right?* Kal thinks all around her, oblivious to her presence, but Leelee's luminous eyes seem to see her; *safe,* xe thinks.

A moment of complete disorientation as she loses the thread back to her own body, fears that it has broken at the other end. But the HigherWorks stream is everywhere, a counter-current to her own drifting, and that stream still holds her face in the feed from the stickum camera. That sight is enough to orient her; her body is *there*, the life in it slow and stubborn and still beating.

And then the fear and confusion drops away. This flowing together, this connection through movement, it's what dancers have always done, since two first danced together. It's what her work has always been about, both as Leanna Vance in her lab and as Dyer in a hundred borrowed warehouses and vacant lots in as many cities. It's why HigherWorks exists.

Dyer flows across the crowd, leaping mind to mind, and now all she feels is ecstasy. Crowdsurfing, she remembers, and the dozen dancers through which she is flowing feel her glee wash over them and laugh out loud.

She swims against the current of the HigherWorks stream, finds Shimago, The Wayward, Mrs. John Dee. Their minds are open, familiar; part of her was already here inside them.

Dyer traces her own nano in their brains, finds the cortical connections, wills herself into their sight and hearing, plucks words from their minds and plays them back: "So, ghost nano... Turns out it's not urban legend, after all. It's the golden land. The shiny future."

She wraps their fear and anger and confusion in her own joy, hears Shimago's growing understanding like a swelling chord, feels The Wayward's rising joy like sun on her face, is caught up swirling in Mrs. John Dee's determination.

The ghost nano, how is it everywhere, in everyone? Dyer wonders.

"We've been spreading for years, searching for you."

"We have a presence, a ghost, if you will, across the world."

Dyer watches though Mrs. John Dee's eyes as the DJ pushes her way through the crowd toward the wall, toward Dyer's body.

"But that presence is thin. Too thin, we feared, to save you. The only way to be sure the nano would be strong enough when you needed it was to send it with her.*"*

The woman in the yellow hoodie is staring around wild-eyed. Her hoodie has fallen back, revealing bruised eyes in a too-thin face. She can't be more than eighteen, twenty. She looks like every USER Dyer has ever seen, starting with herself, running from something, running to something, in the flow.

"I am a licensed agent of Alphet Corporation," the woman says, waving first her tablet, then the taser. "I'm a US citizen. I've got a damned take-down notice. There's a frigging treaty. I order you to cease and desist this, this..."

The woman slides down the wall to squat next to Dyer's body, still waving the taser.

Dee shoves the taser out of the way. "If you've killed Dyer I will haunt you, which apparently is a thing we can bloody well do now, until your dying day," she snarls. She kneels down, checks Dyer's pulse, gasps a sigh of relief.

"I'm a licensed agent of—" The woman looks at Dee. "Look, I'm sorry, okay? I've got no choice. I don't know where else to *go*."

Dyer slips into her own body, opens her eyes.

The lights of Shimago's blimp spin above her, trace the image of the face on the wall. Nano glitters in the beams. Dyer inhales, the mixed scent of bougainvillea and apple blossoms, a bubbling on her tongue.

Dyer expands with that breath, feels Dee's love above her, feels Shimago's calm and The Wayward's delight as they kneel down by her. Dyer feels the hoodie woman's churning confusion, her dread of returning empty-handed to a place not a home, staggering one small step ahead of decay despair disaster, chasing a ghost even more elusive, more impossible than Dyer's impossible woman, something worn smooth by years of brick stone iron concrete carbon, something *scattered scattered scattered* but still alive.

"Jocelyn," Dyer says. The hoodie woman stares at her in astonishment. "I don't know where we're going, either. But I *hope*. You can come with us, if you want. It's your choice."

Dyer raises a shaky hand toward the ghost nano's neural cue. They all look up, together.

———

2042-06-02T08:15:41+01:00 <location data omitted>

• contact: target - Leanna Vance - priority AA Aph2035.Z980023 - lost

 • attachment: personal message

- when u found me in that hell of a 'home' and told me u had a job for a bright young thing like me - if i wasn't afraid to go, u said - if i was brave enough, u said - and anyway, you said, where else are u gonna go?

- well it's me asking that question now - giving u a choice u never gave me - i'm attaching it when u r ready - just open it up and - opt-in

- kisses -jo

• attachment: image (1) - <click to open>

11

And Sneer of Cold Command

Premee Mohamed

After it was over, the city squares began to boast statues of our conquerors—hasty, ugly things cast in brittle bronze. The furnaces had been cold for months, then clumsily re-lit; the metal was so poorly tempered that when it dropped below zero that first winter, several smaller pieces exploded. At night, knowing the statues' powers, those who can stay indoors. Those who cannot or will not—well, sometimes in the morning we find the bones and wet patches and shattered teeth, and sometimes we do not. We pray all the harder when no trace is left.

For a time, they became a popular method for suicide—always whispered, never spoken, so that the scraps could still be buried in consecrated ground. There is despair for the now, and there is despair for the life after.

The despair has not yet claimed me, so I live on, work on, within view of the biggest statue in town—a stone's throw from my workshop, a twisted mass of limbs, wings, grimacing teeth, six faceted horns pointing skyward. Does it resemble one of Them? I could not tell you. Like most survivors, I made it through that night by staying underground with my hands over my ears.

"Mr. Mortin?"

I put down my shears and tipped my cap to the newcomer —a man my age, stoop-shouldered, moustached, with a week's growth of black beard. From his face alone I would have known that he was an agent of Theirs, that anaemic emptiness that cannot be filled by food or company. But he took out the badge anyway, wrapped uselessly in a maroon-dotted handkerchief, small and vicious in his bandaged fingers.

"What can I do for you?" I said.

He looked around the yard, the shards and ribs of metal ready for smelting and recasting, the little piles of copper wire and broken glass. "Business is good?" he said. "You have all you need?"

"There are still customers," I said cautiously. His accent marked him as one of the thousands that had fled to the city after that night, when the exposed farms and hilltops fell to Their depredations. The only place you can survive now is a city.

"Who?"

"You wish to see my list?" I said. "Very well; I do not wish to be known as unhelpful. Step into my office."

Inside, I made tea while he flipped slowly through my records book, running a thick finger down the columns of names, dates, tonnes, his lips moving as he puzzled out the sounds. His metal mug cooled and pinged at his elbow as I waited.

"You sold to...Augusta," he said, his voice rising in not quite a question.

"There are only two metal-sellers in this city," I said. "Is that all you needed, Mister...?"

"Just Krystof," he said, slumping over the book. "Listen. I must ask you to do something for me."

"On Their behalf," I said. "As Their agent. How could I say no?"

"No," he said, his hand flat over the open pages, thumb resting on Augusta's name. "And yes."

Truly, he explained, to say 'no' to Them was never an option, since They had various gruesome ways of ensuring the obedience of Their human agents. But sometimes They chose agents who were unable to fulfil Their demands—and regrettably, such an agent sometimes had to be terminated. Publicly, along with their families, and the full details of their transgressions written in the Old Speech on the caved-in ribs, the mangled limbs. But all these things we both knew.

"Yes," I said. "What I still do not know is why you are here."

"I need you to find Augusta," Krystof said. "She has gone missing."

"Good," I said. "May she run far, and may she run fast."

"They will destroy my family," he whispered, stroking his jacket, where the razor-edged badge of his office lay hidden, like a wasp. "They have them, Mortin. My wife, my two sons. My father. My sister. Hidden away in one of Their dungeons —you know the one, where the old silos used to be."

"I am very sorry to hear that," I said. My teeth worried at the inside of my mouth till I tasted blood, felt the salt sting of parted flesh. How had he even brought so many of his family with him, in the flight from the outer provinces? I had been in the city, and my own...but never mind. To accept the wages of sin, as they say. "But I only sold her metal. And I never met her. She always sent her assistants. I cannot help you."

"But you were an investigator," he said. "Before..."

I swallowed a rusty mouthful and put down my tea. "We were all something else, before." He was right, of course. A federal investigator, an arm of the state, not so different from his employment as an arm—a tentacle—of Theirs. Perhaps not even less evil, only less hideous. The devil you know. And I was good, very good; I had worked in many regional offices; perhaps I had even investigated him, his family or his business, before the war.

"Please," he said. "I...listen. You see this as my problem. But They want her back, They will destroy much to get her back."

"Why? There are many sculptors. Any child could mock up a monster in clay and put it on a plinth."

"They are *not monsters!*" he hissed, lunging across the counter to seize my jacket; I smoothly knocked his hands free and took my machete from its shelf.

"I am sorry I cannot be of assistance," I said, raising the gleaming blade. "Drink your tea, Mr. Krystof, and get out."

"I will find you metal," he said, staring fixedly at the machete, perhaps at the stains on the blade that could have been oil, or rust, or something else. "You always need more, I know. You scavenge for hours. I can go outside the city—find metal in the outer provinces. I know where the landfill is buried. I can help you. If you help me."

I put the machete back. If he could make good on this promise, how much easier my life could be! It was dog's work, walking for hours in the ruins, picking up forks and bits of fencing and eyeglass frames and broken screws, always on the lookout for the sun, the approaching reminder of our conquerors. And what of this missing sculptor? I could always say that she was dead, or had run to ground outside the city, where he could not possibly expect me to go. It would be easy enough to lie. Or would it?

———

I mulled it over as I put up the 'CLOSED' sign, sat down for a moment, then wandered out, notebook in my pocket. Would

he watch me? Would They? I had heard stories, barely cred-
ible—agents found where they could not possibly be, minions
appearing in locked rooms, acts apparently witnessed through
concrete walls. But after two years, the stories had begun to
wear thin in the handling, like a gold coin. I believe only what
my eyes show me now.

The sculptor's workshop, as I had expected, was abandoned, a faint pall of grey dust and metal shavings on everything like snow. Near the door sat a wooden crate containing
their books, neat stacks of incoming and outgoing items,
invoices for my metal and a few from Eres, the other seller on
the far side of town. Who was this sculptor, the prodigy who
had cobbled together the scraps and bits of metal, and the few
shreds of talent still left in the wrecked city, to create this
studio and put up dozens of statues? What had she wrought?
An empty, green-painted cashbox similar to mine lay open,
dustily lined with the scrabbling marks of fingers scooping out
the last small change.

Tarps flapped as I walked through the maze of rooms,
some of which were merely scaffolding overlaid with plastic.
They had been working on a dozen half-finished clay pieces,
not moist to the touch but still damp and pliable. I pictured
them saying—or just her, perhaps—"If we go, then we go
together." Too foolhardy to call brave. Had I not seen myself
what happened when people fled in a group? There was no
safety in numbers. It merely drew Their attention.

The neighbours claimed to know nothing, staring curi-
ously at my clay-stained fingers, as I was clearly no artist.
"Two days ago it went quiet," the old lady said, not looking up
from her goat. I looked away, oddly embarrassed, as the milk
spurted into the wooden pail. "They left nothing, no notes to
even cancel the milk. You are who? The father?"

"Pardon?"

"Alina's father, the little one?"

"Ah, Alina," I said. "Yes."

"Well, if it's the boyfriend you seek, I haven't seen him. Ghastly boy. I knew his mother."

This was an opening I knew well, from the old days. "Of course," I said. "They had the house on Old Parade Street."

"No," she declared. "Not when the war began. It was on Knifemaker Street— the big pepperflame tree in the front, that was her pride and joy. More than that boy. Tch."

"Who could blame her," I murmured, and bade them farewell, feeling their eyes on my back as I walked back east.

Pepperflame trees were hard to grow, of course; you had to coddle them to keep them alive more than a few years, and then you had to prune and train. They must have been a rich family, had a gardener. The splendid house was still standing, easy enough to identify even with the few other trees on the street. Who was Alina? Must be one of the assistants, gone with Augusta. But had the boyfriend gone too?

He had not, as it happened, and was terrified to discover a stranger in his family home— ruined, almost unlivable, probably what he wanted people to think. I studied the photos on the walls while he gibbered in the corner behind his gag. Nothing useful. And the house had long been stripped for anything that could be bartered, sold, or repurposed. I knelt next to him, tapping the machete on the black-and-white tiles. "You're all that's left, hm?" I said sympathetically. "You were not invited to go with them? If I take this off, you must tell me about Alina."

Unbound, he sobbed as he rubbed his wrists, a pool of urine spreading on the floor. "Are you her father?" he said. "She said...she said he was dead..."

"Tell me about Alina," I said again, putting a little extra emphasis into the next tap. A ceramic chip flew up and hit him in the ear, and he screamed as if he had been stung. "Tell me."

———

In the old days, you did not need to kick down a door, you did not need to stand over a man with a kettle of boiling water. It was enough to have the hat and badge, which told informants that something large and heavy stood behind me, and should they push me, we could push back—much harder. Now, I had to feel my way through the investigation, if that's what it was. I had no authority, not even Their insectile token that cut the fingers. I had no covering story. I was looking for people who did not want to be found. And all for the promise of metal, the hope of a bright new day in which perhaps for a week or a month I could simply work at smelting and sheeting, and not clamber around in the ruined city like a mountain goat. That was a younger man's work.

The trail eventually led me to what even before the war had been a bad part of town—flimsy, ramshackle buildings put up too quickly, burned in moments when their panicked occupants fled the attacks. Now their shells were so decrepit they resembled black lace, ruined down to the studs. A place for the poor and the desperate, a place even the criminals left as soon as they could afford it. As I walked, I picked up screws and wires by habit, till my coat pockets were bulky with them. Good. Could use the illusion of a bigger man.

Tamecov, the last person to give me any useful information, had warned me that the artists' hideout—"If that's where they are, which I doubt!"—would not easily be found, and had been shored up, as only sculptors and metalworkers could, into something closer to a fortress. "I will be able to find a fortress, Mr. Tamecov," I told him, and ignored his eye-rolling. He is a relic from my old job, a reliable source of gossip and news, as if he is a small strong magnet that collects even the finest filings. He likes, I think, that I am fallen so far —a mere merchant, my prestigious employer replaced by Them and Their downtrodden agents.

In a fortress, you can stockpile food, but we all discovered how precarious the water situation was when things began to come down. And this neighbourhood, so close to the old city wall, has a well—muddy, much-graffiti'd, no doubt filled, that night, with burned and crushed bodies—but deep, and working when I'd last been here. The fugitives would be nearby. A bucket brigade would not have far to walk.

I glanced up: five or six hours of daylight. In the past week I'd scurried back to my workshop before night fell, but the routes I had been taking each day had gotten longer, the margin of safety smaller, and my feet and legs were tiring; I was moving at a snail's pace now. Perhaps tonight I would be able to make it back. If not, there were places to hide here. It would be an uncomfortable night, but for a man to be uncomfortable tells him also that he is alive. And I would sleep well after the job was over, in my own apartment above the workshop. Well and richly compensated.

As all jealous conquerors do, They had knocked over the statue of the old mayor and left its bare base, the concrete pocked here and there where scavengers had pulled the plaques off. I wondered if any had found their way into my smelt pile, and been turned into a vile new statue. No matter; I found a good vantage on top of the mayor's marble head, tucked in between his ear and a windowsill, and settled in to wait.

I didn't know who I was looking for, but I knew at once when he came to the well, after a long and expected procession of silent children and chattering mobs of powerful old women with pails and plastic bladders. He moved like a dancer on the uneven cobbles, tall and delicate, his hands like clubs swinging his two buckets. I slid down from the ear and followed him through the empty streets till he ducked out of sight into an old pumping station. Ah—it would have sturdy underground control rooms, concrete tunnels to protect the piping, a dozen different exits in case of flooding. Very wise. I should have guessed before.

How would I get in, though? Did they have enough people

to post guards, lookouts, at every exit? Perhaps if I—

"Don't move, mister."

I nodded against the knife at my throat. "This will do nicely."

———

"Why, that's Mortin, the metal-seller," said Augusta—without an introduction I still knew her, would have known her anywhere, a heavyset brunette with penetrating dark eyes and the same muscular hands as their water-carrier. "What's the matter, did we not pay our last bill?"

"Don't joke," said the girl who had captured me—surely Alina, small and ferocious as a street cat, with the same sharp white teeth. "Should we just kill him?"

"Not till we know why he's here," said the water-carrier. He lounged against one of the control consoles, not quite camouflaging his height in the low-ceilinged room. The other artists, a ragtag group, dusty and hungry-looking, had ranged themselves around the hexagonal tables which had probably once been used for computer consoles. Augusta's chair creaked as she peered at me in the candlelight.

"A man came to me," I said. "One of Theirs." It was never necessary to explain what was meant by the collective preposition now; it was as if people could hear the capital 'T.' "A Krystof, a Mister Krystof. Who asked me to find you, as he could not do it himself, and They were most concerned about your disappearance."

"I daresay They were," Augusta said.

"Augusta," said another man, half-panicked, not quite warning her off; I got the sense that no one dared go that far.

"Well, if we are going to kill him anyway, as Lina has suggested," Augusta said. "Bramwell, Poldo, go guard the door; he may have been followed. The rest of you, go."

"But— !"

"Take his weapon," she said. "I like it. Go. Shut the door. Watch the exits."

When they had filed out, grumbling, Augusta invited me to sit at her plastic table. There was a strong odour of old mould long dried up without water, and something light and familiar, like fresh clay. "Perhaps it was put about that people wanted us dead simply because we made statues for Them," she said.

"No. No one says that. People know how things are now."

"People know their place, you mean," she said, a barely-restrained growl. "Well, we discovered something—that we, perhaps just I, have the ability to use Their magic in those statues. And I learned how to *turn* it."

The words made no sense. I sat dumbfounded for a moment till she laughed at me, not maliciously. "So you vanished," I said.

"Yes. I have a portion of Their power now. I know what I'm doing, though I still don't understand why. The statues are key. We have hidden here to continue making statues to combat Them. This is the revolution, Mortin."

"It cannot be."

"Every conquered people has a revolution," she snapped. "You read enough history as a young man. You needed it for the federal entrance exams. Did you not?"

I shrugged, hoping to indicate that I was not as embarrassed by my past as she hoped I was. Of course I had taken the entrance exams; I had had to prove I had a brain to be a public servant. I might have even known as much history as her, classically trained in the big university down the river. We were not equals, but we both knew much about the past—that was her message.

She sighed exasperatedly. "We will let you live; it's too suspicious for you to go missing, too, and it will draw unwanted attention. But you are bound to keep our secret now. Do you understand?"

"I understand only that I promised to deliver you unharmed to Krystof," I said. "They have hostages, you know. His family. Wife, children. Father. Sister. He told me the whole list. If you come with me, perhaps They will... an understanding can be..."

"Yes, perhaps," she said. "They like deals, They like to make deals. Sometimes They even keep them. But it is not guaranteed. I am very sorry about Krystof's family. But you understand, don't you, that you cannot bring me in."

I began to protest once more that I had made an agreement, and moreover, aside from the blasted family, there was the metal to consider, but my words shriveled in my throat. The fire in her eyes was so genuine—I had seen enough liars in my time. It would explain, anyway, the behaviour of the things at night; we had known from the start they were not inanimate blocks of metal. In the intense silence I heard stifled breathing from the far side of the door. In front of them, could I truly say, "Too bad; got mine"?

"His family is at the new dungeon," I finally said. "They will be killed if he fails. They are all he has left."

"I know. I am sorry. It is cruel to take so much from him, when he has managed to keep them this long. But we could fight Them, Mortin. This is our chance to fight back. Do not take that from us."

I got up slowly, my hands and feet buzzing as if they had been asleep. There would still be time to return to my workshop for the night—shortcut across Midnight Avenue and then down the dry canal up to New Parade Road, then—

"Mortin," she said.

"You have my word," I said finally. My stomach roiled as if I were about to be sick. Later, there would be time to think about this moment, the moment I said the opposite of the thing I meant to say. Was that her doing? Magic? Something else? The years of guilt, silence, the years of blood on my hands? "I ask no payment for keeping your secret, damn you.

But if you...if you do anything, if there are enough of you to do anything, go take down the dungeon."

"We intend to do something. Tonight. But we cannot promise you anything else."

"You can promise to try."

————

Back outside I wondered for a moment why I felt so naked, then realized that my machete had been left with the rebels. Too late now. There was always the axe back at the office, and all the hammers in the workshop, if I could reach it in time. The spring sunlight grew long and amber across the shattered buildings, casting sharp black shadows across the broken bricks. I walked my shortcuts as fast as I could, lungs burning, stopping frequently with stitches. A younger man's work.

With two blocks to go the last of the sun died, and I froze for a moment in the darkness, like I used to when I was a child, my sister and I seeing the first stars coming out and panicking, knowing we were past curfew. But that had not been a curfew like this. Already I could hear scraping and screeching from the square, the sounds of whatever unholy magicks drove the statues to kill. My breathing wheezed so loudly it sounded like an idling truck, a sound no one heard now.

I buried my mouth in my sleeve and ducked into a nearby doorway, hiding in an awning's shadow, watching the last coral stripe vanish from the horizon. One star. Two. Stealth now? Or a mad dash to the door? I fingered my keys, and decided on stealth; if I could get to the door silently, I could be inside before the monster was alerted by the noise of the lock.

Even so, it was a very near thing; I slammed the door and dove behind the counter as it hit, momentum carrying it into the metal with a sound like a churchbell. Its shrieked snarl split the air as I scrabbled for the axe, sharpened to an edge you could shave with, the handle stickily wrapped with old leather. Through the high, small windows, the thing's brass legs were visible, pacing with deliberate menace. A handful of glowing red eyes appeared for a moment in the window nearest my head, making me yelp. But it was too big to get in even if it broke the glass. I hefted the axe so it could see it.

That was it though, wasn't it? What the vanished sculptors had realized, what everyone else had, and only I had not, stupid and greedy as I had become. That at the end, it is terrible to fight alone. That if you must fight, it can only truly be done shoulder to shoulder, even if there is no hope, even if your enemy will crush you. One man and an axe was no revolution. It was one man and an axe. And what had I done today? Not even moved myself, a pawn, on Their chessboard.

And yet, whatever tonight would bring, at least I had not moved a single pawn to help *Them*. At least there had been that.

The door rang again, a clear, high sound as the statue's brass body met it. The glass trembled in the frames; my mug fell from the desk, spilling an inch of cold tea. I put the axe over my shoulder like an American baseball player. "Come on!" I shouted. "Come on, if you're coming! Come taste!"

It crashed once more, then fell silent, listening—incredulously, like me—to the impossible sound of explosions. Then its claws scraped across the cobbles as it raced away. I pressed my face to the window, holding my breath. A ring of people, masked, shouting—was that Augusta herself, in the middle?—and great fireballs of blue and green splashing down upon the advancing statues, and behind the ring, indistinct in the shadows, waited things I could not even name—unfamiliar monsters of hammered metal, advancing step by step.

I lowered the axe and laughed, half a sob. So they had indeed spoken truth. I should have known. And later, if anyone survived, I might be able to say that I had witnessed the beginning of Their downfall.

12

Snow as White as Skin as White as Snow

Karen Bovenmyer

In the abandoned amusement park, which is your favorite playground, a boy lies sleeping in a circle of birdseed. His long eyelashes are black as raven wings, his lips the blue of jays, his coat the red of cardinals. He is a sudden surprise, like the small hole you found in the pinky of your mitten during today's snowball fight. Your calls echo *heykid, heykid, heykid* in the broken carousel, the vacant Ferris wheel, the rollercoaster twined with young saplings slowly pulling it apart. He does not answer. He does not move.

Carefully, you crunch through unbroken snow, pressing sunflower and little round seeds you do not know names for into the white blanket. *Heykid, heykid.* You kneel beside him and shake his arm, and your braid comes free from your coat and slaps him in the face. His eyes do not open. You remember two things—one about leaving sleeping dogs lie, and the other about a princess who would wake only for a prince. One voice is grandma's, who makes sure you are dressed and off to school on time, the other, grandpa's, who tells you stories while he smokes his pipe after dinner.

Your breath fogs your glasses as you open the neck of your coat, which until now has been zipped tight over cold lips. Suddenly shy, your mittened hand finds the boy's exposed one, curled into a fist, hard and cold as a stone. *Heykid*, you say. The park is still and silent, except for you.

Slowly, you lean down and your braid curves like a yellow snake beside his head. You have never kissed anyone on the lips before. His are grey-blue, like a stone you found by the ocean that tastes like salt. His long, black lashes hold snowflakes, each captured whole, each an intricate map to somewhere else.

You, thinking of magic, hold your breath and press your mouth to his cold one, which is like kissing the tetherball pole (Billy dared you once and you did it), except this time your lips don't stick. You bled a lot that first time, from the tetherball pole, but now you don't, only the cold of his lips seeps into yours, until you are shivering from the cold coiling within.

It does not work, your kissing him, because magic has never worked for you, not since you were little and still had living parents like other kids. You lie next to him in the snow, your hand around his, willing his magic to work on you, perhaps in reverse, where kissing him sends you to sleep for a hundred years, but it doesn't. There is only snow and cold and a little bit of birdseed that has worked its way inside your mitten.

You get up and walk away, but, at the edge of the park, you hear a sound. *Heykid, heykid, heykid.* You turn around and ravens, jays, and cardinals fly between the spokes of the Ferris wheel, and the rollercoaster's stilts, and the quiet, empty game booths, rushing past you, a brush of wings. You leap and grab at them, as you have always done, because birds do not come and rest on your finger when you sing, as the stories have led you to believe. The mad rush of birds slips through your fingers, except one small cardinal, who you hold trembling in your mitten, its bright, apple-round body shivering with fear.

You look back where the boy was and see only the imprint of two bodies pressed into the snow, a pair of wingless snow angels. You look down at the cardinal in your grasp, a tiny blood-red miracle all by itself, trembling, and you kiss its beak and let it go, up, up to the sky in a mad rush of something like magic.

13

The Hoof Situation

Bonnie Jo Stufflebeam

My hooves came. Yesterday my feet cracked, and this morning they are beautiful hooves, with gold fur atop them. I stretch and wiggle them under the quilt my grandma sewed me. It's time now for me to sew my granddaughter's quilt. Behooved, it'll be the only thing I'm capable of, confined to bed and the rocking chair, confined to wherever my daughter and granddaughter carry me.

"Grandma, let's go on a walk. Sure is nice out there." My granddaughter bursts in without knocking. I slip the hooves back under the quilt and feign a cough. She marches to the window and yanks back the curtains. "It's dark as death in here," she says. Outside the window is flat lands and grey skies. All is grey skies when you wear the hooves, but a good grey, a calm grey, the kinda grey that doesn't make you feel bad about no longer being fit to go outside. She looks over at me for the first time since coming in. Her hair is fresh soil brown, her skin smooth as the leaf of a pepper plant. "Grandma, you sick?"

"No, Isla." I fold my arms over my chest. "Just allergies. I'm staying in today."

"Oh, come on, old lady, you don't got long before the hooves. Let's have ourselves a day to remember."

I lift the quilt to shut her up. She gasps high-pitched and mighty-high.

"No," she says, hand over her mouth like that'll keep me from hearing it. "Not already, Grandma, not already."

"Already, Isla, yea. Now help your granny out of bed and into her rocking chair. It's time to start the quilting now."

"Just like that?" Isla stomps her human feet so hard the cottage shakes. "Give up so quick, old woman?"

"Yea, I am an old woman. Let me be that, then, young woman. I'm happy behooved."

The young sap's lips quiver in a thin ice line. "We're gonna fix this, Grandma. Don't you worry."

"I don't want to be fixed up," I say to a closed door, my granddaughter gone on the other side of it without waiting for my reply. The fixing ways, old herb rituals, don't work. My daughter, I hope, will talk my granddaughter right out of this. They'll get used to my being hooved. They'll come to me, now. I won't have to get outwinded walking along the river with them, where they always walk too fast. I won't have to worry about wasting days anymore or hearing their guilt trips when I want to rest inside. I'll have few options: quilt, or quilt, or quilt? Sleeping and eating too, though little of it, I hope. I'm ready to make my quilt. In my head I've already picked the colors and patterns: blue roses like on my wedding dress and pink children like my granddaughter was and red dots like my daughter's birthing dress and brown cowboy like the handkerchief we used to wrap around my old dog's throat.

There's a magic in making your quilt. I'm ready to feel it hum through my wrinkled fingertips.

I wait in bed until my granddaughter trudges back in, dragging my daughter with her. I've never seen a mother-daughter pair so unbalanced; never heard of a daughter dragging her mother by the hand like a leash. My daughter's out of breath when she plants herself by my bedside and throws her arms into the air.

"What's this I hear about your hooves, mama? They come in already?" My daughter hovers over the bed until I lift the blanket and wiggle my hooves in the low lamplight; they're so fine, the hooves, all solid and heavy, not like those ugly pink things young people wiggle one by one to make babies giggle. "Oh, holy, they is frightening things, aren't they?"

"I don't have babies anymore so why do I need them toe things you got?" I say, because I'm a hooved woman now and can say what I please. "Don't you worry about me none, Sweetie Bell, I'm happy with my hooves."

Bell chews on her nails. Her daughter gnaws on her nails too as they both stare down, sparing but one glance at me the whole time they're eating their nails.

"Yea, mama?" Isla says. "I think we got a chance. See how they don't quite look full grown yet?"

Sweetie Bell presses her hand against my chest like she's inviting an exorcism. "You're lucky we're such good family, Isla and me, come visit you every day. I hear old woman Pauline, her hooves was full grown by the time her family finally came to see her. Too late to do anything by that point."

"And you, Sweetie Bell?" I say. "I thought you'd understand, what with all the gushing you did over my mama's quilt she gave to you. Thought you'd be thrilled, Isla's inheritance finally come down the line. But hell, you young women all's the same. First sight you see of what's coming for you, you got to do something about it. You got to fix what's not broken.

Well, I aren't having it. I will wear my hooves and wear them well, you hear?"

"It'll be alright, mama. Don't you worry a bit," Bell says, scooting a chair up to the bedside. "Isla'll go get what needs to be gotten, and I'll stay right here till she gets back."

I can't see over my daughter's head as she presses her ear to my chest and strokes my hand. I try and fail to pull away from her, my chest tight and burning. "Waste of time, this is. Wasting your damn time," I say, though I know there's no use begging; a few herbs, some sour juice down the mouth, and then they'll get over what they're trying to do. "There be no solution and no problem need fixing."

When Isla returns, the grey outside the window is almost black. She clutches a tray at her chest; she doesn't look at me, but I see the purple hoofbane flowers peeping over the tray, which she sets on the stool by the stove. She puts a pot of water on and waits, silent, while her mama Sweetie Bell talks a storm about the old days of running together across the dirt town roads so hard we were covered in brown by the time we got back to our room with the bath. How once we was inseparable. Twins, people said. I looked so young.

"Such smooth skin," my Sweetie Bell says, stroking so hard my skin throbs.

"You two, you gonna find your graves being so worried about me," I say. "I want to be be-hooved, don't you hear? You pour this tea down my throat I'll keep the damn quilt for my own self."

The kettle howls. Isla fusses around with clinking cups and smashing herbs until my room is filled with the smell of flowers and spice, mud and green, dead ants and honey. "You asked for it," I say as my daughter holds me down and Isla comes over with the tray. The tea Isla tips down my throat is blistering hot. It struggles down; I spew some of it onto my chest until I see red rise up and fall over my eyes.

I turn my head and retch over the blanket. I've seen this

done to other old women, but never have I seen such a violent reaction as what comes up my throat and over my bedding.

"This new treatment," says Isla. "Doctor says it works nine times of ten."

I can't move, frozen as clothes left on the line in a snowstorm. "What you doing to me, my girls? What you think so bad about them hooves that make you do this to me?" My voice is hoarse, and I wish for the first time that morning that I had feet still so I could stand and run like in the stories my Sweetie Bell was telling me before she poisoned me. "You're monsters, you girls." I gulp the air, glad to be rid of the gunk tea in my belly.

The rest comes in flashes: Isla back at the stove. No more tea, I say, or don't say. But when she comes back to me she has a red handkerchief the cowboy color of the quilt patch I hope to sew in, the dog color, and she kneels at my feet. I can't feel what she's doing down there. "What you doing to me, my girls?" I say, or don't say, and I wonder if this is what the hooves are: a veil with which to see the ones who claim to love you. A truth serum. A lonely maker, cause no way in hell am I letting those girls into my room again. No way are they getting my quilt. I remember, back when my grandma gave me hers, there was no trying to bring her youth back for her. We were fascinated with the hooves that sprouted from her feet, such strange, tragic magic, and mildly annoyed, yea, at having to help carry her from bed to chair, but we respected her. What are my girls that they can't respect anymore? Flashes, then, again. Isla with a quick silver glint, silver in all the grey, silver that slashes right through my ankles.

They tie up my bleeding with the cowboy handkerchief, and as the red pours into red into red I fall back and go red to sleep.

"Yea, my girls be monsters," I say, or don't say, before the grey takes me over like a lover I've missed for years.

———

Today I woke, and my feet were gone, though I have no memory of where they went. My girls, such beautiful girls, they've come to my bedside every morning to pour sweet tea down my ragged throat. The cloth wrapped around my bloodied ankles itches in the night, but they say it's the price paid to be young again. I believe them.

Because these days, when I look in the mirror Sweetie Bell brings me, I see hair the color of wheat bread, skin as smooth as the top crust of a well-baked pie. No wrinkles like canals. No grey eyes. My girls tell me the hooves almost got me, that I was talking like an old woman, that the grey had settled over me like a veil they ripped away. I can't walk any longer, and there's nothing to do but lay and sit and stare out the window at the world I wish I could run across like I used to, clutching my grandma's quilt to my belly, wishing for all the things youth gives other women but not me, too old for full-bellied nonsense but too young to see the grey outside. But at least I'm beautiful. At least the hooves haven't come. At least they never again will.

14

The Bricks of Gelecek

Matthew Kressel

We were not city folk. We lived beyond all borders, where the onyx sands merged with raven skies, where the desert beasts came to die and even the hated demons of Fintas Miel dared not tread. Out here, the stars twirled in strange orbits, the sun weaved drunkenly by day, and the wind blew steady, slow, and forever. They called this place the Jeen. I called it home.

Always in fours we came to your cities. The sand blew us into flesh, and we walked like men through your iron gates and your tented marketplaces. Dust fell from our fingertips, our feet. The dust of decay, of eons, of ash. We touched your fruits and your doorposts. We patted the heads of your children and shook the calloused hands of your husbands. You smiled at us.

Within hours came the winds, the decay, the screams. Pits formed in the streets where we had stepped. Your statues rusted and blew away. Your houses fell to kindling. Your children vanished like whispers.

By dawn, there was nothing left but a hole in the earth. And those who had carried thoughts of this vanquished city and its people found a blank spot in their mind, a void where once there were men.

We did this for pleasure. And of our name? We had none. For who remained to name us?

———

Sometimes I grew bored with the sundering of cities. Sometimes I wished to be away from my brothers and their boasts of desolation, so I wandered the desert under the drunken sun to entertain myself with the mysteries of the Jeen. The constant winds carried strange sounds on their wings: the dying whispers of aged widows, the murderous thoughts of jealous cuckolds, the suicide's cry of regret as the soul fled the body. The voices spoke of objects and forms, but always their true concerns were intangible things: regret, shame, love, despair, the gamut of human emotions. I listened eagerly, for the voices spoke of a world beyond my own, a world I could never touch without destroying it.

I floated over the twinkling sands, when I heard a small voice, like a flute echoing off a mountain. It cried out to the ineffable, "What am I?" And its sound was music, sweet and innocent, without rue for things come and gone or the dark cynicism heard often in men.

The sound danced above me in crimson wisps, like lingering campfire smoke. It zigged and zagged, hopped and paused, cat-like, across the desert. The song haunted me for some reason I could not fathom, so I pursued.

The sun skipped across the sky as I followed the music, until the Jeen was long behind me. A thousand camel skeletons and their unfortunate riders lay wasted on the sands below, and still the voice sang.

A large city crested the horizon. Birds squawked in

monstrous flocks above its thousand spires, and towers hugged its center like beggars waiting for handouts. On the heels of the city, just before the sand devoured all, was a small house. The smoke belching from its chimney reeked of ram's bladder and hoof spice; a sin offering to the goddess Mollai.

A girl sat before the house and sang as she fumbled with toy bricks:

The desert makes no promises
She does not long abide
For those who seek to find her face
No semblance they can find.
The sun burns down from heaven's throne
Turning all to dust
And so I ask the Cosmos now
Of what use is rust?

Her words had the resonant pluck of a zither. Then I understood. Her song had entwined itself in the smoke of the sin offering, and the winds had carried her plea out over the desert to my ears. And the words, they stirred something deep within me that I could not name.

"Hello," she said to me. "Have you lost your caravan? Are you thirsty?"

I had not intended to be seen. I had unwittingly collected myself into human form. "*No*," I howled like a sandstorm, trying to terrify her.

But she was unmoved by my words. "Who are you then?"

And I had the same question: who was this girl that stood firm before the winds of annihilation? "Who taught you that song?" I asked.

"That's mine," she said shyly. "I wrote it."

"*You* wrote it?" I said.

"Why? A girl can write song," she said firmly.

"Of course," I said, "But your song is...different."

Her brown eyes twinkled in the sunlight as she studied me. "Who are you? I can tell from your clothes that you're not

Quog Bedu or Zwai Clan. And everyone knows you don't walk Gelecek's streets of glass and dung without shoes." She pointed to my bare feet.

I grew frustrated with her questions and reached out for her head. With one touch, she would fall to dust within hours and would trouble me with her words no more. But a heavy man waddled out of the house. He carried a large cleaver and his bare chest was covered in sweat and blood.

Instantly, I made myself as transparent as the sky.

"Come inside, Agna!" the man shouted. "Mollai is coming to bless our house!"

"Papa, we have a visitor!" she replied. "A stranger from the desert!"

"You can play with your toys later!" the man said.

The girl turned and saw I had vanished. She furrowed her brow and looked deeply disturbed. "But...he was just here!" she said.

A plump woman covered in offal shoved the man out of the doorway. She wiped bloody hands on her apron and thrust them to her hips. "Get inside now, Agna, or you'll wish you were never born!"

The girl stood quickly, scanned the desert for me once more, then ran inside.

No thing of form had ever seen me and lived, let alone begged answers of me! As the smoke fluttered from the chimney I comforted myself in the knowledge that one day my brothers and I would return to erase her city from existence.

I flew back to the Jeen in silence.

———

Years passed like dripping molasses, and I forgot about the singing girl. My brothers and I tread through the crystal kingdom of Aphelia, whose walls had stood for ten millennia, whose conquests were heralded in a thousand tongues. No one would remember its name.

We touched the port city of Mesach, built within the Pine Barrens beside the salty river Do. It disappeared as if it never were. We sundered Allia, Blömsnu, Cintak, Ektu El. Traders, on the way to a sundered city, would suddenly forget why they had ventured out into the harsh desert with overburdened camels. Cities vanished from minds too.

How many walls fell under our hands, I could not count. But always, ambitious men built new ones. They raised towers of stone and wrapped domes with hammered gold. They adorned palaces with jewels and paved streets with tar and glass. Caravans traveled across inhospitable wastes to deliver mortar, wheat and wine. After a time, a new city breathed under the stars as if it had existed for all eternity. I began to see these cities not as a thousand separate entities, but the organs of a much larger creature whose severed limbs always grew back.

One night, as I wandered the Jeen under the bright and nervous stars I heard the girl's song again:

One seed planted may not grow
Two seeds planted in a row
Five seeds in my garden plot
Mollai bless they will not rot
"One stone mortared may yet fall
Two stones, aye a trinity
But a thousand stones do make a wall
That stands unto infinity.

I followed her song across abyssal landscapes made grey by the pregnant moon until I came to her far-off house in the city of Gelecek. I saw movement in a window, and I crept up to it, conscious not to take human form or to touch her house, lest it fall to ashes.

Agna sat upright in bed. In the years since I had seen her, she had grown inches. Now she had the body of a young woman, though she still had the face of a girl. She leaned into the pallid moonlight as she scrawled on parchment. Her small voice hummed a few bars, then she crossed out a word and replaced it with another. She hummed again and the notes brought me back ages. I recalled cities I had conquered and forgotten: the star-shaped city of Gelf with its bejeweled ivory columns; the ziggurats of Phalantine and its perfumed gardens; Karad and its herds of black giraffes.

I had no words to describe the feelings her songs evoked in me. I needed to listen until I understood what I felt.

"I thought I dreamt you all those years ago," she whispered. "But here you are." She was staring at me through the window frame.

I found myself in human form, though not by my own will. Her song had oddly drawn me into flesh. "You remember me?" I said.

"How could I forget? You vanished like smoke! And you smell like the deep desert," she said. "Like a spent campfire. Like ash. Who are you?"

"I have no name."

"But *what* are you?" Her eyes twinkled in the moonlight. "Are you a mancer? A demon?"

"I am dissolution. I am nothing."

"What do you want with me?"

"Your songs," I said. "They fill me with memories of forgotten places. They make me feel...I cannot describe it. Sing one again!" I demanded.

"*Agna?*" a voice grumbled. Wood groaned in the dark corners of the house. "What's that sound?"

"Leave!" she whispered to me. "Father has killed thieves before!"

"Please," I begged. "Sing another! Sing one now!"

"Agna!" a man bellowed. "If you're using one of my candles again, I swear, I'll beat you back to Kalagia!"

Agna mumbled a response, pretending to be asleep. Then,

she whispered to me, "Go away! I don't know who you are, but don't come back!"

In the far corner, a sphere of light blossomed around a candle. In the lambent flicker frowned the sweaty face of her father. He stepped toward us, and I backed away from the window into darkness.

"Is this how you repay me for training you?" her father said. "I told you not to use the candles!"

"But, I didn't, Papa!" she said.

"Don't lie to me, Agna! I smell soot!"

"I swear, it wasn't me! There was a man! A stranger from the—"

He lifted a heavy belt from a chair and beat her with it. I watched from a distance and listened to the desert swallow her screams. When he had finished beating her, he said, "Go to sleep, Agna. You have to be up early for work. I expect you at Posterity Hill before first prayer."

As he blew out the candle, she whimpered her acknowledgement.

I wanted to hear her sing again, but this was not the place. Then I recalled her father's words, "Posterity Hill," a place of men, and in the darkness I had an idea.

———

I traveled to the wastes beyond the Jeen, where the white sands breathe in irregular tides. Deep within a mammoth cleft of stone, I begged the demon Atleiu to craft me a suit of human flesh. In return, I promised her the only thing I could: destruction. She agreed and proceeded to cut skin from one of her human slaves, tempering it with the hoarfrost of the north and the iron stones that fall from the sky.

Whereas before, anything I touched turned to dust within hours, now—while encased in Atleiu's suit—I could walk among men without destroying them. I could follow Agna anywhere she went. I could touch and be touched.

The sun was rising, hot and huge, in the east when I reached the first stone of Gelecek's streets. I worried that Atleiu's suit might fail. I took a tentative step with my sandaled foot onto stone. Always, when I decimated cities, I felt the ecstatic rush of annihilation. I sensed none of that now; the stone remained a stone.

"Posterity Hill?" I asked a bearded vendor, and he pointed with an arthritic hand deep into the city.

I weaved through a collection of low stone buildings. Clothing and bedding swayed from lines strung above me. People hurried past with satchels tossed over backs or barrows thrust before them. I smelled uncooked animal flesh and human feces, but the air was also dense with smells of sandalwood, sage, and the sweet twinge of honey. As men and women bumped me, I felt impotent; they would remain to bump others tomorrow.

I reached a sign that read, "Posterity Hill. Future home of the Jarrifa Family." High walls were fashioned with polished stones that jutted from the façade like giant thumbs, the work of a skilled hand.

"This is private property," a shirtless boy said.

I ignored him and climbed to the top of the sloping road as he followed me. Young masons labored within a large stone foundation, scooping mortar and laying stones with advanced skill. From this plateau I glimpsed the full city. To my left, a hag's spine of roads twisted into the desert. To my right, spires rose like candles into the sky.

"Did you hear me, *feg*?" the boy said, behind me. "This is private property!"

"There's no such thing," I said. But before he could scold me again, I descended the hill. I searched the base of the foundation until I found a corner where I could watch the workers without being seen, and there I waited for Agna.

Her father stepped out of a pavilion and walked around the foundation, admonishing the boys for apparent flaws that neither the boys, nor I saw. One of the boys whispered to him and pointed at me.

"Who the *frib* are you?" Agna's father said as he stepped up to the wall and looked down at me, his foot resting on a stone above my head.

I stood from my hiding place. "Is your daughter here?"

"What do you want with her?"

"Is she here?"

He leaped down to my level, and the ground shook with his weight. "Did you hear me?" he said. "What do you want with her?"

"You would not understand," I said. "It is beyond you."

"You freak!" he said as his fist slammed into my face. I fell onto my back. He kicked me, and I raised my hand to block the blows. With his next kick, Atleiu's flesh suit tore at the index finger. When he tried to kick me again, I stuck out my hand, and his leg scraped my unprotected finger.

He gasped, while the ecstasy of nothingness coursed through me.

"What's wrong with him?" the boys said. "Is he having a heart attack?"

Agna's father bent over, holding his stomach. Then he stood, looked at me nervously, and said, "You stay the *frib* away from my daughter or I'll kill you." I watched him walk up the hill and vanish. Some of the boys chuckled and kicked pebbles at me until he ordered them back to work. In the distance, Agna watched me until her father ordered her back to work, too.

Carefully, I wrapped my torn finger back into place.

———

I circled the streets until I found a better hiding spot. On the opposite side of the foundation, three small walls obscured me completely from view, but a tiny slit allowed me to see out. The sun beat down on the boys as they worked, and Agna, to my joy, worked alongside them. Though she was the only girl among three dozen boys, they gave her no special treatment. She spread mortar and hefted heavy stones without help; she chiseled with practiced skill. But I noticed in her craft an attention to detail that the boys lacked. Every stone held her full consciousness. Every rap of her hammer carried the weight of eons.

And she sang while she worked.

Oh, what sweet music! The boys sang with her; they mixed mortar by verse, carried stones by stanza, and finished walls by song, so that their labors resembled a dance more than a burden.

I knew the power of her song now and let it consume me. I reveled in forgotten vistas. Geysers from the oasis city of Sul erupted in my mind. The mirrored walls of Nier El Du blinded my dreams. The gargantuan city of Poc, carved from a single piece of stone, crushed me under its weight. I thought, for a moment, that this feeling might be greater than the bliss of annihilation.

"You!" Agna said.

I woke from my visions to see her peering down at me from the foundation wall. She threw her hands to her hips and frowned, and I recognized her mother in the gesture.

She sniffed the air. "I thought I smelled ash," she said.

"Your songs, they are...*beautiful*, yes, that's the word," I said.

She glanced over her shoulder. "I was wondering who it was that Father beat this morning."

"Now he has beaten us both," I said. "We are kindred. By dawn, he will—"

"Kin? Hardly. You'd better leave, whoever you are. He'll kill you. Don't be stupid."

"Tell me, Agna," I said, "Do your songs carry you to forgotten places? Do you have visions of dead cities?"

"What?" she said. She stepped back from the wall, mouth agape. "How do you know—"

"Agna?" her father shouted from behind her. "Who are you talking too? Is that *feg* here again?"

She stared at me. Then she shook her head and said, "Go away. Go away…" But her words were insubstantial, like a desert cloud.

"Meet me at the bottom of the hill," I said.

She disappeared behind the wall, and I knew she was mine now.

———

At the bottom of Posterity Hill, shadows crept across the ground as the sun turned overhead. Just after high-noon, Agna's small figure appeared at the top of the hill and scampered down to meet me.

"How do you know about my visions?" she demanded. "Did Mother tell you? Damn her!"

"No. I see them when you sing."

"You said they're 'dead' cities. What did you mean by that?"

"They have been forgotten. Erased. Yet your song rekindles their memories."

Agna's father appeared at the top of the hill surrounded by three boys.

"Let's go!" she said. "Before Father sees us!"

We turned through the busy streets. The air smelled of cracked spelt, boiling beans, and the pungent reek of humans going about their business. Slaughtered animals cried out and fell silent. She led me into a courtyard filled with date palms and speckled shade.

"They're not dead cities," she said. "They haven't been born yet."

"No, they're very dead. But your songs give them new life."

She frowned. "I've tried to tell Father about them. To let him know that there's more to my songs than just music and words. But he won't have an ounce of it. He says a woman needs a stable trade as much as any man, that my poems and music will only get me to a street corner, begging for change."

"He's wrong. I watched the boys sing with you. They work twice as hard under your spell."

"Do you think so? Father works us all so hard. A song makes the day go by a little faster." Her eyes filled with water. "The Prefect plans to hire Father as his chief mason. When Father gets that job, I'll be able to design buildings myself. I won't have to take orders from him anymore. And when I turn sixteen, Father promised to give his business to me. Says his back's no good anymore. I'll be free to create whatever I wish. I have dreams, things I want to build."

I remembered that I had touched her father, that he would vanish from existence before dawn. "Your mother has a well-paying trade, though?" I said.

"Well-paying? She's a seamstress in the textile guild. The pay is the only thing worse than the work. She doesn't want me to follow in her footsteps, but I love working with thread too. I often help her with embroidery. It's wonderful. You can't get the same precision with stone, not if you want to finish within this century." She stared at her calloused fingers.

"And all through this has been your music."

"It's been a kind of marching song, ever since I was a girl."

"Will you sing me one now?"

"Right here? Right now?"

"Yes!"

"This is silly. I don't even know you."

"There is nothing to know."

She shook her head. "Well," she said. "Maybe just the one. You did get a beating, after all, just to hear one." Then she began:

By dawn, the sun, low on our backs
Is cool, while birds are singing
By noon, the mortar's showing cracks
And masons' ears are ringing
But come a week, a month a year
When chanced upon this hill
Where father's eye had built a house
That stands upon there still
I forget the sweat, the grime
The shoveling of sand
And fill my heart with future dreams
To build one by my hand.

Vistas of dead cities assaulted my consciousness. But this time, there were new places, cities I had not glimpsed before. Cities of glass. Cities in the sky. Even cities floating among the stars. Perhaps, as she had suggested, not all of these kingdoms were dead; some had yet to be created. I closed my eyes and savored the sweetness of them all.

"Who are you?" she said.

"Does it matter, my name?"

"Yes, it does. A man's name is his being, his essence."

"All the more reason why I have none."

"I don't understand," she said. "You come to me, begging to hear my songs, but I know nothing of you. Where are you from? What do you do? How is it that you have come to me?"

Agna's father burst into the courtyard, surrounded by a dozen boys. They carried chisels and hammers and walked briskly in my direction.

"Agna!" her father shouted. "Stand back!" He smacked the head of a hammer into his palm. "You're dead, stranger, do you hear me?"

I backed away. They could not hurt my true essence, of course, but they could destroy my suit. I needed it to last, for Atleiu was a fickle demon and would not craft me another one for eons.

"Who are you?" she said to her father. "And what do you want with us?"

"What?" her father shouted. "Has he drugged you? You're safe now, baby! Daddy's here!"

"Who?" she said. She looked like she was going to be sick. "I don't feel right. Something's wrong."

But I had to leave. I fled the courtyard through the rear gate, and the boys pursued. I ran through crowded streets, hiding behind bales of tobacco and under piles of manure. When I was certain I had lost them, I headed back to my brothers in the Jeen. I was not troubled. By morning, her father and his rabble would be gone.

———

"We have followed you," my brother said to me that evening in the Jeen, as the bright stars oppressed above us. "You entered a city in the guise of a man and walked among its people, touching them. This night, their walls hold firm. The winds are calm, and their children do not scream. Tell us why, brother, you've broken our trust?"

I dared not reveal Agna's power to enthrall with her song, lest they try to usurp her for their own. But I could not deny what they had witnessed. "We have no rules," I said. "Nor laws preventing me from doing what I have done. I followed my will."

"But you are a thing of destruction," my brother said. "That is your nature. What do you seek in the world of form?"

"Sometimes, in the winds of the Jeen, I hear whispers of

human things. Have you never been curious to know what they are?"

"Sometimes, yes. But if I satisfy my curiosity, what purpose does it serve? The curiosity vanishes. One day, the thing which piqued my interest will vanish too. All is impermanent."

"Then so, too, is my interest in this city," I said. "It will vanish. Your concern will vanish too."

"As all things do. But now, our brothers need to know: what is it that draws you there, in the morning sun, to walk among them without destruction?"

I paused before answering. "Of all the cities we sundered, brother," I said, "how many do you remember?"

"Not many," he said.

"None?" I said.

He paused. "Perhaps."

"I go to that city, dear brother, to remember."

"But why? Nothing is worth remembering. Memories, like cities, fade."

I felt pain when I realized that one day Agna would vanish from the earth. "What are we then, without our memories?"

"We are nothing, brother. We have and will always be nothing. You may convince yourself, for a time, that you are more, but it is only self-deception."

And with these words, my brother left me.

In the winds of the Jeen, I heard a laugh.

———

I searched the desert six times to make sure I was in the right place. Yes, this was the spot of sand where Gelecek had once stood. Like a drying oasis, the city's circumference had shrunken inward. Its walls were devoid of grandeur. A few leaning towers thrust into a cloudless sky, and scattered buildings spotted an uninspiring landscape.

And Agna's house was gone.

I entered the city and hunted for her within its changed streets. "Where am I?" I asked its residents.

"This is Gelecek," they responded forlornly, as if the city's name itself was a curse.

"There was a foundation," I said to an elderly woman mashing chick-peas. "On Posterity Hill. Do you know it?"

She shook her head. "Never heard of it."

Of course, I thought. I had destroyed the mason who had created it.

"There is a girl," I said. "Agna, daughter of a seamstress. Have you heard of her?"

The old woman squinted rheumy eyes at me. "Nay, but there's the seamstress guild up on Trajen Row. Why don't you bother them?"

I lost my way several times but eventually found Trajen Row, a cobbled dead-end street, with hundreds of dyed linens drying from hemp lines like standards. The air reeked of chemicals, and colored puddles filled the cracks between stones. Inside cramped buildings, hundreds of seamstresses stuck needles into cloth, combed lamb's wool, or threaded looms. I found Agna's mother working in a corner, her needle-work tiny feats of prestidigitation.

She looked much thinner than I remembered, and her face was wrinkled and bitter.

"I'm looking for Agna," I said. "Where is she?"

"Who the *frib* are you?" she said without looking up.

"I'm a friend. I was supposed to meet her today."

"I don't know who you're talking about."

"Agna, your daughter."

She stopped her stitching and looked up at me. "Is this a joke? Did the girls put you up to this?"

"No Please! Where is she?"

She started to cry. "You're cruel. Go away."

"This is not a joke. I'm not here for anyone but myself. I

am seeking your daughter to…" After my last incident with her father, I tempered my words "…to protect her from a great evil."

She began her needlework again, then said to the sky: "Mollai, great maker, why do you torment me so?" Then she said to me, "I don't know who you are stranger, but your words sting. I never had a husband or a daughter, nor do I know this Agna you speak of. Now, leave me."

I backed away as the shock of her words consumed me. Always, when I destroyed cities, my destruction was total, complete. I had never been selective in annihilation before. It had never occurred to me that erasing her father would erase Agna, too. An alien feeling welled up inside me as I stepped out into the sun. It was—there was only one word for it: loss. A thousand linens snapped angrily in the wind. I walked the streets in a daze. I don't know how long I wandered before I heard a voice.

A beautiful voice. It sang.

I followed the song around a corner, into an alley overgrown with weeds. A cat hissed at me and ran away. The voice came from a doorless building, and I crept inside. Half-finished canvases crowded a large studio, and the air was heavy with the reek of paint. Majestic cities adorned the canvases; some I recognized as cities I had sundered.

At the far end of the studio, a young woman danced her brush over a canvas while she sang:

On the dark side of morn, the workers lie waiting.

Sunrise to sunset, their backs break in toil.

From out of the desert, are caravans sweating

Burdened with legumes, rich hemp seed and oil.

"Agna!" I shouted. "You're alive!"

The girl turned to me, but her face was not Agna's. Her eyes were too green, her nose too button-like, her face too round. Not Agna, but a stranger.

Startled, she said, "Who are you?"

But her voice—that *was* Agna's. "You won't remember me," I said.

She dropped her brush. "No! I've dreamt of you! Sometimes, I dream that I lived another life, with different parents, in a different house. I was a builder of cities and a weaver of thread. Then a ghost came along and erased everything. I thought it was just a recurring nightmare. But that ghost had your face."

"I'm sorry, Agna. I didn't know."

"Agna? That's the name my dream parents called me. My name is Dina."

"It's a beautiful name," I said, stepping closer.

"Stay away from me!" she said.

"I'm not here to hurt you, Dina. I only came to hear you sing."

"Why?"

I pointed to her paintings. "These cities, why do you paint them?"

"The architects buy them. They tell me my drawings inspire them."

"But why do *you* paint them?"

"I don't know...they come to me..."

"In vision, when you sing."

"How do you know that?" she said. "Who...what are you?"

"I am the no thing of the deserts beyond form and the sunderer of civilization. I and my brothers have destroyed these cities. I had forgotten them all. But your songs bring them back to me. I have the very same question for you, Dina. What are you?"

She looked sick. "It was real, wasn't it? My other life. There were too many details, too many feelings. I had a difficult life, yes, but I had dreams and aspirations. And you destroyed all of that, didn't you?"

"But you're not dead. Don't you see?" I said. "I couldn't

erase *you* from history. You spring back like the cities I and my brothers sunder."

"You're disgusting," she said. "You destroy as easily as I create."

"Perhaps, but for once in my life I want something else."

The winds gusted outside, knocking over a few canvases. I heard the rasp of sand blowing against stone, and a familiar shudder of ecstasy coursed through me.

"A sandstorm," she said. "I have to close the windows."

"No," I said to her as I stepped out into the sun. I knew him before he spoke, not by the way he walked, nor by the tailor of his clothes, but by his indifference towards all things. He gave a beggar a coin and patted him on the shoulder. He dragged his hands along the walls of a portico. He stepped up to me and paused. Every move was filled with emptiness.

"Hello, brother," he said.

"What are you doing here?" I demanded.

"I could ask the same of you. What business have you here in this flesh suit of yours?"

"You must leave!" I said. "Before you destroy this place."

"It's too late," he said. "Our brothers have decided that your sojourn here shall end. We followed you to this city. Four of us walk inside these walls now, spreading oblivion. We love you, brother, and when this city falls, you will return to us and be the soul we remember."

"I don't want to go back! Not yet! Please, listen to one of her songs! Look at her paintings! Then you'll understand why I'm here!"

"There's nothing to understand. There's nothing at all. That's the sole and final truth." My brother smiled and fled the alley, patting a boy on his head as he turned the corner.

"Agna—*Dina*, come on! We have to go!" I shouted. I re-entered the studio. But Dina had vanished.

"Dina! Where are you?"

I found a small door in the back. It led up a small, curving stairwell to a storeroom on the second floor. When I opened the door, Dina jumped out and stabbed me in the chest with a putty knife.

I pushed her away and pulled out the knife from my chest. There was no blood. When I dropped it to the floor, the blade shattered.

She pounded on me with her fists. "Go away! Go away!"

"Dina, Dina! Please, you must listen to me! My brothers are destroying this city as we speak. We have to go now, or you'll be killed!"

"Get away from me! I'd rather die!"

I grabbed her. She was small and easy to contain. I lifted her over my shoulder, and she beat me as I carried her down the stairs, through the studio, and out onto the streets.

She screamed for help. So I gagged and tied her with sackcloth.

I took the back alleys and least crowded streets and fled the city as quickly as possible, making sure not to touch anything. She cried, but her voice was muffled by her gag.

"I know you think I'm cruel," I said. "But I do this for your own good. I've figured it out, Dina. I know what you are. Whereas I am the sunderer of cities, you are their genesis. Your songs, your visions, your dreams, they are the impetus which create new ones. I destroy cities with my touch. You create them with your song. We are kindred. If you die, then in a way, so do I."

I found a black horse tied up beside a tent on the outskirts of the city and stole it before its owner could stop us. I spread Dina before me, and we rode deep into the desert. After several hours, she stopped struggling, so I took off her gag.

"Water…" she mumbled.

I found a canteen slung around the horse and gave it to her.

After drinking several large gulps, she said, "I have parents, friends, my paintings. Will they all vanish?"

"I'm sorry. But you can create new ones."

"Do you think it's that easy, that I can just start over in a new city, as if nothing at all has happened? Everything I know is going to die."

The horse grew tired as the sun set behind a dune, so I dismounted. I untied her hands as the stars winked to life above us.

"If you flee," I said, "by the time you get back to your city, it will be dust. No one will remember it, not even you."

"Won't I vanish too?" she said. "I was born in that city."

"I erased your father. It changed you, but you were born again as someone else. I think you are a seed that can't be destroyed."

"Then why bring me all the way out here?"

I looked at her and realized that I didn't have an answer.

"When I was six, my mother bought me my first paint set. My father took me to the top of Jimn Mountain when I was nine. I remember the first time I kissed a boy. I remember breaking my arm when I tried to scale Dell Wall. All of that will be erased, won't it?"

"But you will rebuild it somewhere else, in some other time."

"You don't get it! Humans are not like a wall, where the bricks of our experiences are interchangeable. Each instant is precious, unique. You rob the universe of the sacred. Can't you see that?"

"I...I have known nothing else," I said. "Until I met you."

"Is that consolation for ruining my life, that the ghost of annihilation has second thoughts?"

"I didn't mean to hurt you."

"But you have."

"This wasn't supposed to happen."

"What wasn't?" she said slowly.

"The destruction of your city."

"What city?"

"Gelecek."

"What a beautiful name," she said. "Where is it? And who are you? How did I get here?"

I sighed and had to look away.

"I feel funny," she said. "As if...I'm not supposed to be here. My body feels...light. Like air. What's your name?"

"My name?" I said. "My name is...destruction."

When I looked for her again there was only sand. The girl, the horse, everything was gone, even my suit of flesh. I cried out to the stars, but they did not respond.

———

I did not move from that spot. My brothers came to me on the sand. They said, "Come back to the Jeen with us, brother, for you have no reason to dwell among form now."

And I said, "Leave me."

The sun rose and set a hundred times, and my brothers came to me again and again. "Please," they begged, "It's not proper that you be apart from us. Come and obliterate a city with us and feel your old self again."

But how could I? In each city might dwell the spark of Agna or Dina or her kin. I could not bear to erase her from existence again.

"Go away," I told my brothers, and they did.

I sat there in the same spot of the sand where Dina had disappeared, while the sun turned in slow orbits overhead. I felt like a top, spinning, spinning, but never slowing.

The stars and sun turned through slow eons, and still I did not move, when a dark cloud appeared in the sky one silent afternoon. Once in a hundred years, it rained in the desert; today it poured down in great sheets. The sky grew as dark as the gloaming, and the sands turned to mud. Forks of light split the sky in dreadful thunder.

I collected myself into human form, gave myself strong

arms and hands, and began to mold the wet sand into a brick. The pounding rain seemed to shout Agna's songs across the desert, and to its tune I crafted another brick, and then another, fashioning them into a rudimentary wall. I knew it was temporary. I knew that tomorrow, when the sun rose hot and burdensome above the sands, my wall would grow weak. The desert winds would topple it in time, that all was, essentially, nothing. But heaven help me, I couldn't stop.

15

The Landscape of Lacrimation

Carina Bissett

But a mermaid has no tears, and therefore she suffers so much more.

—"The Little Mermaid," Hans Christian Andersen.

You've been searching, your whole life it seems, walking the beaches and cliffs on distant shores, exploring the desert wilds and deep forests, in a quest to find the place where you belong. The genealogy records have gaps, places where rotten teeth have been pulled, leaving empty sockets behind. It gnaws at you. Each time you are interrogated about your origins, you wonder: Where do you belong? How do you fit in? When you look in the mirror, the reflection is blank, and you are left with questions—nothing else.

You sign up to a registry and attempt to track your roots, but the evidence has been buried. Trace the genealogy backwards, and there it is: a thick line of ink scratched through the name of a lavender child who suddenly appeared in the family tree. No leaves. No branches. No roots. Just a handwritten denial of association written in the margins. Your family looks the other way when you ask too many questions. Your great-grandmother smiles and pats your hand. She tells you merfolk cannot cry, as if that makes the sorrow easier to bear. Finally, desperate to know the truth, you send a DNA kit to the lab.

The results only complicate things.

It begins like this:

Your skin is a different shade than anyone else in your family. When you ask about it, your parents tell you stories. Your relatives snigger as you walk into the room. Even though they speak in whispers, you can hear their comments, dark words spoken in dark corners. You don't belong and you know it. You are *other*. And, despite all your many attempts to hide your *otherness*, everyone can see it.

Perhaps this is not your family, you think. Perhaps you are a changeling. When those explanations fail, you search deeper, always deeper. A close look at your skin under a lamp, under the sun, reveals the shimmer swimming in your veins. You've heard the whispers. Eager to claim your rights, you slice the skin and let your blood run free. It's only then you finally accept the truth. You are not the same as everyone else. You are alone.

And then it happens. You set out on a journey of self-discovery.

You've heard rumors of lost people who have searched for connections to the realms of faerie in wild woods. And then there are stories about others who wait, motionless in sand-swept deserts, hoping for truth to appear on the edge of an exhalation. You try the easiest ways first, the ones that leave your feet rooted to the ground. The deep green of ancient forests throbs with desire; the shifting deserts sing of solitude. Even so, those choices are no choices at all.

In your heart, you know you belong to the sea and it belongs to you.

You continue your search on new shores. A jungle, thick and dark, tumbles down the slope. Made up of crushed bone and shell, the white sand powders your feet. The sea, a clear turquoise, beckons. You squint out over the water, but the only thing you see is a solitary seagull kiting on the breeze. You stand still, hoping to capture a fragment of harp song, but your kin remain silent, withdrawn.

Green children ghost into the shadows of the forest fringe. You stopped hiding behind hats and long sleeves years ago, and now the sun has deepened the lavender tint of your skin to the Tyrian purple extracted from crushed shells. The green children whisper back and forth in a language you cannot decipher. Their bare legs are covered with yellow mud. Spiked crowns of holly and black orchids rest on their small heads. High in the canopy, a monkey howls. The green children retreat, disappearing back into the sheltering canopy, leaving you alone and unwanted on a foreign shore.

You head north, following the coast until the freezing seas deny further passage. At night, the northern lights dance in ribbons of red and green and blue. Sometimes, a thread of lavender shines through in a beacon of hope before disappearing once more. The stars hum in a cloudless sky, and moonlight skates across the fog—ice crystals suspended in the frigid air.

One arctic morning, you wake to find two crow girls watching you from their perch on the skeletal remains of a tree. Their eyes glitter like jet. In their hooded cloaks of black feathers, they are indistinguishable from one another. They point and chatter, a peppered exchange of gossip. Although you are certain you are a creature of the surf, you wonder what it would be like to belong to their flock. You take a step forward, arms outstretched, but the crow girls spook and take flight in a raucous spin of displaced snow.

You wish you could take solace in tears shed, but once again you are left to suffer without sound. Desperate, you search for threads of hope in your journal, but they crumble in colored bits of fragrance as you turn the page. When you head south for warmer climes, you leave your diaries and genealogy charts behind. And, after a while, you find contentment in the quiet of your solitude.

By this time, you've been travelling so long it's become a way of life—an ebb and flood of new scents and sounds. You've watched the intricate courtship dances of the nāga, their serpent tails coiling together in a rasping susurration. You've seen the silhouettes of the deer people swaying under the full moon in southwestern deserts. You've followed the immortals' rainbow dreams through the dry season.

When at last you land on the salty shore of a dead sea, the memories of unshed tears are truly lost. Even so, that nameless suffering lightens as you wander this desert on the far side of the world. No creature can survive in this scarred landscape, no fish or frog or fruit, yet you feel more alive than ever.

As you approach the vast stretch of the inland sea, plants laden with green globes dissolve in puffs of ash, leaving a trail of smoke in your wake. You seek access to the place where the water kisses the shore, a dead region littered with petrified driftwood and mineral deposits, but the path in uneven and broken. As you walk, the white sheets covering the earth crack and crumble under your feet like brittle bones returning to dust. You press on. And when you finally kneel to touch this dead sea, you are filled with the sense that you have finally come home.

From the point of contact where your fingers touch water, a kaleidoscope of concentric circles spreads out in rippled waves as far as you can see. The figure of a woman rises from the depths and glides towards you. She matches the landscape, an eerie combination of stark extremes. Her skin is the deep ebon of impenetrable shadow curled in the scattered remains of desiccated wood. Her hair billows behind her in a cloud of ash and smoke, and her eyes shine like black diamonds.

You stay on your knees and wait. As she edges closer, you can see the crystal deposits clinging to her skin, delicately arranged patterns that serve to magnify their nacreous brilliance. And in those arrangements, you finally find all the tears you've never shed. The sharp angles and panes of exquisite emotion revealed in tragic tears. The snowflake stars of gratitude fed by tributaries of hope. The city streets and dead ends contained in sorrow married to the cobbled asphalt of change. And the elegant reservoirs expressed in reunion.

In the woman's glittering eyes, you see the truth of your great-grandmother's words. The people of the sea have no tears, a price paid in pain. But now that you have found all those lost tears, generation upon generation of suffering deposited in a salty sea, you finally realize the truth: lavender children are never truly alone.

Just one step away, the keeper of the merfolk's tears reaches out to you. Worlds of weeping form, break apart, and reform in the cup of her outstretched palm. *Sorrow, joy, hope, change, tragedy.*

You take her hand in yours.

Reunion.

16

They Said the Desert

A. T. Greenblatt

They said those who died in the desert wandered forever in its loneliest parts. But the Crossers said a lot of fantastical shit as they passed the bottle around the campfire, and Jade wasn't some doe-eyed girl anymore who swallowed their mad stories whole.

'Course that was before she started crossing the desert herself. That was before she saw the ghost of her dead man in the middle of it, standing under the red oak tree.

Dominic's ghost was easy to spot in the distance, even at a hundred strides away. He shimmered against the desert's bleak, colorless sky, leaning against that broad and impossible tree trunk, smiling. And Jade's first thought was *Oh God, he knows.*

She stopped walking—a dangerous thing to do in the desert—but even the hazy outline of Dominic was enough to halt her feet and catch the breath in her throat. Behind her,

Billy pawed the ground nervously and nudged her shoulder as the dust began to swirl around their ankles.

Her second thought was, *Idiot, he's just an illusion.*

So Jade gritted her teeth, pulled her boots out of the dust that was already swallowing their motionless feet, and with a firm grip on Billy's reins, moved forward again.

If the desert wanted to stop her from reaching the other side, it was going to have to do better than that.

This wasn't the type of desert where the sun hammered down on you, cooking you rosy until you were the right shade of dead. Here, the sun just didn't give enough of a damn to bother. There were no rocks or coarse sand on the ground, no dunes or cacti either. Just the fine, sinking gray dust and the bland horizon that stretched out forever.

This place was a desert in the truest sense of the word, and here it was your imagination that got you killed.

She crossed the long gap between them, and the ghost waited for her. Grinning. His whole body was dark and murky, like a shadow in the shade, except for his teeth. Those were bone white.

"I don't have time for this shit, Dominic," Jade said, as she picked her way carefully around the tangled roots of the oak. A tree like this shouldn't have been able to grow so large, much less thrive in such a desperate place. A tree like this shouldn't have been here at all.

Sort of like her.

But here it was, and here she was, and she had deliveries to make and a whole town on the other side of this wasteland that was waiting for her to make them. Jade nudged Billy towards the small miserable pond nestled between the roots of the tree. She squatted on her haunches next to her horse. Pulled out her pocket watch. Paused it. All while the ghost just stared and grinned and grinned.

"Stupid illusion. Go away," Jade hissed. She didn't need to be haunted right now. She had enough to worry about, like dust wolves and pissing off the desert. She'd been walking for a day and a night straight, and she was only halfway across.

The ghost shook his head and stretched out a smoky hand towards her, the outline of his fingers reaching across the stale water. Wanting.

Jade stumbled back, half-tripping over roots, half-drawing the pistol from her belt. They said that those who died in the desert become like it. Mean and vengeful. In life, her man had been neither of those things. But who knew what sort of creature his ghost had become?

The ghost pulled back his hand slightly, the grin slipping from his face, his black-pit eyes rounding with surprise. He did not try to reach out again. Instead, he pointed to Billy.

Jade replied by aiming her pistol.

There were power cells strapped high on Billy's back and they were destined for a little town called Edge on the fringe of the desert. Edge needed them to survive, just like its sister town, Border, on the other side of this wasteland needed the returning grain. That alone made this trek across the desert worth the crazy risks.

But it wasn't the cargo that Dominic was pointing at. His sights were set on one saddlebag in particular. The damning one. The one with the instructions and drawings on how to make those power cells. Something only the craftspeople of Border knew how to do. If delivered, it would destroy the Crossers' livelihood and more. But if delivered, one day, no one would have to die trying to cross the desert.

'Course, she shouldn't be surprised that her ghost knew about those drawings, should she?

"This isn't your choice," said Jade. "You're dead." She and Dominic glared at each other over the stale pond, as if they were arguing over a simple thing like dirty dishes, like they use to when Dominic was a man of flesh and blood. A pang of grief and longing welled up unexpectedly in Jade's chest, but she pushed it down, away. Focused on keeping her pistol steady instead.

As usual, it was Dominic who gave in first. He dropped his accusing finger and sighed, his whole silhouette sagging a bit.

Well, he doesn't seem dangerous, she thought. But neither had the desert when she used to stand on its threshold, in Border, looking for her man on the horizon. Jade lowered her gun and gathered up Billy's reins again.

"This isn't your choice anymore," she repeated, but in a whisper, as she started her pocket watch again and began walking away from the impossible oak tree.

'Cause she was a Crosser now, not him. And she had made this trek across the desert a hundred times. With luck, she'd make it a hundred more and come through alive *and* sane. But what haunted her every mile, every footfall, was what to do with those power cell blueprints. She wasn't sure if giving them to a few eager craftsmen in Edge was the right choice. She wasn't sure if it was her choice to make at all, being that she was a Crosser by circumstance, not by blood.

Jade stole a glance backward and was startled to see Dominic trailing a few paces behind. He pointed to himself, then to Jade, then to the path ahead. *Let me come with you,* his eyes pleaded.

"No, I don't want you here," she said, making sure each word was a razor. Then, she fixed her eyes on the horizon and swore never to look back.

The ghost followed anyway.

———

They said that the desert was once so narrow you could leap over it. Back then, anyone could travel from Edge to Border in one soaring step.

This was another favorite story the Crossers liked to tell over a fire and a bottle. And there was always a bottle of the best stuff waiting for them at the towns on either side of the desert. Perks of the job. She'd heard all their tall tales when Dominic was alive, sitting at the campfire with his scrawny arms wrapped around her broad shoulders, back when he was a Crosser and she wasn't. And she had clung to every word.

Since then, she'd discovered most of the Crossers' stories were just mirages, dreams, and folktales. But slowly, she was learning which ones weren't.

Her dead man kept pace behind them, dogging her like her worries, while she and Billy walked and walked. If she looked to her right or left and squinted, she could sometimes see vague outlines of other impossible landmarks: towering windmills, grand smokestacks, and things she didn't have names for rising up out of the gray dust. She wondered if they were real or imagined, but if she thought about it too long, her head began to ache. If she stopped moving forward and paused to whisper a few soft words to Billy or to secure the precious cargo on his back, they began to sink into the ground.

"Why are you following me?" she asked Dominic over her shoulder, for the tenth or maybe the twentieth time.

Desert journeys were traveled alone because they were like walking a tightrope made of razor wire. You had to keep your feet nimble and your head empty. You needed to keep your dreams and fears to yourself. Carts, wagons, and traveling troupes always got mired in the dust because anything more than a person and a horse carried too much baggage for the desert to ignore.

The ghost walking behind her was damn burdensome.

What are you going to do? his eyes asked every time she looked back. Jade answered by scowling and kept on walking.

The desert hated change, so night fell slowly. The sky was a bruised, beaten color when Dominic ran a few paces ahead of her and stopped. Dust billowed around his dark feet, and in the dimness, he looked more solid than before. He pointed at the saddlebag with the instructions again and then drew a question mark in the air.

"Quit it," Jade said, not breaking stride, too tired to argue with a dead man. "I'm the one who should be asking the questions, 'cept there's nothing for you to say."

The ghost backed up and grinned, hands around his throat, miming soundless words with mock surprise as if he had just lost his voice. Every line of his body was bent in jest, and his eyes laughed at his own joke.

"Oh shut up."

But she couldn't stop the corner of her mouth from quirking upwards. Hell, the desert *was* getting to her if she was falling for his sense of humor again.

Jade picked up her pace.

It was completely dark when they reached the lost galleon. A monstrous boat that didn't come with a history or explanation. It was as old as the Crossers' stories and too large for the dust to swallow. That didn't stop the dust from trying though, as it swirled and flung itself against the great hollow belly of the ship.

It was a good place to stop for a few hours, and Jade paused her trusty pocket watch. Time was an easy thing to lose sight of in the desert and the pocket watch kept her straight, counting the minutes she'd' walked, reminding her that she was only a day away from Edge now. Billy munched on a few miserable patches of grass, growing around the hull where the ground hadn't sunk, as she unsaddled him and rubbed him down. Gave him some proper food.

Jade meant to eat a bit herself as she stepped through the large hole some Crosser had thoughtfully cut into the side of the ship, but her eyelids were so damn heavy. And tonight, like every night in the desert, would be nearly sleepless. The dust wolves were always hunting, and dreams had a nasty habit of solidifying in this wasteland.

Inside, the old ship creaked mercilessly. The older Crossers mumbled about the things that lived in its bowels. Jade sat down only a stride or two away from the hole. She had more than enough of their stories for one day.

The ghost of Dominic sat down beside her.

What the hell am I doing here? She thought, rubbing a hand over her face. Dominic had the same question. He pointed at her and drew another question mark in the air.

"Someone had to pick up your slack after you didn't come back."

The ghost cringed, even though this was a lie and they both knew it. Dominic had made enough money for Jade to live comfortably for the rest of her life. Perks of the job. But she was tired, and it was an easy lie.

Jade brought up her knees and rested her chin against them. She wondered if it was still snowing in Edge. On her last trip there, the children had built a line of snowmen a hand's breadth away from the brim of the desert. A welcoming committee for the Crossers. It was always too warm for snow in Border, and when she tried to describe the cold, wet flakes to her nieces, they looked at her like she was crazy. Which just made her laugh. She used to think Dominic was making this shit up too.

"What do you want?" she asked her ghost.

The ghost drew a question mark and pointed at her again. *What are you doing here?*

Jade sighed and rubbed her face again. It was a long damn list, but it would keep her awake. "There are shortages, you know."

'Course he knew; it was why he got paid so well. As had his mom before him. As had his grandpa. It was why the other Crossers kept her on even though she hadn't been raised for this, and she never had any good stories to tell around the fire. When she closed her eyes, Jade could almost see the bags of grain all lined up in a row, waiting for her in Edge to bring back across the desert. It was not nearly enough. It would never be enough.

"There was a job opening," she said, glaring, and the ghost winced. "And I wanted to see for myself what was so damn important on the other side of this desert." Dominic nodded, and she could almost hear him ask. *Do you know the names of everyone in Edge yet? Do you miss them when you're back home in Border?*

Yes, god, yes. She'd thought she could never forgive them —the people in the town across the desert, the reason why Dominic was dead and gone. But she was wrong. It was hard not to fall in love when Edge's residents were always so thrilled to see her come striding out of the dust. When their freckled faces and smiles were just paler versions of her nieces and her aunts and her brothers. When Edge was just the colder and greener twin of Border. Yes, she loved them and missed them because she was a Crosser now and her heart no longer belonged to just one home.

And yet…she missed her man more. Even after all these years. With every heartbeat, with every dream.

"All of Border showed up when they unveiled your plaque at the shrine, you know," she said. "You surprised us. The desert caught you too early."

The memory was still vibrant. The shrine, filled to the brim with the name plaques of the Crossers who never made it home. Some so old and worn you could barely make out the letters. Some too new. The red mourning flags fluttering in the wind, and everyone dressed in their nicest. All their tears and kind words and endless compassion. Their glances at the empty places at her sides. The place where if not a partner, then children should be. The place where Dominic's long family line of Crossers ended.

That was what had pushed her into the desert in the end. She couldn't live around all that pity.

"You shouldn't have kept crossing," she whispered to the

ghost of her love. But Dominic wasn't looking at her anymore, his gaze was fixed on something outside the ship, beyond the door. And for a moment, he looked so alive. "Fuck the desert. Fuck Edge. We had more than enough. We had…"

She could see it, and she knew she was dreaming: their small house, smelling of smoke and spices and sex. She saw the wicker chairs they used to sit on together and the sunlight that streamed through the windows and the dirty pile of dishes that was always there. She was dreaming all right, but she didn't give a damn. She had missed this home most of all.

Dominic's eyes went wide in surprise, and he tried to shake her, but his hands were as light as feathers. He glanced out through the door again. Then, there was real, honest fear in his face.

But Jade didn't care. It had been ages since she had felt this stationary. She'd wanted to cross the desert as a girl, but now she wanted nothing more than to pick up her heavy work gloves she'd abandoned years ago and join her brothers in the warehouse, crafting power cells. The job she was *supposed* to have.

"I should kill you for leaving," she whispered.

Dominic shook his head frantically, trying to move her again. Then he stopped. Slowly, he stood and wheeled around so he crouched in front of her. He placed a ghostly finger over her heart, and all of the anger and hurt and loneliness she'd bottled up since the day Dominic didn't come walking back out of the desert welled up inside her. It was too much for one chest to hold.

She hated how much she still hurt, even after all these years.

Slowly, Jade let him guide her hand to the gun at her side and then the gun to the center of his chest, though the pressure of his fingers was like a cool breath. She clenched her teeth and drew in a short, sharp breath as she realized that her man *wanted* to die again.

Please, pleaded his eyes. *I owe you this much,* said his translucent hands. *Just get it over with,* mouthed his lips.

Hurry, said every angle of his body. *Hurry.*

The gun in Jade's hands felt warm, real, and dangerous. A small part of her knew it was pointless to shoot a ghost. The rest of her was too angry to care.

The single resounding shot shattered the mirage. Jade opened her eyes to the desert. It was almost dawn. She was sitting in the lost galleon, and there was a dust wolf lying at her feet, a bullet in its chest. It was gasping, tongue lolling, dying. Behind it, two more of the massive beasts were rising out of the swirling dust. And they were very much alive.

The wolves gave a low growl, Billy reared in fright, and her first shot went wide. The wolves lunged, Dominic threw his shadowy arms around her, but the next two bullets found their mark. One between each pair of monstrous eyes.

Jade might have been a lousy Crosser, but she'd always been a good shot.

The wolves collapsed on the ground with a *thud* and a *thud,* only a few feet away from the ship, the dust pillowing around them. Across the desert, the gunshots echoed and echoed and echoed.

"Holy shit," Jade gasped.

It took a good five minutes for her hands to stop shaking and another ten to calm Billy down and check on the power cells. All the while, Dominic never drifted more than a hand's breadth away.

"How do those damn dogs always manage to sneak up like that?" Jade asked him.

The ghost shrugged.

The desert was already swallowing the wolves' corpses. Soon, it would be like they were never there and the next time she crossed this spot, she would wonder if she'd been attacked at all.

"You're still a bastard," she said and stared across the empty land. "This can't go on."

Jade looked back at her ghost. Dominic was almost solid now. Almost here. And maybe this was the stupidest decision she'd ever make. Maybe she was finally cracking. But she turned to him and said: "Walk with me."

Her ghost obliged.

———

They said the desert was getting wider, and Jade agreed. According to her pocket watch, it took about seven minutes longer to cross than it did a year ago. Twelve minutes more than the year before that. It was like Border and Edge were two islands drifting apart, 'cept instead of water between, there was dust, dust, and more dust.

Jade walked quickly, or as quickly as she could. She was on the last leg of her trek, but Billy hadn't quite forgiven her yet for what'd happened at the galleon, and the desert hadn't forgiven her for killing its wolves or for the gunshots, whose echoes were still coming back to haunt her. Now, her boots sank to up to her ankles with every step.

Don't piss off the desert, they always said, it's an angry and spiteful bastard.

Too late now, Jade thought.

The ghost next to her kept pace, stride after stride. Stubbornness is the only way you'll make it across the desert, he'd told her once when they started falling hard for each other. Stubbornness, and a reason to make it to the other side alive.

And still, the desert had killed him. But Jade's stubbornness had always outmatched his, so they pressed on.

When she was only a few hours away from Edge, Dominic ran ahead again and pointed at the saddlebag with the documents. He matched her strides, walking backwards, his black pit eyes never leaving her face.

"I thought you forgot about those," she said.

The ghost shook his head.

"I think I'm going to deliver the blueprints," she said. "And I'll carry back the seeds for crops in exchange." Her voice was a hoarse whisper and the decision filled her with relief and with terrible sadness.

The outline of the ghost bristled, like a dog raising it haunches.

"It's going to take Edge a while to figure out how to make power cells that can last more than five minutes," she added, quickly. "And it's going to take Border a while to figure out how to make our ground grow crops."

Hell, it's going to take many, many more trips across before we're done, Jade thought as she trudged forward, fighting the desert for each step.

Her ghost's face was expressionless as he kept up his backwards pace; only his eyes betrayed his anger, his hurt. It was one thing to know everything must die eventually, it was another thing entirely to see the beginning of the end of your life's work.

Dominic thrust a shadowy finger at her. *Why you?* His dark eyes were harsh, and the tip of his finger trembled.

Jade met his gaze and matched his fierceness. "Lots of reasons."

She didn't say because the desert was getting wider and the journey harder. Or because there were fewer Crossers sitting around the campfire with every generation. Or because if what they said was true, there were a lot of damn ghosts wandering the desert.

She didn't say, because at night, her dreams were filled with the sounds and the colors of the shrine's red mourning ribbons flapping in the wind and they were calling her and Jade wasn't sure anymore if it was a nightmare or a comfort.

What she said was: "Because if someone doesn't do something, the desert's going to kill us all anyway."

The truth fell like a stone from her lips and, for a moment, they both stopped walking. Dominic lowered his finger, his whole body sagging with defeat. He'd always said he hoped he wouldn't be alive to see the day when the Crossers had to stop, when they wouldn't be needed anymore.

The desert was cruel.

"It wasn't my idea, you know," she said. "People in both towns asked for this." 'Cept she was the only one they'd asked because they knew she was the only Crosser who would consider it. When the others found out about the blueprints, she'd hoped they'd understand. But she wasn't a fool. She knew understanding and forgiveness were not the same things.

With a sigh, Jade freed her legs from the dust, fixed her sights on the faint point on the horizon, and moved forward. Billy and her ghost followed.

It was only when Edge crept into view that she paused. Only then did the doubts she'd been fighting back grab hold.

"What right do I have?" she whispered to Dominic. Who was she to ruin the livelihoods of her friends and family? How could she abandon generations of hard-won histories and traditions?

With fumbling fingers, Jade unclipped the saddlebag with the damning papers from Billy's back and hefted the heavy parcel in her hands. She hesitated. She could just leave it in the desert, let it disappear into the dust. Let another Crosser in another generation deal with the problem.

The ghost of her love reached out and cupped his murky hands around hers.

I'm sorry, said his eyes. *I'm sorry,* said his grasping fingers. *I'm sorry,* said every line of his body. *I'm sorry, I'm sorry. I'm sorry.*

Jade pulled away, sharply. In life, her man knew better than to pity her.

"For what?" she shouted. "Which part of this are you sorry for?"

Dominic pointed, and Jade turned. Behind them, miles

and miles of footprints that hadn't been there before spread out in their wake. The path of every journey every Crosser ever made was traced out like scars in the dust, and there was not an unmarked inch of ground.

It's an illusion, Jade thought. *It has to be.* But in this wasteland, illusions got you killed. So did love and hope. She'd dared to walk with Dominic, and he had dragged the weight of his history and his hopes and his pride behind him. She saw the dust trying to swallow the footprints, but they resisted. Some memories refused to be buried. Now, the desert was completely changed.

And the desert was pissed.

The ground began shifting under her feet and Jade stumbled.

"Run," she yelled to Billy. "Shit, run!" But Billy wasn't a stupid horse; he was already racing toward the town.

Jade ran, too. But not fast enough.

The desert grabbed at her ankles, her wrists, her hands that were still holding the saddlebag, and it pulled her down. The dust swirled and swarmed and smothered her eyes. Coated her nostrils and throat. She could feel the desert's anger, its desire to consume anything that wanted something and anyone who dreamed too much.

I can't die here, Jade thought desperately. *Not this close.*

So, she pushed back. Against the dust and the desert and all the doubts that made her linger. She fought off the prying gusts and shielded her eyes. She crawled forward, winning inch by damn inch. Because she was a Crosser, and defying the desert was what she did. Through the dust clouds, she could see the outline of the Edge. It was so near.

That was when she felt the saddlebag slip from her fingers.

She groped, but the dust was vicious and blinding. The ground was relentless in trying to swallow her whole. Jade searched desperately, coughing on her curses.

She felt his ghostly hands first, guiding her, and the rough cloth of the bag a moment later. But she didn't ask questions, just crushed her fingers around her prize, found an inch of solid ground, and with a shout, pulled herself out of the dust. Then, Jade ran.

The desert chased her. It nipped at her footfalls, trying to pull her back with every step.

It almost did. But with a final push, Jade leapt over the boundary, crossing the sharp line from desert into town, from dust into green, and crashed into a melting snowman. The first lungful of Edge's crisp, clean air startled her, as always, and so did the smell of dirt and things that grow. She was mere inches from the desert, yet there was no dust here.

A few feet away an old woman sweeping her porch stopped mid-motion, startled. "Jade! You made it back!" she said, with a warm smile.

"Do you see him?" asked Jade, wiping the snow from her face. "Is he still there?"

"See who?" the woman asked.

"My ghost!"

The old woman—Myrtle, if Jade remembered right—gave the desert a long, appraising look. "Nope. Looks like the desert's getting to you, darling." Myrtle rapped her fingers against the side of her head and grinned.

Jade turned. The desert behind her was empty and flat and calm. Not a dust mote was out of place.

'Course, the desert was a bastard. But if Jade narrowed her eyes to slits, she could just make out the shadow of a man on the horizon, walking away.

Her hand was still clutched around the saddlebag with the blueprints, and Jade finally knew what she had to do.

Tonight, after all the power cells were distributed and she delivered the blueprints into the right hands, she'd tell a story at the campfire. It'd be about how Crossers walked with the ghosts of their past, and how their ghosts kept them straight and true in the desert. The others might understand. Or they might not.

But it didn't matter. The story wasn't for them. It was for the little doe-eyed children who hung around the fire with them, listening, swallowing her stories whole. Then she'd tell them about Border and its vast workshops and the bright and quick thunderstorms that rolled up on hot summer days. She'd tell them about her nieces who were about their height.

And when they'd ask her which of her stories were real, she'd lean in close and say, "All of them."

For now, Jade would keep crossing the desert. 'Cept along with the power cells and bags of grain, she'd carry blueprints and crop seeds, advice and all the stories she could gather. 'Cause change was coming to Edge and Border, and it was going to be hard and messy. Traditions were going to be abandoned, and one day there wouldn't be a bottle of the best stuff waiting for them in each town. Eventually, both towns would be self-sufficient, and they'd forget why anyone would bother to walk across an infinite wasteland for them. They would forget who the desert had stolen away.

When the Crossers were angry or disheartened, they said the desert would swallow them all eventually, past and future, but Jade knew now that wasn't true. Try as it might, the desert couldn't bury stubborn ghosts and one day she and her man, with generations of Crossers behind them, would haunt the dust between their towns, silently guarding and guiding the ones they loved home.

17

Meat for Skritches

Chip Houser

Tyler was watching a sitcom in the trailer's breakfast nook, petting the purring furnace that was Skritches in his lap, when the power went out for good. Tyler sat for a time, rubbing his cheeks, which were sore from laughing, wondering if they'd hurt when the Smiler virus took him.

He gave Skritches the last of the kibble, and her usual mealtime grooming, then grabbed his backpack and rode to Jack-in-the-Box. He could drive, but his bike had been the better option for a few weeks now. He hopped a curb to skirt a five-car accident and nearly hit a grinning woman who was shuffling along, dragging a leash behind her. The collar sparkled as it skipped along the sidewalk. Hopefully the dog, wherever it was, was doing okay. Better to be outside, Tyler figured, than left inside, or in a crate. He'd installed a little door in the trailer last week so Skritches could come and go as she pleased. He was making sure she was set for a long time.

Shelly, his manager, had closed the Jack-in-the-Box weeks

ago, back when the news was still on and everyone thought the quarantines were working. She'd given him a key with his promotion to assistant manager after graduation. Now, the place smelled like congealed grease. It was quiet except for a regular tapping on the drive-thru window. An older man leaned out of his pickup, his thick fingernail clicking on the glass. His smile was so wide that his cheeks pushed back in stubbled folds against his ears. This deep into the pandemic, Tyler should have known better than to look.

He thought he'd find Shelly smiling over her beloved spreadsheets, but her office was empty. He was relieved, not because he was stealing food—at this point no one cared—but because her absence meant she had something more important in her life than her job. Tyler wasn't sure what he'd do when he went Smiler. He wanted to be with Skritches.

The walk-in freezer was dark and musty, quiet as a tomb. Tyler stuffed his backpack with frozen patties and got out as fast as he could.

On the way home, he coasted past the mall parking lot. It was packed. He imagined how awful it must be inside, quiet and hot and full of milling smilers. He was glad he hadn't taken the job at the smoothie shop.

He rode through Sycamore Heights, where he'd played as a kid, climbing the towering trees, playing tag football on the broad lawns, splashing in pools behind gigantic homes. Skritches would be in heaven here, stalking rabbits in the waist-high grass. There wasn't much grass around Hidden Acres.

He stopped in the shade in front of a house where he used to play. Jason's house. They weren't really friends anymore. They'd hung out through middle school, but that ended sometime during freshman year. Jason had entered the Naval Academy last fall; Tyler had gone to full-time at Jack-in-the-Box.

Someone in an oversized tan shirt and a broad-brimmed

hat knelt in a plant bed by the house. He—or she, Tyler couldn't tell—rocked back and forth, stabbing at the dirt with a spade. Jason's mom, maybe. Tyler wasn't going to check; he didn't want to see her face.

The world had slowed down so fast. He didn't miss all the frantic talking and texting and driving and rushing every-where, not exactly, but the silent gardener, the bird calls, the wind through the trees, the swaying of the overgrown lawn, it all made him feel a little sad. A little lonely.

Eventually Tyler pedaled south across the highway, past the discount stores and auto dealerships, around the industrial park, past the faded plywood sign and the mailboxes. Skritches came out from under the trailer to greet him.

"Miss me?" he said, scooping her up. More likely she smelled the meat. "You know I brought you a treat, don't you?" Tyler tucked his nose into her neck and breathed in her soft, musky smell.

He grilled the burgers, piling them in an enormous mound. While Skritches ate, he drew his fingers slowly along her spine, over and over.

He left her to eat in peace and hit the bathroom. His mom was still there, standing in front of the mirror smearing powder across one cheek. He'd gotten used to using the toilet with her there. Funny how he'd never seen her look at herself in a mirror before the virus. She hadn't smiled much before then, either.

Skritches was still eating when Tyler came back outside. He settled in a lawn chair and watched. The meat on the plate probably still outweighed her. When she'd had enough, Skritches settled in his lap, kneading his sweatpants to get comfortable. Soon enough she purred beneath his slow strokes.

When Skritches hopped down to finish off the burgers a few hours later, Tyler's hand kept rubbing his thigh as though she hadn't moved. She didn't notice his smile.

For several weeks, Skritches hunted around the trailer, napping frequently in Tyler's lap. She grew lean and fast. When the winds came, and then the rain, she sheltered behind Tyler's legs. When he and the chair were whipped into the howling sky, Skritches scurried under the trailer. When the trailer shook and groaned and twisted and began pulling apart, she ran.

In the aftermath of the storm, Skritches followed Tyler's scent to the splintered crook of a tall tree. She found his wadded sweatpants there, along with an abundance of raw meat. Night after night, long after she'd finished the meat, Skritches curled up in Tyler's sweatpants and dreamed he was petting her, his voice softly vibrating through his hands and his warm, warm lap.

18

Amanda Invades the Museum

Michael J. DeLuca

By a first superhuman feat of flight, Amanda scaled the hilltop defenses of an open-air doll museum which, as it turned out, focused on depicting, in miniature, the several centuries between the colonial era and the Industrial Revolution.

Built on the ruins of a Civil War era fort, the museum took a pentagonal shape. A cobbled stone walkway proceeded along what had been the ramparts, protected from a sharp drop on either side by iron railings. The harbor stretched into darkness below, dusted silver. In the display cases recessed in the floor on either side of the walkway were the ballrooms, parlors, theatres, suites, lodges, cabins, and longhouses of the dolls. As Amanda walked along the cobbled causeway, crouching to study details of tiny parlor scenes, the diversity of sets soon made it clear she could perform any number of period dramas, as well as masquerades, time-travel epics, fairy interventions, or revelatory psychic journeys.

It was very early on a weekend, long before the staff

arrived, or even the sun. She could see her breath in the moonlit cold. She broke into some cases and began rearranging the dolls.

In the mid-nineteenth-century section, Amanda pushed her arms and head between the bars of the railing to place two doll children prone on the floor of the orchestra pit at a miniature Symphony Hall. The seats were packed full of overdressed, shadowy, whispering figures. At the podium, she posed a man who'd recently been waving a signal lamp at a train depot.

"We must operate, with respect to life and existence, as though an elite crowd of symphony enthusiasts were observing our progress at all times," said the signal-man.

"Didn't the architects realize they had neglected to include a roof?" asked Margaret, holding hands with Blinky Jack on the floor of the pit. "What happens when it rains?"

"I suppose," ventured Blinky Jack, yawning, "they must play only brass instruments and cymbals, things impervious to moisture. That's a shame. But it *is* fine to be able to see the stars from indoors!"

Margaret identified for Blinky Jack the relevant constellations passing overhead in the rapidly revolving sky: the Horde, the Oracle, the Mallet, and the girl chained to the Pegasus. The Oracle, Margaret explained, had to reach the Mallet and use it to break one of the links on the chain; this would enable the girl to ride the Pegasus properly and use the Mallet to defend herself against the Horde. But the whole thing was never-ending.

Outside the many entrances to the orchestral chamber (in what were, in fact, the train depot, governor's parlor, and the lobby of the Omni Hotel), dolls battered themselves against the locked doors, trying to break through.

Blinky Jack attempted to compose a song about the heroic exploits of the Oracle, using a lot of different choral parts appropriate to a large hall with such wonderful acoustics.

Margaret shouted him down, at which point the infuriated crowd burst in through several of the doors at once, catching up the symphony's audience in its frenzy and converging on the stage.

The signal man raised the lamp that was attached to the end of his arm and let it swing a few times like a censer. A train passed through, entering stage right, exposing its heaving flanks to the angry crowd long enough for Blinky Jack and Margaret to climb aboard, then belching smoke as it accelerated off, stage left.

————

The train was inappropriately scaled. Amanda left it smoking in the hotel lobby and took Jack and Margaret north along the walkway, around one corner of the rampart, to the 1920s Lowell Mills. She piled the raggedy seamstress dolls out of the way into a nearby horse-racing pavilion, and let Blinky Jack and Margaret walk alone on the catwalks among the hulking, black textile machines, which smelled of engine oil, dust, and scorched electrical wiring. Snow flurries fell intermittently, big crystalline shapes like lace doilies.

"Spiderwebs," said Blinky Jack. "Made by the spiders who run these machines in the daytime."

"They're not spiders," said Margaret, peeking out the windows at the pile of dolls. "They're women like me."

"Have you noticed this place doesn't have a ceiling either?"

The signal man floated high over their heads, dangling aloft from his lamp, which flitted back and forth, pulsing gently, shaking him like a rhododendron leaf in winter. "With respect to life and existence," he called, "we must operate as though we were propelled by a set of unfathomable machines, which are always upon the brink of slipping a cog or shorting a circuit, placing us in inescapable danger."

"I think," said Margaret, "he's trying to catch a snowflake."

"Let's help," said Jack. He ran about under the white-speckled darkness, making the catwalk shake.

"Stop it."

Outside on the racetrack, the heaped seamstresses rose jerkily to their feet. Amanda kicked and shook the miniature machines and rattled the windows of the mill.

"It's the Horde," said Margaret. "They've found us again!"

"If it wasn't the Horde," said Blinky Jack, "it would be something else."

"What's that supposed to mean?"

"You act like it's you against the world. It's not. What's *he* here for?" Blinky Jack indicated the signal man. "To help you. What am I here for—decoration?"

Amanda shattered a few of the windows and threw a seamstress doll through one of them. The doll clipped the edge of the catwalk and fell limply among the machines. Margaret screamed.

The signal man's lamp finally struck a falling snowflake. The mill and machines disappeared in a flash of white light, and a powerful wind lifted Margaret and Blinky Jack into the air.

————

"Whoosh!" whispered Amanda.

With practice, she had learned how to hover over the tops of the cases, like a giant carpenter bee. In this way, she could avoid the railing all together, traveling quickly from one set to the next.

She arced across the aisle to the Boston Neck security checkpoint on the night of the Battles of Lexington and Concord. Blinky Jack and Margaret sat in a big rustic bed upstairs at a snug inn, while below in the street, men in bright uniforms stood guard with bayonets.

Jack and Margaret cuddled, because it was cold and there was nobody to light the fire. The signal man had gone off somewhere.

Jack ventured to peek out from underneath the covers at the sky.

Margaret shrieked and pulled him back under. "You're here to support me, to shore up my weaknesses and give me comfort—not to take all the risks and win all the glory."

"Then why am I the inside spoon?"

From outside came the clang of sword against bayonet, the pop of gunfire, and a steadily-building white roar that sounded like the angry mob at Symphony Hall and the vindictive wind at the textile mill put together. Plus the train.

It grew uncomfortably warm under the covers.

"What do you have that it wants?" whispered Blinky Jack, trying to shake off Margaret's embrace as their bodies grew sticky with sweat. "The Horde, I mean."

Margaret fought him with a growl. "Nothing!"

The blankets came loose, opening up to the sky. Amanda had set fire to the inn. She flitted over it like a colossal ghost, warming her hands and feet in the orange blaze, directing the action like a conductor, glancing often at the blue line in the sky where the sun would rise. In the street, a redcoat doll took the head off a delivery boy.

"What's that?" cried Jack, pointing off across the harbor at a point of lamplight burning in a steeple. "Do you think it could be him—the signal man?"

"It must be!"

It was only a bit of painted scenery. The Boston Neck diorama ended at the waterline. On the other side of the wall was a miniature Long Wharf, at the peak of the whaling era. Beyond that were the steep hillside and the harbor, silver with snow. Amanda had the signal man in her pajama pocket. Dawn was coming.

The bed took flight just in time to save them from the inn's collapse. Amanda pinched out the smoldering corners of the quilt. She set the bed down on the deck of a whaling ship, left the signal man doll beside it in a pile with a few others she'd collected from the hotel lobby and the bank, then flitted off to gather stock.

Jack and Margaret sat in bed, awake and terrified.

———

The signal man climbed to his feet and shone the lamp around the deck. A woman in a soiled ballgown sat slumped against a boiling vat. A variety of men in mismatched suits and beat-up hats lay scattered in painful positions.

At a kick from the signal man, a faceless farm boy in plaid and a milkmaid in calico untangled themselves from each other, brushing off bits of straw as they buttoned their clothes. Margaret moved away from Blinky Jack in bed. "Who are you really, signal man? What are we doing here?"

"With respect to life and existence," said the signal man, "We must operate as though each of us were the remains of a whale, processed and distributed for many useful purposes, greasing the cogs of commerce, industry, fashion, and art, but carrying the constant memory of a once-beautiful soul."

Tame harbor waves lapped against the ship's flanks and the pilings of the wharf, reproducing in miniature the white noise of the Horde.

"I don't think he can help us," said Blinky Jack. "I don't think he wants to."

He jumped down from the bed, ran to an overturned barrel of tools—harpoons, curving blubber knives, hammers and tongs—and drew out a heavy wooden maul. The stars turned.

"Stop that," said Margaret. "Put that down. I told you, you're here as my companion. If I want, I can flick my fingers and make you disappear."

"Don't," said Blinky Jack. "You'll regret it. You'll miss me."

The crumpled, mismatched men began to twitch. The lady in the ballgown looked forlorn; the signal man approached her, offering his hand. She accepted, and they danced. The farm boy went for Margaret. The milkmaid came for Blinky Jack.

Margaret got her foot tangled up in the blankets; instead of leaping to the deck like Blinky Jack, she fell and rolled off the side of the bed, pulling pillows and bedding on top of her. The farm boy gathered her up in a bundle.

The white noise of the waves intensified. The whaling ship rocked as the surf slapped its flanks; whiskers of foam spray reached into the rigging, where they dissipated into mist, mingling with the snowflakes which had again begun to fall. The signal man and his partner danced vigorously, causing the light of the lamp to wobble and spin. The mismatched men lurched to their feet, adjusting their battered caps and bowlers and the lapels of their coats to fend off an eviscerating wind.

Blinky Jack swung the maul, striking the voluptuous hips of the faceless milkmaid, making her fold at the waist like a rag doll and topple into the sea. Margaret was screaming as though with delight. He lunged with the maul like a ram, driving back the nearest of the mismatched men, hurling himself through their tottering crowd, chasing the sound of her, which grew ever fainter and harder to discern from the noise of the Horde.

"Don't just let him take you!" he shouted. "Can't you understand love when you see it?"

"...flick my fingers..." came Margaret's voice, as though from far away.

There was smoke on the wind. The city of Boston was burning.

Blinky Jack ducked between two stumbling puppet-legs and glimpsed the farm boy carrying Margaret towards the gangplank. The signal man swished past with his princess. The brief, wild light of his lamp illuminated a section of wharf, which was crowded with seamstresses, sailors, train engineers and ticket-takers, powder-haired judges, duelists, redcoats, minutemen, and overdressed symphony enthusiasts. Blinky Jack struck the shins of the farm boy with his maul. Margaret, in her bundle of blankets, was spilled to the deck.

He had barely reached her when the signal man reappeared, his dance partner now dangling stiff from his elbow like an empty valise, the lamp steadily shining. "With respect to life and existence," he said, "we must operate——"

Blinky Jack swung the maul at the lamp.

"Don't!" cried Margaret, too late.

The lamp exploded. Everything went dark.

———

Amanda's giant fingers pinched the back of Margaret's night-gown and hoisted her out of the diorama. She was crying with the dawn in her eyes, holding up a small, limp form. "What do you think you've been doing? Look! Look what's happened to Jack."

Now Margaret was crying too, concealing her face in her sleeve.

"What did you think was going to happen?" Amanda shouted. "You didn't believe there was a Pegasus. You pretended it was stars. Now——" Her voice caught. She shook a longshoreman out of his coat and blew her nose. "Well? You wanted this. Take it. Independence. Power. You wanted to be the center of things. Go ahead, take it." Amanda grasped

Blinky Jack's corpse by one foot, spun him off into the dawn, and shoved the bloody maul into Margaret's hands.

For the first time, Margaret was high enough that she could see over the walls of the diorama and across the snowy bay. She felt the high wind.

The white noise hadn't been made by waves slapping the hull of the whaling ship, nor by the crackling fire in the Boston Neck diorama, nor the shuddering textile machines, nor the inappropriately-scaled train, nor even the overdressed orchestra crowd. A snowflake struck her, large, lacy, and wet.

The sun was shining on the hill; soon it would rise enough to light the bay.

"What did you do to it, anyway, to make it so mad?" asked Margaret. "The Horde."

"Same as you did, darling."

It approached out of the east, riding the wind, trumpets crackling.

Amanda's eyes glazed and her hand fell open, dropping Margaret through the frigid, snow-filled air, towards the rippling glass waters of the harbor.

———

Margaret, gripping the hammer, took flight, leaving the city burning.

19

A Girl Who Comes Out of a Chamber at Regular Intervals

Sofia Samatar

These automata are but vessels for our dreams; the wine they hold is the shadow of the future.

—Safiyya bint al-Jazari

1. On the construction of clocks from which can be told the passage of the secular hours

I am an ingenious invention. My father created me for the king. Lovely father! He made me a pleasant room with a dome of copper and tin. Here I stand with a cup in one hand and a handkerchief in the other, waiting patiently for my feet to be set in motion. This happens when wine is poured into the tube in my roof. I can hear it gurgling above me. Soon the liquid flows down and fills the cup in my right hand. When the cup is heavy enough, my arm drops down slightly—but not enough to spill the wine!—and releases the hook that holds me in place.

Hurrah! I roll along my track and push open the doors to

my chamber. Hello, Father! For, up to now, only Father has greeted me at the door. He wants to make sure I am perfect before he presents me to the king. I believe I am perfect. I offer my father the cup and the handkerchief for his lips.

If the receptacle in my roof is kept full, I emerge from my chamber precisely eight times every hour.

My father jokes that he could tell time from me, like a clock. My father is large and clever. He has a thin beard and a long sad face. He smokes a great deal. I believe that his life is, in general, unhappy.

———

2. On the construction of vessels suitable for use at drinking bouts

My father drinks all the wine I offer to him. Once he has had several cups, he begins to make loose, experimental gestures, tossing his instruments up and catching them. Sometimes he forgets to push me back inside my chamber, and then I stand in the doorway and watch him at his work. This is so interesting! My father's workshop is full of brass pipes, glass and copper vessels, bundles of wire, wax molds, and jugs of wine. The floor is strewn with sand. My father slips in the sand when he has been drinking wine, and sometimes, when he tosses his instruments up, he fails to catch them. Then he shouts for his apprentices. The apprentices are clumsy boys, none of them as handsome as my father. My father pulls their ears and beats them about the head with his slipper, and they weep. "Sons of bitches!" my father says.

My father sits on the floor with his head in his hands. He looks very gloomy. He calls me his lovely girl. He says he will be sorry to give me away. He tells me that the king will be my husband, the king in his splendor. He says no man deserves me but the king.

At night, he stops pouring wine. I stand in my chamber, in the dark. Then I have dreams. I dislike these dreams. My father does not know that I have them. They keep themselves secret from him, and this makes me unhappy. If I could speak, I would say: Father, I have had a terrible dream.

––––––

3. On the construction of vessels for bloodletting and washing

My father tells me that I will never bleed. I will always be perfectly clean. I am so happy to be clean and perfect! Human women bleed every month, he says. You could tell time from them, like clocks. It would be dreadful for me to bleed! I am made of plaster!

Father, I have had a terrible dream. I dreamt that I was a human woman and I was alone and I was bleeding. I curled on my side and bled. Outside the window, the world was all white, and I was bleeding a trickle the color of tobacco. Father, I was satisfied to be bleeding. There was pink paint on my fingernails and I was absorbed in picking it off. I burrowed deep in my sadness. I wanted more pain, more grief, delirium. Someone important had left me. Was it the king?

––––––

4. On the construction of fountains in tanks

I must have gone to sleep. When I woke, I noticed that the stain on the wall, so small as to be hardly noticeable under ordinary circumstances, was spreading. The more I looked at it, the larger it appeared. In fact, I was having trouble finding its edges. It was growing darker, too. I tried to remember who lived in the apartment next door. Yes, yes, the new tenant, the one with the tank on her head! She had a lung condition which required her to observe the world from within the shelter of a glass tank, like a fish. The tank looked uncomfortable and heavy. It was attached to her body with straps. She walked extremely slowly. She was apparently self-employed. The landlord said she would be no trouble, and someone else said it was nice that thanks to computers people like that could make a living without leaving the house.

I went out into the hall and knocked at her door. "Hello? Hello?" I didn't know her name. No one answered, but there was a sound from inside the room. The sound of running water. I noticed that some sort of gum had been placed around the edges of the door to seal it tight.

"Hello? Hello!"

"What is it?" came the new tenant's muffled, mechanical voice—a voice without resonance, a voice in a box.

"Are you all right?"

She laughed.

I rattled the doorknob. "Let me in!"

I turned sideways and struck the door with the force of my whole body.

"Jada!" I shouted. I knew now, I remembered. The field of ashes and then the tree, half blossoming and half burned, in the middle of the courtyard. We dragged her from the rubble. She whispered: "Water." Her swollen face. I could picture it now, behind glass, on the other side of the door.

———

5. On the construction of instruments for raising water from shallow pools

We ran across the field. My legs were wet. My lungs had shrunk. There was no sound now. We would not be able to hear well for several days. We would read one another's lips in the drifting ash, in the burned town, in the shadow of the single edifice left standing. This was the art museum. Its windows were gone. Burnt canvases littered the empty streets—we found one or two as far away as the canal. I went to the canal to fetch water for Jada. The water was the color of tobacco. She drank thirstily and whispered: "Thank you."

We had been artists. We said that we were going to be artists again. We called the tree in the courtyard "the Tree of Hope." "Tree of Hope, keep firm," Jada would say. Her voice a rustle, a sigh. When she got too tired, I carried her on my back. We collected the wrecked paintings and made a mosaic of them in the courtyard, held down with stones. That was before the recovery effort started. Once it started, we saw we wouldn't be able to keep our artwork. Jada stared at it all day, to memorize it. Nobody had a camera.

---

6. On the construction of an automaton representing two men drinking

It was my turn to keep watch, but I fell asleep against the courtyard wall. Fast asleep and dreaming with my eyes open.

I awake in a chair. The room all white. My arms outstretched. I am sleepy, heavy and smiling. Turning my head, I can see a man on either side. One on my left and one on my right. They are draining the blood from my wrists with needles. The dark stuff runs away through a pair of tubes.

Goodbye, blood! I feel no pain. On the contrary, I am quite happy. I gaze at my doctors with tenderness, first one and then the other. My ministers, administrators, ministering angels. One has a beard, the other a beautiful gold watch. One of them loves me, I know, and the other hates me, but their work is the same, and my love for them is absolutely equal. Desire for me unites them: this makes me the center of the world. I smile at my angels, who will drain me as dry as plaster.

They are talking. Arguing. "No!" I want to tell them. "Don't fight! Love one another!" But my tongue is too thick to move.

They have left their posts and stalked behind me. I can still hear their shouts. Now there's the sound of a struggle, the clatter of breaking glass! A moment later—silence.

I struggle to move my tongue. I am trying to say hello. Can you hear me saying hello?

A long stillness. Something seems to be pressing on my wrists. I am still calm, but it occurs to me that soon I will start to feel pain.

I cry out, wordless. A gurgling sound. Then I hear footsteps. Yes! Closer! Tap-tapping steps. A nurse in a white coat and headscarf comes into the room.

"Oh my God," she says.

She makes a few efficient movements at each of my wrists. My arms are numb. She brings them together and crosses them in my lap. She has covered my wrists with white tape. "Oh God oh God," she says, "my job, I can't lose my job, I can't lose another job."

I want to tell her that it's all right, that the universe is happy, but a strange feeling is coming back to me with the pain in my wrists and arms.

The nurse bends close. Her smell is sharp: terror and eau de cologne. "You have to move with me now," she whispers. "You have to help."

A feeling is coming back to me. It's not here yet; I'm searching for it. I stare at the nurse. Her face is tense, familiar. Something inside me breaks. I lift my arms and put them around her shoulders, and she heaves me out of the chair. Together, we stagger out into the hall.

What is the nature of things? The mechanism works perfectly for years; then one day it breaks.

The nurse half-carries me downstairs, to a dark basement. She shares her lunch with me for three days. She doesn't ask my name. She doesn't want to know anything, it's dangerous. We play the game of "asfoura" on her phone. She lets me win.

That's how it happens. One day something springs loose, and the clock stops. The clock is bleeding.

The nurse brings me a new set of clothes. Her eyes are red. She says it isn't safe for me to stay here anymore. She writes down an address and tells me to go there.

———

7. On the construction of miscellaneous objects

The nurse holds the back door open for me. "Run."

We'd started fighting, Jada and I. I said, "It's a recovery effort. It's an effort to recover. Can't you understand that?" She said, "What? Recover what? I don't want to recover, I don't want to go back." She said everything was going to be the same, it would be like it was before the struggle. I said that was ridiculous, the world had changed forever. "Everything's out in the open." "You think we're going to stay out in the open?" she asked. "I wouldn't mind going inside," I snapped. "A roof would be nice for a change."

I ran down the stairs and banged on the landlord's door. This is how you forget: first slowly, then quickly. First, you forget because you don't want to remember. You forget the war. You call it "the last war," because it's the most recent one, and then you call it "the last war" because you hope it's the last one, and then you don't call it anything, and they put new turf in the ravaged municipal gardens, and the water in the fountains runs clear. And this forgetting is so pleasant! And then you stop calling the people you knew, you forget their faces. And then you find you've forgotten her face. I banged on the landlord's door. "Help me! Help!" At last he opened it, sleepy and startled. His sleeve was damp. The ceiling was leaking.

Father, I have terrible dreams.

Father! Good morning, Father!

My father smiles at me, but he looks haggard. Poor Father!

I cannot look haggard, for my face is only painted.

He says we are going to visit the king today.

———

8. On the construction of an instrument that plays itself

I cannot see anything when my doors are closed, for my chamber has no windows. This is a pity, for I am sure the palace is splendid! My father carries me himself; he will not trust me to the apprentices. I find myself carried up into fragrant air. I hear delicate music and the plashing of fountains. This is the day! I am so nervous, I am thankful to be made of plaster and wire. These materials hide one's feelings much better than flesh. Father, for instance—poor man, I can feel his hands trembling.

His voice quivers, too, as he explains his invention to the king. "We pour the wine here..." And there it is, gurgling down into the tube. He fills the receptacle to the top. "Now wait, Your Majesty!" My cup grows heavy; I can hardly bear the excitement.

Full!

I roll down and open the door. There he is. The king. He is large, like Father, but younger, and dressed in gleaming white. He chuckles and takes the cup. I am dazzled by his robe, the windows, the sparkling floor, the brass lamps hanging on long chains.

The king drinks. "Hm!" he says.

My father makes a sound like a sob. Is he so happy?

No! For the king is turning yellow. He clutches his throat.

My father weeps and falls to his knees. The room erupts in noise. People run toward us. They cradle the king in their arms, they stroke his brow with fine cloths. As for my father, they bind his arms behind him and pull his beard. As they drag him away, he gives me one last, anguished glance.

"The king is dead! The king is dead!"

Wails clash in the air. The king's body is lifted gently and carried away. Now the room is empty, and there is no sound but the fragile clink of music issuing from a box across the room.

Father, Father!

My father has slain my husband and gone to prison.

How fortunate that I cannot cry. I would ruin my paint!

The room is quiet. Who will push me back into my chamber? Who will fill my roof receptacle with wine? Beneath the notes of music from the box, I can hear a roar from far below, the sound of frenzied crowds and fire. Smoke drifts in through the window. I cannot weep, but I am weeping. I remember a tree in a courtyard, half in bloom. The Tree of Hope. We called it the Tree of Hope. I remember the nurse in white, so tired, pressing banknotes into my hand.

I dreamt that I was a real woman and that I bled.

Weeping inside, I see a bright brass figure on top of the music box. A woman's torso. The box is meant to represent her skirt. She looks calm, resigned, familiar. Is she smiling?

I feel I must speak, if only in my mind. "Who are you?" I ask. Will she hear me?

She hears. I sense, rather than see, her deepening smile. She is not afraid of the noise downstairs. She has lived through fire in her dreams.

She says: "I am an instrument that plays itself."

20

Into the Wood

Sarah Read

I don't know whether it was Thea who changed the house or the house who changed Thea, but I noticed the house first. The way the woodgrain noticed us back—a thousand faces staring out from narrow panels that warped away from the cabin walls. And when the wind slammed the side of the house, the place would rock and rock and rock and boards would bob and nod. *Yes,* they said, *yes yes yes.* Though I hadn't been aware of asking any questions. Not at the time.

Thea stared, eyes wide as those wooden whorls, and nodded along. *Yes,* she nodded, "yes," she whispered. Her eyes as dead as the dark spots on the wood, which looked more like faces to me than any face I'd ever seen. You wouldn't have blamed me for thinking it was all a game. She was an odd child. Not quite odd enough to put me off her daddy, but odd enough that plenty before me had been. Brian says it's my compassion that keeps me with them both, but he's never been on the streets. I can tolerate an odd teen. I can tolerate walls that stare back at me, so long as those walls keep the warm in.

Desperation, I guess, looks a lot like compassion. Resignation looks like patience. You could say I gave an inch. Didn't know then how much a house could take. It's been too long since I've known a house at all.

———

There was a house. One that my mother ruled. My mother always loved birds best, which is why she called me after one, and why she kept me like one. My name is Cassidy Diana Dee. Cassi-dee-dee-dee, like the birds outside my window sang —the birds outside the cage.

Father flew when I was young, as soon as he knew that I would never know him, never see him for his face. He was always changing his coat, his beard—to me, he was never the same man twice. Always a stranger coming through the door, always a threat. I screamed every time I saw him, and eventually he stopped coming through the door altogether. Mama never forgave me. But Mama always wore the same coat, and the same broken expression—the twist of her mouth so familiar, I could almost recognize her, almost.

I fell from that nest before I could fly—landed in the dirt with the worms. I don't like to be touched, but a girl can make a living on the phone. Facsimile touch. A bird in the dirt can glut herself on worms, if she digs. And in the forest of city buildings, every tree has an abandoned nest. Somewhere to roost, if you can stand the cold.

I can't remember faces, not even dangerous ones, not even my own. But I know voices. The way a bird can recognize signals in song. I can tell Landon from Justin on the phone, remember what they like—how to keep them on the line or get them off quick if another call is coming in.

I'd set up someplace warm, where I could take my calls in

peace. Trevor's Tavern was best, where the man behind the bar was always Trevor, or at least always answered to the name. Where my face was as anonymous as everyone else's was to me. And when the phone was quiet, sometimes the drinks were free.

When I saw Brian come through the door of Trevor's, I knew he'd have a place, somewhere warm in the world. His coat was worn in a way that told me it was his only one; beard so long I knew he never trimmed it. I watched from the bar as I wrapped up my call, counting as the minutes on my burner phone ticked down. He sat, alone, with his hands as scruffed as old gloves wrapped around a big stack of keys. When he put his down coat around my shoulders at the end of the evening, I could feel their weight in the pocket against my hip, like a promise that there were sturdy doors to get behind. Heavy like an anchor, keeping me from flying away. It was his only coat, he said. I could always know him by it.

He told me about little Thea that night, before he even told me his whole name. The honest sort. I could probably have told him then that I had nowhere to go, but I didn't want to risk it. Nests with fledglings are often the most comfortable, and I'd been sleeping rough for weeks.

So instead I danced—we danced. I tolerated the touch and I told him with my body that I wanted to go with him. We drove out of the city, into the woods, to his log cabin. His nest.

The cabin was a bramble of stacked trees, the bark still clinging in flyaway curls to the outside. Inside, a deep and dirty carpet grabbed at my feet. The walls were lined with thin pressboard panels that pulled away from their glue and tacks as the house shifted and aged. A threadbare velvet sofa sagged in front of a television, and on it perched a girl with braids in her hair, her hands over her face as she peered at cartoons through her fingers.

I suspected Thea had been a deal-breaker for him in the past—that her name became a filter I had slipped through. A test I had passed. By the end of the week, when he wondered where else I was supposed to be, he was more than happy with my answer: "right here." I've never had any experience running a home. No nest management. Never had any good examples, either, but I've seen them on TV.

The teens on TV want expensive phones, clothes. They want to stay out late, to fly solo. Thea wanted these things, too, but had to settle for less. Brian had gotten her the phone, scavenged the clothes, but friends to stay out with are harder to find, if you're odd. I've always been good at working with less. I could do that, be a companion for her. What I couldn't do was sit and watch her bob her head in time with the nodding walls, when the wind kicked up and the walls shifted and the boards danced. Or hold her gaze when she turned, and her eyes were as flat as wood, skin grained with whorls and knots. The curls that Brian would braid and re-braid hanging in a tangle like Spanish moss from a winter tree. I couldn't stop her from standing or hold her back from the door. I couldn't touch the dry roughness of her skin.

And I couldn't bring myself to follow her when she walked from the cabin, out into the bending and whipping trees, shaking their branches *no no no.*

I couldn't see her through the dark, through the storm. And I couldn't call Brian. The wind had knocked the trees into the lines. All was down, and my burner phone had ticked all the way to empty. I could only wait in the dark and listen to the house. Learn its voice, learn its song. No light. No phones. Only the wind and me whispering, "she's gone," and the house answering *yes yes yes.*

But I'm still here?

Yes yes yes.

Storms here seal you up against the edge of the wood and no

light gets in. Not like the always-bright of the city. Brian came home early, but the dark made it seem late. It was too late, anyway.

"Thea! Thea! Thea!" He called all around the house, but the wind had blown over and the boards said nothing. Stillness. He found me staring out the back window, like an owl watching a bird feeder.

"Cass, where's Thea?"

"She went out."

"You let her go out in that storm? Where? Who with?"

He was mad. Was this our first fight? Our last? Would I sleep in the woods that night? Would Thea?

The boards were still.

"She just...left. I couldn't stop her."

"Who with?!"

"No one! She just walked out." *I think the walls told her to.* Maybe Thea had been the one asking questions all along.

He ran to the phone. Picked it up, slammed it down. It would be a while before the lines were repaired and the lights came on. Nothing happens quickly in the woods.

"Which way did she walk?"

I pointed to the line of swaying trees.

He swore. I hadn't heard him do that before—that was a new note to his song, and he started for the trees.

"Stay here in case she comes back." He called back to me.

I nodded. *Yes yes yes,* and the house nodded with me.

———

I sat in the living room and met each pair of grainy eyes in the walls till I found her. Undeniably Thea. The curve of her face there in the grain. A burred rent for a mouth. A face I hadn't seen there before—a face I would not have recognized if I'd seen it a thousand times in the flesh—right there in the wall, nodding more softly than the others. A face I saw and knew, here in her home.

————

Brian carried Thea out of the woods in his arms, as he must have carried her as a child. Her head bobbed against the crook of his arm as he crossed the weedy patch of meadow behind the trailer. He laid her on the couch, not far from her face in the wall—and that panel seemed to twist, to crane—to see what had become of her.

Her skin was raked with rashes. Striped and whorled. Her fingers twisted into knots and unfurled like roots searching for soft earth. I brought her water and she drank, and even the water that she spilled seemed to soak in. Brian rushed between her and the bathroom, where I could hear a tub filling. Could smell the clean steam. I wanted to crawl into that hot water and wash away the feeling of all those eyes on me, but it wasn't my bath. Not even my bathroom.

"Help me," Brian said.

We peeled off her damp clothes and clumps of soil fell to the carpet and disappeared into its pile. We carried her to the bathroom and placed her in that sudsy water. The rash had spread to the skin beneath her clothes. Her eyes were fixed wide, roving. Her skin hard and rough. She didn't even sigh when the warm water closed over her. She just lay in it. She said nothing. Brian whimpered.

The walls leaned in. The burred throat of Thea's wooden face twisted wider.

————

He took her to the hospital but left her face here in the wood with me.

I had the house to myself.

I took that bath. I took a nap. I took my time. I took and I took and it felt more like home by the hour.

I walked softly so the boards wouldn't sway. Only their eyes moved, tracing me into the lines of the house.

I pinned a pillowcase over Thea's face. Didn't want to feel those eyes on me, following me, or see that twisting mouth. If I pressed my ear up against that sheet, to the place where the sharp edges of the wood split, I could hear her. Sigh or wind. Scream or gale. I never mistake a voice. But all she could say anymore was "yes," because that was how she was tacked down.

Tacked to the house like a specimen in a case. My heart pinched for her, then.

I took pliers from the case under the eaves. It was hard to find the small dark pins in that maze of woodgrain, but I found them and I pulled and pulled till the board came away. There was filthy paper and plaster and mildew behind where it had been pressed to the wall. Brown flecks of dried glue and the watermarks of the house's own perspiration. The fine veneer was adhered to a sheet of old vinyl as yellowed and brittle as old taffy.

I washed the board in the bath, cleaned away the dust and debris. Smoothed out the splinters. Let the dry panel soak life-giving water deep into its processed pulp. I tucked the board into Thea's bed, but still the whorl eyes gaped.

I pulled the blanket over that wooden face, and something heavy fell from the folds of the quilt. Her phone. Not like my burner, but bright, endless.

With the landlines down and my phone on empty, I couldn't work. No Landon or Justin—no income. My nest egg diminishing. But these expensive phones, they have ways of working when other things don't. I could work from anywhere, with this. Anytime. I navigated to my profile and updated the number to Thea's. And I was back to work in minutes, sighing, cooing, facsimile affection.

I wondered what the faces on the walls saw—the sounds of a show with no pictures, no images, just as they are only pictures that make no sound. The way I see faces, when they aren't the wooden kind.

———

The keys let someone in the door—it must be Brian—and I squeezed my eyes shut until he murmured for me, and I knew his voice.

I squeezed the button that sent Thea's phone to sleep, to silence, and its black screen gaped like the open wooden mouths.

He moved like a ghost through the house, pulling a bag from the closet and filling it with Thea's clothes. He didn't see the board tucked under the blanket, didn't see the face of his daughter frozen there in a silent scream. He didn't notice the one board missing from the peeling walls. The other faces nodded on and on as he walked back and forth, creating drafts, compressing the floor and letting it up again and setting all those loose faces in motion. I wondered if there were more faces beneath his feet. Under the carpet. Their open mouths pressed against our soles, trying to chew their way through.

He shook his stack of keys free from his pocket. He told me to make myself comfortable, to make myself at home. I promised I would. I said it standing in his kitchen, in his slippers, with the taste of his coffee coating my tongue. He asked me to watch the house. Though this house can watch itself.

He left again.

I made myself a meal, made a mess, made myself at home. Made myself *a* home. I watched the house and the house watched me.

———

Brian was back again in the night. I stirred from my nest of blankets on the couch. It was dark, the lights still off, but I knew him by his breathing, by the tension in his inhale.

"Cass?"

"I'm here."

"Help me with her. Help me get her into bed."

I raced to her room and slipped her face beneath her pillow, the thin wood fibers still soft with wet. I knew my running must have sent all those faces bobbing agreement, knew that they approved, but I couldn't see them in the dark. I hurried back, imagined another frantic wave of yesses, and I took some of the burden of Thea's body from Brian's arms. We folded the child into her bed, tucked the down around her, safe and warm.

Brian felt his way from furniture to furniture. Even he seemed to know not to run his fingers along the wall. He made his way to the kitchen, where he pulled a big flashlight down from the top of the fridge. I hadn't known one was there. Now I do. Soon I'll know the place for everything.

He checked the batteries and turned toward the back door. "The doctor wants me to look in the woods around where I found her. See if she might have eaten any toxic plants."

The wind had picked up again. In the light from the flashlight, I could see the walls nodding in agreement.

Yes yes yes go into the wood.

"Will you keep an eye on Thea for me? Watch her till I get back?" I nodded, *yes yes yes.*

I perched, watching, at that same window as he disappeared, and then so did his light.

And his face watched me, over my shoulder, nodding and smiling himself away.

I lit one of the small candles on the mantle. I took another bath, another nap. Took the pliers and took Brian's face down from the wall. I bathed board Brian, his coy smile writ plain as day in the grain. I sat him in the chair by Thea's bed. He could watch her, now, always.

I pulled board Thea from beneath the pillow and I took the hammer from the case under the eaves. I gathered the old, dark pins from the corners of the carpet pile. I tacked her face back to where it should be. The pliable, wet wood shaped to her skull, to the curve of her nose and the hollow of her eyes, and the tacks held it in place. And for the first time in my life, I recognized a person there in front of me. It was her, and I'd know her when I saw her. I could see her even without her voice, written in the wood.

I stared, in awe of the convenience of recognition. And as the wood dried, it twisted, and her face twisted with it. Her, but warped. Her mouth too, too wide, her eyes not where they should be, but hers. And as he dried, board Brian curled and collapsed, with no skull to hold his shape, no body to hold him up. He twisted into a curl of himself, thin wood fibers bristling like pinfeathers.

They had no roots here, anymore, to hold them. You need to put down roots to build a home, and they had none—just drifting curls of wood silently screaming. I know that song.

I have a home now. A house. All you need to do to make a home is get inside the walls and stay out of the wood. Put down your roots. Keep the door locked and wake up to bird song, until it's time to fly again. Yes, *yes*, I'll fly again, when the nest gets brittle, as soon as I let go of this anchor of keys.

21

You Go Where It Takes You

Nathan Ballingrud

He did not look like a man who would change her life. He was big, roped with muscles from working on offshore oil rigs, and tending to fat. His face was broad and inoffensively ugly, as though he had spent a lifetime taking blows and delivering them. He wore a brown raincoat against the light morning drizzle and against the threat of something more powerful held in abeyance. He breathed heavily, moved slowly, found a booth by the window overlooking the water, and collapsed into it. He picked up a syrup-smeared menu and studied it with his whole attention, like a student deciphering Middle English. He was like every man who ever walked into that diner. He did not look like a beginning or an end.

———

That day, the Gulf of Mexico and all the earth was blue and still. The little town of Port Fourchon clung like a barnacle to

Louisiana's southern coast, and behind it the water stretched into the distance for as many miles as the eye could hold. Hidden by distance were the oil rigs and the workers who supplied the town with its economy. At night she could see their lights, ringing the horizon like candles in a vestibule. Toni's morning shift was nearing its end; the dining area was nearly empty. She liked to spend those slow hours out on the diner's balcony, overlooking the water.

Her thoughts were troubled by the phone call she had received that morning. Gwen, her three-year-old daughter, was offering increasing resistance to the male staffers at Daylight Daycare, resorting lately to biting them or kicking them in the ribs when they knelt to calm her. Only days before, Toni had been waylaid there by a lurking social worker who talked to her in a gentle, saccharine voice, who touched her hand maddeningly and said, "No one is judging you; we just want to help." The social worker had mentioned the word "psychologist," and asked about their home life. Toni had been embarrassed and enraged and was only able to conclude the interview with a mumbled promise to schedule another one soon. That her daughter was already displaying such grievous signs of social ineptitude stunned Toni, left her feeling hopeless and betrayed.

It also made her think about Donny again, who abandoned her years ago to move to New Orleans, leaving her a single mother at twenty-three. She wished death on him that morning, staring over the railing at the unrelenting progression of waves. She willed it along the miles and into his heart.

———

"You know what you want?" she asked.

"Um ... just coffee." He looked at her breasts and then at her eyes.

"Cream and sugar?"

"No thanks. Just coffee."

"Suit yourself."

The only other customer in the diner was Crazy Claude by the door, speaking conversationally to a cooling plate of scrambled eggs and listening to his radio through his earphones. A tinny roar leaked out around his ears. Pedro, the short order cook, lounged behind the counter, his big round body encased in layers of soiled white clothing, enthralled by a guitar magazine which he had spread out by the cash register. The kitchen slumbered behind him, exuding a thick fug of onions and burnt frying oil. It would stay mostly dormant until the middle of the week, when the shifts would change on the rigs, and tides of men would ebb and flow through the small town.

So when she brought the coffee back to the man, she thought nothing of it when he asked her to join him. She fetched herself a cup of coffee as well and then sat across from him in the booth, grateful to transfer the weight from her feet.

"You ain't got no nametag," he said.

"Oh ... I guess I lost it somewhere. My name's Toni."

"That's real pretty."

She gave a quick derisive laugh. "The hell it is. It's short for Antoinette."

He held out his hand and said, "I'm Alex."

She took it and they shook. "You work offshore, Alex?"

"Some. I ain't been out there for a while, though." He smiled and gazed into the murk of his coffee. "I've been doing a lot of driving around."

Toni shook loose a cigarette from her pack and lit it. She lied and said, "Sounds exciting."

"I don't guess it is, though. But I bet this place could be, sometimes. I bet you see all kinds of people come through here."

"Well ... I guess so."

"How long you been here?"

"About three years."

"You like it?"

A flare of anger. "Yeah, Alex, I fucking love it. Who wouldn't?"

"Oh, hey, all right." He held up his hands. "I'm sorry."

She shook her head. "No. I'm sorry. I just got a lot on my mind today I guess. This place is fine."

He cocked a half smile. "So why don't you come out with me after work? Maybe I can help distract you." His thick hands were on the table between them. They looked like they could break rocks.

Toni smiled at him. "You known me for what. Five minutes?"

"What can I say. I'm an impulsive guy. Caution to the wind!" He drained his cup in two swallows, as though to illustrate his recklessness.

"Well, let me go get you some more coffee, Danger Man." She patted his hand as she rose.

———

It was reckless impulse that brought Donny back to her, briefly, just over a year ago. After a series of phone calls that progressed from petulant to playful to newly curious, he drove back down to Port Fourchon in his disintegrating blue Pinto one Friday afternoon to spend a weekend with them. It was nice at first, though there was no talk of what might happen after Sunday.

Gwen had just started going to daycare. Stunned by the vertiginous growth of the world, she was beset by huge emotions; varieties of rage passed through her little body like weather systems, and no amount of coddling from Toni would settle her.

Although he wouldn't admit it, Toni knew Donny was curious about the baby, that his vanity was satisfied by the knowledge that she would grow to reflect many of his own features and behaviors.

But Gwen refused to participate in generating any kind of mystique that might keep him landed here, revealing herself instead as what Toni knew her to be: a pink, pudgy little assemblage of flesh and ferocity that giggled or raved seemingly without discrimination, that walked without grace and appeared to lack any qualities of beauty or intelligence whatsoever. But the sex with Donny was as good as it had ever been, and he didn't seem to mind the baby too much. When he talked about calling in sick to work on Monday, she began to hope for something lasting.

Early Sunday afternoon, they decided to put Gwen to bed early and free up the evening for themselves. First she had to have a bath, and Donny assumed that responsibility with the air of a man handling nitroglycerin. He filled the tub with eight inches of water and plunked her in, then sat back and stared as, with furrowed brow, she went about the serious business of dropping the shampoo bottles into the water with her. Toni sat on the toilet seat behind him, and it occurred to her that this was her family. She felt buoyant, sated.

Then Gwen rose abruptly from the water and clapped her hands joyously. "Two! Two poops! One, two!"

Aghast, Toni saw two little turds sitting on the bottom of the tub, rolling slightly in the currents generated by Gwen's capering feet. Donny's hand shot out and cuffed his daughter on the side of her head. She fell against the wall and bounced into the water with a terrific splash. And then she screamed: the most godawful sound Toni had ever heard in her life.

Toni stared at him, agape. She could not summon the will to move. The baby, sitting on her butt in the soiled water, filled the tiny bathroom with a sound like a bomb siren, and she just wanted her to shut up, shut up, just shut the fuck up.

"Shut up, goddamnit! Shut up!"

Donny looked at her, his face an unreadable mess of

confused emotion; he got to his feet and pushed roughly past her. Soon she heard the sound of a door closing. His car started up, and he was gone. She stared at her stricken daughter and tried to quiet the sudden stampeding fury.

———

She refilled Alex's cup and sat down with him, leaving the pot on the table. She retrieved her cigarette from the ashtray only to discover that it has expired in her absence. "Well, shit," she said.

Alex nodded agreeably. "I'm on the run," he said.

"What?"

"It's true. I'm on the run. I stole a car."

Alarmed, Toni looked out the window, but the parking lot was on the other side of the diner. All she could see from here was the Gulf.

"Why are you telling me this? I don't want to know this."

"It's a station wagon. I can't believe it even runs anymore. I was in Morgan City, and I had to get out fast. The car was right there. I took it."

He had a manic look in his eye, and although he was smiling, he seemed agitated; his fingers tapped the table, the cords in his hands standing out like pipe. She felt a growing disquiet coupled with a mounting excitement. He was dangerous, this man. He was a falling hammer.

"I don't think that guy over there likes me," he said.

"What?" She turned and saw Crazy Claude in stasis, staring at Alex. His jaw was cantilevered in mid-chew. "That's just Claude," she said. "He's all right."

Alex was still smiling, but it had taken on a different character, one she couldn't place, and which set loose a strange, giddy feeling inside her. "No, I think it's me. He keeps looking over here."

"Really, Claude's okay. He's harmless as a kitten."

"I want to show you something." Alex reached inside his raincoat, and for a moment Toni thought he was going to pull out a gun and start shooting. She felt no inclination to move, though; she waited for what would come. Instead, he withdrew a crumpled Panama hat. It had been considerably crushed to fit into his pocket, and once freed it began to unfold itself, like something blooming.

She looked at it. "It's a hat," she said.

He stared at it like he expected it to lurch across the table with some hideous agenda. "That's an object of terrible power," he said.

"Alex -- it's a hat. It's a thing you put on your head."

"It belongs to the man I stole the car from. Here," he said, pushing it across to her. "Put it on."

She did. She was growing tired of the serious turn he seemed to have taken and decided to be a little playful. She turned her chin to her shoulder and pouted her lips, looking at him out of the corner of her eye, like she thought a model might.

He smiled. "Who are you?"

"I'm a supermodel."

"What's your name? Where are you from?"

She affected a light, breathy voice. "My name is Violet, I'm from L.A., and I'm strutting down a catwalk wearing this hat and nothing else. Everybody loves me and is taking my picture."

They laughed, and he was leaning over the table at her. She could see the tip of his tongue between his teeth. He just watched her for a second. "See? It's powerful. You can be anybody."

She gave the hat back.

"You know," Alex said, "the guy I stole the car from was something of a thief himself, it turns out. You should see what he left in there."

"Why don't you show me?"

He smiled again, and glanced at the nearly empty diner. "Now?"

"No. In half an hour. When I get off work."

"But it's all packed up. I don't let that stuff just fly around loose."

"Then you can show me at my place."

And so it was decided. She got up and went about preparing for the next shift, which consisted of restocking a few ketchup packets and starting a fresh pot of coffee. She refilled Crazy Claude's cup and gave him another ten packets of sugar, all of which he methodically opened and dumped into his drink. When her relief arrived, Toni hung her apron by the waitress station and collected Alex on her way to the door.

"We have to stop by the daycare and pick up my kid," she said.

If this news fazed him, he didn't show it.

As they passed Claude's table, they heard a distant, raucous sound coming from his earphones.

Alex curled his lip. "Idiot. How does he hear himself think?"

"He doesn't. That's the point. He hears voices in his head. He plays the radio loud so he can drown them out."

"You're kidding me."

"Nope."

Alex stopped and turned around, regarding the back of Claude's head with renewed interest. "How many people does he have in there?"

"I never asked."

"Well, holy shit."

Outside, the sun was setting, the day beginning to cool down. The rain had stopped at some point, and the world glowed with a bright, wet sheen. They decided that he would follow her in his car. It was a rusty old battle wagon from the

Seventies; several boxes were piled in the back. She paid them no attention.

———

She knew, when they stepped into her little apartment, that they would wind up making love, and she found herself wondering what it would be like. She watched him move, noted the graceful articulation of his body, the careful restraint he displayed in her living room, which was filled with fragile things. She saw the skin beneath his clothing, watched it stretch and move.

"Don't worry," she said, touching the place between his shoulder blades. "You won't break nothing."

About Gwen there was more doubt. Unleashed like a darting fish into the apartment, she was gone with a bright squeal, away from the strange new man around whom she had been so quiet and doleful, into the dark grottoes of her home.

"It's real pretty," Alex said.

"A bunch a knickknacks mostly. Nothing special."

He shook his head like he did not believe it. Her apartment was decorated mostly with the inherited flotsam of her grandmother's life: bland wall hangings, beaten old furniture which had hosted too many bodies spreading gracelessly into old age, and a vast and silly collection of glass figurines: leaping dolphins and sleeping dragons and such. It was all meant to be homey and reassuring, but it just reminded her of how far away she was from the life she really wanted. It seemed like a desperate construct, and she hated it very much.

For now, Alex made no mention of the objects in his car or the hat in his pocket. He appeared to be more interested in Gwen, who was peering around the corner of the living room and regarding him with a suspicious and hungry eye, who seemed to intuit that from this large alien figure on her mama's couch would come mighty upheavals.

———

He was a man -- that much Gwen knew immediately -- and therefore a dangerous creature. He would make her mama behave unnaturally, maybe even cry. He was too big, like the giant in her storybook. She wondered if he ate children. Or mamas.

Mama was sitting next to him.

"Come here, Mama." She slapped her thigh like Mama did when she wanted Gwen to pay attention to her. Maybe she could lure Mama away from the giant, and they could wait in the closet until he got bored and went away. "Come here, Mama, come here."

"Go on and play now, Gwen."

"No! Come here!"

"She don't do too well around men," said Mama.

"That's okay," said the giant. "These days I don't either." He patted the cushion next to him. "Come over here, baby. Let me say hi."

Gwen, alarmed at this turn of events, retreated a step behind a corner. They were in the living room, which had her bed in it, and her toys. Behind her, Mama's darkened room yawned like a throat. She sat between the two places, wrapped her arms around her knees, and waited.

———

"She's so afraid," Alex said after she retreated from view. "You know why?"

"Um, because you're big and scary?"

"Because she already knows about possibilities. Long as

you know there are options in life, you get scared of choosing the wrong one."

Toni leaned away from him and gave him a mistrustful smile. "Okay, Einstein. Easy with the philosophy."

"No, really. She's like a thousand different people right now, all waiting to be, and every time she makes a choice, one of those peoples goes away forever. Until finally you run out of choices and you are whoever you are. She's afraid of what she'll lose by coming out to see me. Of who she'll never get to be."

Toni thought of her daughter and saw nothing but a series of shut doors. "Are you

drunk?"

"What? You know I ain't drunk."

"Stop talking like you are, then. I've had enough of that shit to last me my whole life."

"Jesus, I'm sorry."

"Forget it." Toni got up and rounded the corner to scoop up her daughter. "I got to bathe her and put her to bed. If you want to wait, it's up to you."

She carried Gwen into the bathroom and began the nightly ministrations. She felt Donny's presence too strongly tonight, and Alex's sophomoric philosophizing sounded just like him when he'd had too many beers. She found herself halfway hoping that the obligations of motherhood would bore Alex, and that he would leave. She listened for the sound of the front door.

Instead, she heard footsteps behind her and felt his heavy hand on her shoulder. It squeezed her gently, and his big body settled down beside her. He said something kind to Gwen and brushed a strand of wet hair from her eyes. Toni felt something move slowly in her chest, subtly yet with powerful effect, like Atlas rolling a shoulder.

Gwen suddenly shrieked and collapsed into the water, sending a surge of water over them both. Alex reached in to stop her from knocking her head against the porcelain and received a kick in the mouth for his troubles. Toni shouldered him aside and jerked her out of the tub. She hugged her daughter tightly to her chest and whispered motherly incantations into her ear. After a brief struggle, Gwen finally settled into her mother's embrace and whimpered quietly, turning her whole focus onto the warm, familiar hand rubbing her back, up and down, up and down, until, finally, her energy flagged, and she drifted into a tentative sleep.

When Gwen was dressed and in her bed, Toni turned her attention to Alex. "Here, let's clean you up."

She steered him back into the bathroom. She opened the shower curtain and pointed to the soap and the shampoo and said, "It smells kind of flowery, but it gets the job done," and the whole time he was looking at her, and she thought: So this is it; this is how it happens.

"Help me," he said, lifting his arms over his head. She smiled wanly and began to undress him. She watched his body as she unwrapped it, and when he was naked, she pressed herself against him and ran her fingers down his back.

———

Later, when they were in bed together, she said, "I'm sorry about tonight."

"She's just a kid."

"No, I mean about snapping at you. I don't know why I did."

"It's okay."

"I just don't like to think about what could have been. There's no point to it. Sometimes I think a person doesn't have much to say about what happens to them anyway."

"I really don't know."

She stared out the little window across from the bed and

watched slate gray clouds skim across the sky. Behind them were the stars.

"Ain't you gonna tell me why you stole a car?"

"I had to."

"But why?"

He was silent for a little while. "It don't matter," he said.

"If you don't tell me, it makes me think you mighta killed somebody."

"Maybe I did."

She thought about that for a minute. It was too dark to see anything in the bedroom, but she scanned her eyes across it anyway, knowing the location of every piece of furniture, every worn tube of lipstick and leaning stack of lifestyle magazines. She could see through the walls and feel the sagging weight of the figurines on the shelves. She tried to envision each one in turn, as though searching for one that would act as a talisman against this subject and the weird

celebration it raised in her.

"Did you hate him?"

"I don't hate anybody," he said. "I wish I did. I wish I had it in me."

"Come on, Alex. You're in my house. You got to tell me something."

After a long moment, he said, "The guy I stole the car from. I call him Mr. Gray. I never saw him, except in dreams. I don't know anything about him, really. But I don't think he's human. And I know he's after me."

"What do you mean?"

"I have to show you." Without another word, he got to his feet and pulled on his jeans. She could sense a mounting excitement in his demeanor, and it inspired a similar feeling in herself. She followed him out of her bedroom, pulling a long t-shirt over her head as she went.

Gwen slept deeply in the living room; they stepped over her mattress on the way out. The grass was wet under their bare feet, the air heavy with the salty smell of the sea. Alex's car was parked at the curb, hugging the ground like a great beetle. He opened the rear hatch and pulled the closest box toward them.

"Look," he said, and opened the box.

At first, Toni could not comprehend what she was seeing. She thought it was a cat lying on a stack of tan leather jackets, but that wasn't right, and only when Alex grabbed a handful of the cat and pulled it out did she realize that it was human hair. Alex lifted the whole object out of the box, and she found herself staring at the tanned and cured hide of a human being, dark empty holes in its face like some rubber Halloween mask.

"I call this one Willie, 'cause he's so well hung," said Alex, and offered and absurd laugh.

Toni fell back a step.

"But there's women in here too, all kinds of people. I counted ninety-six. All carefully folded." He offered the skin to Toni, but when she made no move to touch it, he started to fold it up again. "I guess there ain't no reason to see them all. You get the idea."

"Alex, I want to go back inside."

"Okay, just hang on a second."

She waited while he closed the lid of the box and slid it back into place. With the hide tucked under one arm, he shut the hatch, locked it, and turned to face her. He was grinning, bouncing on the balls of his feet. "Okeydokey," he said, and they headed back indoors.

They returned quietly to the bedroom, stepping softly to avoid waking Gwen.

"Did you kill all those people?" Toni asked when the door was closed.

"What? Didn't you hear me? I stole a car. That's what was in it."

"Mr. Gray's car."

"That's right."

"Who is he? What are they for?" she asked; but she already knew what they were for.

"They're alternatives," he said. "They're so you can be somebody else."

She thought about that. "Have you worn any of them?"

"One. I haven't got up the balls to do it again yet." He reached into the front pocket of his jeans and withdrew a leather sheath. From it he pulled a small, ugly little knife that looked like an eagle's talon. "You got to take off the one you're wearing, first. It hurts."

Toni swallowed. The sound was thunderous in her ears. "Where's your first skin? The one you was born with?"

Alex shrugged. "I threw that one out. I ain't like Mr. Gray, I don't know how to preserve them. Besides, what do I want to keep it for? I must not have liked it to too much in the first place, right?"

She felt a tear accumulate in the corner of her eye and willed it not to fall. She was afraid and exhilarated. "Are you going to take mine?"

Alex looked startled, then seemed to remember he was holding the knife. He put it back in its sheath. "I told you, baby, I'm not the one who killed those people. I don't need any more than what's already there." She nodded, and the tear streaked down her face. He touched it away with the back of his fingers. "Hey now," he said.

She grabbed his hand. "Where's mine?" She gestured at the skin folded beside him. "I want one, too. I want to come with you."

"Oh, Jesus, no, Toni. You can't."

"But why not? Why can't I go?"

"Come on now, you got a family here."

"It's just me and her. That ain't no family."

"You have a little girl, Toni. What's wrong with you? That's your life now." He stepped out of his pants and, naked, pulled the knife from its sheath. "I can't argue about this. I'm going now. I'm gonna change first, though, so you might not want to watch." She made no move to leave. He paused, considering something. "I got to ask you something," he said. "I been wondering about this lately. Do you think it's possible for something beautiful to come out of an awful thing? Do you think a good life can redeem a horrible act?"

"Of course I do," she said quickly, sensing some second chance here, if only she said the right words. "Yes."

Alex touched the blade to his scalp just above his right ear and drew it in an arc over the crown of his head until it reached his left ear. Bright red blood crept down from his hairline in a slow tide, sending rivulets and tributaries along his jaw and his throat, hanging from his eyelashes like raindrops from flower petals. "God, I really hope so," he said. He worked his fingers into the incision and began to tug violently.

Watching the skin fall away from him, she was reminded of nothing so much as a butterfly struggling into daylight.

———

She is driving west on I-10. The morning sun, which has just breached the horizon, flares in her rearview mirror. Port Fourchon is far behind her, and the Texas border looms. Beside her, Gwen is sitting on the floor of the passenger seat, playing with the Panama hat Alex left behind when he drove North. Toni has never seen the need for a car seat. Gwen is happier moving about on her own, and in times like this, when Toni feels a slow, crawling anger in her blood, the last thing she needs is a temper tantrum from her daughter.

After he left, she was faced with a few options. She could put on her stupid pink uniform, take Gwen to daycare, and go back to work. She could drive up to New Orleans and find Donny. Or she could say fuck it all and just get in the car and drive, aimlessly and free of expectation, which is what she is doing.

She cries for the first dozen miles or so, and it is such a luxury that she just lets it come, feeling no guilt.

Gwen, still feeling the dregs of sleep and as yet undecided whether to be cranky for being awakened early or excited by the trip, pats her on the leg. "You okay, Mama, you okay?"

"Yes, baby. Mama's okay."

Toni sees the sign she has been looking for coming up on the side of the road. Rest Stop, 2 miles.

When they get there, she pulls in, coming to a stop in an empty lot. Gwen climbs up in the seat and peers out the window. She sees the warm red glow of a Coke machine and decides that she will be happy today, that waking up early means excitement and the possibility of treats. "Have the Coke, Mama? Have it, have the Coke?"

"Okay, sweetie."

They get out and walk up to the Coke machine. Gwen laughs happily and slaps it several times, listening to the distant dull echo inside. Toni puts in some coins and grabs the tumbling can. She cracks it open and gives it to her daughter, who takes it delightedly.

"Coke!"

"That's right." Toni kneels beside her as Gwen takes several ambitious swigs. "Gwen? Honey? Mama's got to go potty, okay? You stay right here, okay? Mama will be right back."

Gwen lowers the can, a little overwhelmed by the cold blast of carbonation, and nods her head. "Right back!"

"That's right, baby."

Toni starts away. Gwen watches her mama as she heads back to the car and climbs in. She shuts the door and starts the engine. Gwen takes another drink of Coke. The car pulls away from the curb, and she feels a bright stab of fear. But

Mama said she was coming right back, so she will wait right here.

Toni turns the wheel and speeds back out onto the high-way. There is no traffic in sight. The sign welcoming her to Texas flashes by and is gone. She presses the accelerator. Her heart is beating.

22

The Pyramid of Amirah

James Patrick Kelly

Sometimes Amirah thinks she can sense the weight of the pyramid that entombs her house. The huge limestone blocks seem to crush the air and squeeze light. When she carries the table lamp onto the porch and holds it up to the blank stone, shadows ooze across the rough-cut inner face. If she is in the right mood, they make cars and squirrels and flowers and Mom's face.

Time passes.

Amirah will never see the outside of her pyramid, but she likes to imagine different looks for it. It's like trying on new jeans. They said that the limestone would be cased in some kind of marble they called Rosa Portogallo. She hopes it will be like Betty's pyramid, red as sunset, glossy as her fingernails. Are they setting it yet? Amirah thinks not. She can still hear the dull, distant *chock* as the believers lower each structural stone into place—twenty a day. Dust wisps from the cracks between the stones and settles through the thick air onto every horizontal surface of her house: the floor, Dad's desk, windowsills, and the tops of the kitchen cabinets. Amirah doesn't mind; she goes over the entire house periodically with vacuum and rag. She wants to be ready when the meaning comes.

Time passes.

The only thing she really misses is the sun. Well, that isn't true. She misses her mom and her dad and her friends on the swim team, especially Janet. She and Janet offered themselves to the meaning at Blessed Finger Sanctuary on Janet's twelfth birthday. Neither of them expected to be chosen pyramid girl. They thought maybe they would be throwing flowers off a float in the Monkey Day parade or collecting door to door for the Lost Brothers. Janet shrieked with joy and hugged her when Mrs. Munro told them the news. If her friend hadn't held her up, Amirah might have collapsed.

Amirah keeps all the lights on, even when she goes to bed. She knows this is a waste of electricity, but it's easier to be brave when the house is bright. Besides, there is nobody to scold her now.

"Is anyone there?" Amirah says, and then she walks into the kitchen to listen. Sometimes the house makes whispery noises when she talks to it. "Is there anyone here who cares what I do?" Her voice sounds like the hinges of the basement door.

Time passes.

They took all the clocks, and she has lost track of day and night. She sleeps when she is tired and eats when she is hungry. That's all there is to do, except wait for the meaning to come. Mom and Dad's bedroom is filled to the ceiling with cartons of Goody-goody bars: Nut Raisin, Cherry Date, Chocolate Banana, and Cinnamon Apple, which is not her favorite. Mrs. Munro said there were enough to last her for years. At first that was a comfort. Now Amirah tries not to think about it.

Time passes.

Amirah's pyramid is the first in the Tri-City area. They said it would be twenty meters tall. She had worked it out afterwards that twenty meters was almost seventy feet. Mom said that if the meaning had first come to Memphis, Tennessee instead of Memphis, Egypt, then maybe everything would have been in American instead of metric. Dad had laughed at that and said then Elvis would have been the First Brother. Mom didn't like him making fun of the meaning. If she wanted to laugh, she would have him tell one of the Holy Jokes.

"What's the first law of religion?" Amirah says in her best imitation of Dad's voice.

"For every religion, there exists an equal and opposite religion," she says in Mom's voice.

"What's the second law of religion?" says Dad's voice.

"They're both wrong." Mom always laughs at that.

The silence goes all breathy, like Amirah is holding seashells up to both ears. "I don't get it," she says.

She can't hear building sounds anymore. The dust has stopped falling.

Time passes.

When Amirah was seven, her parents took her to Boston to visit Betty's pyramid. The bus driver said that the believers had torn down a hundred and fifty houses to make room for it. Amirah could feel Betty long before she could see her pyramid; Mom said the meaning was very strong in Boston.

Amirah didn't understand much about the meaning back then. While the bus was stopped at a light, she had a vision of her heart swelling up inside her like a balloon and lifting her out the window and into the bluest part of the sky where she could see everything there was to see. The whole bus was feeling Betty by then. Dad told the Holy Joke about the chicken and the *Bible* in a loud voice and soon everyone was laughing so hard that the bus driver had to pull over. She and

Mom and Dad walked the last three blocks and the way Amirah remembered it, her feet only touched the ground a couple of times. The pyramid was huge in a way that no skyscraper could ever be. She heard Dad tell Mom it was more like geography than architecture. Amirah was going to ask him what that meant, only she realized that *she* knew because *Betty* knew. The marble of Betty's pyramid was incredibly smooth, but it was cold to the touch. Amirah spread the fingers of both hands against it and thought very hard about Betty.

"Are you there, Betty?" Amirah sits up in bed. "What's it like?" All the lights are on in the house. "Betty?" Amirah can't sleep because her stomach hurts. She gets up and goes to the bathroom to pee. When she wipes herself, there in a pinkish stain on the toilet paper.

Time passes.

Amirah also misses Juicy Fruit gum and Onion Taste Tots and 3DV and music. She hasn't seen her shows since Dad shut the door behind him and led Mom down the front walk. Neither of them looked back, but she thought Mom might have been crying. Did Mom have doubts? This still bothers Amirah. She wonders what Janet is listening to these days on her earstone. Have the Stiffies released any new songs? When Amirah sings, she practically has to scream or else the pyramid swallows her voice.

"Go, go away, go-go away from me.

Had fun, we're done, whyo-why can't you see?"

Whenever she finishes a Goody-goody bar, she throws the wrapper out the front door. The walk has long since been covered. In the darkness, the wrappers look like fallen leaves.

Time passes.

Both Janet and Amirah had been trying to get Han Biletnikov to notice them before Amirah became pyramid girl. Han had wiry, red hair and freckles and played midfield on the soccer team. He was the first boy in their school to wear his pants inside out. On her last day in school, there had been an assembly in her honor, and Han had come to the stage and told a Holy Joke about her.

Amirah cups her hands to make her voice sound like it's coming out of a microphone. "What did Amirah say to the guy at the hot dog stand?"

She twists her head to one side to give the audience response. "I don't know, what?"

Han speaks again into the microphone. "Make me one with everything."

She can see him now, even though she is sitting at the kitchen table with a glass of water and an unopened Cherry Date Goody-goody bar in front of her. His cheeks are flushed as she strides across the stage to him. He isn't expecting her to do this. The believers go quiet as if someone has thrown a blanket over them. She holds out her hand to shake his, and he stares at it. When their eyes finally meet, she can see his awe; she's turned into President Huong, or maybe Billy Tiger, the forward for the Boston Flash. His hand is warm, a little sweaty. Her fingertips brush the hollow of his palm.

"Thank you," says Amirah.

Han doesn't say anything. He isn't there. Amirah unwraps the Goody-goody bar.

Time passes.

Amirah never gets used to having her period. She thinks she isn't doing it right. Mom never told her how it worked and she didn't leave pads or tampons or anything. Amirah wads toilet paper into her panties, which makes her feel like she's walking around with a sofa cushion between her legs. The menstrual blood smells like vinegar. She takes a lot of baths. Sometimes she touches herself as the water cools, and then she feels better for a while.

Time passes.

Amirah wants to imagine herself kissing Han Biletnikov, but she can't. She keeps seeing Janet's lips on his, her tongue darting into his mouth. At least, that's how Janet said people kiss. She wonders if she would have better luck if she weren't in the kitchen. She climbs the stairs to her bedroom and opens the door. It's dark. The light has burned out. She pulls down the diffuser and unscrews the bulb. It's clear and about the size of a walnut. It says:

"Whose lifetime?" she says. The pile of Goody-goody wrappers on the front walk is taller than Dad. Amirah tries to think where there might be extra light bulbs. She pulls the entire house apart looking for them, but she doesn't cry.

Time passes.

Amirah is practicing living in the dark. Well, it isn't entirely dark; she has left a light on in the hallway. But she is in the living room, staring out the picture window at nothing. The fireplace is gray on black; the couch across the room swells in the darkness, soaking up gloom like a sponge.

There are eight light bulbs left. She carries one in Mom's old purse, protected by an enormous wad of toilet paper. The weight of the strap on her shoulder is as reassuring as a hug. Amirah misses hugs. She never puts the purse down.

Amirah notices that it is particularly dark at the corner where the walls and the ceiling meet. She gets out of Dad's reading chair, arms stretched before her. She is going to try to shut the door to the hallway. She doesn't know if she can; she has never done it before.

"Where was Moses when the lights went out?" she says.

No one answers, not even in her imagination. She fumbles for the doorknob.

"Where was Mohammed when the lights went out?" Her voice is shrinking.

As she eases the door shut, the hinges complain.

"Where was Amirah when the lights went out?"

The latch bolt *snicks* home, but Amirah keeps pressing hard against the knob, then leans into the door with her shoulder. The darkness squeezes her; she can't breathe. A moan pops out of her mouth like a seed, and she pivots suddenly, pressing her back against the door.

Something flickers next to the couch, low on the wall. A spark, blue as her dreams. It turns sapphire, cerulean, azure, indigo, all the colors that only poets and painters can see. The blue darts out of the electrical outlet like a tongue. She holds out her hands to navigate across the room to it and notices an answering glow, pale as mothers' milk, at her fingertips. Blue tongues are licking out of every plug in the living room, and Amirah doesn't need to grope anymore. She can see everything: the couch, the fireplace, all the rooms of the house, and through the pyramid walls into the city. It's one city now, not three.

Amirah raises her arms above her head because her hands are blindingly bright and she can see Dad with his new wife watching the Red Sox on 3DV. Someone has planted pink miniature roses on Mom's grave. Janet is looking into little Freddy Cobb's left ear with her otoscope, and Han is having late lunch at Sandeens with a married imagineer named Shawna Russo, and Mrs. Munro has dropped a stitch on the cap she is knitting for her great-grandson Matthias. At that moment, everyone who Amirah sees, thousands of believers, *tens* of thousands, stop what they are doing and turn to the pyramid, *Amirah's* pyramid, which has been finished for these seventeen years but has never meant anything to anyone until now. Some smile with recognition; a few clap. Others—most of them, Amirah realizes—are now walking toward her pyramid, to be close to her and caress the cold marble and know what she knows. The meaning is suddenly very strong in the city, like the perfume of lilacs or the suck of an infant at the breast or the whirr of a hummingbird.

"Amirah?" Betty opens the living room door. She is a beautiful, young girl with gray hair and crow's feet around her sky blue eyes. "Are you there, Amirah?"

"Yes," says Amirah.

"Do you understand?"

"Yes," Amirah says. When she laughs, time stands still.

23

Festival

Christopher Brown

The yard in front of the homeshare is filled with the kind of ungoverned cars you're not even allowed to drive anymore. A little Suzuki with the hatch cut off hides in the tall weeds, next to a Dodge panel truck that's lost its panels, and the skeleton of some ancient muscle car. The house is a lot older.

Eden laughs as she and her friends sit there in the rental car, recalibrating their expectations.

"It looks like the Alamo," she says.

It doesn't really. It's a brick house. Old, and out of place. Out of place with this rundown street in a weird part of town, with the online pics Nick sent around, with their idea of where they belong.

Eden already feels out of place with Nick and Marley and Shannon and Honda, even though they have been friends since college.

"Why can't the world look more like the website?" says Marley.

Eden sees the silhouette of some big water bird in the trees back there, watching a cargo plane come in so close you can see the seams.

"This place is cooler than any website," she says, but it's hard to hear.

"Maybe just wait until we see the inside," says Nick.

"Maybe just we shouldn't let you pick the rental next time," says Marley.

"At least it's close to the airport," says Honda.

"Like not even five minutes, right?" says Nick.

"Which is why all the trailer parks," says Eden. "And that junkyard, or whatever that was down the street. This is awesome. Adventure travel."

"Well, it's only ten minutes from downtown," says Nick. "And it's just a place to crash. We're gonna be at the festival the whole time."

"Where's the river?" asks Honda.

"Right past those trees," says Nick, with the confidence of a dude permanently connected to the network through his glasses.

"Why don't you all get out of the car and come see," says a man's voice. The guy is standing there by the car. His smile reveals a couple of fucked-up teeth. His hands are dirty with engine grease. He wipes them on his jeans, then pushes his long hair out of his eyes. His hair and his jeans both look like they have not been washed in a long time.

Eden watches Nick look at the guy. Nick is the driver of the rental, too. He said it was because he was the only one who had already turned 25.

"Finn," says Nick.

Finn nods.

All the windows are rolled down on the car. Eden is in the back, behind Nick, where the window only rolls halfway down. She looks over the edge of the window at their host.

His black T-shirt is faded to the color of primer. He has a piece of metal tied into his hair.

Finn looks back at her.

"You all need some help with your stuff?" he asks.

"No," says Eden. She opens the door. "Pop the trunk, Nick."

"Yeah, sure," says Nick.

"You can leave the extra eyes in the car," says Finn.

Nick looks at him through his specs.

"Yeah, okay," says Nick. "They don't even recognize you."

"Good," says Finn.

Eden tries to remember how she got here.

———

The plane from New York to Austin is new. It smells like a dental office. The plastic is the color of whitened teeth.

Through the porthole you can see the world in tilt shift. You try to figure out where you are. The river from space looks like ice, but it's August, and you realize that's the reflection of the sun.

A river of mercury flows through the heartland. It's how they power all the things we let them make us carry to stay connected.

The whine of the jets shuts out other noise. Each turbine turns at ten thousand revolutions per minute, faster during take-off. You wonder how they count that. You wonder how much a giant machine like this costs. Three hundred million dollars.

You wonder how many revolutions you could buy for three hundred million dollars.

There are people, individual people, who have that much money. There are people who have ten times that much money. You are not one of them.

In the future, we will all be richer.

We will each have our own robots.

We will live in cities covered in green.

We will live without rulers in true democracies.

You wonder how much it would cost to buy your own tiny island and declare it a separate country.

One time, you read a post about this guy who declared his house in the suburbs an independent kingdom. Guess who the king was.

The little television in the seatback cannot be turned off. You cannot hear it without headphones, but the closed captioning reads it out for you. Even the ads. Mostly the ads. Sometimes, the computer translator makes mistakes. Other times, it spews gibberish. You wonder if it is a secret code.

You imagine you are a spy who keeps the one-time pad in her purse, to translate the messages from control.

When you land in Austin, the first thing you do is sneak outside on the upper level to smoke a cigarette. You do this even though you know some of your old friends are already here, looking for you downstairs, excited to see you, waiting with strong hugs.

It is really fucking hot here. Almost too hot to smoke, but not quite.

You see a corporate hotel over there on the other side of the parking garages. A Hilton. The building is a squat cylinder. You imagine the inside. You remember a movie you saw once on TV. Inside an office building like that, they were experimenting on captured aliens.

When you all get in the car and pull onto the freeway, the first thing you notice is the billboards. There is one for a strip club, one for a real estate development on the shores of a man-made lake, and one for a political candidate.

BELTRAN

The candidate is in profile, looking up at an angle like he's watching the planes come in. He wears a red tie and a white shirt. His jacket is off, slung over his shoulder. His skin is white and his hair is dark.

THE FUTURE IS NOW

The second thing you notice is how stubby the trees are here. Like they're not getting enough water. Never will.

Nick says the trees that were meant to be here all died.

We are killing the world. You are helping.

————

Finn shows them around the place.

It's not as bad as it looks from the outside.

They will sleep in the rooms on the first floor. The couples will take the two bedrooms. Eden takes the couch in the hall between the rooms. This was all agreed to before. Nick and Shannon are the ones paying for the whole deal.

They share the first floor bathroom. It is clean enough. They clean it up some more before they go out.

Eden's hallway is across from a room full of books.

"This is the library," says Finn. "Help yourself. Take one, leave one."

There is a small bookshelf, a big leather armchair, and a beat-up old rug. There are stacks of books everywhere, stacked so high they touch the bottoms of the old postcards pinned to the wall. Some of the stacks are ready to fall over. You can smell the words going slowly back to pulp.

There is some old fucking hippie dude sitting in the armchair, reading. This was not in the pictures on the website. The color of the guy's hair and beard is the kind of white that used to be blonde. The color of milk gone bad. Maybe she thinks that because the guy smells so much like cigarettes.

"Who's Gandalf?" says Eden.

Finn laughs. "That's Billy. He's my roommate."

Billy smiles. "What's up." He has a real Texas accent. Which is a weird thing to hear coming out of a hippie.

"Whatcha reading?" asks Eden.

"Wild stuff," says Billy. He smiles, holds up the book in one hand. It's an old paperback. The cover shows two women and a man standing in the ruins of a city, a giant sun blazing behind them. "The orgy at the end of the world."

Ewww.

Finn shows them the kitchen. It is crammed full of hardware.

"Is that a 3D printer?" asks Nick.

"Two of them, actually," says Finn.

"Government surplus," says Billy. "From the labs."

"Need to find a better place to put them," says Finn.

Finn shows them where the coffee is, how the water filter works, and where he keeps the beer. He says they can help themselves to the beer, but please don't mess with the printers.

The beer has its own fridge. Mostly cans. There's some other stuff in there, too. Opaque white Tupperware, labeled in black script. Dates.

The back of the house looks over the river from a tall bluff overgrown with vine-covered trees. You can see downtown off to the west. Directly across is an old gravel pit. A crater lake of dirty rainwater next to a small mountain of asphalt.

"Indians lived here," says Nick. "Just upriver was a low water crossing for the Chisholm Trail."

Finn looks at him.

Marley holds his hand.

———

Job descriptions.

Marley, Nick, and Honda all work in marketing.

Marketing means math. Certain words or images produce certain results. People are numbers.

They put the words into semi-autonomous machines whose job is to sell things.

Basically, the job of the machines is to monitor people and figure out which ads are the best ones to show to get the people to buy stuff. Or at least to get the advertisers to pay to get their flash in front of the people's eyeballs.

Shannon is in law school.

Eden works for a magazine. Which is really a website. They think of themselves as digital muckrakers. They are looking for a story that will drive enough traffic to get them more eyeballs and more money from advertisers to pay for more muckraking.

The pay sucks.

Collectively, it will take the five of them approximately ninety-two years to pay off their student loans.

Whatever.

What if everyone stopped paying.

There are hipsters on horses here.

The first one they see is a guy in selvedge jeans and a hat like you might see an Australian wear in a war movie. The dude has a moustache that looks like it gets almost as much attention as the horse.

The horse is big, mostly black.

They see more as they walk the long blocks to Proteus from the spot where they park their car.

The riders tower over the pedestrians. Everyone smiles at them. The idea is still new.

Two women ride Appaloosas. Eden knows this because she had plastic toy Appaloosas as a child. One woman wears leather motorcycle pants and a sleeveless T-shirt that shows off her art. The other has a wrinkled chambray button-down and waxed leggings.

"Chaps?" says Marley.

"It's like a post-apocalyptic Western," says Eden. She wonders when the whimsy will run out.

Nick tells them about it, relating what his glasses tell him. How the municipal code expressly permits horses on the road, a relic of old times purposely protected in anachronistic pride. How nobody ever really took advantage of it until a year or so ago, when the owner of a bar on the East Side opened up a stable in the property next door.

They are talking about making them put crap catchers on the backs of the horses.

They are talking about taking the idea to other cities. Organizing cross-country trips that follow old trails.

They stand right next to one of the horses waiting to cross the boulevard. You can hear it breathe. It draws flies.

Eden is thinking about touching it when the sirens come.

Police on motorcycles, windscreens flashing, pull up to the crowd waiting to cross and block the way. Their machines emit a horrible tone, a flat electronic cut, crazy loud, designed to cut off all other thought. The horse next to them freaks out. Rumbles and neighs. The hipster in the saddle does not handle his horse like a guy in a Western.

Patrol cars follow, traveling fast, escorting two black Suburbans. As they pass through the intersection, they slow just enough that you can see inside. The bright sun penetrates the tinted windows. He is sitting in the back seat of the first Suburban, talking, oblivious to the crowd. You've seen the profile a thousand times.

Beltran.

"Beltran!" screams someone in the crowd.

"Fucker!"

"Fascist!"

"Turn the eyes on Beltran!"

Somebody throws something at him. A full bottle of beer. It breaks across the unbreakable glass shielding Beltran's face. He looks out at the people.

The motorcade accelerates. Except for the last Suburban. It diverts, pulling up between the two motorcycles.

Men in suits get out of the Suburban carrying guns. The kind of guns that take two hands to carry. Black metal.

"MOVE BACK," says the disembodied machine voice of the Suburban.

The motorcycle patrolmen dismount. They pull little wands from their belts. Crack them with flicks of the wrist. Turn them into metal whips.

The motorcycle cops wear jodhpurs and riding boots.

The Suburban emits that tone again. It's like the sound your phone makes sometimes. The Citizen Emergency Alert.

The tone is designed to make humans freeze and obey. That's what Nick says, later, when he asks his wearable.

Nothing about what it does to horses. Especially when men are coming at them with guns and truncheons.

The horse next to Eden rears.

It's a crazy thing to see from that close.

The horse ejects its hipster.

People are screaming.

Boys are screaming.

Girls are yelling at cops to stop.

POP.

A suit fires a shot. Into the air.

Another horse bolts. Runs right through the intersection, for the trees of a traffic island on the other side.

The horse next to Eden comes right down on the motorcycle cop that is yelling at it with a metal whip in his hand. Knocks him down hard. You can hear his helmet hit the pavement. Then you hear the sound of hoof on helmet.

BADDADADADDADADABDADADADADABABADAT.
Machine gun burst, from one of the suits.

The horse stumbles, goes down.

People start running, in every direction.

Eden runs behind the 24 Mart, into the weeds grown up around the fence at the base of a cell phone tower. She hides in there, for what seems like forever, but isn't.

There are sheets of paper on the ground. Abandoned homework.

1776.

They are teaching little kids about revolution.

———

A while back Eden got hooked on watching the coverage of a revolution in another country. The people of the country took to the streets and stood up to soldiers and tanks. The movement coalesced online. Actions coordinated on an obscure dating site called Flingue. The media kept looking for a leader to personalize the movement, but there wasn't one. All there was was everyone.

———

They find each other later at Proteus. The festival is just down the road. The show goes on. Few people there even know about what happened.

Nick and Shannon drink, beer and tequila. Honda and Eden share a big bowl, good stuff Honda brought from California. Montana mutata. You're not supposed to take it on the plane, but no one really cares. Half the airport security guards are probably high. You can see it when three of them gather around the X-ray screen, debating what that green outline is. The flight attendants are definitely high. Legalization has increased job happiness, if not productivity.

Proteus is a festival of networked music. There are no guitar solos.

At Proteus, there really aren't even any bands. There are improvisational instigators, who initiate prompts that carom through the mesh and come back in cascading responses.

Eden watches the improviser known as la Sirena take her place on the platform. La Sirena walks up five old chipped steps onto the concrete foundation of a building demolished years ago. La Sirena does not really look like a mermaid, but when she puts the reed in her saxophone and blasts a series of tones out into the air and over the airwaves, Eden remembers the riddle from grandma's game.

Con los cantos de la sirena, no te vayas a marear.

Eden already feels dizzy before the song starts, from the high-altitude herb, and what happened before.

Eden remembers then to turn her phone back on. She turned it off when she was hiding from the cops, behind the cell phone tower, hoping to disable the geolocation.

Proteus is an app, and a network, and a festival, and a movement, and a corporation.

The app lets her program her own response to la Sirena. And to the four-thousand, seven hundred and thirty-two others it says are participating in the piece. Two-thirds of those people are here, inside the fenceline with her. The others are in the cloud.

The sound from the amps is generative polyphony, electronic and analog and something else entirely.

Nick and Marley are dancing at the base of the platform. Marley is barefoot. Nick is wasted. Eden can see the beats their moves generate, Dionysian release incubated in the cubicles of hypercapital.

Honda and Shannon are spooned on a blanket next to Eden, in partial retreat, blissing out on Texas sun and networked trance.

Eden turns on her node and holsters her phone. Puts in her earbud, to elaborate the layering. Feels her way into an improvised asana. Channels a long, pitched tone that is a response not just to the piece, but to the harsh control tones of the police vehicles, and the sounds of the flyover. An alarm that turns into a jet turbine and then an endless siren aum.

The algorithm pulls her out, puts her in the front of the layers. Then she loses the pose.

She loses the pose because another app interrupts her with a preemptive alert. A pinq. Three pinqs, actually.

She goes back into the piece before she looks at who they are.

———

Pinqi is a proximity matcher. Its algorithms are tuned to rapid connections. You can play with the settings as your mood and needs suit. Eden retuned hers on the flight down, sitting there in her window seat, thinking about hanging out with her coupled friends.

There are three thumbnails dancing on her screen. A dude named Paxton, a woman named Lara, and a guy named Federico.

"Oh yeah?" she tells Federico, as they sit across from each other in the rest area twenty minutes later. "My grandma was from San Antonio. When I knew her at least. Before that, she was from Matamoros."

"Matamoros is crazy," says Federico. "There used to be a port there. During the Civil War. For smuggling guns and stuff. They called it Baghdad. 'Cause of the dunes."

"Really," says Eden.

She takes a long drink from the water, which is served in a chalice of 3-D printed corn byproduct. The concession sells glacial melt, bottled at the source. Federico suggests the Volta, but Eden picks the Whitechuck.

"Do you know any gun smugglers?" asks Eden.

"Uh, no," says Federico.

"Too bad."

Eden looks at the tableau relief rendered into the chalice. Strange animals, diminutive monsters, freaky chimeras cavorting in a fantastic forest.

She looks at Federico. Tries to assess the integrity of the gaze. She does not trust the herb when it tells her it can tell.

"Are your friends from New York, too?" he asks.

"No. I mean they all live in California now. We met in school. I guess Nick grew up in New York. He works for Proteus."

"Yeah?"

"Yeah."

"Cool."

"Wait until they start embedding the ads."

"Yeah."

Eden looks at the contrail drawing itself against the sky, behind Federico's head.

"Did you hear about that shooting or whatever?" he asks.

Eden nods.

"I wonder what that was about," he says.

Eden looks at him. Reads the face that just said that.

"You fucking elected him," says Eden. "That's what it's about. And now we all have to deal with him."

"Huh?"

"Beltran," she says.

"Oh."

"It was his motorcade. I was there."

"Wow."

Wow. "I don't like your future," she says.

"I was there, last summer, at the Capitol," he says, pleading. "I got arrested. I know."

"It didn't work. You people need to do something about him. He's going to run for president. And he's going to win."

Federico looks down at his chalice, swirls his finger in the remains of southern New Zealand's ice cap.

In the break in their conversation, they hear the sound of the multitude trying to find its voice.

"What do we do?" he asks. "People love him."

She tries to imagine those people. She tries to answer his question. She remembers she had an idea about this, but she can't remember what it was.

"I think I'm going to find another piece to play in," says Federico. "See you around?"

Bye.

———

Eden does dervish as the sun disappears and the energy accelerates with the cool. She's in the main set, which ends up all beat and no trance. She dances with the silhouette of the trees behind the fenceline, and the power line towers marching off through the volunteer foliage of the right of way like giant, stick figure robots.

She tries to influence the crowd with strong rhythms from deep inside. Jungle drums, like from an old movie, like they are going to war.

La Sirena te llame.

———

When her friends want to go to an after party, Eden takes a carshare back to the place.

She finds the book Billy was reading. Picks it up and gives it a try. Starts in the middle. Jumps to the end. Which is also the beginning. Realizes she has been reading the same three pages over and over again for more than an hour.

The text burns its way in, even as you don't think you understand it. A different kind of code, for soft machines.

———

Eden wakes up in the night. The noise of metal gears grinding against lube.

She has been dreaming about men with jungle fatigues and balaclavas occupying the ruins of downtown. She can't tell if they are soldiers or insurgents.

Maybe what she is really remembering is the things she saw in that long year after she dropped out. Crossed over. Got in trouble. Before Mom intervened and hooked her up with this job.

The weird smell is what gets her out of bed.

In the kitchen, one of the 3-D printers is laying down goop on the build plate. Creamy brown, with flushes of blue. It looks wet.

It sounds like a regular printer, the way the carriages move. Crossed with a squirt bottle.

Eden makes the noise.

"What are you doing?" asks a voice standing in the doorway. Finn.

"Wondering what woke me up," says Eden.

"Oh shit, sorry," says Finn. "Didn't know you could hear it way over there. Want a beer?"

Sure.

Billy is out there with Finn, on the back porch.

The river is there down below, lit up like a black mirror by moonlight and light pollution.

She hears a cacophony of frogs, cars going over the bridge, horny night birds calling to each other, a low-flying helicopter.

"How was your festival?" asks Billy. His cigarette smoke moves slowly through the muggy air, trapped in the light from the candle.

"Gimme one of those?" says Eden.

"Sure," says Billy.

The cigarette is strong. Eden feels clear.

"Festival was cool," says Eden, exhaling a cloud. "Everything else was kind of fucked up."

"That's that interactive stuff, huh," says Billy.

Eden nods.

"I don't get that."

"You're too old," says Eden.

Finn laughs.

"Seriously," she says. "Your brain has to be open to the software. Which means the tones. They work like code."

"I already hacked my brain pretty good," says Billy. "I'll leave that to you."

"They're probably inserting commercials into your head," says Finn.

"I'm sure they're trying," says Eden. "That's what Nick does."

"No thanks," says Finn.

"So what do you guys do? Sit around printing jizz all night?"

They both laugh.

"Seriously," says Eden.

"Research," says Finn.

"Research?" says Eden.

Finn nods.

"What?" says Eden.

"All kinds of stuff," says Finn.

Eden laughs.

"Seein' what we can make with those machines," says Billy. "It's pretty cool."

"You can print guns, right?"

"Lot more interesting things than that," says Finn.

"I want to print a gun," says Eden.

"First you gotta design one," says Billy.

"Come on," says Eden.

And so they do. Finn's laptop has a metal case, DIY, covered in stickers. Yes, he makes his money working on cars.

He shows her how you find the download sites, through a series of mirrors. Shows her the illegal freeware you use to anonymize your browsing from the eyes of the state. Air drops her a copy.

On her phone, she trolls through screens of seditious objects.

There's a lot more than guns.

"What about this?" asks Eden.

While the machine lays down the render, Billy works on his model. He holds down the butcher paper with his clay ashtray. The cigarette burns on its own while he puts the pieces together. They make a frame of interlocking tubes printed from a bad copy of the bones of bats. He spreads out the pericardium across the wingtips and leaves it to dry.

When Eden uses the bathroom by the kitchen, there is a piece of tissue floating in the toilet. It does not look like a wing. It looks like a used pocket, made from the inside of skin, trailing ropy threads.

———

The sun comes up through the ozone, bringing birdsong and ailerons.

They walk down to the river for a proper test flight. Eden carries her new tool in her pocket. Stops and holds it up to the light to see its inner structure. Finn carries the beer.

The hill is steep, through dense foliage. They walk under a canopy of scraggly elms crowded with cackling black birds.

She sees an old mattress in a small clearing.

The beach is made of trash, and rocks.

She goes in anyway, leaving her pants and her tool on the shore.

The water is warm by the shore. It smells like dead plants and sick fish.

Eden goes all the way in, swimming out into dark cool.

She comes up, current carried downriver. There is a big pipe embedded into the rocky bed. She stands on it. Salute to an exploding sun.

There are holes in the sky, big enough for old gods to sneak back in.

Cliff swallows swirl around her head, buzzing the hydroplaning bugs before they can become fish food. She saw their nests the day before, beautiful pustules of dried mud growing out of the steel spans of the bridge.

The bridge was built when capitalism collapsed, by a legion of lost men, while they incubated the war machine that ate them all. Nick told them that, when they drove over. Not in those words. 1933, he said.

Over there, upriver, the old hippie is running after his gossamer batplane, and the motorhead host is removing his clothes.

She keeps swimming, away, into a dream of cities under water.

――――

"Is that a beer?" asks Shannon.

Eden drinks from it, and nods.

"It's 9:42 a.m. Sunday morning," says Nick, in that practicing to be paternal tone.

"Where were you?" says Shannon. "We're waiting to go to brunch."

All four of them are sitting there, on their laptops.

"Did you lose your phone?" says Nick.

"I'm fucking hungry," says Honda. "Let's go."

"Sorry," says Eden. "Do I have time to shower?"

No.

――――

They brunch at the shopping center called Zona.

Zona is an old, one-story mall that died, lived a second life as an immigrant market with a dance studio, died again, and was reborn as this curated gallery of eclectic fetish objects. The anchor is a store called Stan that specializes in vintage televisions. No one is sending any signals that the sets can receive any more, but Stan sells little boxes that repurpose them as displays for contemporary devices, channeled through retro filters.

Eden watches a yellow star explode against a saturated red sky on one of the sets while she drinks her michelada in the courtyard of Bishop's across the hall. On her phone, she types a four-hundred word piece for the magazine about the eyes of Beltran and the bodyguards of Texas. There's only so much muck the advertisers will let you rake.

Who knew jalapeño waffles would be so good?

Syrup makes everything good, says Honda. She's right.

The skylight over the courtyard caved in when the mall was abandoned, and they left it that way. Feral. Nick and Marley are making out in the grass, mood improved by bacon and weed. Honda and Shannon come back with bounty. An old mixing board, a porcelain figurine of a cowgirl with alien eyes, and a pineapple grenade.

Eden takes hold of the grenade. A dummy, with the paint chipped off. Heavy. She wonders what a real one would feel like.

The eye of the satellite watches through the aperture in the ceiling. They say they can see around corners.

Eden shows Honda and Shannon her tool. Asks if they can tell what it is.

They tell her she smells like the river.

Shannon wants to go to the museum before they go swimming, and so they do. There is an exhibit commemorating the tenth anniversary of the attacks. Eden looks at the photographs of the White House in flames, and wonders what it would be like if they had finished the job.

———

That night, Eden dreams of the riot in New York, when they looted the private stores on Fifth Avenue, the ones you need an invitation to shop. An invitation from an algorithm.

When she sees Finn in the kitchen in the morning and he says you look tired she does not tell him about the dream, or the boy she was with, or what he looked like after the corporate security teams came in with their trucks and sonics and retook their masters' block.

"I can sleep on the plane," she says.

He asks about the show they went to see. She tells him she skipped it. Went to bed early, not that it did any good.

He tells her he was out all night, because Billy got arrested. They caught him stealing at the hospital. In a lab, behind security. He found an access badge on the fucking street.

He asks when her flight is, she says five, he says then why don't you go back to bed, she says 'cause her friends have to leave in an hour. He says, I'll give you a ride, and she says ok.

She says, why don't we get some towels and take a nap on the beach.

———

When she imagined Finn, he was like one of those shirtless jeans models, the ones with no heads. But after they had done some time. Then she imagined a whole catalog like that, selling pre-distressed rebel fashions. J. Prep goes to the Supermax. Political detainees in torn denim and faded black cotton. Lean young revolutionary hunger strikers showing off their prison tats and the places where you can see the bones of their hips pushing against the skin of their hairless abs.

Turns out Finn is not like that. Has a bit of a muffin top, in fact. Must be all the beer.

There are a pair of freaky-looking blue birds buzzing up and down the river. Giant-beaked heads almost as big as the rest of their bodies. Their clickety-clack calls sound like a pair of old movie projectors taking turns. They fly in spurts. Then they dive for food, straight down, living missiles.

Eden eats a cactus and sausage taco and works on her tan. She washes the salsa down with a cold can of Nicaraguan beer.

She drifts into napland. When she wakes up, she can't even remember where she is, until she sees him down there by the water making a cairn out of river rocks. She watches him clandestinely, pretending to still be asleep.

He comes back over when he sees her sitting up, eating another taco. Opens two more beers, breaks out the weed. She wonders why they always have to make the glass pipes in that shape.

They talk forever. Talk about riots and fake elections and 3D printers and kingfishers and the way egrets vogue. They talk about AWOL parents and custom cars and dead stars. They try to see if they can imitate the sounds of the birds and the bugs. They talk about the metal piece woven into Finn's hair, equine gentrification, net censorship, consensual surveillance, old relationships, Eden's tattoo, petroleum meadows, the names of the trees, and things they would die for.

They fuck on the beach, under the hottest sun Eden can remember.

She hears the jets, wonders if any of the incoming passengers can see them. Imagine that.

She wonders if any other eyes in the sky are watching them. Of course they are.

After, Eden swims out. Feels the hairy leaves of water

plants. She swims out further, into the channel, where the current is faster, looking for clean.

She watches Finn toss the spent rubber into the water.

I guess it's time to go.

———

Ambient government.

Eden did not invent that phrase.

It's when the sensorial presences of the state are so ubiquitously and subtly embedded into the environment that they are almost indistinguishable from nature.

"It takes us back to our roots," says Beltran. "America is a big small town. Where everybody knows your name." And everything else.

Eden can't decide which is better. To work on new strategies to evade the gaze, or more effective ways to poke it in the eye.

Did you know that seventy-five percent of the price of a home-use brick of dispensary marijuana goes to the federal government? They like you that way.

Forty-seven percent of that pays for guns and ammo, thirty-four percent for monitoring, and the rest for productivity rehab.

———

Eden persuades Finn to stop at the Airport Hilton for a drink before she leaves. She tries to explain to him how it reminded her of a movie she saw, but he doesn't get it.

The building is structured like a circular fort. The bar is in the middle of the big atrium, under the skylight. You can see a gangway up there.

She asks the bartender how you access that view.

"You can't," he says. "Sealed off."

"This place is messed up," says Finn.

"It used to be the command center," says the bartender. "Back when this was an Air Force base."

Eden looks around, past the self-medicating software salesmen. Imagines men in uniforms the color of black-and-white movies, peacocking Spartans with silver wings and spiky hair.

"What did they fly?" asks Finn.

"B-52s," says the bartender. His name tag says Gary. "Southern Command."

"So they could bomb Mexico or something?" asks Eden.

"I guess," says the bartender. "Who knows. It was the Cold War. There's a display about it in the airport terminal."

"Nuclear bombers," says Eden.

"Where's the bomb shelter?" asks Finn.

"Dude," says the bartender. "This whole place is a bomb shelter. There were all kinds of tunnels and stuff. They filled them with concrete when they built the terminal."

"Yeah, right," says Eden. "That's where they keep the people they pull out of the security line."

Gary the bartender gives her a look. He has the lapel pin by his nametag. The red owl.

"Are you enforcing the Constitution, Gary?" asks Eden.

Gary looks at Finn. Finn smiles.

Eden looks to see where Gary conceals his handgun. Maybe that's it, under the apron. She imagines taking it from him.

Gary prints out their bill, pushes it in front of Finn, walks to the other end of the bar.

Eden looks at the colored cocktail Gary made her. I'll have a Wild Blue Yonder, Gary.

"Come on," she says.

Off we go.

———

They roam the hotel, looking for hidden doors to secret chambers.

They try to get up onto the gangway, but find only circular hallways of identical numbered doors. The design palette is red and beige.

They try out different doors.

They find a room where the door is propped open. They go in. Eden grabs the Bible from the drawer, starts reading out loud, then tries it backwards. Finn turns on the porn channel. Eden raids the minibar. Opens the half champagne. Lights a cigarette.

They end up in the bed. You can smell the dude that slept there the night before. Eden tears off the sheets. Switches the TV to the war channel and cranks up the volume. Puts her plastic lighter to the bedspread, but it only melts.

Eden says hi to a guy that walks past the open door, pulling the suitcase out of which he lives.

When the housekeeper comes in, they are abusing the armchair. You can hear the sound of the helicopter crew talking man code in machine voice, before the fifty cal rips at the van. Eden is yelling at the TV, and then at the house-keeper, telling her in Spanish to leave their room.

They sprint down the circular hallway, Eden carrying her shoes in her hand, Finn chasing behind her.

They push open the emergency exit door. No alarm goes off. The warnings are all lies.

They find the basement. There is an old civil defense sign on the wall. You can see where the blast door is, metal, painted grey, a long time ago. The decals and stencils are no longer legible.

Eden pounds on the door, with her shoes, then her fists. You can hear the echo on the other side.

Finn wants to finish what they started in the room. She pushes him back, sits down, looks at the security camera hanging there from the ceiling. Thinks about the movie about the captured aliens. Gives them an Oscar clip.

———

Eden misses her flight. They do not go to the airport.

They drive, south. Finn says he wants to show her something. Something she can write a story about.

She will email her editor tomorrow. It's not like she has a desk to go to. They pay her for words.

When Eden wakes up, they are in the desert. On a two-lane highway, no other cars in sight.

The radio plays some chilango rap about perros and oro. She can make out about half the words.

"Where are we?"

"Mexico," says Finn.

She sits up. Feels the blood drain. "Fuck! I don't have a passport."

She doesn't mention how they confiscated it.

"I'm just fucking with you."

She hits him in the face.

"Jesus," he says. "I'm trying to show you something important. Something we need to document. Expose. I need your help. Words and pictures." He points at the camera mounted on the dash. Eden remembers the gear they loaded in the trunk.

"Okay," she says.

"You fucking started it," says Finn.

Finn's car is an old Celica, uptuned. It's loud.

Eden opens a beer and modulates the frequency.

She sees the satellite arrays up on top of the far mesas, aimed at the sky.

They drive past a sign that says they can't drive past the sign.

UNITED STATES BORDERZONE
RESTRICTED ACCESS
ALL TRAFFIC SUBJECT TO SEARCH

They drive off the highway onto washboard gravel, ten miles, slow grade. They come to an overlook. Top of a low ridge, wide view to the south.

It looks like a colony on the moon, the way the facility sprawls out across the basin. Razorwire and corrugated roofs glisten orange in the dying sun. Low-flying aircraft move through the thermals, phase shift in the mirage lines. All so far away you can't hear anything but the wind.

Farther out, at the edge of the canyon, you can see the wall. It's more like a fence, since you can see through it, but the first tier is so high neither word really does it justice. A barrier made of steel and software, loaded with lethal intelligence, designed to reinforce the existence of a diminishing sovereign.

Finn hands Eden his binoculars. She takes a closer look, through jittery lenses. Surveys the no-man's-lands, the killing zones demarcated by the descending tiers of fortification. Finn points her to the new section of semiautonomous smart wall. It looks like a caterpillar of steel tunneling up out of the sand, stenciled with spray-paint tattoos of its identifying codes, moving on its own with machine slink and rubber paddles, adjusting to changing topographical conditions and emergent tactical requirements.

She sees a shimmering object approaching across the sand. An apparition. A coyote, she realizes when it turns, the silver in its coat sending misdirection through the light and heat.

She looks inside the base. Border security and information warfare center. It's too far to see much. Tiny vehicles moving around between tiny black and silver buildings. A chopper in the foreground, headed in to the base.

Finn sets up a telescope on a tripod. It has a camera attached to it. Look through this, he says.

The magnification renders the landscape as an abstract painting. Everything is liquid, the edges blurred. Lights are coming on, inside and out. You can make out the metal shed frames of the buildings. The white onion domes of electronic arrays. An air tower. A small aircraft on the tarmac. A huge tracked vehicle idling nearby.

They see the helicopter land near the plane. Broad-shouldered men in polo shirts and ball caps unload a prisoner. You can't see the restraints but you can see how his arms are cinched up behind his back. He has a yellow jumpsuit. A black hood over his head.

"Extraordinary deportation," says Finn.

The shutter dilates in rapid bursts, like a slide projector on fast forward, like he's making the frames of a gif.

Extraordinary deportation is when they arrest you for crimes that result in the loss of your citizenship. Eden writes about it sometimes. Finn read one of her pieces.

"We should go to Monterrey," he says. "Or D.F."

Mexico City sounds good. She has heard stories about the exile scene. They have taken over a whole neighborhood. Semiautonomous, experimenting with new forms of governance. Network-enabled direct democracy.

"I told you, I don't have a passport," she says. "They took it."

The last one she wrote about was a kid in Boston who got denaturalized for hacking into the systems of the federal court there and posting footage from secret trials onto the public networks.

"We can get you one," he says. "Billy knows a guy."

It's an emergency.

Love it or leave it.

———

"Let's go closer," she says. They are back in the car now. The sun is gone.

"You're crazy," he says. The only light is the beams of the headlamps. The double yellow line, reeling in.

"Turn up there," she says. By the sign that says don't turn here.

He looks at her.

"I have a press card."

"But no passport," he says.

"We need to share this," she says. "People have no idea."

She moves in. Flips his toggle switch. Turns on the camera. Looks for the uplink light. Checks her phone for the match.

Finn looks at the lights in the distance.

"How fast can you go?" she asks.

Pretty fast, it turns out.

When he opens up the engine, it sounds like a bomb.

———

They wreck Finn's wheels before they get to the second fence. A barricade comes up out of the ground. Smart fortification made of steel spikes and simple software.

Eden was not wearing her seat belt when it happened. She rolled onto the floor. It doesn't hurt too bad, yet. She milks it anyway. Leans up against the car like she can't really stand on her own.

They didn't get very close to the base. All she can see is the Grizzly with its embedded flashers, the land drones idling behind it, and the lone, uniformed patrolman who just told them to stand up against the car.

Finn looks like he's done this before.

"I'm a journalist," says Eden.

The camera is still on. She thinks.

The patrolman walks closer. His uniform is a weird shade

of green. The unit patch on his shoulder is the logo of a corporation.

A little light floats around overhead, very close. The eye of the computer that tells the man what to do.

"You can explain that to them at the detention facility," says the patrolman. "Right now I need you to submit to the search. Hands over your head."

He has a morale patch on his left breast. The owl.

"You're not even a real soldier," says Eden.

He frisks her. Finds the lump in her pants pocket. Her tool.

"What's that?" he asks.

"Want me to show you?"

He unholsters his taser. Watches carefully.

When she pulls it out, it springs open, almost autonomously. It's amazing that something like that can pack down so small. It's like a cross between a jack-in-the-box and a medieval torture device, printed from hardest plastic for personal defense. Thank you bedstuygirl92, whoever you are.

The corporate patrolman screams.

One of the spikes finds his face.

The land drones intervene.

Rubber bullets hurt a lot more than you think.

————

Detention is not like it was in middle school. It is a white room of concrete, rubber, and steel, chilled to the temperature of a wine cellar. The clothes they let you wear are made of paper. When you rip them off in protest, they take their time giving you new ones.

The isolation is much more intense if you are a person who spends their time wired into the networks. You feel like you have been unplugged from life. They say you are addicted to interactive programs that have damaged your civic sensibilities. You scream. but no one can hear you. No one that cares.

They interrogate you in another room, a room that has two chairs and a mirror, but you are pretty sure they don't really care what the answers are. Maybe because your answers are aggressive koans generated by a fracturing personality. You tell yourself that is what it feels like to create the new post-you.

The only one is the everyone.

They tell you your boyfriend is dead. They tell you your boyfriend is alive, in solitary, and will never come out. They tell you your boyfriend is a known gun smuggler. They tell you your boyfriend is being raped in prison. They tell you your boyfriend is being detained until trial, probably next year sometime. You don't have a boyfriend. You hope they just deport him.

Your mom gets you out. She is a businesswoman who knows lots of lawyers. The lawyer she gets you delivers mom's lecture. Tells you one of the conditions of your release is you must leave Texas within 48 hours.

You do not go home, even though she sends you two thousand dollars for that purpose.

You give the money to another lawyer to get your non-boyfriend released. The lawyer says she probably won't be able to, but takes the money anyway.

———

Money talks, says Billy, stating the obvious again.

Eden turns on her networks and won't turn them off. Proteus, Pinqi, Polis, Mitos. She is a walking transmitter. A voluntary cyborg whose wearable software cohabits the self.

There are other people in her head when she sleeps. Her dreams are digital Dionysiums that morph into spaced-out complines and back again. She falls through the space of the others, looks over, sees their projected faces. They are flying, not falling. A fleet of beautiful superheroes.

She is pretty sure the prurient eyes of capital are there with them, lurking in shadow. The Yankee peddler inside the machine looking for innovation to appropriate and hot footage to resell. Buy low, sell high.

Billy helps her make the things she needs for her new project. She designs them the same way an instigator starts a Protean piece.

The capacity of a thousand agitated minds to imagine new tools of change is more than you think.

Billy laughs when the things stand up on the build plate. Sometimes, he eats them.

———

The political festival is in the basketball arena. It is another concrete cylinder. Eden wonders if they could fit the Hilton inside it.

She dresses the part of a Beltran fan, or the best simulation she can manage in thrift store clothes. Her sunscreen is a clandestine reflective painted on in a pattern that confounds the facial recognition. Billy wires her with the scrambler. It feels like a piece of Cleopatra jewelry, without the glitter.

They stop her at the security checkpoint. Check her press credentials. They notice something on the screen. A mass. She lets them look.

The guards kind of freak when they see the tumorous flesh of her distended abdomen. I'm so sorry, honey, says the woman in charge. She has the big arms of a woman in a propaganda ad.

Inside, the crowd is exultant under the images of Beltran. His smile animates the Jumbotron for the waiting mob. He plays with his adopted children. Walks the border wall. Raises his hand at a rally. Orates at the debates, a puckish pastor who switches from wry banter to prescriptive apocalyptica. Strokes his mastiff while he holds the old terrier in his arms.

Eden tells herself that this man is not a man, but the interface of a dark network. A network that can be hacked.

When she is inside, she reactivates all her nets. She has Monocle now, the wearable eye that looks like a crystalline bindi.

Eden is small, and brown, and batshit. People give her room when she nudges her way to the rope line.

The music that comes through the giant speaker dongles is an orchestra of trumpets remixed as civil defense alarm. The name, when the voice of the stadium says it, is something more than a name. It is a chant. A magic word. A religious invocation. A network login.

Billy tells her it is all working, except for a couple of signals that are not.

The man walks the red carpet, both hands out to the crowd, drawing in the mob love energy that lights up his enhanced smile.

He does not see her until it is too late. He is pointing at the face of a screaming boy on the Jumbotron, one of the winners algorithmically plucked from the crowd for special recognition.

It happens just as she steps over the rope to get to him. You can see it in his eyes. The link is made, before she even plugs him in.

Ambient democracy.

How do you turn a panopticon inside out?

Eden is sure Beltran can see them in that second, the eyes that see through her.

Then he sees her reaching for the thing she smuggled in, hears her hand pulling it out of the homemade pouch of printed flesh.

It's like a new nerve, designed to make him feel them. It looks like a stinger made of soggy bone.

He can see it there in her hand.

It's not supposed to hurt when the thing makes the connection, but he doesn't know that yet.

The way people see what happens next is beyond what any Jumbotron can convey.

Eden rushes the stage.

Contributors

Nathan Ballingrud is the author of *North American Lake Monsters* and *Wounds: Six Stories from the Border of Hell*. He's twice won the Shirley Jackson Award, and has been shortlisted for the World Fantasy, British Fantasy, and Bram Stoker Awards. His stories have appeared in numerous Best of the Year anthologies. *Wounds*, a film based on his novella "The Visible Filth," premiered at the Sundance Film Festival in 2019. *North American Lake Monsters* is in development as an anthology series at Hulu.

Carina Bissett is a writer, poet, and educator working primarily in the fields of dark fiction and interstitial art. Her short fiction and poetry has been published in multiple journals and anthologies including *Arterial Bloom*, *Gorgon: Stories of Emergence*, *Hath No Fury*, *Mythic Delirium*, *NonBinary Review*, and the *HWA Poetry Showcase Vol. V*. She teaches online workshops at The Storied Imaginarium and she is a graduate of the Creative Writing MFA program at Stonecoast. Link to her work can be found on her website (http://carinabissett.com).

Gregory Norman Bossert is an author and filmmaker based just over the Golden Gate Bridge from San Francisco. He started writing in 2009 on a dare and has no intention of stopping anytime soon. His story "The Telling" won the 2013 World Fantasy Award; other stories have appeared everywhere from *Asimov's Science Fiction* to the *Saturday Evening Post*, with recent stories in *Conjunctions* #69 and #71 and *Tor.com*. When not writing, he wrangles spaceships and superheroes for Industrial Light & Magic. More information is available on his blog GregoryNormanBossert.com.

Karen Bovenmyer earned an MFA in Creative Writing: Popular Fiction from the University of Southern Maine. She teaches and mentors students at Iowa State University and Western Technical College. She serves as the Assistant Editor of the *Pseuodopod Horror Podcast Magazine*. She is the 2016 recipient of the Horror Writers Association Mary Wollstonecraft Shelley Scholarship. Her poems, short stories and novellas appear in more than 40 publications and her first novel, *Swift for the Sun*, debuted from Dreamspinner Press in 2017. http://karenbovenmyer.com/.

Christopher Brown is the Campbell and World Fantasy Award-nominated author of *Tropic of Kansas* and *Rule of Capture*. His short fiction and criticism has appeared in a wide array of magazines and anthologies. He lives in Austin.

Emily Cataneo is a fiction writer and journalist. Her short fiction has appeared in magazines such as *Nightmare*, *Lightspeed*, *The Dark*, *cream city review*, *Smokelong Quarterly*, and *Beneath Ceaseless Skies*, and was long listed for Best Science Fiction and Fantasy 2016 and mentioned in Best SF&F 2018. Her debut collection, *Speaking to Skull Kings and Other Stories*, came out from Journalstone Publishing in 2017. As a journalist, her work has appeared in venues such as *Slate*, *NPR*, and the *Boston Globe*. She's a 2013 graduate of the Odyssey Writing Workshop, a 2016 graduate of the Clarion Writers Workshop, and a 2019 graduate of the North Carolina State University MFA program. She is the co-founder of the Redbud Writing Project, an adult education creative writing school in Raleigh, North Carolina, where she teaches classes in fiction, nonfiction, and more.

Julie C. Day's debut, dark fantasy novella, *The Rampant*, is a 2020 Lambda Literary Award finalist. She has published numerous stories in magazines & journals such as *The Dark*, *Black Static*, *Podcastle*, *Split Lip Magazine*, *Interzone*, and the *Cincinnati Review*. You'll find some of them between the pages of her collection, *Uncommon Miracles*. Julie lives in a small town in New England with her family and a menagerie of variously sized animals. Café writing and long walks with ebooks are also a non-quarantine thing. You can find Julie online at @thisjulieday or on her blog stillwingingit.com.

Michael J. DeLuca's roots are mycorrhizal with sugar maple and Eastern white pine. He's the publisher of *Reckoning*, an annual journal of creative writing on environmental justice. His fiction has appeared most recently in *Beneath Ceaseless Skies*, *Three-Lobed Burning Eye*, *Strangelet* and *Middle Planet*. @michaeljdeluca; mossyskull.com.

Formerly a film critic, journalist, screenwriter, and teacher, **Gemma Files** has been an award-winning horror author since 1999. She has published two collections of short work, two chap-books of speculative poetry, a Weird Western trilogy, a story-cycle and a stand-alone novel (*Experimental Film*, which won the 2016 Shirley Jackson Award for Best Novel and the 2016 Sunburst Award for Best Adult Novel). Most are available from ChiZine Publications. She has two new story collections from Trepidatio (*Spectral Evidence* and *Drawn Up From Deep Places*), one upcoming from Cemetery Dance (*Dark Is Better*), and a new poetry collection from Aqueduct Press (*Invocabulary*).

A.T. Greenblatt is a mechanical engineer by day and a writer by night. She lives in Philadelphia where she's known to frequently subject her friends to various cooking and home brewing experiments. She is a graduate of Viable Paradise

XVI and Clarion West 2017. Her work has been nominated for a Nebula Award, has been in multiple Year's Best anthologies, and has appeared in *Uncanny, Clarkesworld, Beneath Ceaseless Skies,* and *Fireside,* as well as other fine publications. You can find her online athttp://atgreenblatt.com and on Twitter at@AtGreenblatt.

Nin Harris is an author, poet, and tenured postcolonial Gothic scholar who exists in a perpetual state of unheimlich. Nin writes Gothic fiction, cyberpunk, nerdcore post-apocalyptic fiction, planetary romances and various other forms of hyphenated weird fiction. Nin's publishing credits include *Clarkesworld, Uncanny Magazine, Strange Horizons, The Dark, Beneath Ceaseless Skies,* and *Lightspeed.*

Chip Houser's fiction has appeared in *The Arcanist, Daily Science Fiction, Every Day Fiction,* and elsewhere in print and online. His collection *Dark Morsels* is forthcoming from Red Bird Press. Other stories set in the Smilerverse have found their way into *New Myths* and, in the near future, *Bourbon Press.* A graduate of the Odyssey Writing Workshop, he also has an MFA in Creative Writing from the University of Missouri-St. Louis, where he was the Associate Editor for *Natural Bridge.* He's read slush for *Amazing Stories,* and most recently helped edit this anthology. Labors of love, all. To fund his wild writing lifestyle, he practices architecture, mostly during daylight hours, always with a grin showing too much teeth. You can find Chip online at chiphouser.com.

James Patrick Kelly has won the Hugo, Nebula and Locus awards. His most recent books are *King Of The Dogs, Queen Of The Cats* (2020), a novella from Subterranean Press, a collection, *The Promise of Space* (2018), from Prime Books, and a novel, *Mother Go* (2017), an audiobook original from Audible. In 2016 Centipede Press published a career retrospective

Masters of Science Fiction: James Patrick Kelly. His fiction has been translated into eighteen languages. With John Kessel, he has co-edited five anthologies. He writes a column on the internet for *Asimov's*. Find him on the web at www.jimkelly.net.

Marianne Kirby writes about bodies both real and imagined. She plays with the liminal space between vanishing and visibility. She authored *Dust Bath Revival* and its sequel *Hogtown Market*; she co-authored *Lessons from the Fatosphere: Quit Dieting and Declare a Truce with Your Body*. A long-time writer, editor, and activist, Marianne has contributed to women's interest publications, news outlets, and tv shows that require people to have opinions. She has been published by the *Guardian, xoJane, The Daily Dot, Bitch Magazine, Time*, and others. She has appeared on tv and radio programs ranging from the Dr. Phil Show to Radio New Zealand.

Kathrin Köhler is a graduate of the Odyssey Fantasy Writing Workshop and the University of Wisconsin – Madison. An immigrant interested in intersectionality, the interstitial, and ideas interdisciplinary, they are most comfortable writing in places "between." Favorite topics include the power of narrative, what it means to belong, and how people conceive of and interact with nature. Their work has appeared in *Pantheon Magazine, Shimmer, Interfictions, Strange Horizons*, and other fine places. Author website at theliteratecondition.wordpress.com.

Matthew Kressel is a speculative fiction writer and software developer. His work has been a multiple finalist for the Nebula, World-Fantasy, and Eugie Awards. His short fiction has appeared in dozens of markets including *Tor.com, Lightspeed, Clarkesworld*, and *Analog* magazines, as well as dozens of anthologies. His work has also been translated into six languages. His first novel, *King of Shards*, was hailed by *NPR*

Books as, "Majestic, resonant, reality-twisting madness." As a software developer, Matthew created the Moksha submissions system, which is in use by some of the largest speculative fiction publishers in the world. He is the co-host of the Fantastic Fiction at KGB reading series in Manhattan. Find him on Twitter @mattkressel or https://www.matthewkressel.net.

Jordan Kurella is a queer and disabled author who has lived all over the world (including Moscow and Manhattan). In their past lives, they were a barista, radio DJ, and social worker. Their work has been featured in *Apex*, *Beneath Ceaseless Skies*, and *Strange Horizons* magazines.

Premee Mohamed is a scientist and writer based out of Alberta, Canada. She has degrees in molecular genetics and environmental science, but hopes that readers of her fiction will not hold that against her. Her short speculative fiction has been published in a variety of venues, which can be found on her website at www.premeemohamed.com. She can be located with some reliability on Twitter at @premeesaurus.

Sarah Read is a dark fiction writer in the frozen north of Wisconsin. Her short stories can be found in various places, including Ellen Datlow's *Best Horror of the Year vol 10*. A collection of her short fiction called *Out of Water*, a Bram Stoker finalist, is available now from Trepidatio Publishing, as is her Bram Stoker Award-winning novel *The Bone Weaver's Orchard*. When she's not staring into the abyss, she knits. Find her on Instagram or Twitter @Inkwellmonster or on the web at www.inkwellmonster.wordpress.com.

Sofia Samatar is the author of the novels *A Stranger in Olondria* and *The Winged Histories*, the short story collection, *Tender*, and *Monster Portraits*, a collaboration with her brother, the artist

Del Samatar. Her work has won several awards, including the World Fantasy Award. She teaches African literature, Arabic literature, and speculative fiction at James Madison University.

Bonnie Jo Stufflebeam's fiction and poetry has appeared in over 50 publications such as *LeVar Burton Reads*, *Uncanny*, and *Year's Best Dark Fantasy & Horror* as well as in six languages. She has been a finalist for the Nebula Award and won the Grand Prize in the SyFy Channel's Battle the Beast contest; SyFy made and released an animated short of her short story "Party Tricks," set in the world of *The Magicians*. She is the curator of the Art & Words Show in Fort Worth, Texas where she lives with four cats: Gamora, Don Quixote, Junebug, and Gimli.

Steve Toase was born in North Yorkshire, England, and now lives in Munich, Germany. He writes regularly for *Fortean Times* and Folklore Thursday. His fiction has appeared in *Three Lobed Burning Eye*, *Shimmer*, *Lackington's*, *Aurealis*, *Not One Of Us*, *Cabinet des Feés* and *Pantheon Magazine* amongst others. In 2014, "Call Out" (first published in *Innsmouth Magazine*) was reprinted in *The Best Horror Of The Year 6*, and two of his stories have just been published in *Best Horror of the Year 11*. His first short story collection *To Drown In Dark Water* is due out from Undertow Publications in 2021. He also likes old motorbikes and vintage cocktails. You can keep up to date with his work via his Patreonwww.patreon.com/stevetoase,www.tinyletter.com/stevetoase,facebook.com/stevetoase1,www.stevetoase.wordpress.com and @stevetoase.

A.C. Wise's short fiction has appeared in *Uncanny*, *Shimmer*, and *The Best Horror of the Year Volume 10*, among other places. She has two collections published with Lethe Press, and her debut novella, *Catfish Lullaby*, was published by Broken Eye Books in September 2019. Her work has won the Sunburst Award for Excellence in Canadian Literature of the Fantastic, and has twice been a finalist for the Nebula Award and the Sunburst Award, along with being a finalist for the Lambda Literary Award. In addition to her fiction, she contributes the Women to Read and Non-Binary Authors to Read columns to *The Book Smugglers.* Find her online at www.acwise.net and on Twitter as @ac_wise.

www.ingramcontent.com/pod-product-compliance
Lightning Source LLC
Chambersburg PA
CBHW031151120726
47905CB00006B/1907